Charles Dobson lives in Glasgow. He served in the British Army in the UK, Europe and South East Asia. This was followed by a period teaching English and History in secondary schools and then practised as a solicitor before giving up employment. Relaxations are reading, travel and encountering interesting individuals.

In memory

of

John Hart

Margaret Pawley

and

Simon Hall R M

Charles Dobson

SHALA

Wot Do They Understand?

AUSTIN MACAULEY PUBLISHERS™

LONDON • CAMBRIDGE • NEW YORK • SHARJAH

A CIP catalogue record for this title is available from the British Library.

ISBN 9781528984409 (Paperback)
ISBN 9781528984416 (ePub e-book)

www.austinmacauley.com

First Published (2020)
Austin Macauley Publishers Ltd
25 Canada Square
Canary Wharf
London
E14 5LQ

Chapter 1

The knock was sharp.

The journalist was surprised to have a visitor so late at night. She stopped writing her notes, put down the pen, rose from the cane sofa and crossed the room to the window. Easing open the curtain just enough to peer out to the left side, she could not identify who was at the door. She spotted the usual police guard Land Rover parked across the street and to the right. The two policemen standing close to the vehicle did not seem alarmed. She relaxed.

A second impatient knock.

"Hello, Tony." Her expression was asking what he was doing there.

"Jennie, can I come in?" Without waiting for an answer, he walked past her into the living room.

"Susan is in bed so you need to be quiet."

"Do you have anything to drink?" He sat down in a cushioned bamboo rocking chair.

Jennie surmised that he had been in the room before. Why not? To be expected. "You have a blunt approach to girls." She smiled. "Is that why you're such—"

"Oh, for God's sake!" Tony Hockin stood up and walked to the door. He paused and half turned towards Jennie Croxham. His voice was quiet. "I came here because I had had enough of smart, glib talk tonight. I thought I would be able to talk to someone from the real world, not this pantomime called Shala." He smiled. "Better known as Belhaven's last outpost."

She lowered her eyes. "I'm sorry." She looked up. "What about that drink?"

He smiled, turned and sat back down in the same chair facing the sofa.

She went to a small table behind the sofa. "Susan seems to have only martini and brandy."

"Brandy please."

"Dry ginger?"

"No thanks." He lit a cigarette and belatedly asked, "Do you mind?" Jennie shook her head though she did.

As she fixed the drinks, Hockin wondered what the best way would be to explain to this pretty girl the frustrations caused by seeing the same people for the last fifteen odd years, not just in Shala but also back in England.

Jennie brought the drinks over. She had a martini. She sat on the sofa, closed her notebook and slipped it into the bag to her right. She observed him as he sipped his drink and smoked his cigarette as if in a trance, looking to his left

7

towards the dining table flush against the back wall. Then, he laughed, more of a chuckle.

"Something I said." Not a question.

"Oh. I was just thinking of the Belhaven lot and I realised that you are the only real outsider I have spoken to in a long time. Well, apart from one or two others but that was business." He took a sip of his brandy and turned towards her. "I'm boring you?"

"No." She wanted him to go on, her professional mind sensing that this could be her opportunity to break into the real world of Shala: to pierce the screens and curtains that the expatriates had erected to protect themselves and their lifestyles from ridicule, even condemnation. At a time of economic hardship at home, some of the British press were more than willing to criticise those living lives of luxury and privilege in the fading empire. Their affluence and comfort had been secured by exploitation and theft. They were the undeserving rich! Anyone aware of her family background could charge her with hypocrisy. But she was a journalist. Who better to be her first arrow than Tony Hockin, estate owner, *raison d'être* of Shala. Without the estate, there would be no Alston, no Godden, no Sutch, no colonialism.

"I got pissed off with them tonight. They drink my booze, eat my food but think they can…" He shook his head. "It was so stupid." He told her the story ending with him outside her door. "You know, in many ways, it's Eddie Jerome's fault."

An odd statement.

She wanted to ask him why he had decided to come to her but that could wait. She pushed her personal life to the back of her mind as she recalled the name Jerome. He had been the one-time manager of the estate. She was eager to hear more. Hockin needed no prompting, seemingly oblivious to the fact that she was a journalist.

August of the previous year was hot and humid. Shala was a fantastic place to live and work. No murders or rioting, unlike in the capital to the south. The southerners were always volatile. The northerners were honest, hardworking, maybe drank a little too much, especially as most of them were Muslims—well, nominally. There were no imams in or around Shala. Allah would understand. They were happy and content. And they respected the white tuans who always spoke to them. Shala was the epitome of British benevolence.

Nowhere was this benevolence more evident than at Hockin's estate. Hockin was willing to listen to and resolve the problems of his workers, although he had to ensure the plantation made money. Jerome was the estate manager, the workers' tuan, always representing their case to the big tuan. Housing, wages and food were the best in the country. Their productivity was the highest. They didn't mind when tuans Hockin and Jerome, usually accompanied by Sutch, Bendixson and the pretty white girls, climbed into the open-top Land Rover and the battered, old station wagon always loaded with crates of ice-cold beer to drive the thirty miles to Jacques Bay to spend the day swimming and drinking.

They didn't mind when sometimes they returned and sang their funny, loud British songs, even though it disturbed them in their estate houses close to the big house.

Jennie remembered something she had read, possibly by a French journalist, who in the 1930s had described the young, upper-class English as silly and obnoxious.

Theirs was a happy life and they could not understand why the southerners were always complaining. They did not work hard enough. And were always talking of politics. What was politics? There was no place for politics in Shala, and even less for Shi Baru with his talk of freedom, equality, workers owning the plantation, the struggle against imperialists. And he had been educated in England. Tuan Jerome never used such words and he was concerned about his workers. No. Shi Baru was too clever by half, not like his father, Dato Chia bin Baru, from the local aristocracy who probably was going to become the first prime minister of their independent country. The elder Baru knew that it was in his country's interest to work with Hockin and Jerome. But life would be even better if there was another collection point in the tiger segment.

The plantation had four working segments: snake, monkey and elephant to the west of the Kanu river and tiger on the eastern bank. In each segment, there were either three or four collection points where the tappers would bring their latex, emptied from the small bowls into a canvas bag. There were also resting and cooking facilities at these points, which had been introduced by Jerome so that the tappers could rest and eat before returning to their assigned patch. From these collections points, the latex would be taken by vehicle on the logger's track or on the perimeter roads to the plantation complex consisting of Hockin's house, stores, garages and some of the workers' houses. But in the tiger sector, there were only two collection points: one on the bank of the Kanu River opposite the plantation buildings on the higher ground and the other on the eastern perimeter road leading to the convent. There were no motorable logger's tracks in the tiger sector and the workers had to walk long distances to get to one of the collection points. It was a problem Hockin and Jerome were trying to resolve. The option was to make a track and cut a clearing but that would mean destroying many valuable rubber trees and Hockin was not prepared to do that until he had recovered the money spent on the last series of improvements in the workers' conditions.

Jerome was glowing when he joined Hockin on the veranda for a pre-dinner drink. He had been out on the boat on the Kanu with Mehad, the foreman. They had stopped at a clearing on the east bank when they spotted smoke. Beyond the clearing hidden by the trees was a hut inhabited by an old woman. Jerome was happy: the days of anguish were over and the workers' plight would be eased. It would be easy for the workers to take their latex to the clearing, which could be transported by boat a short way down river to the plantation complex. Jerome and Mehad were sure that the old woman would accept a financial incentive and being relocated to a new dwelling near the government clinic. Of course, Hockin would have to consider it but agreed that it sounded promising. Hockin would visit the site. The workers in the tiger segment had heard, no doubt due to Jerome's and Mehad's enthusiasm.

The next day, accompanied by Mehad and another worker, Hockin visited the clearing. Mehad and the other worker went into the old woman's hut. Hockin wasn't sure why he did not go into the hut. He told himself that it was the smell of the cooking odours, the urine and excreta: the convenient excuse of an Englishman. He remembered the clearing and hut from an earlier trip when he had been on a shooting trip with Arthur Godden. If only he had remembered the clearing and hut when discussing the matter with Jerome and Mehad. He was honest with himself: he wasn't as committed to the workers' welfare as Jerome. He owned only twenty percent of the plantation. His father's debt had resulted in having to sell the remaining shares to uncles who were interested only in profits. They had no interest in the welfare of the workers: the natives, the wogs, were a means of making money. He maintained the pretence of the sole owner. He knew that he should have told Jerome but he at times found Jerome's 60s' liberalism irritating. However, when the new collection point was finished, it might satisfy Jerome and end his incessant demands for improvements in the workers' conditions. Mehad, without informing his employer, had told the old woman of her good fortune of moving to a new home in Shala. It was a Friday and Hockin told Jerome that he was going to the capital for the weekend to do some business and to see Godden. The decision on the new collection point could wait; after all, they had waited a long time and a few more days wouldn't make any difference.

The weekend was boring and he found Godden more smug than usual, almost insufferable. Godden had been at Belhaven though he was two years ahead of Hockin. He had been surprised and delighted when he had encountered Godden in the capital, now a senior police officer. They had struck up a friendship and initially, Hockin had found him amusing company. Godden had introduced him to his sophisticated and influential friends including senior government officials. Godden enjoyed Hockin's hospitality on his rare visits to Shala. However, Hockin found the police officer was becoming more aloof and less willing to share information. Instead of going straight back to the plantation on the Monday, Hockin decided to visit Dr Tom Alston, another fellow pupil from Belhaven, hoping for an invitation to lunch, which was duly given. Unlike Godden, Hockin and Alston had been in the same year. He considered Alston probably to be his best friend though he felt that his friend was constrained by his wife with her petty prejudices and her concern with the pecking order amongst the British community in Shala and in the wider colonial society. She had attended the local girls' school near Belhaven and had met Alston at a school dance. They had married before he had completed his medical studies. Hockin had encouraged him to apply for a post in the government clinic in Shala and had used his influence to secure the post for him. He was a dedicated doctor and by his efforts obtained more government money to expand the services offered by the clinic, which was now though not in designation a cottage hospital.

His wife had never settled, complaining of the heat, the smell and especially the hygiene of the locals.

Almost as an afterthought at lunch, Alston informed Hockin that old Raza had told him that he would like to speak to Hockin about an old lady. Alston thought that he might be as usual looking for money and it might be best to ignore him. The expatriates called Raza 'Merlin', though Sutch referred to him as 'Gandalf', which, according to Jerome, was the sole benefit of the District Officer's Cambridge education. The mention of the old woman touched a chord in Hockin and he decided to meet Raza.

He smiled at Jennie, his eyes fixed on her slim, classical face. "I'm sure that I'm boring you." He was seeking a positive reaction from her.

She smiled. "You know, talking to old Raza was exhilarating. Probably my first real meeting with the East."

His eyes fixed on her. "I count it as one of my greatest experiences." A smile of slight embarrassment. "Probably until meeting you."

Jennie blushed but retained her professional instinct, asking, "You can tell me about it?"

Hockin, after a short internal debate, said, "I have never told anyone else and I wish I had told Eddie Jerome. He might have understood."

In the intense August heat, Hockin had been sweating by the time he had reached the town square. He felt not just a foreigner but an interloper amongst the people bustling around the square. His eyes searched the square and finally latched upon Raza sitting on a low stool surrounded by a pack of children in the middle of the west side of the square opposite the post office. Hockin approached the old man feeling nervous and thinking he should just return to the plantation. Feeling self-conscious, he stood behind the children until Raza's eyes trapped his. Hockin thought he had never before seen such fine, clear, incisive eyes. Raza spoke quickly to the children. Hockin heard 'Tuan Hockin' and the children stood, turned to stare momentarily at him and then ran away towards all corners of the square.

Raza stood up and extended a bony hand, which Hockin grasped lightly and released quickly. "Good afternoon, tuan. It's very hot."

Hockin was surprised at his perfect, accent-less English and Raza knew his thoughts. "If one is to know the East, one must learn not to be surprised. It's hot. I am sure you would like a drink, a beer." Before Hockin could reply, Raza had called to a boy of around thirteen years who ran off quickly and returned even quicker with two large bottles of beer and two glasses as well as a stool. "Please, will you sit, tuan?" The old man filled the glasses and handed one to Hockin who sat down facing Raza. He took out a packet of cigarettes. Raza refused the offer and Hockin lit one for himself. "Cheers." He smiled and relaxed a little.

Raza spoke, "People look at you and say there is the powerful tuan Hockin speaking to that old, foolish man Raza." He smiled. "I hope soon they call you not powerful but the great tuan."

Hockin was curt. "Doctor Alston told me that you wanted to see me…saying something about an old woman."

Raza ignored the young man's impatience and spoke of the history of the plantation, the segments and the problem of collection points in the tiger segment. Raza noted Hockin's expression. "You are surprised, tuan. Please don't be. The police have their spies but Raza has more spies than anyone."

Hockin, still impatient, spoke, "You want to ask me something?"

Raza remained unruffled and spoke quietly, "Time, young man"—Hockin was no longer the tuan— "well, what remains is everything to me. I am trying to make each day happy but soon happiness will be distant to Shala. There will be misery and death." He laughed and his voice became louder. "But that is for the future when we will not be as one…but for the moment, I hope we will be for the same."

Hockin thought of Merlin and smiled. "And the old woman?"

Raza first took a sip of beer. "Let me tell you a story." Raza raised himself off his stool and then sat down as if getting comfortable. He took another sip of beer. Hockin decided that he would not interrupt him.

There was a girl born to a poor peasant family in Choyhung near Canton. Her family knew Sun Yat Sen's family because it was his home village. She worked with her parents on their small piece of land, which provided enough to sustain them. The girl had the voice of what the English would call a nightingale. She began singing in Chinese operas in Canton. She married and had two sons. She did not forget her roots, in particular the poverty. Even though she was rich and famous, she continued to undertake secret and dangerous work for Sun Yat Sen. She was on the gunboat with him when he escaped from Canton down the Pearl River. She continued her singing career. There was no happier family in all of China. That life came to an end when her beloved husband fell afoul of a local warlord and was murdered. For her family's safety, she travelled to Hong Kong. Not having the connections in Hong Kong to restart her singing career, she took on all types of jobs but never stealing or being dishonest in anyway. She struggled but managed to create a comfortable home for her sons and gave them an education. Misfortune struck again. She was urged by a cousin in Canton to take in her son. He was dishonest and deceitful. She paid his debts on the promise that he was waiting for money from Canton from the sale of his business. She knew that she was being foolish but felt loyal to the family. Soon she was penniless. She came to Shala with her sons.

Raza paused and took a mouthful of beer. Hockin said nothing, continuing to drink and smoke.

She had in Hong Kong once worked as a tailoress. She did so again, supplying many people with good, cheap clothes. Though she spoke English as well as her native Cantonese, she made the effort to learn the local languages. She opened a restaurant below her home, now the post office.

Raza gave Hockin time to turn to look at the post office, a solid two-storey building directly opposite where they were sitting.

Her elder son became a teacher and the other one a tailor, both married with children. The Japanese came. Despite their mother's objection, the sons joined the movement fighting the Japanese. This resistance was organised by the British Army, which, despite retreating, had left some officers behind in the jungle. The British supported these officers by parachuting into jungle clearings more men and supplies including arms and ammunition. The Japanese garrison in Shala was small and could not patrol all the clearings and tracks. The individual soldiers were not of the same quality of those fighting in other areas such as China and Burma. The local commander, Captain Koichi, resorted to cruelty and bribery. The sons were betrayed. All of the family including the three children were paraded in the square outside their home in front of an assembled, terrified audience. The sons were beaten with whips and rifle butts by four soldiers. Their commander continued to issue a barrage of orders. The sons were bayoneted repeatedly in the body and head by the same four soldiers. The wives, screaming in deafening anguish, tried to shield the faces of their children from the horror. The four soldiers violently tore the children from their mothers' arms. Their grandmother tried to gather the children around her, again trying to shield their view but the four soldiers grabbed the children, holding them in front of their mothers. A soldier came running from the direction of the Japanese headquarters and handed a sheet of paper to his commander. He read it and shook his head. He barked out orders. The bayoneting was swift. The grandmother was kneeling, grasping her head with both hands, howling, in utter despair at the sight of her butchered family. A soldier moved towards the last, living member of the family but was stopped by Koichi who walked towards her. He removed a pistol from the holster on his belt. The old woman still on her knees took her hands from her head and clasped them together over her heart. She stretched her body up, with her head looking up defiantly at the Japanese officer whose pistol was aimed at her head. She stopped weeping. The officer looked around at the crowd, a sneer on his face and spoke a few words. He turned back to the woman, hit her with his pistol on the left side of her head and reholstered his pistol. He gave orders to a sergeant to get the soldiers off the square as quickly as possible.

Raza was staring at the middle of the square, the place of execution. He said, "That is the only time I have ever seen the devil in human shape." Hockin realised that Raza had been a witness. The Englishman felt empty and worthless. "I mustn't keep you. You are a busy man. I will finish the story another time," said Raza.

"No. Please go on."

An English-speaking Japanese soldier later told some people that his commander had decided not to kill the woman because she would suffer more by

13

having to live with the death of all her family. Some brave villagers in the night helped her up to the river north of the town. They found a small clearing opposite the almost derelict plantation buildings on the other side of the river. There was a 70-yard strip of secondary jungle running along the river's east bank before the rubber trees. Raza and others constructed a shelter for her in the trees just beyond the clearing. They brought her food. The Japanese patrolled the river in boats but seldom stopped and then only on the west bank. Remarkably, the woman recovered her strength and determination quickly. She survived on fish and edible roots. Koichi had been replaced by a major. A few days later, another Japanese captain came to Shala. It became clear that the captain's role was to get the plantation working. He moved into the estate house that had been empty since the British owner had fled on the approach of the Japanese. The new area commander allowed some restaurants and two bars to reopen. The estate workers and others were forced to return to work. One bar was for the exclusive use of the soldiers. Beer and rice wine revealed that Koichi had been removed because of his failure to get the plantation producing again. Rubber was essential for the Japanese war effort. It was said that Koichi had been sent north to Burma. The new commander was cold but proper in his treatment of the people. Punishments continued for infractions of the rules but there were no more executions. The people hoped that the British would not engage in minor and futile attacks. It was such actions that had caused the deaths of the two brothers and their families.

Raza stopped visiting the clearing at the woman's request. He did not know then that Major Donald Fleming, with his stay-behind party of three other soldiers, had come across the woman when reconnoitring the Japanese activity on the estate. When they returned to their base in the mountainous jungle so they could transmit their reports, the woman continued to note Japanese activity, especially the frequency and times of their boat patrols. She found different positions from which to observe the Japanese, using her skills gained whilst working for Sun Yat Sen. On one visit, Major Fleming was struck down with malaria. The woman insisted that his comrades return to their base to report back not only Fleming's condition but the information she had gathered. They agreed, being satisfied that Fleming was in good hands. Over the next few weeks, thanks to the woman's care, Fleming recovered his strength. The pair resumed their observations of the Japanese, selecting fire positions from which to attack the enemy's boats and also points to cross the river to destroy the buildings and stores. Three months after becoming ill, his men returned accompanied by another major. The British were advancing down through Burma. The Americans with their island-hopping tactics were closing on the home islands of Japan, which were being subjected to an extensive and sustained air bombing campaign. Japan was close to defeat. There were to be no attacks on the Japanese and specifically on plantations. The original owners would be reclaiming their property and production could not be interrupted. Fleming was furious and supported by his female co-warrior, considered launching one final attack. But the orders were specific and that was why another officer had returned with his men. The British were considering landing a sea assault force to retake the capital and Shala. Fleming's party was to link up with another party of soldiers and make their way to Jacques Bay where they would be picked up by submarine. Fleming urged his devoted and loyal companion to come with him. She refused. This little area of jungle was now her home. He knew she would not change her mind and admired her steadfastness. He wrote a few sentences on a signals message pad, let her read it, placed it in a leather pouch and gave it to her with the instruction to give it to the first British officer she met. He would tell his headquarters of all she had done to help the British. She thanked him. He stood wanting to convey in a physical way his admiration for her fortitude, her stoicism in adversity and her courage. He felt ill at ease and finally saluted her.

The day the British Army returned to Shala, the woman stood with Raza in the square. She had shown Fleming's written statement to Raza. She approached a tall, young, red-haired second lieutenant who was standing at the edge of the square with a sergeant and corporal, watching another company march through Shala.

"Excuse me, sir." The officer turned and was surprised the speaker was a Chinese woman, her clothes suggesting a beggar, a vagrant. He had found it difficult to gauge the ages of the natives, especially the Chinese. She was certainly old enough to be his mother, possibly his grandmother.

"Yes, ma'am. How can I help you?" His voice was English public school but deep for a young man. Raza thought it had been the most distinctive English voice he had ever heard and it had carried authority.

"Sir, will you read this?" She asked handing him Fleming's statement. He read it quickly, paused, astounded, look down at the woman and read it again slowly:

'I, Major Donald Angus Fleming, declare that Fong Siu Wai has been my brave and loyal comrade. She nursed me back to life when I was ill. She has provided valuable assistance to the British Army. Her two sons fought the Japs. They, their wives and children were brutally killed by the Nips. She now wants to end her life in this small piece of God's earth. I ask, no beg, that she be allowed to do so. I would hope that we or the civilian authorities could build a more permanent home for her. I will provide more details in my op report.'

It had been signed and dated 25 May 1945. Fleming was from the same regiment but attached to special operations.

To no one in particular, he stuttered, "We must honour this obligation." He turned back to the woman. "Eh, Miss Fong, I am Gordon Buchanan-Henderson." He shook her hand then saluted her. He refolded the paper and requested, "May I keep this to show to my company commander?" Fong Siu Wai nodded her consent. "Sergeant McHarg, look after this lady. I need to speak to the company commander." He turned and strode purposefully towards his company commander.

McHarg, in a Highland lilt, spoke to the corporal, "Wonder what that's about?"

The corporal replied, *"Who knows. He's an arrogant sod! He thinks he's the CO."*

"Soon will be, knowing GBH."

They watched as Buchanan-Henderson allowed his company commander to read Fleming's statement. There was a discussion and the senior officer seemed reluctant to comply with Fleming's request. *"The old man doesn't seem happy,"* the corporal said.

"He'll come around. Doesn't he always for GBH. He won't want to upset GBH's family, a brigadier and a general."

A few minutes later, Buchanan-Henderson said, "I will ensure it is done." Then in almost a dismissive tone. "Thank you, sir." He saluted his company commander. The young officer ensured the commitment was honoured. He persuaded some Royal Engineers to build the hut exactly the way Fong Siu Wai wanted. She said that she would pay for the hut but Buchanan-Henderson in his charming manner told her that he was given medals but she was given a hut. He wasn't sure what was better. He did think that she deserved a medal, which probably would depend on how Fleming's operational report was received by the generals. Although the Buchanan-Henderson family had produced generals and brigadiers, the young officer had not been impressed by most of the senior officers he had encountered. On commissioning, he had turned down the opportunity to be on Mountbatten's staff in Ceylon—on the social circuit of cocktail parties, dinners and balls. Like his father, he preferred to be led by a proper general, Bill Slim, even if he was not of blue-blood stock.

Raza, who had borrowed it, gave the original paper to Hockin to read.

Fong Siu Wai continued to work as a tailoress in Shala but never stayed there. Eventually, she sold her former home to the government. She was now mostly financially independent. As she grew older, Raza would ensure that food and other supplies were taken to her by some of the young men and women of Shala, which was an expanding town. Raza visited her at least once a month when she would pay him for the goods. As she grew older, the visits to Shala became rarer and had stopped recently.

The light was fading. Raza finished his beer. "So, tuan Hockin, there's an old woman, once young and pretty, who has had to restart her life from nothing not once but three times." His eyes, still strong and fierce, focussed on Hockin and pleaded on behalf of the old woman. "Please let her stay in her last home. She is going to die soon."

Hockin looked away. "But I have to think of my workers."

"Yes, that is true. You are right. No old woman should stop progress for the many. Even if it breaks the commitment given to her by the British Army."

"Damn you, Raza. She can stay but you're coming with me to tell her." He stood up.

Raza, a glint in his eyes, spoke quietly, "I am an old man. The journey—"

"Don't give me that," Hockin interrupted. "You are not that old. You are the only one who can give her my assurance. I will pick you up tomorrow morning at ten. Here! If you are not here, the deal is off."

Raza stood up and bowed slightly to Hockin. "I must tell you one more thing. You will meet a woman and your lives will be together unless you choose a different path. Then you will regret and be sad. But sadness is part of being British no matter how much they try to hide their feelings."

Hockin scoffed. "Forget the soothsayer bit. I will see you tomorrow morning."

"So the old woman stayed. She is still there. Jerome refused to continue as manager."

"I think that was noble of you." Jennie was sincere.

He sighed. "I wish it was but it was guilt. The owner who deserted the plantation when the Japanese came—my grandfather."

Jennie offered words of comfort. "You can't be held responsible for the actions of your grandfather."

"I know."

Jennie continued as if she was writing one of her moralising opinion columns, "Your name is not blackened. In fact, by your action, you are restoring the family name."

"Jennie, stop." He shook his head. "The guilt comes from knowing that I would have done the same as my grandfather. I would have…deserted my workers." There was silence for a period broken by Hockin saying, "Look at the time, I had better be going." He smiled, his boyish face returning. "You have your reputation to think of." He stood up and went to the door. "Do you have to leave tomorrow…I mean, today?"

"I have to catch a flight to Hong Kong and then file my story."

Alarmed, Hockin inquired, "You won't include what I told you?"

"No, not unless you want me to."

"No."

"It's really about Chila Baru and the future."

"You know, this is his home."

She smiled and replied, "That's why I'm here."

"Of course. Sorry." He held out his hand, which she accepted. "It was great meeting you. Really it was."

Another smile. "Thank you. I enjoyed listening to you."

He said hopefully, "Maybe I will see you in Hong Kong. I must go there sometime."

"Yes. I am easy to find… Wait." She retrieved a card from her bag and gave it to him.

"Thanks." He hugged her quickly. "Sure you're not coming back to Shala? Not even for the soldiers?" Immediately, he regretted betraying Bendixson's confidence.

She concealed her surprise and interest. "Not even for the soldiers."

Chapter 2

The introduction to the police officer in mufti had been perfunctory. The young captain maintained a proper rank relationship with the major sitting behind the desk. During the major's briefing, both officers' eyes drifted occasionally to the medium-built man in civilian clothes sitting to the major's left. The briefing was shorter than usual and not in the usual orders' format for an internal security operation but Captain William Oldham knew there was more to come. Instructions were simple and already known to him. He was to take his platoon north to Shala and undertake normal internal security duties in support of the local police.

After clarifying some points concerning transport, ammunition and stores, Oldham asked with a slight hint of irritation, "Is that all, sir?"

The major ignored Oldham's tone, looked at the man to his left, then down at his desk and said in a weary tone, "From me anyway but I am sure Mr Godden has something to say."

Two days earlier, a jaunty Lieutenant Oldham had been sitting in the Commanding Officer's office. He was handing over his platoon today, being promoted to captain at midnight and no doubt was going to be told his new job. The adjutant had indicated possibly the operations officer but more likely to be a company second-in-command. He had hoped for the reconnaissance platoon but there had been a recent change.

Lieutenant-Colonel Bob Marchant did not engage in pleasantries or small talk. "You are remaining C platoon commander." He had not allowed Oldham time to respond. "I have been told to deploy a platoon to Shala. I think it should be a company." The colonel had looked down at his desk. When he spoke, it was as if he had been thinking aloud. "Not sure why this is not a job for Grievous' boys." He looked at Oldham. "Not important. It's not a place you have been to on your travels around the country. There have been no incidents up there apart from some minor demonstrations. The police are in control. There has been no military there, not even a field intelligence NCO for five years, possibly more." The stunned young officer was trying to formulate questions in his mind. His commanding officer did not give him time. "I know you will be disappointed but it's a good challenge for you. You will be on your own. You'll like that. And you will be a captain."

Oldham could not suppress a smile. "Thank you, sir, colonel."

"I thought of keeping young McMasters in place but I suspect you won't have time to look after a new second lieutenant and it would probably just confuse the soldiers. I am giving you an additional section, Corporal Jubb from Bravo platoon. Is that okay?"

"Major Slater happy with—"

"Leave that to me. Also, you will have a detachment from the signals platoon under Sergeant Williams, six mt drivers, two chefs and a couple of medics." He adopted a pensive look. "I think you should have an intelligence NCO. The IO felt he couldn't spare anyone. So Sergeant Knight will go as your Int guy. I know that he hasn't done the relevant courses but he has done enough ops and knows how SB works." Oldham did not try to suppress the smile. "William. Let me make it clear that Knight is not returning as your platoon sergeant. Nash has to earn his spurs."

"I understand."

"Now I have to tell Knight that he will not be going to the depot as an instructor."

"I don't think he'll be too disappointed."

"William. Only you and Knight will know of the real reason for this deployment. I had to go to the Head of SB even for you two to be told. I will brief Knight. No leaks. Don't let me down on this." Colonel Bob pushed a large, brown envelope across his desk towards Oldham. "It's a briefing on Shala, mainly the history and pen-pictures of the personalities, British and natives. And the cover story. Shala is quite different from the rest of the country." Pointing his right index finger at Oldham, he declared, "Read it!"

"Colonel."

"You are not there to take over from the police. You have spent the last nine months supporting the other companies. Your platoon has experience in all aspects of IS and counter-insurgency. Probably you have my most experienced NCOs and soldiers." Oldham did not interrupt the colonel to point out that these experienced NCOs and soldiers get promoted into other companies or platoons, go on postings or leave the army. It would be considered whinging to do so. One was expected to crack on. "I know that under your sophisticated and calm veneer, you're itching to get into a fight!" Again, he jabbed his right index finger at him. "Don't…unless you have to."

"Yes sir."

"Probably nothing will happen and you will be back here in a few weeks. How many ambushes have we done based on good intelligence and nothing happens?" He answered his own question, "Hundreds! Any questions?"

"No Colonel. Not at present."

"Sort out with the ops officer and QM your weapons, stores and so on. Take additional ammunition and any other kit you think necessary. Any problems, let the adjutant know." He paused, folded his arms and leaned backed in his chair. He seemed concerned, worried, not an expression normally associated with Colonel Bob, "Your OC will give you formal orders on Wednesday morning. You will also receive a briefing from a Mr Godden. He is a senior Special Branch officer. He has a lot of experience of this country. He has the ear of senior officials not only here but in London." He leaned across the desk, his eyes locking with Oldham's. "He is not a kinglehead!"

"Sir." Oldham smiled inwardly at the colonel's expression, though it was not unusual for him to use odd or unknown expressions. The officers tended to refer to the white colonial police officers as blockheads and worse. They were regarded generally as either failed candidates for commissions, inept at any profession, or black sheep despatched to the colonies by their families to avoid scandal.

Godden pushed the hair back from his forehead, uncrossed his legs, stood up and stuffed his left hand into his trouser pocket. He smiled. "It is very simple, Captain. Politics!" Oldham grimaced mentally. Now, politicians told the military how to fight a war and even gave it a new name of Internal Security, which—back home—conjured up images of a few kids throwing stones. He had been reared in the tradition of the military. He yearned for the days of his father and grandfathers when the politicians started a war and the soldiers were allowed to get on with it, albeit he knew that politicians had always interfered in military operations. Political interference was a trusty excuse for the generals when things went wrong.

Godden continued. "Shala is the home of Dato Chila Baru, leader of the National Democrats, and we hope prime minister when independence finally comes. As you no doubt know, these people base their life on the family." His tone was matter-of-fact, not smug and condescending as Oldham had anticipated. "We come to the crux. But I want to be clear. This is only for you and Sergeant Knight. Your soldiers are to be given the cover story." Godden had agreed reluctantly on disseminating this information because he was told that Oldham and Knight were likely to see through the cover plan once in Shala. Dissemination of intelligence was a matter of judgement. He had been assured by their CO that they had received Branch intelligence before and there had never been any evidence of a leak. Neither of them gossiped in their respective messes. The CO had stated that he would personally remind them of the sensitivity of this information. Godden moved to the map on the wall behind the major. "We have had reports of communist terrorists, CTs, estimated around eight, moving into the jungle here," pointing at the area with a thin stick, a wand, which he seemed to have produced from nowhere, "northwest of Shala, obviously having crossed the border or about to." He beckoned Oldham around behind the major so that the captain could see the map more clearly. The major made a half turn towards the map but appeared disinterested.

"How long before they reach Shala, sir?" Oldham felt a 'sir' appropriate.

"That depends on their experience. Possibly working to a set date. Hopefully, if they are like the army, it will take them weeks…or even never to find Shala." Godden grinned. He was referring to the times army patrols got lost or never reached a location. Complete platoons had been lost in the jungle and there was a report that a company from a northern regiment had become lost when trying to locate a lost platoon. The major snorted. The Special Branch man ignored him and continued, "Hopefully, we can give you some warning when they are close to Shala. But we need to be prepared. Their target is likely to be this large, rubber plantation between Shala and the border. The plantation is owned by Anthony Hockin…a rather independent chap who, unlike the other planters, won't want the military all over his land." Godden turned away from the map. "The plantation is the main source of employment for Shala and the surrounding area. We must stop the terrorists from intimidating the locals and driving them away." He paused. "If they do, Baru, who is already under pressure seeing we can't protect his own town and people, might throw in his lot with the communists."

"Would that be so bad." It was a comment, not a question. Oldham, politically conservative, thought it might be best for newly independent countries to have a sort of form of communism, though he thought of it as a form of British paternalism.

Godden ignored Oldham's remark. "If it did happen, we would probably lose our base and eventually our business interests, which are considerable."

"We couldn't let that happen." A sneer.

Godden was too adroit and experienced to be drawn into an argument with the army officer. "I shall be up from time to time to see how you are getting on."

"My CO wouldn't have given me this job if I couldn't do it." Anger in his voice.

"I am quite sure you are capable or I would not have approved you." Godden's face was expressionless.

The officer's anger turned into frustration. He looked at the major expecting support but none came. "Is that all?"

Godden nodded and the major murmured, "Thanks, William." Oldham saluted and turned to leave.

"One other thing, Captain." Oldham turned his head towards Godden, who continued, "Bendixson, the chief inspector in Shala, don't expect too much of him. He is good but has his limitations, pedantic. That's why he's in Shala—out of the way." Now the tone was condescending.

Oldham nodded and left the office. He paused, feeling annoyed with himself and angry especially with his company commander for his failure to support him against Godden. Major Slater was not even at the back of the queue when backbones were being issued. He would issue orders and inspect his platoon tonight with a final check in the morning before moving out. He had to find Sergeant Nash, his new platoon sergeant.

He watched as his platoon sergeant supervised the embussing of C platoon. He was amused by Pete Nash, a dapper, prissy, earnest man with black hair and a pencil moustache who called him 'sir' at every opportunity. He seemed efficient to his platoon commander but thought it unlikely that he could share a few beers with him. He was also unsure whether Nash could relate to the soldiers especially the Jocks, Paddies and Cockneys. The regiment recruited its soldiers from towns such as Leicester, Nottingham and Mansfield who were mostly dependable and amiable. Over the years, due to a fall in recruitment, the regiment had had to take recruits from Ireland, Scotland and London. Oldham felt the reinforcement was not just in numbers but in steel. He felt the 'outsiders' were generally tougher than the Midlanders, especially the Cockneys though he knew few of the Londoners were real Cockneys having East European ancestries but anglicised names. His musings on the quality of the British soldier continued as he watched his platoon. He did not like Northern or Welsh regiments. He believed their soldiers to be temperamental, up and down, and their officers second-rate. He smiled at his arrogance, four years commissioned and he could pontificate on the quality of the British infantryman. He did make an exception to this harsh verdict for one northern soldier who was approaching him, his platoon sergeant before Nash.

Sergeant Phil Knight had come from Wigan, or at least according to his records, had been born there. He was intelligent but taciturn. Promotion had come quickly. They had formed a good relationship. When they had a few beers together, Oldham had talked openly and eagerly of his background: public school in Bedford, his military family, holidays in France, his liking for Calvados and Sandhurst. Knight had never seemed bored by the repetition of the same stories and had encouraged the young officer to expand on his stories and family. However, Knight would steer the conversation in a different direction when Oldham asked him of his background and family. Oldham liked to speculate that Knight had a dark, family secret of which he was ashamed. Nevertheless, the officer suspected that Knight had found him amusing just as he found Nash amusing.

"Good morning, sir." Knight saluted.

"Morning, Mr Bond." A caricatured Eastern European accent. Knight shook his head at the reference to the fictional spy whose films were popular. Knight reminded him that the CO had decided he would be the community relations NCO to avoid annoying Special Branch, which held a low opinion of the army's intelligence people. He replied, "I always wanted to say it."

"Bond. The most *known* secret agent in the world. I thought the clue was in the word *secret*. Read Graham Greene's stuff, *Our Man in Havana*."

"Saw the movie. Alex Guinness. Was that after or before he screwed up on the River Kwai!"

Knight ignored the typical Oldham quip. "There's John Le Carré. A new writer. *The Spy who came in from the Cold*. That's more realistic. We fuck up."

"You know I only read Part One orders…*Commando* and Sven Hassel." It was part of his image crafted for the platoon, reading war comic books known as training manuals and a novel about a German panzer penal battalion purportedly based on the author's experiences.

Knight returned to *Bond*. "So I get the girl this time."

"Good try but I'm still the officer and gentleman."

"So more like the road movies." Knight responded to Oldham's quizzical look, "Forget it. I'll tell you sometime."

"All set?"

"Yes. The Shala brief is quite interesting. It's—"

"Bored with it after the first paragraph."

Another shake of the head by Knight. He changed the subject. "How come you managed to scrounge so many Armalites?" The Colt Armalite rifle, designated the AR-15, was a semi-automatic weapon unlike the automatic M16 used by the American soldiers. The British had bought the AR-15 because it was cheaper. British soldiers called it the Armalite or 'my gat', which referred to the infantryman's personal weapon, usually a rifle. Most of the platoon and section commanders of the rifle companies had been issued with the American weapon. Knight had had one when he had been a corporal in recce platoon and had retained it when he became C platoon sergeant.

"I persuaded the ops officer that Shala was our Da Nang. So the section two ICs will also have them. Also half a dozen spare and three extra gimpies."

"Did 'make them pay' not object?" The nickname for the Technical Quartermaster.

"He couldn't. You know old Ally and me are mates." Ally was Alistair Matheson, the Quartermaster. "'Make them pay' wouldn't argue with the CO and especially not with Ally. Shouting at private soldiers and lance jacks is his level."

"What about zeroing in?"

"Done yesterday." Oldham adopted a mock dismissive tone, "Sergeant Knight. You leave the soldiering to me. Stick to your briefing papers."

"Sir." Sgt Nash was there. He saluted. "Loaded and ready to leave, sir."

Oldham returned the salute. He looked at Nash and then Knight. "Let's go!"

Chapter 3

The first thirty miles out of the capital was on a good tarmac road. The convoy consisted of four long-wheeled based Land Rovers, of which two were fitted for radio (FFR), two short-wheeled based Land Rovers, both FFR, and three Bedford three-ton trucks. Except for Oldham's, the Land Rovers had trailers attached and one Bedford lorry pulled a water-bowser. Two of the Bedfords would return to the capital with their drivers and escorts from HQ Company accompanied by two police vehicles. The vehicles, except for one short-based Land Rover, had had their canopies and frames removed. The benches on the Bedfords were positioned back-to-back in the centre with the soldiers facing out as required for anti-ambush drills.

Oldham was in the leading Land Rover, though he should have been in the second, which was the covered Land Rover with the signals detachment. Knight considered mentioning this to his former platoon commander or to Nash. He decided to say nothing: he hoped that he did not regret it. Nash's Land Rover was the last vehicle in the convoy.

The next twenty-five miles were on a tarred road but not of good quality followed by about sixteen miles on a dusty, dirt-logging road that climbed up leaving behind the flat paddy fields. The soldiers were unhappy, grumbling because of the heat, the road and that it was always their platoon that was given the hardest and dangerous tasks. It didn't matter that they had become accustomed to the heat, the roads and the 'hard and dangerous' tasks. They scanned the passing fields for any signs of an ambush or terrorist threat. In fact, the greatest threat to their safety was the speeding, unstable, loaded logging trucks going south and the unloaded ones overtaking them going north. Knight was again reading the brief on Shala, though his mind wandered to the conversation in the rear. Cook, a cocky Londoner, was again relating his conquests. His tales were peppered with 'not kidding'. McGraw from the tough Raploch district of Stirling retorted, "Yu'll be leavin' here wi mair than a suntan."

Cook was bemused. "What are you talking about, Jock?" Knight smiled.

"A dose!" McGraw shook his head. "VD. Ye'r a bampot!" Cook did not respond. The conversation turned to football, which was dominated by McGraw though Cook had to have his say on his beloved Chelsea. Usually, Knight joined in the banter but his thoughts were on Shala. He felt resentful going up to protect some plantation owned by a posh boy from a minor public school. He remained infected by Wigan.

The final ten miles into Shala was on another good tarmac dual carriage road through the forest. The plantations began about five miles from Shala with the road going downhill towards Shala, which sat in a plateau bowl with rubber and tea plantations rising gracefully up the surrounding hills. The ground to the north was more mountainous and clad in primary jungle and beyond the border. As the convoy neared Shala, on both sides of the road were shacks built of wood or tin or both. Each shack appeared to have its own plot of land to grow—not cultivate produce to sell in the market—to sustain them. There was a large Coca-Cola sign dominating the beginning of Shala proper. To Knight, there was something peaceful in the fields dotted by the shacks but a peace in ignorance. The convoy made its way down the main street between the mostly two-storey stone buildings, many with verandas, through the square was enclosed both by commercial and residential buildings, again mostly two-storeyed. There were shops and restaurants as well as bars to the soldiers' surprise and delight. After ten metres, the convoy turned left into a street leading into the market-place, usually a babbling, bustling noise of bargaining but the stalls were silent. The street continued, passed London Crescent to the right, residential area for the white government officials, to the police station twenty metres beyond the market-place.

The station was a cream-coloured three-storey building set in the middle of a square compound and enclosed by a ten-foot high metal fence bordered at the top by barbed wire. On each corner above the fence was a half-enclosed turreted sentry post accessed by open steps. There were two single-storey wooden accommodation huts, one on either side of the stone building but of a slightly shorter length, and each hut five metres from the perimeter fence. The one-way road circuit was between the accommodation huts and the main building. The guardroom and reporting desk for the public was a two-room single-storey building. The carpark was at the rear of the building.

The convoy entered the compound going to the left around into the carpark. Despite three police Land Rovers and two paddy-wagons, there was sufficient space for the army vehicles. Oldham had already instructed Nash on what he wanted on arrival. The platoon and attachments paraded in front of their respective vehicles. Nash called them to attention, turned and saluted Oldham. "Thank you, Sergeant Nash." Oldham had spotted the police officers at the rear entrance to the station on driving into the carpark. He about-turned and waited at attention.

A tall, gangling police chief inspector approached Oldham. He was dressed in the normal grey shorts and shirt wearing a black Sam Browne belt with a holster attached. Oldham thought he looked out of place and uncomfortable. His shoulders drooped and it seemed a constant battle to keep his head erect. He stopped, not quite a drill halt, one pace in front of the army officer who saluted him. The return salute was hesitant and sloppy, amusing the onlooking soldiers.

"Welcome, Captain Oldham. I'm Chief Inspector Bendixson. Please call me Terence." He was more at ease extending his arm. The whole action of extending his arm, shaking hands and withdrawing was graceful. Oldham speculated that

Bendixson was more at ease out of uniform, probably at social functions. Bendixson introduced the two men flanking him, one a local inspector and the other his station staff-sergeant whose role was a mix of sergeant-major and company quartermaster sergeant.

"Shall we go inside so I can brief you?"

"I would like to get my men settled. Sort out accommodation and get some—"

Bendixson interrupted him, "Staff Ho will see to that." He explained that the soldiers would be in the accommodation hut on the one-way circuit out and that most of the top-floor accommodation would also be available. "Ho is a good man. Chinese. Served in the army. His English is very good. Has organised a meal for your men." Bendixson was eager to convey all this information probably to show his efficiency.

"Thank you. Sergeant Nash!" He told Nash to get the section commanders to supervise the unloading of weapons and that he should supervise the unloading of the weapons of the attachments following which he was to liaise with Ho to get the men into their accommodation and feed. He would hold an orders group later.

He turned to Bendixson. "I'm ready. But you don't mind if my Sergeants Knight and Williams attend?"

"No, not at all."

He called over the two sergeants and introduced his signals sergeant who saluted and then shook hands with Bendixson. "This is Sergeant Knight. He's my political officer—well, the terrorists have them." Bendixson's laugh was forced. "He is my community relations NCO. A sort of liaison officer. You know, 'hearts and minds'."

"Oh! Good."

On either side of the rear door was an L-shaped concrete wall with steps leading down to the basement, to the left were cells and interrogation rooms that covered most of the basement and to the right some small storerooms. The policeman chuckled that the cells were hardly used. Oldham refrained from quipping because it was easier to shoot their prisoners. The first- and second-floor windows had metal shutters with a round firing port in each half of the metal shutter. The windows were open. The front and rear entrances had metal doors.

The four men entered the building. Bendixson had told the inspector he could continue with his duties. On the ground floor to the right was a door leading into a kitchen from which came the smell of cooking, resulting in approving nods from the three soldiers. Opposite, under the stairs, was a metal door to the armoury. Next to it was another door behind which were stairs leading to the cells. At the main entrance on the right was the door to the dining mess for the police with seating for forty people. The door beside the stairs up to the first floor was a briefing-cum-games room.

The first floor was divided. At the top of the stairs to the right was a double-frosted glass swing door into the operations room. Inside to the left along the back wall a table with three telephones and a radio set. A police sergeant sat at a long table with empty chairs on either side of him; above him on the wall, a map of the town and one of the whole police area. The latter map had areas shaded in different colours and round markers with numbers pinned on different locations. Behind the sergeant in the middle of the room was an oak desk with three telephones and a radio handset and a black, soft swivel chair. Behind the oak desk, the room had been partitioned by a balsawood wall with three offices accessed by glass doors. Each office had a metal desk and three chairs, though all the offices looked unused. The other half of the first floor contained a suite of six offices. The chief inspector's was the largest, furnished with an oak desk, three soft armchairs, a sofa, two bookcases and a coffee table. The inspectors shared one office, the sergeants another and the secretarial staff in another. The other two offices were designated for the Special Branch and CID, though neither department had personnel in Shala. SSgt Ho had requisitioned the Special Branch office.

The third floor was accommodation with four single rooms, three two-men rooms, three four-men rooms and a small officers' mess with dining table, six chairs and a small bar, though it was seldom used. In the middle of the corridor was a spring-swing ladder to the roof with the flag pole above the front main entrance, flying the Union Flag. There was a metal water-tank. A low wall around the roof gave protection if kneeling though an individual with a modern rifle could fire onto the roof from the high ground to the north. When built, the station had been isolated from the town but was now surrounded by new settlements though not two-storey stone buildings.

Bendixson sat at the oak desk with the army officer to his right and the two sergeants to the left facing the map. "I will keep my briefing short because no doubt you have read the briefing paper."

"Yes." A lie! "Take as long as you want. I can't always take it in when it's on paper." Knight looked at the floor wishing to avoid his officer's eyes.

The policeman explained that Shala covered a much bigger area because the three kampongs had expanded. The kampongs are named after the original village headman or dominant family with two to the East and the other to the West. Kampong Megat to the southwest was where the logging depots were located and most of the loggers lived there. Kampong Lai in the southeast was the centre for textiles, having two or three small factories as well as individual family businesses all producing different types of clothes and bedding. Kampong Tengu to the northeast had been a hamlet and was now a shanty town, a gubuk, with most of the shacks built from corrugated metal, plywood, cardboard boxes, sheets of plastic and other functional items. The dwellers, mostly Chinese, were almost all casual and transient workers though some were simply squatters or vagrants.

The police and the whites tended to refer to them as X, Y and Z in an anti-clockwise direction due to the previous Irish Special Branch officer. "He was always drunk and probably couldn't remember or pronounce the names." He changed the subject. "The make-up of the population of Shala is very similar to the rest of the country. Around sixty-five percent indigenous natives and roughly twenty percent Chinese and the rest Indian. Of course, the Chinese and the Indians have been here for generations. They are hard-working whereas the natives can be lazy. Why do something today which can be put off till tomorrow?" Knight noted mentally that this view, a cliché, was shared by most of the white community. The police officer continued, "Like the rest of the country, the Chinese and Indians own most of the commercial premises, shops and restaurants. Relations between the communities at present are fine, calm but the tensions bubble away beneath the surface. My officers come from all three communities, which helps keep the place calm. Again my best officers are Indian followed by the Chinese. There are a number of different languages spoken here such as—"

Oldham (impatient): "Yes, yes, Terence. I know about the languages from the briefing paper." Another lie! Notwithstanding, Oldham knew of the language differences from being on operations throughout the colony. "I would prefer if you get to the security aspect."

"Yes. Of course. I understand." Bendixson paused, re-ordering his thoughts. He preferred to keep to his prepared brief. He was going to tell the soldiers that the accommodation was underused because most of his police officers lived in the town and beyond, being married or in relationships. Only one inspector, two sergeants and thirty other rank officers lived in the station. "Right." Bendixson tended to ramble, not being precise and to the point, dwelling on matters that were obvious to the soldiers.

The sergeant at the ops table was the duty officer. The telephones were direct secure lines: one to the operations room in police HQ in the capital, another to the police observation post in the hills above Shala and the third to Hockin's plantation. Bendixson said he had the same direct lines in his office as well as a normal civilian telephone. He moved to the map. With a pen, he indicated the junction on the main road where the convoy had turned left to reach the police station. The right turning led to the government compound, which contained two buildings, one the government offices, the other the government clinic that people simply called GAB, the government administration building. The main road continued to and ended at the plantation with the River Kanu to the east of the road. But before the plantation, about a mile from Shala, another road branched off to the right, northeast, curving through the fields and the newer settlements then twisting around through the hills to the police observation post. A coloured pin marked the post on the wall map. Just before the main road reached the plantation, another secondary road went left, west around the plantation up into the jungle but still on the British side sometimes referred to as the border road. It became a logging track after crossing the wooden bridge over the Kanu but ended abruptly almost in line but below the police OP.

The police mounted mobile patrols in the town and on the three roads. There were also foot patrols in Shala. There were no foot patrols around the plantation, in the settlements or in the jungle. He apologised. "I have not enough officers. Just not enough."

Oldham smiled. "I never have enough soldiers but I still have to do my job." He caught the quizzical expression on Knight's face but continued speaking to Bendixson. "As you know, I have only a watching brief at present. If the situation changes, then…" He did not want to expand that would be for later in private with Bendixson nor did he know how much Bendixson had been told about the platoon's deployment. "I will not be mounting any mobile patrols except for my men to get to know the ground, key points and so on."

"I understand."

Oldham could see that Knight, who was now at the wall map, was still distracted. "Sir," Knight was addressing Bendixson. His telescopic pointer was directed on a green map-pin below the OP map pin "This road to the left just before the OP, where does it go to?"

Bendixson peered at the indicated map pin. "Oh. That's the convent."

Oldham raised his voice, not quite shouting. "A bloody convent! What, with nuns? What's it doing here?"

Chapter 4

The chief inspector was uncomfortable. He shook his head several times before replying, "It's a school and sort of clinic, mainly for the children in the settlements, the official term for the shanties. They pick up the overflow from the government school and medical facilities. They don't charge for any of their services." Knight refrained from asking why the convent was not included in the Shala brief. Bendixson continued, "There are two European sisters—one quite old and a young one. Think they are Irish. And some local sisters." He paused again, looking at the map, more shakes of the head. "We don't think they are at much risk. They look after the people who are more likely to support the communists."

Oldham, not convinced, asserted, "It has not stopped them in other areas. Intimidation! Any resistance by the locals or even hesitation in supporting the terrs—'You not help us, then you'll not have a school.' What do you think?" To Knight.

"You could be right, sir." He thought for a moment then said, "A few hard nuts, especially if they are not local, might think slotting a couple of white nuns would quickly have the desired effect on the locals. And an additional bonus, think of the effect on the expats. The—"

"Surely not?" Bendixson interrupted. "It would be the one thing that would turn the people in the shanties against them."

Oldham and Knight exchanged astonished glances. Oldham, looking directly at Bendixson, asserted, "That will not happen! These people are ruthless! They will not tolerate any dissent!" The officer pointed at Knight and then at himself. "We both know that from experience." A pause. "Anyway, how can we protect people in the kampongs—or the shanties as you call them? You know that, I know that, the CTs know that…and the people know that. Even if we set up protected villages, we don't have enough soldiers or police to guard them." Bendixson nodded resignedly. There was silence for a few minutes.

"I could go up tomorrow, sir?"

"Yes. Good idea. Do that."

"The nuns don't want us around and I think it is even less likely they would want the army," Bendixson said, "and the OP overlooks it so we provide some security."

Knight smiled. "I'll wear my 'hearts and minds' hat."

Bendixson was not impressed but Oldham interjected quickly, "Think time now, Terence, for a one-to-one."

The meeting did not take long. Bendixson did not provide any additional information on the security threat. He confirmed with the army officer that both had the same cover story, which was that the army was being deployed into Shala because it was the only district where there was no military. This was contained in a press release to the local press and radio as well as the BBC. Both potential first prime minister of the soon-to-be independent country had stated that the fledging national army should be in every district. Baru's rival for the post, Onn bin Jafar, had claimed that his opponent, supported by the British, was exploiting the lack of a military presence in Shala to become prime minister. It was true that Baru had claimed it demonstrated his ability to unite the various communities, thereby preventing racial conflict. Now he argued the deployment was not just for security but that the national army was a symbol of national unity and also all should share the economic benefits from defence spending. The colonial government officials were briefed to respond to questions on why British soldiers had been deployed to Shala and not the local soldiers by observing that the more experienced British soldiers had been the first into every district, which was true.

Bendixson agreed to the three offices in the ops room being used by the army; each of the initial familiarisation patrols being accompanied by a police officer with a good knowledge of the area; there would not be a joint ops room; but with the platoon command post in one of the requisitioned rooms, a joint ops setup could be initiated quickly; a section would be deployed to the police OP having confirmed sufficient accommodation for both police and army; the soldiers would not participate at present in guarding the police station but would provide a quick reaction force at immediate notice to respond to any attack on the station; a separate weapons loading and unloading bay would be constructed for the army; and admin issues would be left to Staff Ho and Sergeant Nash. Oldham would draft SOPs for his platoon but accepted that they required Bendixson's approval as he remained for the present the senior officer of the security forces.

Bendixson became wary when Oldham stated that Knight was not only responsible for community liaison but also for the collection of intelligence. Oldham explained, "The army always does this. A way of keeping us busy. You must know this from your own experiences with us."

His neck sunk into his shoulders, open palms extended almost in supplication, the policeman said quietly, "Actually, no. I came here as an inspector. You are the first military here for some time." His head pulled his neck out of the shoulder, fingers intertwined in a loose clench. "I was then a staff officer for the Commissioner. Establishment tables. Manning and such things." A pause. "Of course, I had some dealings with the military but not on..." He searched for the correct words. "Internal security operations." Another pause, his eyes looking down but not directly at the shorter Oldham. "I was promoted and came back here as Chief Inspector about six months ago." Oldham suppressed a smirk but not the thought, *Probably good at cocktail parties and flattering the Commissioner. Same promotion route for some army officers.*

"I am sorry, William, I will need to consult Godden about the intelligence thing. He's the Special Branch officer responsible for Shala."

"I know. I have met him." He had the urge to say, *He talks highly of you.*

" Oh. Right."

"You'd better run this past him as well…and get his consent." The officer wanted his soldiers to be able to go out to the bars and restaurants in Shala. It had been Knight's suggestion. Soldiers frequented the bars in the capital and other towns even where there had been attacks. It would look odd if off-duty soldiers were not seen in the bars of the most peaceful town in the country, and no doubt there were watchers who would report back. The policeman nodded his head in agreement. He justified it further by reminding Bendixson of the cover story and asked Bendixson to get approval from Godden as a matter of urgency.

His platoon sergeant loitering outside the ops room when Oldham left Bendixson's office snapped to attention and saluted. "Sir. The platoon and the attachments are assembled in the briefing room downstairs as requested."

"Thank you." He hid his annoyance. He was sure that he had said 'an orders group'—the commanders not the whole platoon. "The boys fed?"

"Yes sir. Just chicken, rice and some vegetables. Chinese."

"Sounds good. Any left?"

Nash said in a surprised tone, "Getting cookie to rustle up a meal for you and the senior NCOs."

"No need." His annoyance seeping out. "I just want to speak to the commanders. The others can go back to their bunks." To avoid any misunderstandings. "I just want the four section commanders, Sergeant Williams, the MT, cook and medic corporals, Knight—"

"Sergeant Knight?"

Knight's voice thanking Staff Ho as he left his office stopped Oldham from expressing his annoyance. Instead, he turned and shouted, "Knight!" still glimpsing Nash's disapproving look.

"Yo!" Knight also noted Nash's look.

"That Knight," Oldham said, now smiling. "And yourself, of course. Give me five minutes. I want a word with Sergeant Knight."

"Yessir." He saluted and went down the stairs.

They waited until they heard the clamour of the platoon exiting the briefing room. Oldham expressed his frustration with his new platoon sergeant's conduct including his constant saluting. Knight did not respond, not being the right time, and instead he asked, "How did it go with the chief inspector? Find out anything new?"

"He's rather short of the requirements for this job. He was a staff officer for the commissioner before coming back here as chief inspector. A bit prissy." He expressed his earlier thought. "Probably bloody good at cocktail parties and sucking up to the commissioner. It's not just the army that—"

"Sir. What did he say about the Int thing and the boys going out?"

"He has to get permission from goddamn Godden." An imperceptible half-shake of his head, lips curled in tightly, looking straight ahead, the Oldham sign of irritation or frustration. He changed the subject. "How did you get on with Staff...eh...forgotten his name."

"Tony Ho. Brought up in Liverpool. Well—"

"God! A scouser!"

"He spent some time there. He was in the Malayan Army during the Emergency. Federation regiment or something. Think he might be helpful."

"Unlike his boss."

"I would like to use the CID office. To get to know him. Also it keeps me away from the platoon. Think that might help."

Oldham knew it was to help Nash get established with the platoon. "Okay. I'll ask Terence. Probably bloody needs to clear that with Godden...I wonder why he doesn't just drop the last three letters." He chuckled, a self-satisfied look spreading over his face. Knight ignored it, knowing as Oldham did that it was probably not original.

"You know, Ho cooked that meal for the boys himself."

"Did he." Expression of surprise, not a question. "Hope there's some left. Though Nash didn't seem to approve of it." In an accurate mimic of Nash's voice, "Better with steak'n'kidney, sir." Knight smiled but knew he would need to speak to Oldham about his attitude to his new platoon sergeant. It was finding the right moment. At that moment, they saw Nash lingering at the bottom of the stairs. Oldham knew it had been more than five minutes but it was just an expression. The word 'pedantic' whizzed into Oldham's mind.

"I'll get on," said Knight. He ran down the stairs, nodded at Nash, went into the briefing room, found his allocated seat and was told by Sergeant Williams the form.

When the platoon sergeant called the room to attention, the others stood up to attention wearing headdress—soft jungle hats, sometimes called floppy hats. He saluted the platoon commander. The platoon commander returned the salute and said, "Thank you, Sergeant Nash." He sat at a table facing the others who were seated in two rows, the four section commanders and the platoon sergeant behind sat Knight and the four detachment commanders.

"Sit down, you jungle bunnies. Relax. Remove your hats." He paused. "It's been a long day. Not giving formal orders. Not prepared any. Not had time. Anyway, the platoon sergeant and I are going out on the piss. Taste the delights of Shala." The others laughed or smiled except Nash who frowned. Oldham flipped opened his small, black notebook. He wanted everyone to get a good night's sleep, though there would need to be a guard, more a fire-piquet. He reminded them of why they were there but in typical army style they would still train so that they would be ready in case the Chinese army crossed the border. The soldiers laughed though most of them probably didn't realise the Chinese border was three countries away.

The first task was getting to know the ground, Shala and the roads around it. Mobile patrolling would begin from 1200 hours the next day. There would be a policeman with each patrol. Only two double mobiles at any time, one in the town, the other in surrounding roads and tracks including the rubber plantation.

He didn't want to alarm the locals. The platoon sergeant was to draw up the patrol programme. One section would provide the QRF and fatigues. The signallers, drivers and medics would take part in these patrols as well as taking their share of fatigues. Initially, Cpl Jubb's section would man the police OP. He would brief Jubb separately but Jubb's section would not deploy there for forty-eight hours to enable the section to complete familiarisation patrols and to allow the corporal to recce the OP. He added that Jubb would be deploying with two GPMGs. Oldham would have his platoon signaller. Knight would also need a signaller and a FFR Land Rover with driver. Oldham would set up his office in one of the rooms in the police ops room but he wanted to avoid too much movement there because the police had to go about their normal business. The platoon ops room was to be in the far office of the police ops room, ready to convert to a joint police-military, polmil in the jargon, ops room. The signals sergeant advised that communications had been established with the battalion. As well as the normal platoon net, Oldham and platoon HQ would be on the battalion net, not the company net. Individual callsigns were confirmed and a separate callsign for the OP.

He dealt with other matters including feeding and positioning of vehicles and fuel. He would have a separate meeting with each detachment commander to address their specific problems. He acknowledged that procedures and routines were likely to require adjustment so they would meet in a couple of days to review matters, time to be announced. He would inspect the accommodation and other areas at 1000 hours the next day but it would be a working inspection. He stressed the importance of getting on with the police and the locals, 'hearts and minds'. Further, he said that it was not C platoon and detachments but one unit. Personal weapons were to be carried at all times and if not, being held no more than an arm's length away. There was to be no saluting outside even within the police compound. "I don't want people standing to attention every time I appear. The morning and possibly one at the end of the day would suffice though no need to wear hats inside. If I am displeased with someone, he'll soon know. We need to be professional and alert. Hopefully, we will have a few days to settle in, sort ourselves out. There are no changes to the Int briefing we received." He turned to Knight. "Unless you have something, Sergeant Knight."

"No sir."

"I will produce sops." He looked around, smiling. "For the benefit of the base wallahs, that's standing operating procedures." It was for the benefit of his platoon sergeant. "Oops. Broke my own policy." He looked down at his notebook for a moment, then asked, "Any burning questions…no…good. Thank you, gentlemen." Some perceived him as an arrogant young officer; others as a confident, competent officer; two thought it was both.

There was some food left. In an otherwise empty dining-hall, Oldham and two sergeants were enjoying Staff Ho's food. Nash did not join them because he had some admin tasks to finish and had eaten earlier. The three were having a general discussion on their first impressions. Then Oldham focussed in on their numbers. "We have sixty-one including us." The sergeants nodded though neither knew the exact strength. "I have four sections, though Jubb's…well, to begin with…will be in the OP. One section on QRF, which also will be the guard. Later, we might need to share perimeter guard duties. But at the moment, two sections for patrolling. Not enough." He pondered the problem. "I would like to form another section." Solving problems stimulated him. From slouching with his elbows on the table, he sat back, body erect with his palms flat on the table. "I don't need all my HQ. My runner and light mortar team. That's three. Two drivers. Quite a few in the platoon can drive. Can't they?" He was not looking for a reply but merely thinking aloud. "Anyway, I want to get us on foot." He turned to Sergeant Williams, asking, "Pronto, can you spare one of your guys?"

"Yes, a private or lance-jack? Suppose I could manage on twelve-hour stags but depends how long—"

"If it drags on, we'll need reinforcements or be relieved. There will also be casualties just from accidents and sickness. Good. Thanks." He took out his notebook, flipped open to a fresh page and made a list of the numbers and the detachments. When finished, he looked up. "Who else…the medic private. Anyway, all our sections have done first-aid, the basics, treating gunshot wounds." He made another entry. "That's…" He counted down the page using the tip of his pen. "Seven. Any ideas?"

Knight opined, "Maybe when Jubb has done his recce, he might not need his whole section in the OP."

Oldham shook his head and replied, "Not happy with that. He's from another platoon. Saying to the guy, we're fucking you off to an OP on your own, and by the way, you're not taking all your guys. He wouldn't be happy and I wouldn't blame him. He would go whinging back to his boss."

"I know Jubb, sir, and I don't think he's like that. He's on the ball and very professional. If he thinks it's for a good reason, even if it's not, I don't think he would complain. He did that detachment to Sarawak. I had to teach him Morse."

"Did he? I didn't know that." To Knight. "None of our guys went on that. Why not?"

Knight replied, "We argued that we could not afford to lose any of our NCOs because we were always being tasked." Knight deliberately used 'we' out of loyalty. In fact, he had been unaware of it because he had been on a two-week attachment to the Jungle Warfare School in Malaysia. Oldham had complained to Major Slater who had told him that if he felt so strongly about it to speak to the battalion second-in-command, which he had. The 2ic in his languid, emollient manner said that it was not a problem but thought he was being foolish in denying one of his NCOs an excellent and challenging opportunity. Knight had told him the same on his return from Malaysia. Oldham was unhappy with his platoon sergeant going to an exercise in Jungle Warfare School considering that he had been there before on a course as well as on the battalion's six-week training exercise before deployment. On that occasion, he was advised quietly but firmly by the adjutant not to question it. It was the CO's decision.

"OK. I'll look at that when I do my recce at the OP and discuss it with Jubb. Anything else?"

Knight again. "If we are doing local patrols, just in Shala and with the police, we might not need to send out a full section. We have done that in other places."

"I know…but I was never happy about that." Oldham did not trust the police or rather their British officers. "I suppose for local patrols or QRF, a section of eight would be enough. So got seven. Need a corporal. Any ideas?"

"Don't think 'first parade' Groves," said Knight, referring to the MT corporal known as 'first parade' because if there was any problem with a vehicle, it was because first parade maintenance had not been carried out or not properly.

"What about my Corporal Horrocks?" Williams suggested. "He did the same detachment to Sarawak as Corporal Jubb."

"I didn't know that. Did you?"

"Only after he had been casevac'd," said Knight.

Williams continued, "He's only with the signals platoon because he was casevac'd from Sarawak about a month before the end. He wasn't fit enough to return to a rifle company so he came to the signals. He could do Morse and knew radio procedure. He picked up the maintenance side of the sets quite quickly. He's smart." Williams did not like the blond-haired, moustached corporal. His hair was longer than normal. Most soldiers and even officers kept their hair short because of the heat and especially when operating in the jungle. Williams thought that he was arrogant and wanted to stay in the signals platoon because it was cushy. He was a bit of a wheeler and dealer. He would be glad to see him go.

"What do you think?" he asked Knight.

"I don't know him. I know of him. From what I hear, some think he's good, others that he's a bit flash." Knight had not heard it from Williams. "But must have something if he was selected for Sarawak." There had been whispers of him having relationships with the wives of SNCOs, even an officer's wife.

"OK. Thanks. I'll give it some more thought. I'll speak to Jubb and Horrocks first. You don't mind me speaking to Horrocks?"

"No sir," replied Williams.

"It's a big area and I'll need as many available for patrol as I can get," Oldham said. This prompted Williams to say that he was surprised by the size of the shanty towns outside of Shala. He had spotted them when on the roof putting up the antennae for the radio sets.

"There are two to the…" He paused, his hands moving across his body to get his directions right and being met with some gentle—had been a long day— abuse from the other two. "Two to the east and the other to the west, more southwest." The other two agreed they would need to look at it. In an effort to regain some standing, Williams said, "They are not really marked on our maps."

"Well observed, Pronto."

Oldham joined in. "And can send Morse."

"He'll be wanting one of these next," Knight said, indicating his Armalite.

Williams stood up. "You can…er…" He didn't know Oldham well enough to use an expletive even if it was good-natured. He knew officers could be funny:

36

taking part in the ribbing but taking offence quickly if they felt a soldier was overstepping the mark, tramping on their dignity. "I'm going to bed."

"Make sure you sort out my mosie net. Tuck it in tightly."

"You can fuck off." He was looking directly at Knight.

"Goodnight, Lewis."

"Goodnight, Sergeant Williams."

"Goodnight sir…Phil." Williams left them. They could hear him singing as he was going up the stairs. Both resisted the temptation to make a Welsh comment. It had been a long day.

"Think I'll do the same."

"Are you sharing a bunk with Pronto?" Oldham asked.

"Yeah."

"Who has the other single room?"

"The platoon sergeant."

"You're senior to him. Surely Pronto is as well."

"Sir, he's the platoon sergeant and—"

"Don't I know that." A curt tone.

Knight knew this was the opportunity. Knight said, "Sir, can I give you my last piece of advice as a platoon sergeant?" A nod of consent from Oldham. In a quiet voice, Knight said, "Sir, see it from his side. He's already done three months as a platoon sergeant in another company with a senior lieutenant. I know it was only because Barnes got casevac'd. I heard he did OK. He gets to C. Knows after a couple of weeks; he's getting a baby Rupert. Already met him. Probably planning how to mould him. Just one more day with you." Knight saw the familiar Oldham sign of irritation but pressed on in Nash's defence. "Then. You're staying…and now a captain. He has never done an op with you?" Oldham shook his head in confirmation. "First op is a deployment miles from the company. Not just the platoon but attached dets, almost two platoons. He has to administer and account for weapons, stores, fuel, ammo and wagons. There's feeding and accommodation. He's a mini CQMS and CSM."

"You're probably right. Anything else?"

"I know, sir, that you will guide him. But you are going to have a lot on your plate. Normally, a platoon sergeant can get help from his fellow sergeants. Also from the CQMS but especially the CSM. Got a problem, the CSM can usually sort it. Sometimes just a chat is enough. He can't go to Pronto. What does he know about being an infantry platoon sergeant! He won't come to me. And I wouldn't blame him. Up here, he doesn't have anyone to turn to."

"At least we have that in common." It was an intended slight of Knight. "Any suggestions?"

"Maybe Pronto could help. Responsible for the wagons. It's his radio equipment."

"He's Welsh," Oldham said in a playful manner.

"He's not real Welsh."

"Might work."

"Suggest—"

"Speak to Nash first. I will." He stood up. "I'm going to get some shut-eye." He walked to the door, paused and half-turned towards Knight. "You are right about one thing."

"Sir?"

"That's the last piece of advice you give me about my platoon." He was gone.

Knight knew Oldham intended it as a slight, a rebuff: he was saying this is my platoon now. Their relationship had ended. Knight was not offended. It was the nature of the army, especially of an infantry battalion. Relationships changed or ended. The bond between a platoon commander and platoon sergeant was unique. Knight thought sacramental was the more accurate adjective albeit he did not accept this description, being part of the myth-making prevalent in the army. Platoon commanders and sergeants did not always get on. Nevertheless, he had been fortunate in that he had enjoyed a good relationship with Oldham. He respected him and regarded him as a good officer who established an excellent rapport with the soldiers. Some officers found it difficult to relate to the soldiers though it did not necessarily make them bad commanders. But with Knight and Oldham, it was their similar attitude to soldiering that had created their relationship, not a shared sense of humour. They were demanding of their soldiers in training, concentrating on fitness, minor tactics and shooting, especially snap-shooting in jungle lanes. The platoon did have one difficulty in mastering the platoon box formation for riot control. All were amused by the need to unfurl banners giving warnings. They hoped the platoon would not have to use this tactic in an actual riot.

They were fortunate in the quality of most of their JNCOs and soldiers. Sports did not play much of a part in C Platoon's life unlike most of the other platoons. Their company was the battalion's reserve but it seemed only to be their platoon that was ever deployed. There were grumbles by the soldiers that it was always C Platoon because the OC Major Slater resented Oldham. However, the real reason was the CO did not trust the other two platoon commanders, being kingleheads. Major Slater did not resist the Colonel. He was weary and worn-out due to not just his past service but also tragic circumstances in his personal life. Knight had learned this from his company sergeant major though it had become an open secret in the battalion but it had not engendered sympathy for the major from the newly promoted captain.

Chapter 5

Gordon Buchanan-Henderson, at first 'GBH' to his soldiers but now 'Grievous', not in his presence though some officers did use the soubriquet in conversation with him. Notwithstanding an officer, no matter how senior, would need to be sure he had gained or earned GBH's respect or he would be met with the withering 'You will call me sir or colonel' or 'Sir, I prefer you call me by my name or rank'.

Two months on from Hockin's decision on Fong Siu Wai, Colonel Gordon Buchanan-Henderson was in his office waiting for a visit from Jimmy Doherty, the Special Branch officer responsible for Shala. The previous year, during a joint army-police conference in JWS, Doherty had told him about Shala. He did not disclose that he had been in Shala. Doherty who had been in Singapore ostensibly on leave for a few days had telephoned wanting to see him but unofficially. It was a short trip in his hired car across the Causeway to the Jungle Warfare School in Ulu Tiram on the Johor Baru-Kota Tinggi Road, a familiar route. After a brief but warm greeting, the Ballymoney man had launched into a tirade against the usual targets: the colonial officials, the senior police officers and the army officers, all English public schoolboys with the same sexual preference. GBH found him boorish with an excess of expletives even for an Irishman, yet a good Special Branch officer. He had proved his worth in Malaya during the Emergency: his intelligence had led to a number of kills and captures. GBH had served in the locally recruited Federation Regiment and benefitted from this intelligence. Doherty had on occasions delayed an operation until GBH's company became available. They socialised together but for the army officer, it was duty though he did concede that at times he found Doherty diverting company. Indeed, Doherty called him Grievous. According to Doherty, the CTs were planning to attack Shala, the most prosperous, stable and peaceful district in the country.

"A fuckin' blind man can see that…and it's Baru's home. They're gatherin' a fuckin' band on the other side of the border. They going to fuckin' hit Shala, especially the plantation. It's owned by Tony Hockin…another fuckin' posh boy." He paused, then to bolster his position, "My intelligence is good. It might not be soon. The bastards are waiting for something…maybe more fuckin' hard guys… We have taken out some of their fuckin' experienced guys… Maybe they want to improve their network in Shala… Get more fuckin' touts, especially from the fuckin' chinks in the shanties…or something." He was shaking his head and exclaimed, "The bastards won't listen!"

GBH asked, though he regretted it straightaway, "Why not take your Int directly to the Commissioner?"

"Fucksake. Are you serious! He'll tell his fuckin' staff officers. Then, at the next fuckin' cocktail party, if he doesn't, one of his bumboys will tell a fuckin' army officer…'just between you and me'…fuckin' right! Every fuckin' coolie would know. My sources would be blown, probably killed." He shook his head vigorously in frustration, calming himself then said, "But that's not what I have come to see you about. Well, it's connected. I need your help." He explained his misgivings about the army but with fewer expletives. The army officer listened in silence.

"Jimmy, I'm in a non-job here. I have no influence." Doherty's expression was one of disbelief. "Jimmy, it's true. Look, the CO of the next battalion is a good man. I know him. I can speak to him—"

"Yes yes, but it's not him. It's the fuckin' younger ones. They don't have it." He clenched his right fist. "You've done it. You know what is fuckin' needed."

"I'll see what I can do but don't—"

"I know you won't let me down." He had cheered up. "You never let me down." He leaned forward, a glint in his eyes. "What about a few drinks? Start down the village, then onto to JB…those places still there?"

"So I'm told but those days are over for me. Anyway, you say it's urgent so I had better crack on." He stood up, followed quickly by Doherty.

"Thanks." They shook hands. "Oh, by the way, I've got Tony Ho up in Shala."

"Who?"

"Fucksake. He was in your company. A sergeant. The only one who spoke proper fuckin' English."

He remembered. "Yes, yes. A good man. I had forgotten about him going to the police. I think I had to write a reference for him. Give him my best wishes."

"Rather not. Want to keep this meeting on the qt for now."

"I understand."

"Though Ho wouldn't say anything. He's the only chink I trust…in fact, he's the only fuckin' peeler I trust. Well. Good to see you again."

"You too."

"I mean it." Doherty was now clasping the other's hand with two hands. GBH thought he detected a tear in Doherty's eye. "Grievous. You are first-class." Then turned quickly, opened the door and left, leaving the door open.

GBH sat down, centred a blank sheet of paper, not official Jungle Warfare School headed paper, and picked up his pen. He had decided his course of action whilst Doherty had been explaining his concerns with which he had some sympathy. His letter was to the Commander of Far East Land Forces. He knew he was going outwith the chain of command. It was not the first time but would probably be the last. It was not an act of recklessness but a calculated risk. He had learned from his sister not to be reckless.

The Buchanan-Hendersons were a venerable but not a well-known Scottish family with a lineage back to Sir Andrew de Moray. However, like many Scots families of their class, they were anglicised in speech, manner, education and attitudes. Gordon had been happy growing up in the Northeast of Scotland. His father David had had a 'good war', reaching the rank of brigadier at an early age, almost certain to emulate his father in becoming a general. Shortly after his second child was born, he decided to leave the army saying that he sought a new challenge and returned home to run the family estate. He wanted to make money in order to provide a more comfortable life for his family than the one provided by his father who seemed always to be scrimping and cutting. Legally, his father, the General, remained the owner of the estate but he was content to leave the running to his son, especially as it prospered, bringing a substantial increase in profit. Although on occasions, he expressed regret at his son abandoning his military career, he was aware that it was his son's management of the estate that had allowed him and his wife to enjoy their retirement in London and their biannual trips north, living in a cottage on the estate.

Another motivation was to provide work for those returning soldiers, the Jocks of his own local regiment, and also for the families of those Jocks who would not be returning or could not work. This motivation was never articulated, left unsaid, the proper conduct. He continued to take an interest in regimental affairs and attended reunions where his once subordinates were eager to seek out Brigadier David's advice on all aspects of regimental life. Never complaining on the few occasions his advice was ignored. He vetted prospective regimental officers. He was considered more rigorous than General Sir David who was less probing in his questioning. Although he sought the best officers for the regiment, the Brigadier on occasions advised the candidate that he was better suited to the artillery or the new tank corps even if it meant losing a potentially good officer for the regiment. Indeed, he had advised his elder son—also David—to join the Brigade of Guards. He hoped that his younger son would break with tradition by eschewing an army career and follow him in managing the family estate and business.

The estate continued to thrive, producing good quality food that was supplied predominantly to hotels. However, the estate opened its own shop initially in the village and then further afield. Income came from issuing fishing permits and the holiday renting of some cottages, some around the village. There was no renting to 'Hooray Henries' or shooting parties but to former officers as well as lawyers, including the odd judge, bankers and academics usually from Edinburgh, Aberdeen and sometimes Glasgow. David and his wife Elizabeth never entertained the guests, no matter how exalted. GBH's mother observed that it deterred visitors from London. David had formed a close working relationship with a French colonel, Charles Planet, which had developed into friendship and mutual admiration. After the war, he corresponded with Planet who was one of only two former comrades with whom he maintained a relationship. Following his first visit to the estate, Planet promised that he would make his friends and neighbours go there, to the most beautiful place in the world, and they would pay. He did not break this promise.

Gordon loved his sister Fuffy, then Fi but had to be 'Fiona' when his grandfather, the General, and his grandmama visited from London as well as in front of Mr McPhail and Mr Thompson, the ministers of the Church of Scotland and the Free Church of Scotland respectively. Fi protected Gordon from his brother David's bullying and Gordon was secretly pleased when David went away to prep school. David spent many of his holidays with his grandparents in London. When he did come to stay, he announced often to his siblings that he was grandpapa's and grandmama's favourite, and that he would inherit the family estate. They would be reliant on him. Gordon did not understand and Fi just laughed at her elder brother. David did not play with him because Gordon was four years younger than him, still a baby though it did not bother Gordon, and anyway he had his sister who was only two years older. She never ignored him.

The success and expansion of the estate business resulted in an increase of staff including domestics for the cottages and drivers for the new vehicles required to deliver the produce to the shops. David employed a young, energetic assistant manager who quickly demonstrated his abilities. Soon David was delegating so many tasks to him that he made him manager but he retained overall control, ever mindful of his ultimate responsibility. This allowed David and Elizabeth to spend more time with their three children. When their father added a wooden-bodied estate car, a Woodie, to the Hillman Minx, there were more family outings, usually on a Saturday and even further afield. They indulged their children, especially their daughter Fiona, the first daughter in the family for over one hundred years. Sometimes she was allowed to stay up to spend more time with her parents. Their father responded to the sons' protests by saying good-naturedly that he had never had a sister.

Other times, Fiona accompanied her mother to Dundee where they would spend one or two nights. Their maternal grandmum, now widowed, lived there. His father explained that it was a trip only for ladies followed by a wink. Young David, unlike Gordon, appeared to understand his father's explanation. Gordon thought his grandmum was fun. Fi said she was dotty, only later did Gordon understand the meaning. There were a few ladies' trips to Edinburgh and London. Even when they visited Uncle Charles in France—a long but exciting journey by train and aeroplane—there was a ladies' trip to Paris, though this time their father went. Uncle Charles explained their father had to pay the bills.

Gordon followed his sister to the local primary school. Mr Robertson and his wife were the teachers. Due to the size of the school roll, there were only two classes, though sometimes they came together for some subjects or the classes were mixed up according to the ability of the children. The two teachers emphasised the importance of the 'three Rs', reading, writing and arithmetic. Even Mr McPhail on his visits to the school would mention the importance of the 'three Rs'. Geography and history, including Scottish history, which was seldom on the curriculum in most Scottish schools, were taught. During one lesson by Mrs Robertson on William Wallace and King Robert the Bruce, Fi put up her hand. Mrs Robertson expected a question. Not a question. Fi addressed the class, telling them that the greatest Scottish hero was not William Wallace or Robert the Bruce but Sir Andrew Murray, sometimes called Sir Andrew de Moray.

At school, Fi defended her brother against potential bullies. Gordon was aware that Fi and he spoke differently from the local children and that they lived in a much bigger house. Nevertheless, they got on with most of the children. Fi played all the games and accepted all the dares even those just for boys. She was not reckless. If she thought a dare was too dangerous, she challenged the darer to go first. She never dared anyone unless she knew that she could do the particular leap or climb. She became the leader of all the pupils. Gordon idolised her.

The Buchanan-Hendersons were Episcopalians but his father thought it was his duty to attend the local churches, or Kirks as the ministers called them. On a Sunday, the family attended the nearby Church of Scotland, except one Sunday each month when they went to the Free Church—though when visiting, their grandparents never attended the Free Church. Mr McPhail was a quiet and kindly man but always seemed sad even when he visited the school. He spoke quietly and his sermons were short. In contrast, Mr Thompson of the Free Church was loud and his sermons were very long and depressing. To a small boy, he was always angry, leaning forward over the pulpit, his fists clenched out in front of him. Gordon kept expecting him to jump out of the pulpit. Everyone was a sinner. He spoke often of betrayal and leaned forward, accusatory at Gordon's father and mother. At the end of the service, Mr Thompson walked down the aisle to wait outside the Kirk door. His father's handshake with Mr Thompson was fleeting accompanied with a curt 'good morning'. He could not recall his mother ever exchanging a handshake or words with Mr Thompson whereas both his parents would chat to Mr McPhail for a few minutes. He came to tea occasionally and that was the only time Gordon ever saw him smile, even laugh for which Fi was responsible. He seemed to be in a carefree trance as he listened to Fi's stories. In contrast, Fi mocked Mr Thompson by impersonating him. She would do it in the kitchen in front of their cook, Mrs Mackenzie, who would laugh until tears came to her eyes. Gordon clapped and asked for repeats. On one outing to the cinema, on seeing a newsreel of Adolf Hitler addressing a rally, Fi cried out, "It's Mr Thompson's brother!" Gordon laughed. Heads looked around. It was the only time Gordon could recall his father speaking sternly to his daughter though the rebuke was for disturbing other people and not the association.

One day after school, Gordon said to Fi that Mr Robertson must have visited many places in the world because he knew all about them. Fi laughed and told him not to be silly. He had only read about them. Fi decided there and then that the two of them would visit these places, go on expeditions. In preparation, they spent hours in the library poring over maps and books with Fi recording in a black notebook the details of their journeys: the places to visit, the routes, when to go, the length of each leg, the clothing and equipment required. After expeditions to North and South America, Africa, Arabia, their final one would be to follow in the footsteps of Marco Polo on the Silk Road through Samarkand onto Peking. But they would continue to Shanghai, possibly Hong Kong because they had an uncle or cousin in one of those places. The family did not speak of him. Mrs Mackenzie had said that he was 'the black sheep of the family' but Fi was not to repeat it to anyone. Gordon was not anyone. They assumed they could travel anywhere in the world. They were British and no one would stop them. Fi told Gordon of Mungo Park and David Livingstone who were Scottish and anyway, many Scots had travelled and settled in other countries. That was what Scots did. They were adventurous: she had no knowledge of the Highland Clearances. Fi decided they would need some training in living off the land so asked her father for permission to approach the cook's husband Mr Mackenzie whom her father called the warden though in other estates called the gillie. The warden took them stalking over the hills measuring distances, identifying plants that could be eaten, lighting fires, erecting a tent but not shooting. Once, Mr Mackenzie's son Jamie came with them. He spoke only to Gordon and never to Fi but Gordon noticed that he looked at his sister in what he thought was a secretive way. Two nights under the stars were enough for Gordon.

At Easter, Nigel Staveley, the second former comrade friend, visited. Gordon was told by his mother that his father wanted to see him in the study. His father, seated behind his desk, asked Gordon to sit in the chair on the other side of the desk. He wanted to tell him something. His parents had been invited to accompany Uncle Nigel and his wife on a cruise to New York. It was the first cruise of a new ship. Fiona had been invited as a companion to the Staveleys' niece or someone. Uncle Nigel had been given only six tickets. David could not go because it was an important time for him at school. Gordon was confused because he had heard his parents saying it was an important time for Fiona at school because it was her last year at primary school and she had to sit the qualifying examination for secondary school but his father knew always to do the right thing. They would be away for a month. His father gave him a choice either to live with his grandparents in London or remain at home and be looked after by Mrs Mackenzie and Morag, the maid. His grandmother would be there most of the time but sometimes she would need to go home to Dundee. It was his choice. Another point, a carrot, he would have only to go to Mr McPhail's church on a Sunday, not Mr Thompson's. Gordon decided that he would stay at home.

At the beginning, he missed his parents and especially Fi who had left him a list of tasks to undertake in preparation for their expeditions. The tasks were mostly recording information from named books, sometimes being assisted by his grandmum. His grandmum and Mrs Mackenzie were like friends. She would spend a lot of time in the kitchen talking to Mrs Mackenzie. His mother and grandmama never did that. Sometimes they would lower their voices so that Gordon could not hear what they were discussing.

His grandmum took him on outings to new places, pointing out buildings, streets and fields and telling him of people who had lived there or events that had taken place in the past. They went on the bus or were sometimes driven by one of the estate drivers. One day, they went to Dundee. Mrs Mackenzie was with them. They stopped in a street where the buildings were grey and dirty as were the people, especially the children. A group of children who, to Gordon were unwashed and dressed in rags, gathered around the car. They were like the beggars he had read of in books and seen in pictures but worse. The driver was telling his grandmum that they should keep going but she ignored him, telling Gordon that people lived like that because of the greedy capitalists. Immediately, Mrs Mackenzie in a stern voice told her to stop and reminded his grandmum that she had been present when her daughter had given her strict instructions not to mention politics. Mrs Makenzie ordered the driver to take them home.

When his grandmum was not there, he slept in the MacKenzies' cottage. Jamie Mackenzie was now working for the estate. He loved working on the cars and tractors, being able to strip and replace the engines. He told Gordon that he was going to join the army. He said that there was going to be another war because Hitler had to be stopped. Sometimes he asked Gordon about Fiona. On Sundays, Mrs Mackenzie took Gordon to the Church of Scotland. She sat with Gordon in the back pew, standing up or sitting down with the rest of the congregation. She did not put money in the collection plate but made sure Gordon did. She would acknowledge Mr McPhail but not shake his hand. Gordon realised that was the first time he had ever seen any of the Mackenzies at church.

He was overjoyed when his parents returned laden with presents for him. He sensed that his parents and Fiona were different, sad. Mrs MacKenzie told him that they were just tired. Soon Fi was her usual energetic self, full of fun and telling him stories of the ship and New York. Mrs MacKenzie had been right.

That year, their grandparents arrived in July, not August. They explained that they had no need to wait for David because he was spending the first three weeks of his holidays in Dorset with a school chum and they were desperate to hear about the American trip. During tea on the second day of their visit, after revealing her likes and dislikes of New York, Fi announced that she had now settled on her heroines: Florence Nightingale and Mary Slessor—nod of approval by grandmama; Gertrude Bell and Amelia Earhart, a surprised look; Emmeline Pankhurst and Mrs Eleanor Roosevelt, much tutting and shaking of the head then an admonition for her son for allowing Fiona unrestricted access to books and newspapers. "Goodness knows what she read in New York!" Next, her daughter-in-law's mother was responsible for Fiona's behaviour. "One should not be surprised. She is originally an Elphinstone." His mother Elizabeth did not respond. Morag was told to take the children downstairs to Mrs MacKenzie.

"Have you decided Fiona's school?" asked grandmama. "It's time she went away to school. To be with her own kind." There was no response from either parent. "Downe House would be suitable. It's in Berkshire. Rodean is probably out of the question. We have heard good reports of Beneden."

David was about to say that Fiona did not want to go away but thought it tactful not to. "Mama, we would prefer that Fiona does not go away to school."

She was aghast. "You mean, go to the local school. To be educated beside…the sons and daughters of farm labourers, cooks, domestics, shopkeepers."

He remained calm and spoke softly, "Those are the same people who fought and died in France for us." He looked at his father who seemed uncomfortable, then at his wife who gave him a slight nod of approval and encouragement. "I was going to say we would prefer if she did not go away but we know the local school is not right for her. We have found a school, Kilgraston."

"I have never heard of it. Have you, David?" To her husband who responded by shaking his head.

Her son said, "It has a good reputation. We were impressed by the commitment of the staff and the school's ethos." He paused and then hesitantly said, "It's a Catholic school."

"What! You mean Roman Catholic?" Grandmama was even more aghast.

Grandpapa expressed mild disapproval, "Not sure that's in keeping with the family tradition."

"It's certainly not in keeping with this family's traditions nor mine. My brothers will be appalled. What will our friends think!" A reproving stare at Elizabeth. "This is your mother's fault!"

"My mother does not know about it."

She was not deflected, just changed her line of attack. "What will the estate workers and villagers think! They will feel betrayed!"

"Mama. You sound like that fool Thompson." His mother was wounded by this comparison. He did not give her time to recover. "One of the bravest acts, if not the bravest, I ever witnessed was a Roman Catholic priest—from Glasgow, I think—tending the wounded whilst under fire. He didn't ask or care what the man's religion was. He was simply tending to a wounded, sometimes dying, soldier. He received…no, he earned his DSO." He paused for a moment to find the right words. "My, no, our daughter, your granddaughter needs that care now."

"David, I think they are entitled to know," Elizabeth said. Her husband nodded in consent. "Fiona has a defective heart."

After a brief silence to absorb the impact of the news, she said, "Thought that was only a scare when she was born?"

"That's what we were told," David said in reply to his mother. "She had been complaining about feeling tired and she didn't seem to be putting on weight. Just before she started school, we took her to Dundee—"

"Dundee?"

"They *are* the leading heart specialists," Elizabeth told her.

David continued, "Their diagnosis was that there was nothing they could do. It was a matter of time, probably around two to three years." He chuckled. "They didn't know our Fiona."

"To be fair," said Elizabeth, "they did say that there are always new techniques and they would continue to monitor Fiona, which they have done."

"Why the trips to Dundee…not to subject her to Elphinstone's malign influence."

The trip to France was because Planet had recommended a specialist in Paris. The recent trip to New York was also for a specialist to examine Fiona. Staveley had arranged and paid for a specialist to come down from Michigan to see Fiona. Both specialists had concurred with their colleagues in Dundee. Staveley's 'niece' was a nurse, which was merely a precaution. She too had been infected by Fiona's zeal. Fiona had wanted to visit New York because she had read so much about it and seen some pictures, movies. Fiona met Mrs Roosevelt, which had been arranged by Staveley using his extensive business, political and social contacts. That explained Fiona's inclusion of the President's wife in her pantheon of heroines.

When his wife began to complain about not being told, especially with Planet and Staveley knowing, General Buchanan-Henderson silenced her with an authoritative, outstretched open palm towards her. David saw that his father was hurt and also seeking an answer. "Papa. At first, we thought it might just be a scare like before. So there was no need to worry people. But after a number of tests—and believe me, those doctors wanted to be wrong…and hoped that they could come up with a new procedure, technique—"

Elizabeth interrupted, "Some of the medical profession think it's unethical to interfere with the heart." David nodded agreement. "Anyway, when we finally accepted…well, Fiona was six. She did not want us to tell anyone, especially Gordon. She knew Gordon to be sensitive and gentle. He apes her and she protected him, especially from David and later at school."

"Papa. We were torn. We discussed it often. We knew it was unfair to you and Mama but…it was happening to Fiona and we felt we had to respect her decision. She has been… is so brave."

"I understand. I do. But why tell Planet?"

"He suspected something was not right," said David in reply to his father, "and he asked. I felt I could not lie to him especially after…well, you understand."

From his father a slow, purposeful nod, from his mother, "You lied to us." Hurt tinged with bitterness.

"No. We *did not*," Elizabeth retorted.

"Elizabeth is right… And Staveley?"

"I approached him. I knew of his contacts not just in business. I knew that he wouldn't refuse me…because of Loos. But I was using him because he is rich and can open doors. I was being selfish but I would have done…would do anything if I thought it would save Fiona."

There followed a few minutes of silence, each in their own thoughts, avoiding any eye contact. Sir David stood up and said, "I think it would be good for Gordon to go away to school."

"No, Papa."

"Elizabeth, David, hear me out." He outlined his reasons in particular that Fiona would not be around to look after Gordon, that he was not robust enough

47

for the local secondary school and it would give them more time with Fiona. After some discussion, it was agreed that it was a sensible course. However, Elizabeth wanted to discuss it with Fiona and gain her consent. Despite light resistance from Mama, this was also deemed a sensible course.

Elizabeth raised a possible obstacle. "Gordon is too old to begin prep and too young—"

"You leave that to me. The Headmaster would not dare to defy a Buchanan-Henderson, especially this Buchanan-Henderson. And if he did, he would lose his best pupil. Followed by others once I had spoken to some chums." There was a glint in his eyes. He had not had a meaningful purpose for a long time. He was back in command. "One of the governors, Bedlam?...Bellows?...yes. He was one of my brigade commanders in fourteen div. He'll do what he's told...or I'll tell the truth about him." His wife watched him approvingly. He was not finished. "I *shall* brief some of the masters. Make sure they look out for Gordon... And I will speak to David when he arrives here. Where is he? Oh yes, he's spending time with Lord Pirie's grandson in Dorset. Pirie! Another useless guardsman! I shall make sure David understands his duty towards his brother." He paused, looking at others. Then a twinkle in his eyes, he declared, "And if that little bugger...or any of the masters do not follow my orders, they will be...denied chocolate cake!" He was pleased with himself. The others chuckled. He glanced at the grandfather clock. "I will telephone the Headmaster now. He should still be in his study. Bloody well should be." It was agreed that her parents would speak to Fiona now and that Gordon should not be told until a place was confirmed.

A short time later, the adults had reconvened but this time in the study. The parents reported that Fiona had understood why her grandparents had to be told. She thought that David as the elder son should also be informed. She agreed to Gordon going away to school but she wanted to be there when he was told.

"I think this calls for a celebratory dinner... And the children will join us."

His wife frowned but Elizabeth said, "I think that's a good idea. I'm sure Fiona and Gordon will be thrilled."

"What's cook providing tonight? Doesn't matter. Just bread will do me...with whisky. No wine or champagne...or those bloody cocktails! I have had enough of going to cocktail parties and endlessly boring dinner parties." He looked directly at his wife. "And I am not ever going back to bloody Henley."

"Papa, I trust you will curb your language in front of the children." It was a teasing rebuke from his daughter-in-law.

"Fiona probably knows more bad language than me...from that local school."

Elizabeth and David thought it was likely that he was right. "For Gordon's sake?"

"You are right, Elizabeth." His next comment was directed at his wife. "I hope we hear more of Fiona's opinions. She will probably spoil your dinner, my dear." To the other two, *sotto voce*. "Aided and abetted by me."

The dinner was a success. It was the first time Fiona and Gordon had sat down to dinner with their grandparents. Only a small part of the long dining table was used with both head of the table chairs unoccupied: their grandpapa flanked by Elizabeth and Fiona on the side facing the door and on the opposite side back to the door, grandmama flanked by David and Gordon. Fiona told some stories but it was grandpapa who dominated. He told army stories. Gordon thought the army to be one big playtime in which people had silly names, played sports or pranks on each other, always eating and drinking. He wondered why his father never spoke of his time in the army. His grandpapa did not just tell his stories but acted them out with facial expressions, mimicking other characters mentioned in the stories. Gordon was whooping with laughter and several times his mother or grandmama had to calm him.

After pudding, Grandpapa declared that the ladies were not leaving the table and that there would be no port. He would stick to his wee drams though Gordon did not think they were very wee compared to the small whisky his father drank. Gordon, adopting a serious expression, asked, "Are we a cavalier or roundhead family?" Glances were exchanged amongst the adults. Fiona explained it was in a school lesson.

Grandpapa replied, "Cavalier, of course. The roundheads cut off the king's head…Puritans…bloody miserable buggers." He leaned towards Gordon and in a conspiratorial whisper said, "There are roundheads in parliament today who got rid of the King and replaced him with his clot brother and his ghastly, common little wife."

"David. That is disgraceful. They are *our* King and Queen."

His son knew his mama's comment would encourage him to more contentious comments. "Papa! Remember. No politics in the mess."

"Sorry, brigadier." He winked at Gordon. "What rank am I?"

Gordon shouted, "A general!"

"In my day, generals gave brigadiers orders. Times must have changed." Another laughing spasm by Gordon. His mother was laughing also and thinking that she had not seen this side of her father-in-law for many years. Her husband, though witty at times, was staid whereas his father had a puckish persona. Fiona and Gordon on their way up to bed agreed that it had been one of the best nights of their lives. They had not known that grandpapa was so funny. Gordon was still excited and found it difficult to sleep. He loved his grandpapa who made him laugh so much.

He would have seen another grandpapa if he had gone downstairs. In darkness, the old general sat in the armchair in the study, a whisky in hand, weeping. He wept for his friends and all the other men killed in the service of their country in faraway places but mostly in France. He wept also for his granddaughter, the bravest individual he had ever met. He knew that her behaviour and outlandish opinions irritated others including himself and in particular his wife who came from good Kentish landed stock. She had adapted well to army life and had indeed embraced the role of a CO's, then brigadier's and finally a general's wife. She held Elizabeth's mother responsible for Fiona's behaviour, which at times amounted to disrespect for the family name and its place in society, akin to insubordination. A guffaw amidst the tears. *And* he would encourage Fiona's insubordination for the remainder of her days.

The Headmaster could not have been more helpful. Of course, a place was available. There might have to be some cramming for Gordon to catch up with the other boys but that would not present a problem. Gordon was seated in the same chair for the second time in the study across from his father. His mother and Fi were present. His father explained that his sister was going away to school. Gordon did not mind going away to school, especially if Fi was not going to be there. When he arrived from Dorset, David would help him prepare for his new school and look after him at school though Gordon was unsure whether he liked that part but said nothing. His mother said there was much to be done: he needed new clothes and labels required to be sewn on his clothes. Fi told him that all those snooty boys in England would not be a match for him. David was attentive to Gordon although he did not like his brother's first observation. "We will need to do something about that accent. You sound like Jamie Mackenzie." Thereafter, David told him about the school: the 'dos' and 'don'ts'; the good Masters, the bad ones and the mad ones; the helpful boys and the ones to be wary of; the sports; and the clubs and societies. Gordon could not take it all in but he did acquire respect, even admiration, for his brother though he could at times still be pompous.

Gordon's initial qualms faded as he realised his reading and writing was not behind the other boys and probably ahead of most of them. His knowledge of history and geography was generally in advance of the others. He had no Latin and so was well behind but his brother and others were helping him at night. Fortunately, it would be the following term when the class would begin Greek. Some of the younger masters expressed astonishment at Gordon's ability and knowledge considering he came from a village school in Scotland. An irascible, Scottish master, his right arm with his palm opened flat, pointed in their direction, enlightened them, "Your Reformation led only to a change of name on the door." A pause for them to take in, and for his hand to curve in towards him. "Our Reformation created the finest education system in the world." He then crossed his arms across his chest with his hands hidden in the folds of his gown in his customary combative stance. The longer serving masters, including some previous recipients of the same assertion, smiled or tittered behind their cups and saucers, hoping for some challenge to the assertion, which would be refuted by further assertions plucked from his gown. The spectators were disappointed because no challenge came and they returned to the monotonous chitchat of the staff common room.

Gordon started each day with the intention of writing to his parents and of course Fi but he was always too tired at the end of the school day. He did after several weeks send short letters to his parents and Fi. They were not concerned because David had kept his parents and grandpapa informed of his brother's progress. To his sister, he wrote that she was right that the snooty boys were not a match for him. He told her that he was learning Latin but it was difficult. Fi replied that she too was learning Latin and they could learn it together during the Christmas holidays. Not an appealing idea for him. If Gordon knew his history and geography, the same could not be said about his knowledge of the events taking place in Europe. Almost all the other boys knew about Hitler and what had occurred at Munich. Despite attempts by the masters, discussions were not curbed and pupils of all ages had opinions, though predominantly their fathers', with the majority opinion being support and admiration for Chamberlain as well as Hitler. He had heard many boys saying that we needed a 'Hitler'. Gordon thought it prudent not to mention that Hitler was Mr Thompson's brother. David Buchanan-Henderson was in the minority and Gordon heard his brother declaring the dictators had to be stopped, which led to arguments with others, some his best friends. Gordon was certain that he would never be able to argue like his brother.

The boys spent their mid-term break with their grandparents in London. There was sightseeing but he was not as excited as he had expected on seeing Parliament, the Tower and Buckingham Palace There was also relief amongst everyone that there was not going to be a war. It was not his grandpapa of the recent dinner and he appeared just to comply with grandmama's wishes, more like instructions. One Saturday afternoon following the mid-term, Sir Nigel and Lady Olivia Staveley came to the school to take them to tea. Gordon thought the lady was Sir Nigel's daughter until she was introduced as his wife. She did not seem much older than their maid, Morag. David and Sir Nigel discussed the situation in Europe with both of them agreeing on the need to stop Hitler. Again, Gordon thought it was sensible not to mention 'Mr Thompson's brother'.

Fiona settled into her new school quickly and found most of the pupils friendly. There were about the same number of pupils as in the village primary school though no boys. She recognised the names of some of the pupils who were from distinguished Scottish families. She had to concede that some of the pupils knew more than her. The teachers were strict but approachable and made lessons interesting and enjoyable. Latin and French were two new subjects for her. She was beginning Latin and French at the same stage as the pupils of her age though most of her peers could speak French, some fluently. She wished that she had listened to Charles Planet more when he had spoken French to her. Most weekends, she returned home as agreed with the school. After badgering her parents, most weekends were spent travelling in Scotland visiting different places including Edinburgh, Aberdeen, Inverness, Fort William, Glencoe, even Glasgow, which she found dark, grimy and depressing apart from the university perched on the hill above Kelvingrove Art Gallery. Her only slight disappointment was that neither of her parents knew the history of the places visited except for basic information. Usually, they would spend at least one night in a hotel and sometimes with family friends though she resented their prying about her life. Her parents consented to her request to stay only in hotels. Her father, in response to her questioning how he could spend so much time away from the estate, told her that the manager was doing an excellent job, which was true. Fiona enjoyed especially the drive along Loch Lomond. It had been a sunny, dry day. The more places she visited, the more she considered herself Scottish rather than British, or as grandmama sometimes said—English, even grandpapa did.

She enjoyed going to Dundee to see her grandmother who seemed to know everything about Scotland and her history. Despite her father's reluctance stemming from her 'not having the room', they sometimes stayed overnight. Fiona thought it was quite a large house, being a terrace house of three storeys with a small front garden and quite a large one to the rear enclosed by stone walls. Fiona and her brother David, when younger, had been cautioned against mentioning her grandmother's deceased husband unless she mentioned him, which she never did. Fiona was stirred when she discovered her grandmother's Christian name was 'Deoiridh', the Gaelic for 'pilgrim'. To Fiona's question whether she had ever been on a pilgrimage, she replied, "Yes. Mine is a pilgrimage through life and I am nearing its end." Fiona felt inspired though there was an intake of breath and the arching of eyebrows by her father.

Her mother smiled and said, "Yes mother. You will live until you are a hundred." She then told her mother that Fiona wanted to ask her some questions about Scottish history, adding that unfortunately her husband and she had little knowledge of it. Deoiridh curbed her impulse to make a comment about their 'English' schooling. She understood David's comment about not tiring Fiona and that she was off-duty. After briefly pondering the matter, she decided that rather than Fiona asking questions, she would narrate *their* history.

Fiona asked if she should take notes but Deoiridh, the timbre of her voice one of passion, insisted, "Scottish history is not like others simply to be recorded as dates of battles or names of kings or queens. It's not for the mind." Tapping both her temples with fingers of each hand. "One has to listen…then absorb it…into your heart and soul." Now both hands clasped, right over left, over her heart. "It is like sniffing a fine wine before imbibing it…or smelling the peat of a malt whisky before tasting it."

"I have never tasted whisky," Fiona said. A little, white lie. Deoiridh looked at Fiona, then at her parents and began to laugh. The other two adults joined in. It lightened the mood. Fiona had, as in the past, noticed an uneasiness between her parents and her grandmother. That day, Deoiridh spoke of Alexander III and the Maid of Norway. On following occasions, it was Wallace, Bruce, Andrew Murray, Reformation, Mary Queen of Scots and the Act of Union. Fiona's parents reined Deoiridh in if they considered she was expressing unacceptable political, social or religious opinions.

With spending most weekends away, the Buchanan-Hendersons were seldom in the two local churches on a Sunday. Their absence was noted in particular by Mr Thompson and he made references, though never by name, to the daughter of an upright Protestant family attending a *Roman Catholic* school. His usual reference to betrayal but still for the moment remained a family of good standing. Several Sundays later, the minister in a sermon, more furious than normal, told his congregation that not only was it a *Roman Catholic* school but it was run by an order of *French*…splattering those in the front pew…*nuns*. A perfidious act of treachery! It was the destructive influence of the *papish* grandmother, *the harlot*.

Elizabeth through Mrs Mackenzie was aware of the growing hostility of some towards the family. Her husband remained insouciant but the family would never enter that church whilst Thompson was the minister. Mr McPhail, aware of the tensions, attempted to mediate but was rebuffed by David who was not even prepared to discuss it. He told his wife that he would not treat with anyone who accused him or his family of treachery, and she was to obey his command. Initially, she was angered and shocked. Unlike other marriages of their class, they were a partnership with no major decisions taken unless agreed by both. She had never seen before his expression, which was without emotion but one of determination. This decision was made known discreetly without any explanation to friends and others. When Mr Thompson heard, he was infuriated because he had expected some appeasement in order to restore the family's standing in the community. When Mr Mackenzie, usually a reticent individual, heard, he declared, "Thompson's a bloody fool. He always was."

Before her school broke up for Christmas, Fiona asked her parents if they would mind not coming to take her out at weekends. Fiona felt there was some resentment of her by some of the girls because she was allowed out of school almost every weekend, the others only once every four weeks unless it was a special family day such as a birthday or wedding. In fact, the resentment did not really bother her, she wanted to make friends. Most of the girls had one or two close friends. She realised that she had never had a female friend, the ones at primary being dull and mostly stupid. Her parents agreed, though it would be a trial period for the first month.

Chapter 6

On the first Sunday after the Christmas holidays, she was in a classroom reading. Non-Catholic pupils were not required to attend mass or other services. They could attend the local churches and the school provided transport. Her parents had agreed that she did not have to go to church. Una McFadzean from her class came into the room. Fiona wondered why she was not at mass because she had seen her going into services during the school week.

"You a proddy? So am I."

Surprised, Fiona said, "I have seen you going into the chapel."

"Yes. I normally do. But in Kirk a few times over the holidays. I needed a rest."

"Why do you go?"

"To keep in with them, the nuns. My father told me that. He's a businessman… He's a bad man!" Fiona thought that was the first time she had ever heard someone criticising their father. Even the boys and girls sometimes who were beaten by their parents always claimed their fathers and mothers were the best in the world. "Old Sister Felicity has hopes that I will become a pape. No chance. Also sometimes in chapel, they announce things about the school and other things, which they forget to tell us proddies. Father says you need to know everything that's going on. He calls it the 'form'." She sat down opposite Fiona. "I like singing and they have some good hymns…better than our dull ones." Fiona was told by Una that she was to have lunch with Catriona Mitchell and her. "She's my best friend. Cat is fun even though she is a pape. You don't have to tell us anything about yourself." She smiled. "We'll find out."

Fiona was surprised by how quickly the two adopted her as a friend. They were in the choir so Fiona joined it, which led to many hours of fun and enjoyment, especially when singing the Scottish and French songs. Catriona's father owned a small estate near Edzell and owned some properties in Aberdeen. Una commented, "They are neighbours of the King and Queen and go for tea." Accompanied by a mock, exaggerated curtsy.

"We do not! More likely you go." She spoke directly to Fiona, "Una's father is the richest man in Scotland."

"Not yet!" Una chuckled. Una's father had recently taken over the family business, which had originally been engineering but now had many factories producing different things. Fiona was elated and honoured when both girls said that they did not come from an ancient and noble family like her. They spent most of their free time together and helped each other with their schoolwork.

Fiona thought Catriona was the cleverest, which she artfully concealed, notwithstanding her friends who said that Fiona was much cleverer and knew more than them.

"Especially in history," Catriona said.

"That's because her family was there." Una as always with a simple explanation. They laughed so loudly in the corridor that it brought a rebuke from Sister Marie-Therese that young ladies do not laugh in that way. Fiona noted that the other two girls were far more physically developed than her but they did not comment on it though they would tease other girls making Fiona think that they knew about her health. She considered asking Sister Felicity who at the first meeting had said that she would not divulge the information to anyone without the consent of her parents and in particular Fiona's. She did not think that Sister Felicity would break a commitment. She speculated that if Una's father was so rich and powerful, he would have influence and could have found out. She recalled Una's comment on 'knowing about everything'.

On two occasions, arrangements were made for the three girls to visit Deoiridh for tea. Fiona's father was concerned about what his mother-in-law might say to the girls and thought about a chaperone but was dissuaded by his wife who told him that she had warned her mother about her conduct. Deoiridh continued with her history lessons starting from when she had finished on Fiona's last visit making no allowance for the other two girls, telling them that if they didn't know it, then Fiona would tell them. Fiona knew by informing her of the backgrounds of her friends that it would control her grandmother. She had come to know and understand her well, feeling sorry for her because she thought that she was lonely. Deoiridh did not say anything inappropriate though she had to restrain herself when recounting the 1745 rebellion; she did make an aside that the Hanoverian George was the rebel. Fiona discovered that her grandmother could sing. She had told her about them being in the school choir so Deoiridh decided after tea that they would entertain her by singing. They sang Scottish songs and one French one. Deoiridh joined in the singing. The girls were polite, telling her that she had the best voice. Fiona was further surprised when, on Una's suggestion that they sing a few hymns, her grandmother knew all the words of the hymns. On the second visit, they had tea in the garden followed by singing. Deoiridh seemed to sing the hymns louder than the other songs. When Catriona worried about disturbing the neighbours, she was told, "Don't worry about them. They are all old and deaf." Prompting laughter from the girls. She made one request that the three friends sing *Loch Lomond.* She sat in her chair but made the girls stand, facing West towards Loch Lomond, which was to the front of her home. The three girls linked arms spontaneously. When finished, Deoiridh said, "Thank you. That was beautiful. You have made an old woman happy." Triggering more laughter from the girls.

David Buchanan-Henderson was at Kilgraston to collect his daughter for the Easter holiday. The school put on an afternoon tea so that the parents could mingle and talk to the teachers whilst the girls were completing their final lesson and collecting their bags. He saw a man with a young lady who seemed to be coming towards him from the other side of the hall. He knew who he was from photographs in the newspapers, Alastair McFadzean, the Glasgow industrialist.

"Hello. Brigadier Buchanan-Henderson? Fiona's pater?" An extended hand.

"Yes." A handshake.

He expected to be known and recognised. "This is my wife, Kitty." Another handshake. "Kitty, off you go to speak to Sister Felicity but don't promise her any money this time." He watched her going towards the nun. "Pretty little thing…from Missouri originally but moved to New York. We did business— still do with her father." He turned his attention back to Buchanan-Henderson. "She's not Una's mother…sadly…childbirth…so delicate…but life needs to go on…especially for Una's sake." A smile, more a leer. "And mine." He did not give Buchanan-Henderson time to respond. "I hear Una met your mother-in-law." He saw the emergent frown on the other man's face. "Don't worry. Una loved her though thought she was batty. Deoiridh is not the dangerous radical or communist people think she is or she pretends to be."

David's impulse was to rebuke him for referring to his mother-in-law by her first name, which was inappropriate. McFadzean continued, "My grandfather sent my father to Dundee to expand the business…think about 1908 and we went with him. Baird was our banker there. I went to the same school as Andrew. According to my father, Baird was the dreariest man in Scotland. No wonder Deoiridh joined the suffragettes…for a bit of excitement. It seems the lot in Dundee were very active and caused trouble. It was said that Deoiridh passed the egg to the woman who threw it at Churchill… He was the local MP at the time. She probably made it up. There were photographs of her in the papers. She was arrested once or twice but never appeared in court. Baird had influence. Though he couldn't stop the criticism by some of the ministers… She probably never got over the death of Andrew at Gallipoli?" Buchanan-Henderson nodded, relieved his wife was not present. Her father had died shortly after her only brother's death and thereafter, his wife's mother had reverted to her maiden name, never mentioning again—as far as he was aware—her son's and husband's names. Elizabeth seldom mentioned her brother but it was his loss that had made her determined that Fiona would go to a nearby school. McFadzean was not finished. "Probably blamed his death on Churchill…suppose it was." The other man thought it was disrespectful and crass of McFadzean to speak of Andrew's death in this way.

The industrialist had changed direction and now smiling declared, "Got the order of the boot from the General, your father in France…said I was the worst, no, the most inept officer ever under his command. Sent me as an ADC to Dublin Castle. Got there a few months before the Rising… Mind you, I was down in Kildare…trying out a new filly." A lascivious smirk that appalled Buchanan-Henderson but he remained silent, *for Fiona*, he told himself. "I didn't get back to Dublin until it was almost over…transport problems." Another smirk. "Thought Dublin looked better after the shelling…then that old duffer Maxwell decided to shoot them. Would have shot most of them if London hadn't stopped him… That didn't go down well with the locals."

Buchanan-Henderson was seething inside. He thought it had been lawful and right to execute them because they had been aiding the enemy, Germany. He and his fellow officers, including the Irish Catholics serving in France, had thought the rebellion was 'a stab in the back'.

"Then they release the others. Nearly all were out by about seventeen... What did they do! Did the politicians think they would say, 'Thanks sur, never do it again'." An exaggerated Irish accent. "They picked up their guns... Know what I would have done! Dumped them all in Boston harbour... Tea-party in reverse... Paid for their families to join them... Mind you, dined out on the Rising in Belfast when over on business. Thought I was responsible for crushing the rebellion. Helped business." He tacked away and asked Buchanan-Henderson, "Are you a Mason, Orangeman?"

"No." He was aware that in some Scottish, and even English, regiments, there were lodges. He would not have allowed one in his battalion believing it to be detrimental to good order and discipline with the danger of causing splits and resentment.

"I'm not. My grandfather and father were. They joined because they knew it would be good for the business. Don't need them now... Was invited to join the Orange Order as a grand master of something... Told them the colour orange hurt my eyes...there were some expressions of sympathy until they realised I was teasing them... Most of my managers and foremen are masons or orangemen or both. They were unhappy when I employed papes as engineers and in other technical jobs. I said if they could find me Protestants who could do the job as well and for the same pay, I would get rid of the papes. No takers." He laughed. "If they knew about Una being here, they would be despairing of me."

"Why did you send your daughter here?" He realised it was a mistake immediately.

"It's a very good school... Also Kitty likes going back home quite often, especially now on the Queen Mary. So I tend to live in my place in Glasgow rather than the pile in Strathblane. My man in Glasgow is very discreet...dinners, parties...plenty of company... If Una was at school in Glasgow, then probably want to spend time in Glasgow...bit inconvenient. Like it that they lock them in here most weekends. On her weekends, off she goes to her aunt near Stirling. She has horses and Una likes to ride. But now she likes to spend time with your Fiona and Cat Mitchell, of course." Another tack. "Looks like war. Terrible. Glad don't have a boy. You have boys." It was a statement. "Enough young men gone the last time. What a waste!" Buchanan-Henderson empathised silently with him and detected a flash of melancholy in his eyes. "Bloody fool! Chamberlain! Saying we will defend Poland. If Czechoslovakia was a faraway place of people of whom we know little or whatever he said. So is Poland... Heard one wag in the foreign office or somewhere said something about having to put wheels on Royal Navy ships to get to Poland or something like that. I could do that...actually, we are doing rather well with the increased expenditure on armaments and it will get better. Probably could get your boys into reserved occupations." His listener was once more appalled at the lack of a sense of right and wrong. Another tack. "I forgot. My brother Angus was in your battalion. Think he came to you because you needed company commanders." Buchanan-Henderson remembered him, a fine and gallant soldier who had been wounded. He had not associated him with Alastair McFadzean.

"A brave officer. Respected by all. How is he? Give him my best wishes."

"No, not well. Mostly in a wheelchair. Memory is going. Just sits there, looking at his medals… Not much good they do him now… Oh…the chaplain. Must go and say hello. Only clergyman of any religion who laughs at my jokes. Hope to see you again. Bye."

David Buchanan-Henderson considered him to be the most amoral and dishonourable man he had ever encountered. Although McFadzean appeared to be a runaway Vickers machine-gun spraying in every direction, it was not impulsive and unstructured but a controlled performance used at a first meeting with individuals. He changed the order as well as omitting or adding bits depending on the victim. Its sole purpose was to intimidate. To make the listeners aware that he had no moral compass so if they had authority or influence, not to obstruct him. Past experience had demonstrated that he did not need to change this tactic.

In April, Jamie Mackenzie and the estate manger enlisted—the former to the Royal Tank Regiment and the latter to his county regiment. David had tried to dissuade them by pointing out that their jobs were reserved occupations. He heard a cock crow in an inner recess of his mind though he justified it to himself in that the supply of food would be essential in any coming war. After conscription was introduced in May, he went to London in a futile attempt to return to active service. The explanation was the necessity to maintain food production with the added acknowledgment that his estate was one of the best food producers in Scotland, if not the whole country. Indeed, he was likely to be appointed as a sort of area commander to oversee food production in the area. His experience and skills were the right mix to motivate people and meet targets as well as knocking heads together when necessary. Buchanan-Henderson understood the logic but felt still that it was the settling of old scores by some because of his premature leaving. However, Charles Planet had been recalled to the colours and sent to London to work on the joint Anglo-French military plans committee, which was because of his outstanding cooperative work with the British in 1917 that had, in fact, been simple cooperation between two adjoining units. The only upside was that his wife was allowed to join him. His son, his only child, was due to graduate from St Cyr as a cavalry officer.

The recently knighted Nigel Staveley hosted a luncheon for Planet, Buchanan-Henderson and his son David due to leave school and go up to Oxford though if war came, he intended—on his father's advice—to join the Brigade of Guards. Young David was alarmed by Planet's and Staveley's views on the effect of air-power, particularly on the morale of the civilian population if there was heavy bombing of the cities evidencing attacks in Spain. His father's fear was that there would be a reluctance on the part of parents to encourage their sons to serve, which he understood because of the losses sustained in the last war, and further he felt that those officers and senior NCOs who had been in the last war might lack the commitment and necessary steel to prosecute a war, making it clear that he was not questioning their loyalty, honour or courage. They may be cautious, which was understandable given the pusillanimity of their political leaders. More importantly, only a small number had commanded a brigade or above at the end of the war. This was the reason he wanted to return to active service. He was still young enough to command a division and not too old for a corps. He knew what was needed to fight. His son had never seen such coldness and determination on his father's face. Then a relaxation with his father saying, "Just need to stick to growing potatoes." Greeted by the others with forced chortles.

The last occasion Sir Nigel Staveley took the two brothers together for tea was the day their school broke up and both were returning North by overnight train. He felt certain that both sons were proud of their father but that he wanted to tell them why. Their father had been a great battalion and brigade commander. He was a tough and ruthless fighting soldier who made sure his subordinates understood what was required of them. David asked him about the 'look' and was told that it usually meant trouble for someone, usually the hun. When Gordon asked about the 'look', he was told not to concern himself with it. Sir Nigel was now working for the government, planning for the coordination of transport in preparation for war so it was unlikely that he would be able to get up to Scotland this summer. He asked that they pass on his regards to their parents and of course to Fiona. Gordon said that he was looking forward to seeing his sister because she knew more than and was not as boring as the boys at his school. Sir Nigel thought Gordon should have been informed of Fiona's health but he did not have the right to comment unless his opinion was sought. Sir Nigel told David privately that he was anxious on how Gordon would cope with Fiona's passing and how he would cope at school without David being there. David shared these concerns, telling Sir Nigel that some of his chums at school thought Gordon immature for his age, almost babyish, so he had tee'd up several of next term's seniors to look out for Gordon.

Summer was apprehensive and expectant: Fiona was neither. There were two parts to her holiday before and after her brothers arrived. The Scottish school term ended before the English one. In the first part, she spent her day walking, reading and singing. She spent a few days at Catriona Mitchell's home and in Dundee with her grandmother. Her father expressed no misgivings about her spending time unaccompanied with his mother-in-law due to, though not admitted, Alastair McFadzean's opinion of Deoiridh. Her father and mother felt guilty at spending so little time with their daughter but David was managing the estate as well as wider responsibilities and Elizabeth had taken on charity work including helping those families whose sons—usually the breadwinners—had been conscripted as well as becoming the area coordinator for welcoming and placing evacuated children in the event of war. Fiona's enthusiasm and vitality gave them hope that she might have longer. In the second part, Fiona continued the same activities except for the visits but for most of the time with Gordon in tow.

For Gordon, Fiona was even more fun, especially with her singing songs, some in French. He did wonder why she had not grown because he was now the same height. He was peeved when she insisted on testing him in Latin and French but Gordon felt disappointment when Fi told him that they would have to delay their expeditions. She intended to go to Glasgow University to study medicine. Gordon said that was an adventure because some of the pupils in his school said Glasgow was the darkest and most dangerous place in the world. Fi told him that they were ignorant fools. She explained that she was going to become a doctor and go to Africa or China to help people. Gordon, his enthusiasm restored, said that he could go with her to carry her bags. She agreed. On another occasion, in response to Fi's questions, he said that he was not bullied at school but had only one friend, Jonathan Ballingall, whose father was an admiral and his brother was training to be a pilot in the RAF. In another conversation, Gordon said that he was not going to Oxford or any university. As soon as school was finished, he was coming home to work with Mr Mackenzie on the estate and then he would run the estate as his father had promised. David participated in their activities only on a few occasions. Other times, Fi and David would have tea together in their father's study or go to a local hotel sometimes with their parents. Gordon did not mind because each time Mr Mackenzie needed his help.

Her grandparents arrived from London a week before Fiona returned to school, and on the same day Alastair McFadzean telephoned her father. "David, how are you?" Not waiting for a response. "I'm looking for a boon. I have some important…vital business coming up. Kitty is off home today and there is no one to look after Una. School starts next week…and I thought that she could stay with you and then on to school with Fiona…Una would love it and sure Fiona would also. You know what girls are like at their age. Like to be together…chatting about movies, clothes and…" He thought it a prudent tactic not to mention 'boys'. "No one down here can help. Can you save the day?"

David surmised the 'vital business' was cocktails and dinner parties in the Glasgow home. He knew that Fiona would enjoy a visit from Una. "Una is welcome to stay, though it can't be today or tomorrow." He had an image of Una sitting in a nearby hotel waiting on a telephone call from her father. "Tomorrow is our family dinner before the children return to school. Do it each year with the grandparents, and the one rule has always been no house-guests." He considered it as a deception plan. There was a family dinner tomorrow but the first celebratory one had been the previous summer.

"I understand." His voice was flat but only for a moment. "Not a problem. She can stay with her aunt. That's on route. Don't worry about anything. I'll get Una delivered to you…and then both of them back to school…into the safe hands of the nuns." David decided not to say that they would be taking Fiona back to school. "Thanks for your help. Greatly appreciated."

"Hope your business goes well."

"So do I…I'm confident it will. Bye."

David felt that he had gained a small victory over the industrialist whilst rebuking himself for the thought. Fiona was elated and it was decided for Catriona to come down, with the three going back to Kilgraston together. David had given his wife a censored account of his school encounter with McFadzean and asked her to discreetly mention it to her mother. Deoiridh recalled the family but said that she had never before or since disliked so intensely a thirteen- or fourteen-year-old boy, whatever age he was. He seemed to take after his father who regarded human beings as a means to increase his wealth. The other son— she could not recall his name—was a well-mannered young man.

The family dinner was a success but subdued compared to the previous year. The General encouraged Fiona to mention more of her heroines simply to irk his wife. When Fiona spoke of the suffragette Ethel Moorehead, her grandmama expressed complete ignorance of her. Only Joan of Arc received lukewarm approval.

Gordon trailed the three girls but they did not mind because Catriona's two siblings were much older than her and Una was an only child. However, he was excluded from tea with them and also when his brother treated his mother and the three girls to lunch in Dundee. Fiona's parents were delighted that Fiona could spend time with her two friends though when they saw their waif-like daughter between her two friends, their hopes that had been raised at the beginning of the summer seemed forlorn. Two cars were needed to take the girls back to school after summer—one driven by Fiona's father and the other by McFadzean's chauffeur who had been ensconced in a nearby hotel to be on-call to Una for trips but her only call had been to return to school. She had said at lunch one day, to much hilarity, that her father's personal staff came from the Glasgow criminal underworld. Fiona's father did not disbelieve her and on meeting the chauffeur, her claim gained more credibility.

With his brother having returned to London with the grandparents to prepare for going up to Oxford, Gordon was the only one waving off his sister because his mother was also accompanying Fiona to school. When he held out his hand, Fiona ignored it and kissed him on both checks as did Una and Catriona to his embarrassment, which grew when the three girls giggled. The cars had moved about twenty feet when the second one stopped. Fiona exited the car, running back up the driveway. She hugged Gordon and ran back to the car.

"See you at Christmas, Fi."

Gordon with his parents had listened to Chamberlain's declaration of war with Germany. Later that Sunday evening, his father received a telephone call from Gordon's Headmaster advising that Gordon should not return to school for the moment. There were discussions ongoing of moving the school to Devon or Somerset. Evacuation had begun and Elizabeth's time was almost exclusively devoted to receiving and placing the children who were predominantly from Glasgow. Nevertheless, David and Elizabeth discussed the situation and agreed Gordon would not go to school in Devon or Somerset. They arranged with Mr Robertson that he would return to the village school whilst another school was found. The village school operated on a daily two-shift basis with the local children attending in the morning and the Glasgow children taught in the afternoon by their own teachers with the Robertsons assisting. The village hall was utilised both as an overflow for the school and a dormitory for children not yet placed. Gordon thought that they were the children he had seen in Dundee only to be told that they were from Glasgow. Most of the locals were stunned at the condition of the Glasgow children dressed in rags, all seeming sick and thin. Eventually, it was arranged for Gordon to attend a public school that had relocated to Blair Atholl from England. On the first Sunday in October, just before lunch, Gordon was called to his new headmaster's study. His brother David and Sir Nigel Staveley were present. Fiona was ill. David and Sir Nigel had travelled up on the overnight train from London and broken their journey to take him home. Gordon remembered all of it as a haze.

His father and mother were waiting for him in the study. Fiona was dead. She had had a problem with her heart. They and Fiona had hoped that he would arrive home before. She had fought hard. There were words of how only her courage and determination had kept her alive for so long. He should remember the happy times with her. The funeral would be in a few days and he needed to be strong, especially in the church. He asked where Fiona was. She had been laid out in the dining room but he was told by his mother that it would be best if he did not see her and just remember her. He asked to be excused and went to his room.

The funeral had been arranged. On her final summer holiday, Fiona had written down the arrangements for her funeral. Her father had promised that he would try to honour her wishes but that he had no control over some requests. The service would be in the Church of Scotland but Mr McPhail had agreed to the Bishop of Perth conducting the service with a shortened Episcopalian rite. There was condemnation by Mr Thompson of this papish desecration of the Kirk. It was agreed that neither Kilgraston staff nor pupils would attend the church service except for Una and Catriona, but not in uniform. Consideration was given to allowing the school to send representatives to the interment in the family plot on the estate but Fiona wanted only family, her father's two friends, her 'uncles', and the Mackenzies. Also, her father was insistent that people did not travel or go to any trouble because the country was at war. The 'uncles' complied with this request in that their wives did not attend. There would not be after the funeral a reception or what the locals called a purvey. There was hostile murmuring about this decision.

David raised with his father and Sir Nigel the use of the Scottish Royal Standard commonly referred to as the Lion Rampant, which was flown only for the monarch. During his silver jubilee, George V had allowed the locals throughout Scotland to wave the Lion Rampant. Sir Nigel concluded that there would be no criticism of an eminent Scottish military family and if there was, he would have words with wee Bertie.

The morning was cold and crisp. The women were dressed conventionally in black though Elizabeth's and Deoiridh's faces were not covered by a veil. The

General, Staveley and Planet were in full ceremonial uniform. David and his two sons wore dark suits, not morning dress. Fiona's coffin was taken from the dining room out to the waiting hearse and accompanying cars for the short journey to the church. There was a small, respectful crowd outside the church. The coffin draped in the Union Flag was borne into the church by four recruit soldiers commanded by a sergeant from the depot of the family regiment. The waiting congregation sang *The Lord's my Shepherd*. There were two readings, two prayers and a brief eulogy by Fiona's brother, David, then the final commendation. The coffin was carried out of the church and placed on two trestles, which Mr Mackenzie had positioned just before the end of the service. He surveyed the crowd beyond the church's low boundary wall. Mr Thompson was lingering further up the street on the opposite pavement but when Mackenzie's eyes fixed on him, he retreated back to his own Kirk.

The Union Flag was removed and replaced with the Lion Rampant causing in the crowd some, but not adverse, mutterings. The family stood on the top of the church's three steps allowing the rest of the congregation to arc out left and right down the steps to form a semi-circle. Fiona's two school friends stood either side of the coffin with Catriona to the right and Una the left, their backs to the family. Each rested their nearest hand delicately on the coffin. A glance and nod at each other, then they began singing *Loch Lomond*. Deoiridh held Gordon's hand. He tried hard but it began quietly, a few sniffs, some tears and uncontrolled weeping by the end of the song. The coffin was placed in the hearse for the return home for interment. As they waited to get into the cars, his mother arranged with Mrs Mackenzie to take Gordon into the house and not to the family plot. Gordon went straight up to his room but watched from his window as the coffin was carried into the small graveyard to the *Flowers of the Forest* played by a regimental piper. His father held the folded Union Flag and his mother the Lion Rampant while his grandpapa and the other uniformed mourners saluted. He turned away before the coffin was lowered and promised Fi that he would not cry ever again.

Chapter 7

The day after the funeral, Gordon returned to school even though it was the end of the week. He had no friends there and did not try to make any. He exchanged letters with his friend, Jonathan Ballingall, who had moved with his former school to Devon and received the odd letter from David who was undergoing officer training. He considered most of his fellow pupils to be stupid though as he got older; he realised the accurate word was ignorant.

Academically, he did not stretch himself, merely doing enough to get a decent report; on occasion in class if he thought someone was being particularly ignorant on a subject, he would shred their argument displaying a knowledge of the subject to the surprise of master and pupils alike. He played rugby and cricket, becoming skilled to the extent that he was made captain of both sports, first at junior then senior level. He enjoyed being captain with its responsibility, becoming more confident but tried to conceal it. He rebuffed efforts by other boys to become his friend as he advanced up the pecking order. Despite his mother's encouragement, he did not invite anyone back to the estate.

During school holidays, he spent most of his time with Mr Mackenzie who took him stalking though now his father allowed shooting besides the other skills. They erected a tent and on occasions, just built make-shift shelters both on the open hills and the forests. Unlike on previous occasions, Gordon did not complain about sleeping outside and was keen to learn. Mr Mackenzie taught him the importance of wearing the right clothes and boots depending on the weather and terrain. His parents were busy with their war work that sometimes took them away so that he did not see much of them. When they did dine together sometimes with his brother and grandparents present, Gordon seldom participated in the discussions on the progress of the war. His grandpapa and his brother disagreed enthusiastically on who were the best commanders and the where and when of the second front. Gordon was content if the family regarded him as uninterested in these matters. Nevertheless, he listened carefully when his father would expound on the most essential quality for a successful commander—judgement. A commander could be intelligent, brave, have a good eye for ground and a firm grasp of tactics, understand the importance of logistics, which are all important but it is to know the right time to act or the corollary. Seldom does a commander get it right but can succeed because the enemy also makes mistakes.

If his parents were not home, he would eat with Mrs Mackenzie and sometimes Morag would be present, being the only other staff member. Jamie was in North Africa but that's all his mother knew, learning more from the newsreels in the cinema than from Jamie. When Morag was not there, Mrs Mackenzie talked of how she came to be married to Mr Mackenzie and also of being particularly fond of his grandmother in Dundee. Mrs Mackenzie would ramble, leaping from one subject to another, and mention names of people Gordon did not know or could not remember. She was especially bitter towards Mr Thompson. She blamed him for Mr McPhail leaving the village not long after Fiona's funeral but Gordon sensed that was not the real cause of her bitterness. Gradually, he linked names, places and events together into one narrative. He did not ask questions. His mother had told them several times on how to behave towards the staff. She never called them servants though Gordon knew of boys at school referring to their servants. They were never to make fun of or embarrass them, never ask questions and not to have relationships with them. Gordon had been disappointed until Fi explained that he could ask what was for dinner but not about their family or personal life. It was only when he was at school hearing other boys speaking about father or brothers with servants that he understood the import of 'relationships'. Gordon and Mrs Mackenzie made a pact that they would not tell his parents what they discussed. He considered it a bit of fun and unlike his ones with Fi, he would not be bound by it.

During the Easter holidays, his last before leaving school, from his bedroom he saw a uniformed figure in the graveyard. He knew it was not David who was home on leave prancing about in his Guards uniform. On entering the gate, he saw it was a sergeant, the uniform frayed and faded. Sergeant Mackenzie turned before Gordon reached him.

"Hello, Gordon, or is it Master Gordon?"

"Jamie." They shook hands. Gordon was shocked by his appearance: he had aged, his face like his uniform. It was his first time home since coming back from Italy. It was only a short leave and he was going back tomorrow. Just wanted to pay his respects to Fiona. She had been a wonderful girl and before Gordon could say anything, "I hear that you are leaving school soon. What are you going to do?"

"The army. The family regiment. I hope."

Jamie shook his head followed by a faint smile. "I'll just have to kill more Germans to win this war before you finish your basic… Gordon, don't believe all this…nonsense about the war in the desert being clean and the Germans were a gallant enemy. I hate them. That's why I don't call them jerries, Nazis or huns. The Germans started this war and I just want to kill as many of them so that it can end and I can come home."

"Even women and children?"

A look of bewilderment came on Jamie's face at the question. "No. I am a soldier… Your brother's coming." Gordon turned to see his brother coming towards the graveyard. "I better be going." They shook hands again. Jamie put on his beret with the cap badge of the Royal Tank Regiment. He turned back towards Fiona's grave and saluted. It was not a proper salute, a quick throw up of his right hand, the fingers extended wide and a slight touch of the beret. He

65

turned and left, walking directly towards David who had not yet reached the gate. Gordon hoped that if Jamie saluted him, David would not upbraid him as he had other soldiers who failed to salute him properly in the village or once in Dundee. He said they were slovenly.

Jamie gave the same salute, which was returned with a correct one. Gordon saw them shaking hands and David put his left hand on Jamie's right shoulder. There were smiles then another slovenly salute returned with a smart one and Jamie was walking away from David who stood watching him. When Jamie was about ten yards away, David called out, "Jamie! Good hunting!" Jamie, without looking back, raised his right hand above his head, gave a wave, then an advance or follow me signal. Gordon concluded that David's behaviour towards Jamie was because both had seen action.

Gordon persuaded his father to allow him to leave school two weeks early so that he could begin his officer training or he would have to wait another six weeks or travel further afield. He was not old enough to begin training but the army needed men so there was some flexibility in applying the regulations.

Apart from the 'square-bashing', which he found boring but understood the logic behind it, the training was quite easy though he would not admit that to the instructors or indeed anyone. His map-reading skills were better than anyone's though if asked by an instructor to indicate their position on the map, he would convey an image of pondering before giving the position, notwithstanding that sometimes at night, he usually did not know their position. He was thankful for all the time he had spent with Mr Mackenzie. Near the end of his training, he rejected an approach to join the Parachute Regiment, which appealed to him but did so out of loyalty especially to his gandpapa who had been disappointed on David joining the Guards. He received an excellent report though he needed to develop his social skills, a criticism that pleased him, and improve his map-reading, which he thought said more about the instructors than him. His confidence was growing, which would soon be considered arrogance by some, and the seed of taciturnity had been planted. He was posted to the Regiment's second battalion, which was part of Fourteenth Army under General Slim. On his last day of leave, having said goodbye to his mother who had to go to a meeting, he sat opposite his father in the study.

"I had hoped it would not come to this. I had hoped that you would have taken over the running of the estate from me."

"I know."

"You will be pleased that you are not going by troopship? Six weeks or something. Hated boats. Even five days to New York…especially the trip back." He looked down, moving his pen from side to side. Gordon did not speak, knowing both were thinking of Fi. His father looked up. "It was good of Staveley to get you on a flight though you could be thrown off any time for a priority passenger. Not sure what we do then."

"Don't worry, Father. I would arrange something."

"You know it was Staveley who arranged for you to join Mountbatten's staff?"

"I thought it was him. He seems to have a lot of clout for an official in transport."

His father smiled. "Indeed. I had hoped that you would have taken it but I am glad you turned it down."

"You read my report. Poor social skills."

His father laughed. Gordon reminded him of Fiona who was willing to take on responsibility even when she was young and always had an answer or explanation. "I can't advise you on fighting in the jungle. Never did it. But remember three things. One. Look after your men and treat them fairly. Two. You are not their friend. You will have to make decisions that could—will lead to some of them being killed. And finally. Treat your prisoners properly. Don't kill them. Not out of any compassion for them but to protect your own men. If you start shooting prisoners, the enemy will."

"I understand."

"Good. Are you all set?" He glanced at the grandfather clock and stood up. "You better be going." Gordon stood up and put on his tam o'shanter. His father thought his hair was more reddish, an Elpinstone, and he had grown but not quite six feet like his brother. They shook hands. Gordon came to attention and saluted his father.

"Thank you and goodbye, Sir."

Gordon returned home in the spring of 1947. He had met his parents in London who were down visiting his grandpapa who was ailing. His brother was going up to Oxford after the summer. His parents were in the process of selling the estate to an American and planned to move to France close to Charles Planet. He thought it was reckless because from all accounts, France was in a worst condition than Britain, though he did not share his opinion with his parents. His parents concealed their disappointment at his decision to remain in the army. He went home only to collect some personal belongings, to thank the Mackenzies for all they had done for him and to say goodbye to Fi.

He spent two nights at home that had been infested by people: some checking the land and buildings to ensure all were included in the title deeds, others counting the livestock and others going through the accounts and other documentation. They were supervised by two Americans sent over by the prospective buyer. He had to tell them that he had no knowledge of the family business. He spent most of his time with Mrs Mackenzie in the kitchen listening to her stories, some he had heard and some new. She explained that she had left bits out before but now he was old enough to understand. She had been a suffragette in Dundee and that is how she had met his grandmother. She called her Deoiridh though apologising to him sometimes for doing so. She had been only young but Deoiridh had been a respectable, married woman with two children. It had been exciting. The war had come. She had gotten into 'trouble'. It was with a silly lad who was about to go to France. Her family had shunned her on the instructions of their minister, Thompson, the father of the Free Church minister in the village. She was the 'harlot' that the present Mr Thompson spoke of, though most people thought it was Deoiridh. Gordon confessed he never heard what Thompson said because he was so frightened of him and he was relieved when they had stopped going to that church. Deoiridh had heard of her plight. She had empathised with her because her family had rejected her when she had married Mr Baird and had given up her religion. Fi had deduced that their grandmother had been a Roman Catholic and had told him. Deoiridh arranged for the pregnant girl to go to Edinburgh to a hostel. Mr Baird gave his wife the money to pay for it.

"He was a good man. He was much older than Deoridh but they had a good marriage despite what people said about him. He was still grieving for his son who had been killed at Gallipoli the year before."

She had a miscarriage. Afterwards, she managed to obtain a job as a scullery maid with the Buchanan-Hendersons. It was grandmama who had been running the house. Mr Mackenzie came back. He had been the General's batman in France. When the General left France, Mr Mackenzie remained in France and served in Gordon's father's battalion. When he returned, he took over his father's job.

"We started courting—I was now the assistant cook—and he asked me to marry him. I refused but he asked me again. I told him about my past. He just laughed saying, 'I have seen and done worse things.' So we were married." Young Mr Thompson had been minister in the village. He had seen her or someone had told him. He was on his way here to inform his grandmama but Mr Mackenzie was working near the front of the house and intercepted him. He threatened to break his neck. Thompson had been terrified of Mr Mackenzie since that day. They decided that they would tell his grandmama who said it was of no interest to her. Gordon was surprised but pleased by his grandmama's response. "Then imagine my surprise when your grandmother turned up here. Your father had just married your mother. She would sometimes come down to speak to me."

He did not ask but knew she would speak of Jamie who had been killed in Germany near Hamburg not long before the German surrender. He could have had a posting as a training instructor because he had spent so long overseas but had volunteered to stay with his unit for the invasion of France. David had told Gordon of this during their recent meeting in London and this had explained David's conduct towards Jamie outside the graveyard. Jamie had been given a few days leave by his commanding officer because he had volunteered, though it was contrary to orders because units going on the invasion had been gated. Ted Locksley, a friend of Jamie's, had come all the way up from Liverpool, though he said he was from Birkenhead, to tell them about Jamie. The only good to come of it was that Morag was smitten with him and they were married and living in Birkenhead. He had a small family printing business.

Thompson who had criticised their families made sure his son did not have to fight. He obtained a reserved occupation in McFadzean's factory in Dundee. An engineer! He did not know one end of a hammer from the other. This surprised Gordon who did not know that Thompson had a son. He asked how she knew all this. She was the cook in the big house and went shopping in the village. There was always tittle-tattle. And there was Morag who was a member of Thompson's congregation. He was always asking Morag questions about what happened in the big house and she told Mrs Mackenzie everything.

He had said goodbye to the Mackenzies. In the agreement to sell the estate was a clause allowing the Mackenzies to stay in their cottage for as long as they wished and provision for a yearly income once Mr Mackenzie stopped working, which would be quite soon. He visited the graveyard for the last time to say his farewell to Fi. He was being dropped off at the station. In the village, on seeing Mr Thompson enter his church, he told the driver to stop and that he would return in a few minutes. In the church, he did not remove his tam o'shanter. Thompson at the lectern saw him and came walking up the aisle, his hand outstretched.

"Gordon. Welcome back. We are all very proud of you." No doubt one of his informers had told him of Gordon's return. Gordon assumed the at-ease position, his hands clasped behind his back with his blackthorn walking stick tucked in on his left side. Thompson looked up at Gordon's headdress but the soldier's manner cautioned him against asking for it to be removed. Gordon decided he would not waste words on him. He thought how easy it would be to break his neck. In a sharp action, his blackthorn was in his right hand at an angle towards Thompson, alarm in his eyes. Then he remembered Fi's admonition against being reckless. He lowered the stick, turned and walked towards the door. He stopped facing the door and said, "My sister saved your life."

He would concentrate now on killing the King's enemies.

Chapter 8

The Land Rovers drove at a steady speed below 30 mph. Knight wanted to have a look at the ground. His driver was Martin, a tall, burly, Leicester man, and in the rear a signaller from Williams' signals detachment who had been with C Platoon before joining the Signals Platoon. Collins was Welsh and felt that he would never gain promotion while Oldham was his platoon commander, being the 'token Taffy'. Knight considered him to be a very good and tough soldier though he had a brusque manner. The second Land Rover, which was a long-wheeled base, had Cpl Jubb and a half section. He was going to the police OP for his recce. When finished, he would come to the convent to RV with Knight.

Knight's eyes caught the white-stoned OP building. It was like a mini-castle or Beau Geste fort, being one storey but in the centre of the flat roof was the circular observation post. Battlements enclosed the flat roof. A Union Flag flew from a pole above the observation post. There were two smaller stone outbuildings. He surmised that one would hold the generator. There was a ten-foot fence topped with barbed wire surrounding the building. He could spot one pedestrian gate in the fence at a distance of about ten yards from the metal entrance door. He could not see if the ten yards were the same radius from building to fence. They had been told that vehicles could not access the compound. A road cut off from the right towards the convent, Knight stopped his vehicle and beckoned the other Land Rover up the road leading to the police outpost.

"Sarge. Don't think that's a chinky up there."

Knight spotted the man sitting on a rough wooden bench and said to his driver, "Martin, did you miss the 'hearts and minds' lecture? This is the 60s. You know we are required to be positive towards the natives and not call them derogatory…insulting names." Though Knight knew soldiers would not stop.

"People should stop calling me 'Taff'. That's derogatory…I know what that means."

"You are right. I will call you 'Mr Collins' from now on." This was met by a gruff grunt from the rear. He told Martin to stop when level with the European. Knight estimated that he was about the same height as himself but he was broader and a little paunchy. His complexion was dark verging on swarthy, the hair thick and long like a young London executive. Though sweating heavily, he had an elegant appearance for a man stuck out in the middle of nowhere. As the Land Rover came level with the man, Knight asked, "Out for a stroll?"

The man cocked his head upwards towards Knight. "Just having a rest. I'm not really fit for a long walk."

"It's hot...will get hotter. Where are you going if you don't mind me asking?"

"Oh. Same place as you, I imagine... Are you going up to search the nuns?"

Knight smiled and told him, "Jump in unless you're a Communist." He climbed into the back of the vehicle sitting opposite Collins, mutual nods of greeting.

"Seeing you're British, I'll be a capitalist today."

Knight told his driver to go up to the convent and swung around in his seat towards the stranger. "My name is Knight...Phil."

"I'm Edward Jerome, Eddie...traveller, amateur accountant, a two-thirds alcoholic and in simple language, a bum." Jerome turned away from Knight to look back towards the plantation. "No doubt you want young Baru."

The Land Rover halted a few feet from some wooden steps leading up into the convent where a nun dressed in white stood on the porch. Knight was quickly out of the vehicle, up the steps to meet the nun. He noticed another similar single-storey wooden building to his right down the slope. There were children of different ages sitting on benches on the porch of the other building. They all appeared to be Chinese and their eyes were directed up towards the soldiers and the Land Rover.

"Welcome to the Convent of the Holy Rosary." She extended a slim, slightly worn hand.

Knight felt awkward. "How do you do, Sister."

"I am Sister Mary Spinola and—"

She was interrupted by the shouts and squeals by the children who were running from the other building up the slope. The nun smiled, looking past Knight to the Land Rover. He looked around to see Jerome being swarmed by the children. Jerome, it would appear, was being asked to do something. "No, no...later... Yes, I promise...I must speak to Sister." He made his way through the children who were now being corralled back towards the school by two young teachers, one white and the other Chinese. Knight was impressed with Jerome's easy and sincere way with the children, not patronising.

"Hello Edward."

"Sister. Some friends gave me a lift." He smiled. "I think they are here to make sure you are safe from the natives."

Knight, though irritated, did not respond. He called to the other two soldiers, "Let me know when they come down from the OP. And if anything comes up on the net." He knew that he would hear the Land Rover. He looked towards Shala and Williams had been right, the shanties east of Shala formed a sprawling area almost touching the town itself and about one hundred yards from the convent.

"I think we should go inside. It's rather hot and I'm sure you could do with a cold drink."

"Thank you, Sister."

"What about your men?"

"They'll be fine there."

"I'll arrange for a cold drink to be taken out to them." She turned to Jerome. "Cold drink for you?"

"Always."

From the door, a corridor ran down to the back of the building and was crossed halfway down by another corridor from left to right. They entered the first room on the left. The room was bare but its simplicity was striking to Knight, a round table in the centre with four wicker chairs, a fan whirling above the table. On the wall opposite the door, a small table with a crucifix set on a white cloth above a picture of the current Pope and one of the previous one on the wall. Facing the windows was a Victorian writing desk-cum-bookcase. The soldier sat with his back to the writing-desk so that the door and windows were in his line of sight. He placed his weapon discreetly at his feet. Jerome sat opposite him and accepted the offer of a beer with Knight asking for a soft drink. When Mary Spinola returned with a tray of drinks, both men stood up. Having put the tray on the table, she placed a glass in front of each man, a bottle of Coca-Cola for Knight and a bottle of Tiger beer for Jerome. Knight regretted not asking for the beer: he had a long and mostly happy relationship with Tiger beer. But a hot afternoon as well as being armed was not the right setting for the relationship. Knight did notice the nun's easy manner when pouring the drinks, not awkward. She sat with her back to the door, a glass of water in front of her. Knight was the first to speak. "You may be aware why we are here. It is not a secret. Independence is coming and I understand that the leaders of the two parties want their army to be in all parts of the country on independence. We have come up to prepare the way. We are hopeful that there will be no problems and the area remains quiet." His tone was brisk and official. "My boss, my officer is Captain William Oldham. He is hoping that he can come up soon to pay you a courtesy visit but for the moment is having to deal with Chief Inspector Bendixson."

"Wish him good luck with that." A snigger from Jerome, ignored but noted.

He paused and leaned forwards, his elbows forming an inverted V and his hands clasped together. "My job is to be the liaison officer with the civilians. To explain the army's role, clear up any misunderstandings."

"Have you previous experience as a civilian liaison officer?" Jerome asked.

"No, but we all have to start sometime." He resisted the urge to say 'like becoming a bum'.

"Thank you very much for coming to tell us. It's Sergeant?"

"I apologise, Sister. I was distracted by Mr Jerome being mobbed. It's Knight, Phil Knight."

"Yes. Edward is very popular with the children. He has done so much for us. Anyway, what should I call you?"

"I don't mind even just 'Knight'."

"I think I would prefer Mr Knight. If that is fine with you?"

"I'm happy with that, Sister." He was trying to identify her accent, probably Irish but possibly Scottish. An elderly European nun came into the room. Both men stood up.

72

"This is Sister Mary Purcella."

"Hello. Phil Knight."

"A tan." She spoke with an Irish accent but her tone was frosty. She ignored his proffered hand, remaining just inside the room.

"Sister." Knight thought it was a rebuke from the younger nun. He did not understand what the older nun meant so if she had intended an insult, it was lost on him.

"Just to remind you, Sister, that you are due to speak to the infants."

"Oh, yes. I'll be straight over." Purcella was already out of the room. Jerome sat down but Knight remained standing behind the chair with his hands resting on the back.

"I must go. If you would like to wait, I should be back in about fifteen minutes."

"I need to wait for my other wagon to come back. So…if you don't mind, I'll wait."

Spinola smiled. "I shall see you before you go."

After she left, Knight sat down, his eyes roaming the room, enjoying the simplicity. Through the window, he could see the plantation dotted with different sizes and types of buildings. The sun was beginning to set. Jerome observed him and then commented, "It is a beautiful country. Peaceful. The trouble in the South seems so far away…until now."

"My mind was somewhere else."

"Thinking of home and family?"

He shook his head. "I have some family at home."

"Wife?"

"No." He should be asking the questions. "What are you doing out here?"

"I came out to a job, to save money. Go home and get married. I didn't like the job. Didn't want to get married. Had no money but I liked the place and the people…you don't get to know the people. They tend to avoid us except for business or need help. So I stayed and ended up drinking too much."

"How do you survive?"

"I told you. I'm an amateur accountant. Do the books for the bars here and other small businesses. Do some teaching here. In fact, I do some government people out of a job."

"Where do you live?"

"I have a room above one of the bars… *The Golden Eagle*. They're all brothels. They wanted to throw in a girl but think they accepted me better because I refused."

Knight smiled; a mentality different to a soldier's. They arrived in a place looking for drink and women. Though he did think it was inappropriate to mention brothels in a convent. "You must know the other Brits, Europeans around here?" Experience had taught Knight that not all whites were British in British present and former colonies.

Jerome laughed. "Shala is home to old boys of Belhaven School plus camp followers." He sipped some beer. Knight thought it was something that would have been mentioned in the Shala brief though he might have missed it. Jerome caught the soldier's inquisitive look. "No doubt, you have never heard of Belhaven. It's a minor public school...very minor...west of London. I went there and so did Tony Hockin."

"The owner of the plantation?"

"Yes. We were at school together. Don't be fooled by first impressions. He's—"

"I haven't met him yet."

"His family in England are not that rich. In fact, his uncles own most of the plantation. He thinks that I don't know that." Knight noted mentally the hostility towards Hockin. "You see. I came out here to work for Tony. But we never really ever got on...different attitudes to the running of the estate...well, that's by the way."

"Bendixson?"

"He's not one of us but he is a friend of Tony's, part of the clique. He's a nice enough guy but just not up to his job."

Knight refrained from asking how he had come to that conclusion, though Oldham and he had reached the same opinion on the first meeting. Knight did conclude that Jerome might be a useful source of information.

"There's also Doctor Tom Alston." A sentence in the Shala brief. "He's in charge of the government clinic. He's a good man. Married. He was probably Tony's best chum at school. He spends a lot of time with Bendixson now. Their wives get on. Oh! And Arthur Godden."

"The policeman? Know of him but have never met him. Our captain has."

"Policeman! He's no more a policeman than I am. He's a politician or something. Ostensibly, Godden replaced the Special Branch guy. Can't remember his name but was Irish and a bit of a drunk. Spent all his time drinking in the bars, restaurants even with old Raza in the square." He saw Knight's ignorance. "Not heard of him? He sits in the square telling the locals their fortunes...for money. He tells stories to the children. We called him 'Merlin' though John Sutch named him *Gandalf*...you know, from *The Hobbit*." Knight nodded. "Oh. You went to public school." Not a question.

"I certainly did not."

"Of course not. Anyway, Raza is a charlatan." He laughed. "I caught him out a couple of times. One minute telling a story about witnessing an event in the capital and in the next, an event here though both happened at the same time."

"Maybe he is *Gandalf*!" interrupted Knight.

A disapproving look from Jerome, then laughter. "Good one! He is a conman, a crock of shite...like *The Hobbit*." He explained that Godden had been at Belhaven but was two or three years ahead of them. Jerome knew him only to exchange pleasantries though Hockin knew him better, even socialising with him. For the area's only Special Branch officer, Godden spent very little time in Shala. "Though towards the end, the Irish guy was hardly ever here. He came up to the convent sometimes, speaking to Sister Consuella. Purcella ignored him. He had a couple of shouting matches with Father Devine. It was put down to

74

typical drunken Irishmen." Again he noticed Knight's 'and he is…' expression. "A few years back, he would come up to say Mass once a month or so. Then he was gone…out of the country. It was said that he had been recalled to Rome."

Knight wanted to know about the people still here. "How did they end up here? The Belhaven ones?"

"The old boys' network. First there was Hockin, genuine reason, the family business. He persuaded Tom Alston to apply for the government clinic job… Though Godden might have been here before Tony. He's always quite mysterious about things. Well, to me he is…probably just doesn't want to tell me. It always strikes me that he has no friends, just followers. Anyhow. We are the four Belhaven boys, like the musketeers. No, I won't go there. It's pathetic schoolboy humour."

He heard the sound of the returning Land Rover before his driver's call. He stood up, picked up his weapon and told Jerome he had to go. Jerome followed him out to the veranda. "It was good to meet you."

"And you," Knight replied. "I'm sure we'll come across each other again." Knight would ensure that they did. "Say goodbye to Sister for me."

"I shall."

Knight was in the Land Rover and a quick wave to Corporal Jubb in the other one and they were gone but at speed this time.

Chapter 9

After the first few days on recces, Oldham had drafted a plan that was agreed at a meeting with Bendixson also attended by Hockin—the policeman's suggestion. It had been agreed that the army would concentrate on protecting the plantation, though Hockin was insistent that there would be no patrolling through the plantation, and manning the OP allowing Bendixson to reduce the police presence there to two police officers. The reality was that the OP could see just part of the border road, the convent, the government administration building and most of the area around the police station. Although it overlooked the whole of shanty area Z, the buildings were so densely packed together that an armed group could gather without being spotted. The police would continue mobile patrols on the roads around the plantation but after last light, they would stop at the entrance to the plantation.

Godden had agreed to Knight using the CID office and collecting information, which Bendixson reported that in agreeing, Godden had said something about keeping them out of mischief. Oldham would be permitted to use Bendixson's secure phone once per day to speak to the CO or the adjutant; otherwise, reports and requests had to be sent by radio. The area was too large to patrol properly and there were so many tracks through the jungle, mounting ambushes would be pointless without specific intelligence. Godden had seemed confident of knowing when the CTs were close to Shala but he could never be confident in the Branch's information. Despite his reluctance, Hockin accepted that Oldham could deploy two sections each night on standing patrols along the border road but not in the actual plantation. The CTs had to cross the road to reach the plantation. One standing patrol would be near the river in case the terrorists try to slip down by boat. During daylight hours, hopefully any crossing would be spotted by the OP and the police patrols.

Oldham recognised that Sgt Nash had so much admin to contend with that he could not act as the platoon second-in-command even with Sgt Williams looking after the vehicles. He asked the adjutant to canvas with the CO the possibility of Horrocks being made a local sergeant and act as the ground second-in-command but Nash would remain overall second-in-command. He was waiting for a decision. The CO was adamant that Knight was to be kept away from the platoon and not assume *de facto* platoon sergeant, which Knight was determined not to do unless necessary. Most of the platoon were asleep during the day after their night patrols so Knight had little contact with them, and also he was able to construct his own job description. There was the problem of clerical support. Oldham was handwriting his sops and orders as was Knight with his reports. It was not intelligence but trying to understand the personalities and dynamics of Shala. Battalion could not provide a clerk. Bendixson was reluctant to use his police secretarial staff and also thought it wiser not to. With the policy of localisation, the District Officer's Brit secretaries were not overworked. Bendixson said he would mention it to Sutch.

Knight was anxious to establish a relationship with Staff Ho. On the morning of his moving into the CID office, just as Knight finished arranging his desk, Ho came in with two mugs of tea. "A welcome drink? Sorry, no milk or sugar."

"Not a problem. Thanks." He took the proffered mug. "Have a seat." Knight laughed. "Suppose that's a bit of a cheek considering it's your station."

"Not bother me." He closed the door and sat down opposite Knight. He was broad, muscular and tall with closely cropped hair. "As we are going to be neighbours, might as well get to know each other." His English was accent-less. Knight had heard him around the station speaking or mostly barking in Malay, English more pidgin when speaking to police officers and Chinese, which sounded like different dialects though Knight recognised some Cantonese. "We are also the two senior non-coms." Knight noted the use of the American expression though British soldiers were beginning to use American expressions picked up from listening to radio and watching television reports from Vietnam.

"Actually, Pete Nash is the senior because he is the platoon sergeant."

"OK. What's your officer like?"

"Fine." He was eager to get Ho to talk about himself.

"You have seen my chief isn't the best." It was a statement. He asked Knight about his army career, which the soldier rattled through. Ho smiled. "You want to know if I'm really from Liverpool? A scouser? Yes, I'm from Liverpool. Born there."

"There are lots of Chinese in Liverpool and other cities."

"Chinese? You must be one of the few gweilos to listen at the hearts and minds talks. I've given a few of them and heard the comments—who does that fucking chink, gook, slope, think he is telling us what to call them."

"I try not to use them. Some of our soldiers aren't the brightest. Don't want them to be considering some of the things we ask them to do. But if you don't mind me saying so, you can't be one of the newer immigrants?"

Ho laughed. "Because of my age. You want to know what a scouser chink is doing in Shala?" Knight nodded.

His father had been born and brought up between Canton and Hong Kong. He was from quite a wealthy family and a marriage had been arranged with the daughter of a nearby rich family. His father, Ho Kar Kei, was not ready to get married so he made his way to Hong Kong and signed up on a ship of Alfred Holt and Company. Quite a lot of Chinese seamen worked for this company, which was based in Liverpool. His father was a steward at first but ended up working as a chef. He tried to hide his family background and that he could speak English. But one evening when the captain was hosting a dinner for bosses from the company, the chef became ill, Ho stepped in and saved the day. The chief steward's translation of the captain's thanks was so bad and inaccurate that Ho revealed he could speak English.

"You need to understand that my father could spin a tale so need to take this with a pinch of salt. He changed the story now and then: sometimes the chef was drunk or had mutinied. He was a scouser before he got to Liverpool."

His father was made the captain's chef and eventually became the chef on the company's flagship. He ended up just on the ships doing the North America run. He met and married a Chinese girl in New York and brought her to Liverpool. He left the shipping company and set up a restaurant near the docks. They lived above the restaurant. The managers and officers not only from Holt's but other shipping companies would come to the restaurant. They received a discount but Ho still made a profit.

"I think my mother was an illegal immigrant. I think Dad had stowed her away. It was unusual for the Chinese in Liverpool to have a Chinese wife. People turned a blind eye because he had a good restaurant."

Many other Chinese sailors settled in Liverpool and married English women, having Eurasian children. They were considered better husbands than the Englishmen because they seldom drank, which meant there was less domestic abuse though they did gamble. Tony Ho was the only full Chinese boy at his school. There were thousands of Chinese in Liverpool during the Second World War. During the war, the Chinese seamen went on strike to be paid the same as their white colleagues. The strike had lasted for a number of months and after it, the Chinese were viewed with suspicion. As soon as the war was over, the companies and the government exacted their revenge, cutting wages and stopping them from having jobs on shore. Many were forced to go back to China on one-way tickets even though the government said it was voluntary, and most of their wives and children stayed behind. Ho Kar Kei decided to return home because he felt the Chinese had been treated unfairly but the real reason was he felt there would be less demand for Chinese food.

"Well, he got that wrong." An ironic grin. "We didn't go to China but to Malaya near Malacca. My father had a brother there and they set up a restaurant near Terendak, lots of soldiers. You know it?"

"Been once."

Tony had gone to school there but he was bigger than most of the boys and felt out of place. Initially, he spoke only some Cantonese but no Hokkien or Hakka and no Malay. But his cousins and his mother helped him become fluent in all three. He worked in the family restaurant, which explained his cooking skills.

By the time he had left school, the Malay Emergency had been in full swing and against his family's wishes, he joined the Federation Regiment though he had wanted to join the Royal Malay Regiment but that was only for Malays, bumiputras, the sons of the soil. The British officers of the Regiment relied on him because of his language skills and he had been detached to British units on occasions again because of the same language skills. He had met one or two officers and some sergeants who claimed to have eaten in his father's restaurant in Liverpool. In 1954, he had been part of the ambush that had killed a senior personal assistant to Chin Peng. Knight explained that he did know who Chin Peng was or is because he was still alive. Ho was eventually promoted to sergeant. He did not have a high opinion of most of the British officers except for his last company commander.

"But by this time, I had got pissed off with the jungle. Fucking horrible place." Knight thought it best not to disagree though he had enjoyed—probably not the right word—the jungle and felt every soldier should be required to do jungle training.

"How did you get here?"

"There was a policeman, a Special Branch guy. Had tasked us a few times. Sometimes I helped him out with the language at briefings. He was Irish. Went to school with lots of Paddies in Liverpool. He was coming here and he suggested I join the police. Said training would be easy for me and I would be promoted quickly because of my experience. Most of the police here had never dealt with bandits." Knight knew it was a term that had been used to describe the CTs though it had been banned in Malaya. "Think most of the senior white officers came here to avoid Malaya. Jimmy thinks they're all useless…though that's not what he calls them." He put his cup on the desk and looked around the room. Knight was hoping that he would not leave. "Jimmy was here before Godden. Have you met him?"

"Godden?" Ho nodded and Knight said, "No. Heard of him."

"What about Jimmy Doherty?"

"Is he the Irish Branch officer?" Another nod from Ho. "Edward Jerome mentioned him but not his name."

"You've met Jerome! What you think of him?"

"Seems OK. Only had a brief conversation with him."

"Guy who lives in a bar and refuses the services of the girls. Would keep clear of him. Probably didn't have much good to say about Jimmy. Mention his drinking?"

"A little."

"He's right. Jimmy drank a lot and kept most of the bars going here." Ho leaned forwards in his chair looking directly at Knight. "But Jimmy knew exactly what was going on here." He stood up and went to the door, paused, a thought had crossed his mind and he turned back to the soldier. "Your name is Phil Knight. I lived in Knight Street in Liverpool."

"Yes."

Ho came back to the desk and picked up a blank sheet of paper from the desk. "Can I use this?" He laid it on the desk and wrote on it. Knight could see it was both English and Chinese. Ho read it out, "Knight Street 励 德 街 Lìdé Jiē lai dak gaai."

"Thanks."

"You should come out on patrol with me sometime but not yet. Get to know the gwelios first and the layout of the town. Don't mind if I call you Phil?"

"Not at all. And you?"

"Just 'Tony', even 'Ho'." He opened the door and said, "I'll come and get you sometime."

After Ho left, Knight thought he had been friendly but controlling the information and no offer of help if he needed it. Knight decided it had been sensible not to ask any questions.

There was no doubting Ho had a presence around the station and in the town where he patrolled mostly on his own around the square, speaking to people including the shop, restaurant and bar owners. When the soldiers found out that he had been born in Liverpool, they would ask him questions and he could affect a scouser accent on demand. He told the soldiers he had grown up with the Beatles, knew them well and those gullible soldiers believed him. Oldham had both observed and been informed by others of Ho's conduct and when he mentioned Ho's doing his own thing, Bendixson shrugged as if to say there was nothing he could do about it.

Oldham had been invited to dinner with Sutch and Bendixson at the former's home. When Oldham mentioned some points he might raise, he was told that Sutch did not permit 'shop' on these occasions. Oldham told Knight that he was to go up to Hockin's place the same evening to give a general brief on personal security. Knight had done it before in other areas. The civilians had these briefings normally from the police but Hockin thought it might be useful coming from the army who were now 'protecting them'.

Chapter 10

Knight arrived at Hockin's home armed only with a Browning 9mm pistol in a canvas holster with the butt attached by lanyard to his shoulder. Hockin was waiting for him on the veranda that enclosed all of the large bungalow. "Hi. I'm Tony Hockin."

"Good evening, sir. Knight, Phil." A tactic he had used before, giving the civilian the choice. Experience had made Knight wary of the colonial settlers and in Hong Kong, the expatriate businessmen who thought they were tai pans. He detested their sense of entitlement. True, some were not concerned about rank but most treated non-commissioned officers and soldiers as the lower orders though even some commissioned officers were not treated with much respect. The soldiers were there exclusively to protect their business interests.

"Phil. Tony. Thanks for coming up. I'll give them an update from my meeting today with Bendixson and Captain Oldham before you do your thing. Don't mind. Good. Let's go in."

There was a semi-circle of chairs, some armchairs and other dining chairs, most of them taken while others were standing and chatting, some with drinks. There was a single armchair facing the semi-circle with a small table to the right on which sat a glass and a small jug of water. "I'll leave the introductions for later. Do you want a minute or two to prepare?" Knight nodded.

He went to his allotted chair. He removed his floppy hat sometimes called a jungle hat, unbuttoned his right-sided epaulet to free the lanyard, took off his belt, wrapping it and the lanyard carefully around the holster so as not to cause an obstruction to the flap of the holster. He placed the bundle on the table, snapped open the flap and drew the weapon partially out so that the pistol butt was free and close to his right hand. He placed on the table his small, black notebook opened at the page on which he had written a number of points; though he knew them all, he preferred still to have notes in case he forgot. Once he had sat down ready to start, Hockin was telling people to get a drink and take their seats. There were around a dozen people, the majority females and all young unlike other such gatherings where there had been a range of ages. Knight was surprised to see Jerome there, dressed smartly in a lightweight grey suit, glass in hand, and speaking to a redhead and a taller black-haired girl, both very pretty. Jerome was the last to take his seat still chatting to the girls, one on either side of him.

Hockin enforced silence on the audience, gave a short brief on what the army would be doing as agreed today and then introduced Knight as the army's civilian community liaison officer. "Did I get that right?" Knight nodded. "So if you have any problems with or complaints about the army, speak to Sergeant Knight. Phil."

"But go easy on him. It's his first time." It was Jerome. Some people laughed.

"Thanks, Eddie." Hockin was not pleased with the interruption. "I am told that Phil and Captain Oldham have done more operations against the CTs than any other unit so we are in good hands. Over to you, Phil." Knight waited until Hockin had taken his seat in the centre of the semi-circle. He gave the same brief as he had done before to similar audiences, and they had heard the same points before: varying routes, letting people know where you are going, not travelling alone, loose talk, seeing something amiss such as a drawer open when you thought it was closed, the CT being adept at setting booby-traps. They were getting bored having heard it all before.

"I want to finish with three points. First is that the CT have no chivalry as far as young ladies are concerned. It has not stopped them in other areas. A few hard nuts, especially if they are not local, might think slotting…killing a white woman would intimidate the locals and think of the effect on—" He did not have to complete the sentence. "Be alert to any changes in behaviour or attitude towards you by the locals. They might have given you loyal service for many years but the CTs are ruthless and determined. They will use intimidation and threats especially to families to make people commit violence for them. Sometimes changes in behaviour is a warning to you or a cry for help. People living in the kampongs, even in the town itself, know that the Brits can't protect them. If you sense a change in behaviour, then tell someone in the security forces or a friend. I would caution you against asking the individual directly." He could sense the disquiet with some disapproving glances exchanged.

"My final point. It is possible at some time, you might have soldiers guarding you or escorting you home. If you find yourself feeling sorry for the soldiers because they are tired, never show any sympathy and say that you will go home or wherever on your own. It's their job. They would never go out without their personal weapon so don't go out without your escort." His right hand, palm open, came up almost instinctively, pointing at them to drive home his point. He smiled. "Now, nothing might happen. Shala has been peaceful and hopefully it will continue. I am trying to make you security conscious, be alert, ever watchful. Thank you." He took his first sip of water, which was not cold. Hockin expressed his thanks and asked for questions.

"If I may, Tony?" He was Scottish with curly red hair. "Good evening, Sergeant. George Robertson, headmaster of the local government school." He would not be for much longer due to be replaced under the localisation policy. His wife, also Scottish, was a teacher. The Robertsons were very popular teachers with their pupils and held in high regard by the parents but not universally popular amongst the whites mainly due to them having opinions on everything—know-alls. This had been exacerbated when they moved into a bungalow on the same side of London Crescent as Sutch and Bendixson. According to the colonial social pecking order, only the police chief inspector and the chief medical officer were entitled to a four-bedroom bungalow. However, when John Sutch, the District Officer, decamped from his mock Tudor two-storey near the government buildings into a four-bedroom bungalow in London Crescent, the Robertsons asked to move from their three-bedroom bungalow across the street into a vacant, larger bungalow. They justified their application by saying all the married officials would be on one side and would give more space to the single female nurses, teachers and secretaries who occupied the three-bedroom bungalows, six in total on the opposite side of the Crescent. Also, in a reference to Sutch, if one could descale, one could upscale. The single females found it both amusing and depressing. None of the married officers had children. Sutch approved the move despite the intensive lobbying against the move by the wives of Bendixson and Alston, via his wife. "What do you think is the better weapon, the Browning or the Webley 38? I see you have a Browning. Personal choice?"

"I get what the Queen gives me." Deadpan. There was a silence momentarily, followed by some murmurs of disapproval though Knight observed a few of the females smiling. He felt he had to explain. "We have to use what is issued and that's for legal reasons."

"Thank you. Another if you don't mind. What do you think is best, a two- or one-handed grip?"

Not matter. Do it standing on your head as long as you slot him. Knight did not express this thought. "That is a personal choice. It's what you feel comfortable with. Also depends on the ground and location of the target. Might not have time to get into your favoured position."

"Thank you, sergeant. Tony." Being no further questions, Knight stood up, secured his weapon in its holster and was unwrapping the belt.

"Tony. I would like to say something?"

"Go ahead, Tom."

"Sergeant Knight. I'm Tom Alston. I'm a doctor at the government clinic." Knight put the belt back on the table but remained standing. "I think what you said, though quite blunt—"

"No finesse. Not public school." Another interruption from Jerome.

Alston ignored the quip. "Is exactly what we need. Because there has been no trouble here, I think we have become complacent." There were some nods of agreement. "But I wonder if you could give one or two examples of attacks on civilians when they ignore security advice?" Knight sat down. He gave three examples but emphasised that he had not been directly involved in any of the incidents. Hockin concluded the briefing by thanking Knight and inviting him to stay for supper or at least a drink.

Jerome had now joined Tom Alston, his wife Joan and Jill Bendixson, the policeman's wife. Alston's body appeared slight and delicate but he was lean and wiry. He was quiet-spoken and reserved by nature though when angry, a dangerous scowl warned people to take care.

"How's business?"

"Find people seem to be keeping away, which I found a bit puzzling but the army turning up here. Not sure I buy this story of army covering the whole country before independence. Raza was my last patient today."

"What was his tale today! Bit of soothsaying?"

"He's a harmless old man," Joan said in his defence. Jerome gave one of his 'if you believe that' looks.

"He thinks the arrival of the soldiers will bring resentment and ill feeling."

"Does he think there is going to be violence?"

"No, no, Joan. Most of the people up here have never seen soldiers. Even when there were riots, disturbances a few years ago, there were no troops. Raza said something about the Japanese soldiers being cruel and inhumane, the Americans who had been here for a short time after the war had spent money and were always trying to be friendly but the British were indifferent to the people. Raza claims that the imprint of the British soldiers will last for years to come."

"Raza says more than his prayers."

Alston had heard Jerome use this expression before and wondered its origin. "John Sutch and Terence seem to take note of what he says." Jerome shook his head in bewilderment but resisted the temptation to comment on them.

Joan Alston was now perturbed and asked, "The soldiers won't take repressive measures? There have been whispers about incidents down south. My uncle William served in Malaya and said the soldiers sometimes shot unarmed civilians." She looked at Jill Bendixson who gave a demure shrug and did not comment.

Her husband tried to reassure her. "My understanding from Tony. He had a meeting the other day with Terence and the army officer…Oldham, I think. And you heard him tonight saying that they are an experienced unit."

"Don't think they are going to say that they are inexperienced and useless!" Closer to a teasing than a mocking tone, making Jill Bendixson laugh but very quietly.

"That Sergeant Knight seems rather cold…and indifferent." A resonance of Raza.

"Professional?" Alston offered as an alternative to his wife's comment.

"You might be right, Joan. I met him up at the convent the other day. He seemed affable, polite and happy to listen to me wittering on. Then when he was leaving…it was like no more time to listen to you. Into his Land Rover and he was gone. Quite abrupt."

"Professional." An assertion instead of an alternative.

"Julie Ryan seems to be getting on with him." Joan's eyes nodded towards them.

"Indeed." Jerome tried to be light-hearted but felt a twinge of jealousy and regret for never telling Julie how he felt about her. His musing was cut short when he noticed the Robertsons coming towards them. "Think I will rescue Julie from the licentious soldiery." He acknowledged the Robertsons in passing.

Julie had been talking about her life prompted by questions from Knight. She had come out to visit her best friend at school, Eva. Like Jerome, she had been

84

enchanted by the place—a description Knight found baffling—and decided to stay on. She lived in London Crescent, the residential enclave for the overseas government employees. She had hoped to go to art school in London and still hoped to go but was helping out at the Convent and the government's social services.

"Do you feel you are getting to know Shala?"

She understood the implicit, barbed comment. "I know. I spend almost all of my time with them." She meant the British. "You don't approve of them?" He shrugged. "They *are* very snobbish and condescending."

"The last flickering embers of the empire." He looked down, feeling guilty. "That's not fair. It's just that…well…I've had my fill of traipsing around Asia, guarding our possessions, which are not ours but those of a few, a very few."

"I take it that you don't like the army?"

"Phew! I wouldn't say that. I have seen many places that I wouldn't have if I was still back in Wigan or somewhere in England."

"Why did you join?"

"Oh. For adventure, travel, sport, all the usual excuses soldiers come out with."

She arched her eyebrows and said, "That's not why you joined." Not a question.

"No. I'm not really sure." He touched the canvas holster and folded his arms across his chest. She noticed that periodically he would rest his right hand on his holster or just touch it as if checking it was still there. "I do know."

"A girl?"

"Good God! No…maybe a lack of them. Bit like you with art school. But things didn't fall into place. I did a number of jobs then I joined the army. I liked it for the first six months then lost interest. Came out East. Doesn't Kipling have something to say about the East and British soldiers…I enjoyed jungle training. Had noble ideas about fighting the communists, defending the poor people. Then I realised it wasn't communism…well, to a certain extent it is but it's really nationalism. It's the same in Vietnam." He laughed. "You better not report me to Chief Inspector Bendixson. He would lock me up."

"But you said they were ruthless earlier?"

"Yes. They *are*. They are not nice, liberal nationalists. I meant every word I said. Please take it on board."

"Do you think we treat the locals badly? I have heard stories but I have never seen or heard any of the people here abusing the locals. I certainly don't patronise them."

"I'm sure you are right."

"Don't you think we treated our colonies better than the French?" It was an opinion too far and there was another surge.

"Oh yes. Superficially, but we never got to know them. The French realised the dangers of nationalism and tried to impose their culture. We kowtowed to their culture…cultures, and that just increased their respect for their past. We do our bit and then retire to our homes or clubs and talk about the old country. Many

85

of the settlers don't realise that England is changing. It's not the same *old country*, whatever that was. People, like here, just want their freedom but they are told they are not quite ready. That's what's patronising. It's like mothers always hoping their sweet little boys never grow up. We were never fit to run an empire."

She nodded. "I understand now how they can feel patronised. I think that's the common view of the people here. Possibly apart from Eddie Jerome, but in his case he's not quite ready for independence. Means he would have to make a decision." They both looked towards Jerome and his little troupe.

"I apologise. My CO told me to keep my mouth shut up here." When telling him that he was not going to depot but to Shala, the CO had warned him not to upset 'the bloody civilians by spouting his left-wing views', which he just about tolerated especially since there was now a Labour Government. Knight felt relaxed and thought he would have a beer if one was still on offer.

"You probably think females—"

"Phil. You're wanted." Hockin gestured towards the door where his signaller Collins was standing. Knight glanced at his watch, 1900 hours, and went over to Collins who in a clear voice at a volume sufficient for all in the room to hear said, "Sarge. You're needed back at the station." Knight thought, *Fuck*. Collins was always punctual and accurate in his messages that being the reason he was chosen to deliver it and not his driver Martin who would probably had garbled something about you told me to come at 1900 hours to say that you were needed back at the station, thereby revealing the pre-arranged plan to rescue Knight.

"Thanks, Collins. I'll be out in a minute."

Collins stood for a moment peering through his thick, black-framed glasses at the scene with his normal scowl dominating his face, thinking, *White prats* before going back to the Land Rover. Knight put on his floppy hat. Hockin regretted that Knight could not stay for supper, thanked him for his advice and hoped to see him again. Knight saluted, not Hockin but as a farewell to the group.

Chapter 11

The clerical support that Sutch—through Bendixson—had offered to the army turned up at 8 am. There was some confusion because only Oldham and Knight had known about it but had not expected Eileen Kanna to turn up the day after the offer. She was shown to the ops room where Oldham was in his office. After a brief introduction, he explained her duties as the platoon clerk typing sops—a terse confirmation that she knew what that meant—and reports both for him and Sgt Knight in whose office she would be located, at the other end of the corridor. After he dispatched a soldier to get Sgt Knight, she told Oldham that her typewriter and a Gestetner copying machine needed to be brought from the GAB but the army would need to collect it. Further, if the army could not provide paper, then the government would but require to be reimbursed. Oldham, in a disinterested tone, told her to sort it out with Knight who was now present and escorted her to his office. He could see Ho observing them. Knight closed the door. His desk was to the left from the door against the dividing wall with Ho's office. The other desk was beside the window. Knight noticed that she was slim and tanned and her curly back hair reminded him of the shape of a Roman centurion's helmet. She seemed quite school-girlish, out-of-place. He moved the desk away from the window with the chair between the desk and wall with the two desks now forming an L shape with the secretary's desk to his left. He invited her to sit at her desk so that he could brief her.

"I want to explain to you the possible consequences of this work. If you change your mind about working with me or the army, I will not mind in the least." He paused and clasped his hands, elbows resting on the desk in an inverted V. "I want you to remember that you must never mention anything that is discussed here or written down with anyone except myself and Captain Oldham. If people find out what you are doing, you will become a target. Terrorists have no chivalry as far as young ladies are concerned. Always remember never to take any chances. Even in here, if you see anything amiss; for example, a drawer—"

"Opened when you thought you had closed it." She smiled. "I was at your briefing though you didn't notice me. Too busy chatting up Julie Ryan."

"I'm sorry. But it could be dangerous."

She arched her eyebrows, her facial expression one of calm sophistication. "If we are going to face these dangers together, should we not be a little less formal and call each other by our names, first names? Eileen."

"Very well, Eileen. Phil." He laughed in an abrupt manner. "Sorry for sounding melodramatic." He paused, irritation on his face. "You must think me a numpty about…well, you probably have a higher security clearance than me."

"Yes." She clucked her tongue allied with a slight rightwards movement of her head. She told him of the need to collect her equipment. "The dashing captain probably thinks typewriters are beneath him."

"He has a lot on his mind."

"Such loyalty!"

He ignored the comment. "Let's go and meet my…our team. Then they can pick up your gear."

Eileen had been called into Sutch's office the day before and invited to work for the army in the police station. She had confirmed her light workload, could finish it by the end of the day and be at the police station the next morning. She had become a glorified typist, with her time now spent typing up mundane reports without sight of any secret or sensitive information for around three months. It had been an opportunity to escape from the insufferable Miss Garland. Even the senior secretary's workload was lighter due to the DO now writing any secret or sensitive reports, which did not present a problem because his handwriting was extraordinarily neat and exquisite. The DO had ended the interview by admonishing her not to reveal or discuss with the army any information from her work in his office and refrained from thanking her for her efforts because she would continue to be working for the same team. She had concealed her scorn.

Eileen Kanna had been determined to escape from her existence in Bromley. Her parents were decent, respectable middle-class people who believed in the Queen, the Church of England and the Conservative Party, though their trust in the latter had been shaken by the conduct of John Profumo, the War Minister who had shared a prostitute with a Russian military attaché and unforgivably had lied to Parliament. In their minds, this conduct had led to a Labour Government with a Prime Minister who was undoubtedly a Marxist and aimed to turn the country into a socialist state. Even more worrying for them was the intention to legalise homosexuality and abortion. When Eileen informed her parents that she had applied for a post in the civil service in the Far East, her mother suggested that she should contact her 'aunt' Margaret—an indication that she was more than a friend in the Kanna family social circle—who had worked in Malaya. Eileen had been surprised by this information about her staid 'aunt' married to a Church of England vicar; nevertheless, she decided to visit her aunt in the vicarage of her husband's parish in Limehouse.

Her 'aunt' could not have been more welcoming, insisting on Eileen dropping the 'aunt'. To her astonishment, not only had Margaret worked in General Templar's headquarters during the Malayan Emergency but had served in the Special Operations Executive in North Africa and Italy during the war. Eileen made a number of visits to the vicarage to listen to Margaret who was open and honest, which the younger woman found exhilarating and refreshing. Margaret described General Templar as vain and egotistical who claimed credit for successes in Malaya that were in fact due to the work of others. Eileen was flabbergasted when in the year of his death, Margaret criticised Winston Churchill, whom her parents regarded as the greatest ever Englishman. The criticism was even more acerbic in that it was made in a soft, delicate bone-china English voice. Margaret said that she could not give her any advice on the selection and interview process because she had not gone through the same procedure but emphasised that she should be honest in her answers and not give the 'right' answers. If selected, Margaret advised Eileen that she should try to learn some of the local languages. She apologised that she had forgotten almost all of her Malay. On Eileen's final visit, Margaret offered three final pieces of advice: don't make hasty judgements on individuals, remain composed and don't show surprise at the unexpected and remain emotionally detached on the conditions of the local people.

On arrival in the summer of 1966, she was told that the position in HE's office to which she had been assigned was now being filled by a locally recruited civilian under the policy of localisation in preparation for independence, and she was being sent to the DO's office in Shala notwithstanding that post was likely to be localised in the near future. Her relationship with Miss Garland, the senior secretary, was formal and cold. She found the work interesting in that initially she was responsible for collecting and analysing data on the health and education of the locals, which meant liaison with the health and education departments. Eventually, her role was diminished and her duties were restricted to typing with any changes explained and justified under the policy of localisation.

She was not too disappointed because her unspoken aim in life was to find a husband, which would have astounded her colleagues and the other Europeans who regarded her as one of these liberated young women of the 60s. Her initial focus had been on the DO but she discovered he was married to a dull but nice lady; no wonder he would be in his office sometimes by 7 am and would not leave until about 8 pm. She was no more impressed by the other British women, dowdy and limited. As to the two eligible men, she regarded them as overgrown schoolboys who shared an inane sense of humour. Of course, as expected, she attended the various social events that she found boring, reminding her of the middle-class Bromley she had escaped. Consequently, she found herself going around Shala on her own, visiting the shops, eating and drinking including the less salubrious establishments. She found Kampong Tengu, known as area Z to the expats, fascinating and bought clothing and other bric-a-brac there. These trips stopped on advice from the policeman Staff Sergeant Ho who, with his rough and pitted face, was the most intimidating person she had ever encountered.

Her work now consisted of typing reports and platoon orders for Oldham and reports for Knight as well as maintaining the growing card index system. After the first few days, she asked if she could accompany him on what she called his strolls through Shala. His initial reluctance evaporated when he realised that she could speak some Malay and Hokkien. Shopkeepers and others including Old Raza knew her. She introduced Knight to Raza though the latter seemed unwilling to speak to him, simply engaging Eileen in a mixture of English, Malay and Hokkien. Knight's signaller Collins was particularly impressed with her, declaring that she was the only 'only decent civvy there', 'a bit of a cracker' and 'not a white prat'.

She told Knight that she would never ask for information but only ask after their families and health. It was an odd sight, Knight with his Armalite, Collins with his heavy pack radio, Martin armed with sterling sub-machine guns and Eileen in army-style loose cotton trousers with a light-coloured male shirt hanging outside her trousers, a wide-brimmed soft felt hat and a brown canvas photographer's bag across her left shoulder. Knight was impressed by her ability to talk to the locals, being understanding of and being sympathetic to their concerns but tempered with reality and paradoxically seemingly indifferent to them. On return to the station, they would draft jointly a report, which Eileen typed up. Eventually, Martin dropped out due to problems with his feet, Collins left his radio behind, and he and Knight armed themselves only with 9mm Brownings. Despite Knight's advice to all on varying their routes, it was difficult in that there were only two ways out of the police station. There were always police around and any incident would be reported immediately. On two occasions, they dropped into the *Golden Eagle* for tea or soft drinks, chatting with the mama-san and enquiring after Eddie Jerome though on both occasions he had not been there.

Shala remained peaceful and the life of the British expats continued as before. C Platoon continued to mount standing patrols along the northern boundary of the plantation. Oldham, despite the agreement with Hockin and Bendixson, inserted small patrols nearer the Hockin home at night on the premise that CTs could evade the standing patrols so therefore stood a better chance of intercepting them nearer to the house. As ever with the army, if it resulted in the kill or capture of CTs, no one would mind but if Hockin discovered Oldham was breaching the agreement by patrolling the plantation close to his house, then he would no doubt raise it with Sutch and especially Godden. Oldham could be replaced notwithstanding he considered it sound military tactics. Godden had not visited him as he had said during the briefing nor had he spoken to him by telephone. When he broached it with Bendixson, the message from Godden was that there was no change in the situation. Oldham was surprised and a little annoyed that the CO or anyone from Battalion HQ had not visited the platoon. He began to entertain doubts on the reason for the deployment and speculated on this being a diversion, especially as the rest of the Battalion was busy operationally.

Knight continued, with the assistance of Eileen Kanna, to expand his knowledge of the area and individuals. Usually, he had a daily chat with Tony Ho who passed comments on some of the Brits and also some of the locals like the mama-san of the *Golden Eagle* bar but still not an invitation to accompany Ho on patrol. After the chats, Knight wrote down as much as he could remember of Ho's comments. Knight felt he was being fed scraps by a wily police officer though he was not too concerned because of Eileen Kanna's knowledge. Knight and Oldham met almost every night to update each other. The officer speculated that the 'cover story' might actually be the real reason for their deployment and the alleged armed incursion was to keep them on their toes though Knight doubted whether their CO would have agreed to that approach. Oldham was of the view that Godden was mendacious and so devious that he would not inform their CO, which caused Knight some concern that Oldham was becoming rather irrational when it came to Godden.

Oldham and Knight were invited to a cocktail party being held by Bendixson to celebrate some date in his so far undistinguished police career. Knight was surprised but suspected his invite was due to Hockin's influence. Despite his mandatory protest, Knight enjoyed going not so much because of his job but because of the females.

On the day of the cocktail party, Ho invited Knight to accompany him on his afternoon beat patrol; though he was reluctant, he felt it would be churlish to refuse. Ho walked *a la Prince Philip*, his hands clasped tightly behind his back pulling back his broad shoulders, his muscular chest straining against the shirt. Knight was certain civilians and possibly even police officers would not be prepared to confront Ho and no doubt he had inflicted pain on anyone daring to cross him. He pointed out places and people to Knight, which were known to Knight via Eileen Kanna. On occasions, he spoke to passers-by, shopkeepers and patrolling police officers in the same brusque, interrogatory manner. Sometimes he stopped, removed his notebook from his left breast shirt pocket, made an entry and returned it to the same pocket. He had a truculent encounter with Raza in the square; Ho was issuing a warning to the old man partly in English and Knight caught a reference to getting her to hospital. Ho stated it was time for a break that would be in the *Golden Eagle*. Once seated and hat removed, he ordered a Tiger beer though Knight had tea. The policeman had a few words with the mama-san in a mixture of Malay, Chinese and English, then haughtily dismissed her back to her stool at the end of the bar. The two locals in the bar hastily finished their beers and left.

"I wonder if Mr Jerome is in?" said Knight loud enough for the mama-san to hear who shook her head.

"Him!" It was a snort. "Refusing women. You wouldn't!"

Knight wanted to defend Jerome but thought better to humour Ho. "Never been lucky enough to have to make that choice."

Ho eyed him warily and then said, "You're not a fucking public schoolboy?"

Knight laughed. "I'm from the North, Wigan."

"Have a beer then. You've got the chief's cocktail party tonight."

"Why are you not invited?"

Ho snorted again. "I'm a sergeant." A malicious grin. "Don't think it's because I'm a chog, a chink, a slope…because I'm a scouser. They think I would steal their jewels and screw their women." He laughed. "I would if I got the chance." He turned serious. "Hockin invited the local inspectors and sergeants up to his place a couple of times. But my chief and the DO as well as the other fucking gweilos weren't happy about it. Even the much-admired Jerome doesn't really like mixing with the natives. So there were no more invites." He finished his beer and ordered another one. He leaned closer to Knight and said quietly, "Tony Hockin is actually OK. Apart from Jimmy Doherty, he's the only gweilo I like. He's done good things. That's what I was talking to Raza about."

"Did I hear something about hospital and a woman?"

"You've got sharp ears. Yes. I'll tell you about it sometime."

Knight was emboldened. "Can I ask what you think of Raza? There seems to be conflicting opinions amongst the…gweilos."

"He's harmless. A sad old man trying to make his life mean something. There are others the same but not so old. Mind you, Raza isn't as old as he seems or acts."

"Tony. I don't know what is going on here in Shala…and I'm supposed to be our Int guy."

"No one knows what's happening here. There could be fifty armed terrorists in Kampong Tengu and we wouldn't know."

"Why is there not a Branch officer here?" Ho's expression made him think that he had gone a question too far.

"No need. Nothing ever happens up here. Jimmy Doherty made sure of that." A satisfied grin breached his rough pitted face. "Apart from the fifty-armed terrs." He rose from his chair, put his hat on, nodded to the mama-san, each a slow almost ponderous action, and said, "Let's go." Knight noted he did not pay. Just before reaching the station, Ho stopped at the entrance to London Crescent. "Need to check on the memshabs." He faced Knight, at the same time looking around to ensure no one was close to them. "Phil. If you do hear about any specific threats or anything that concerns you, come to me first. Not to your officer and certainly not to my chief."

"Not sure if I—"

"I know you have a chain of command, and I'm not asking you to be disloyal but just tell me first."

"OK but I'm not promising—"

"Good! Go and enjoy cocktails." Ho was almost jaunty now. "Going with Miss Kanna?" Knight walked on towards the station. As he entered the station compound, different and conflicting thoughts swirled in Knight's mind including so that you can warn the terrorists, gain credit, even keep Doherty informed. Notwithstanding that he felt he was being played by this wily police officer, he had not given any commitment: it was for him to decide what was a threat or what concerned him. His first duty was to the army, to his soldiers, not a colonial police officer though he was keen to develop and maintain a relationship with this formidable policeman.

Chapter 12

Hockin was in good spirits, his zest for life having returned. He did not hide that this was due to a female journalist coming to Shala from Hong Kong. She had visited Shala before, not long before the army had arrived and Hockin had liked her. Apparently, he had been pining like a little dog for her and had shunned a couple of females who had envisaged themselves as Mrs Hockin, mistress of the plantation. His good mood had been further bolstered by being told by Tom Alston that Fong Siu Wai had been removed to hospital and was doing reasonably well. Hockin criticised Raza for not acting earlier but Alston thought it was really Hockin's responsibility because she lived on his land and he should have told his foreman Mehad to keep an eye on her; however, he did not offer this opinion sensing it was not the right time. Knight, after a brief chat with Alston, surmised that it was the same woman Ho had mentioned to Raza, making a mental note to raise it with the policeman.

Following another brief chat, this time with Jerome, Knight managed to waylay Julie Ryan though there was no need to see if Eileen Kanna was listening because she had decided to forego the pleasure of Bendixson's cocktail party in order to teach Collins and Martin how to play bridge with her housemate making up the foursome. Although the London Crescent was out of bounds to the soldiers, Oldham had sanctioned it so that in the event of an incident, there was a vehicle and crew outside. 'Good luck with that!' had been Knight's initial reaction to the thought of trying to teach the two soldiers bridge, then, 'Surely not Eileen and Collins!' A twinge of envy that dissipated quickly when Julie declared that she had no interest in Hockin. She became serious asking, "Do you think there will be trouble? Some people say Baru is determined to cause trouble here."

Knight creased his forehead, his eyes almost hidden by not quite closed eyelids. "What do you mean? Baru is on our side. He's the great white hope."

"No. I mean his son. Shi."

Something clicked inside Knight's brain. Hadn't Jerome mentioned the young Baru? He scolded himself for being careless in not asking Jerome. "You mean Baru's son is opposed to his father. Wait a minute. I'm sure I read an article about Chila Baru that mentioned his son. But isn't he at Oxford or somewhere?"

"Yes, but he returned about a month ago. He was seen around Shala but seemed to disappear. There was a rumour he had joined the communists. We thought that's the real reason the army was here." She was partially right in that they had been deployed because of intelligence of an armed CT gang heading

93

for Shala. But he thought this made the situation more dangerous or had potentially more serious consequences if Shi Baru was opposed to his father. "I thought it was common knowledge…well, amongst us. Tony and Eddie know him."

"Excuse me, Julie." He went to find Oldham who possibly knew but hadn't told him, which he thought unlikely. He saw him speaking to Bendixson and his wife. Waiting until he had moved away, he intercepted Oldham. "Can I have a word in private?" They found a quiet corner. "Did you know that Baru's son Shi might be with the communists?" His voice was calm.

"What?"

"I didn't think you did, sir. It appears to be common knowledge among this lot."

"That bastard Godden never mentioned it."

"One other thing." Knight told him about Jerome's comment on the way to the convent.

He sighed. "I think Bendixson said something to me but he just rambles on. Never sure what he's on about. Both of us fucked up." He considered how to proceed. "I'll get hold of Bendixson and Sutch. Have a private chat."

"What about Hockin and Jerome? Apparently, they know Shi Baru."

"No. Not yet. Let's just confirm it first. And you're coming with me. Don't want to be screwed by them with some crap."

The four men were in Bendixson's study-cum-library-cum games room. The walls were painted cream and a worn, light carpet covered the floor. To the right from the door was a small wooden pedestal desk with a swivel chair almost flush onto the back wall and directly opposite on the other side of the room beneath the window, a square, rattan coffee table was sandwiched by two low easy-chairs of the same material. In the centre, facing the door was a square card-table with four black cushioned seats and back support chairs in position for a game of bridge or whist. Set against the wall opposite the door were two chest-level bookcases, not fully used, filling the space between the table and desk and between table and window. The furniture was all standard-issue government items. Bendixson sat at the table, his back to the door, Oldham opposite him and Knight to his officer's left. Sutch positioned himself in the easy-chair to the right of the coffee table, leading Knight to speculate that the District Officer was signalling that this was a polmil matter and he was an observer only. He also took it for granted by Oldham's expression, which he knew well, that it may be a heated confrontation. Oldham was controlled and formal in his question. "Chief Inspector, were you aware that Chila Baru's son may be involved with the communists here?"

"There are rumours to that effect." He didn't look at Oldham. "I thought you knew." His tone tentative. "I thought I had mentioned it."

Oldham was not going to surrender the initiative. "I would have thought it was something that should have been highlighted, not mentioned in passing. One of the key points of your briefing to us."

94

"I think…I may have been distracted when Sergeant Knight asked about the convent."

Knight thought it was a sly ploy; for Oldham, it was old-fashioned lying. Oldham leaned forwards, elbows on the table, his eyes looking up at the taller policeman who sat upright. "I don't think that is a justification for keeping me in the dark." He had made it personal. "Unless you were instructed to play it down." Bendixson was uncomfortable. He knew it had been the wrong decision because the people in the room next door liked to gossip and share secrets, the glue of the white community and its sole pastime in Shala.

"Yes. I was instructed to—"

"By whom?" said Oldham in a curt voice. "Special Branch? Godden?"

"Yes."

"That bastard!" Oldham leaned back and said in almost a whisper, "He's more politician than a policeman."

Knight saw the disapproving reaction of the other two and the remark was certain to be relayed to Godden. It was irresponsible on Oldham's part and he was doing what his CO had warned him against, picking unnecessary fights, though the CO had meant with the enemy not the police. "This possibly could endanger my men if the shooting starts and Baru is behind it."

"Gentlemen, please. Let's remain calm." The low but firm voice belonged to Sutch. "I suggest we discuss what new approach is required, if necessary." He stood up and came over to occupy the last chair at the card-table. Sutch as the District Officer, the DO, for the Shala region was responsible and answerable only to the Governor. He was well groomed and dignified.

After obtaining a history degree from Peterhouse College, he had considered a number of options but he had wanted to be in a structured organisation with a clear career path. The entrance examination and interviews had not presented hurdles to him. He was professional, calm and rational as well as being unselfish in willing to help others. The DO was responsible for the whole gamut of government services such as housing, education, social and health services. Despite his misgivings on some aspects of government policy, Sutch understood that he was there to implement policy, not make it. As a colony neared independence, it was essential that decisions were not made that could be used by the newly independent country as a stick to beat the UK. One had to do one's utmost to secure your country's interest and the new country's goodwill and appreciation. Sutch did not rock the boat. If one was right on identifying a potential problem, then credibility increased but being wrong, being negative was not positive for one's career. Judgment was the most important criteria and it was good judgment not to exercise or offer your judgment too often. Most government posts were filled now by locals under the policy of localisation. He was also the local magistrate but he seldom sat on the bench. He had vacated the DO's mock Tudor two-storey home because of its size and there had also been security concerns because of the encroaching shanty town; now he was occupying one of the bungalows in London Crescent designed for junior officers. His decision was viewed by some in the capital as unbecoming for a man who sat just below God in the form of His Excellency the Governor. However, unbecoming did not stop HE to continue to ask Sutch to write reports outwith his brief such as proposed changes to the overseas civil service. Sutch's reports were precise, comprehensive and scrupulous in that all options were considered. London knew that only the signature was the Governor's contribution.

"I dare say it is regrettable that you were not informed about Shi Baru. However, it is unlikely that I am made aware of all the intelligence. From my experience, the Special Branch are a rum lot. They, like the other intelligence agencies, have one commandment—do not compromise thy source. I do not understand what difference this makes. The position remains that Shala continues to be peaceful. It is not experiencing the violence as in other areas. Nothing must be done that might cause alarm or increase tension, especially between the different races. That is why it was agreed that the expats, the white community, would not begin carrying weapons openly. The same reason why the army is to adopt a low profile. *And* the army here remains in support of the police and under the direction of the civilian authority." He looked at Oldham.

"Understood, sir."

"My understanding is that, apart from Tony Hockin who has been told of a general threat to his property, we *four* in here are the only people in Shala to be aware of the specific threat. *And* that is the way it is to remain for the present." He looked at Knight. As DO for the most important region outside the capital, his equivalence would normally be at least a colonel, not a captain and a sergeant no matter their reputed experience. Nevertheless, he understood that the recent history of Shala with its lack of violence and prosperity together with the cover story necessitated the deployment of junior officers. The present state of Shala could be considered due to his good governance though he would give credit to his able staff.

"Understood, sir," said Knight.

"I am still unsure of the purpose of this meeting."

"Sir, I think we would like to have some more background information on Shi Baru." Oldham was trying to retrieve something after realising he had acted impulsively.

"I recall meeting young Baru once. He was just another serious Oxbridge student." Knight suppressed a smile.

"Hockin and Jerome probably know him better than anyone. It might be helpful if Captain Oldham has a chat with them to get some information."

Sutch considered Bendixson's suggestion, reluctant but decided to allow them to proceed. "Only background information. Keep it low-key. It's certainly not a conversation that I should be part of." He went to the door, then paused. "Terence, you better go and get them." He opened the door, allowing Bendixson out then closed the door, his hand remaining on the handle. "William. I don't think it is helpful to use terms such as 'bastard' and 'politician' when speaking of a senior police officer. From my observation, the army is not immune from these blights." He had left the room before Oldham had understood the import of Sutch's comment.

96

Bendixson asked the first question. "Tony, you knew Baru. What he's like?"

Hockin leaned back, throwing his two hands behind his head. "Oh. I met him about a year ago. His father was my guest and his son was on holiday from Oxford. He graduated about six weeks ago and returned here. I didn't see him and then I heard he had disappeared. I heard some talk about him joining the communists but I didn't give it much thought. His opposition to his father was quite well known up here. But we all probably thought it was just a typical youthful rebellion. I understand university does that… Bloody students! Why? What's he done?"

"Is he popular here?" Oldham's question.

"Yes and no. He's quite a good-looking chap and when he used to come back on holiday, he tried to mix with the locals. Think many of the older people found him rather condescending."

"By older people, do you mean Raza?" At Jerome's mention of Raza, Oldham looked inquisitively at Knight who gave a little shake of his head to say 'not now'.

Hockin ignored Jerome. "No doubt, he felt slightly strange, ill at ease, after Oxford. He doesn't have the same pull as his father but Eddie knows him better. Didn't you have a long conversation with him that night?" It was as if he was saying to Jerome, you doubted me so you have a go.

"He isn't a communist, or wasn't. He believed his father's attitude was wrong. He claimed that independence wasn't real independence if there were still foreign soldiers remaining." It had been agreed that some British troops would remain for a short time after independence to assist in training the national army. "He wants a neutral country…but isn't anti-British." The two soldiers exchanged glances, recognising the usual communist propaganda. "He told his father that there was opposition building up against him from the intellectuals and of the possibility of the communists moving in to exploit the discontent."

"Is this from a recent conversation or from a year ago?" Knight asked.

"At Tony's dinner party. When he came back a few weeks ago, I bumped into him in the square. Thinking he was going to see Raza. Just said hello and agreed that we should meet up for a chat and a drink. Then he disappeared." Knight thought this Raza knew everyone. "There were rumours that he had gone off to join the communists."

"Is there a communist organisation here?" Oldham's question was for Bendixson.

"There are rumours that the shanties area near the convent is a hotbed. Sometimes posters appear in the town denouncing imperialism and capitalism as well as urging the people to rise up against their foreign masters." He gestured towards Hockin. "Thanks to Tony, the workers are content." Knight wished that it was that simple. Even after a few days, he realised the official Shala brief was simplistic and misleading, probably never amended since it had first been written by some staff intelligence officer. His view had been reinforced by his chats with Staff Ho. The loggers and clothing workers in their respective areas outnumbered Hockin's workers and were probably ripe for some agitation, apart from the shanties beside the convent. The reality was no one knew what was going on in there. There were some cottage industries producing shoes, hats, stools and other goods that the hawkers brought to the market. No doubt there would be some with grievances. He told himself that he had to sit Oldham down soon to explain this but he was too busy doing and planning patrols.

Jerome said, "I told you he is not a communist. He just wanted his father to change some of his policies. But his father is quite arrogant."

"A family trait," Hockin jibed.

In response, disdain showed on Jerome's face. "Chila Baru believes the people will always follow him. May be true but Shi's concern was when his father would be gone. Baru is quite a sick man." Another discovery for the two soldiers. Bendixson explained the fear was that if Baru died or was incapacitated, there would be instability in the National Democrats and would likely result in Bin Jafar coming to power on independence, which was not what HE or HMG wanted. The almost imperceptible shake of his head and curved lips, Oldham's irritation was this time with politics.

"This is laughable." Hockin stood up and directed his next comment at the two soldiers. "You weren't told about young Baru. Any chance of a drink, Terence?"

"Yes, of course. What would—"

"G and T."

"Anyone else?" Only Jerome accepted—a whisky. Hockin placed himself in the chair behind the pedestal desk and lit a cigarette.

After Bendixson returned with the drinks, Hockin began. "I am fed up with all this secret nonsense. Everybody in Shala, including the dogs, know or think that Shi Baru has gone to join the communists…the people's liberation party or whatever they call it." He took the first sip of his gin and tonic. "Except for the army who are supposed to be here to protect us. I'm told, hush-hush, that the communists might soon launch an armed attack on my plantation and even possibly try to assassinate me. Though with Arthur Godden these days, who knows what he's talking about. It's all gobbledygook. Is it called byzantine?" The four listeners nodded. "And I can hardly hear what he's saying. No wonder they call it hush-hush." He laughed. The other four were seated at the card-table, all turned towards Hockin as he held court. Bendixson did not complain about Hockin usurping his desk chair and Knight thought him too deferential towards Hockin as he had been to Sutch, which was more understandable considering their respective positions. The army had its 'Bendixsons', neither feared nor admired but ridiculed and almost certainly essential to pave the way for the heroes going up and the failures going down. A wedge for the door. "People know what is going on here. It's not a desert. They just don't tell us, or tell us what they think we want to hear. They read the newspapers. There are Malay, Chinese and English language papers. Wouldn't be surprised if old Raza didn't have the Times sent up. They listen to the radio…Raza no doubt *the BBC*…a few even have television." He omitted to mention that only a few had television because he had lobbied against the building of a transmitter to increase television coverage. He felt it would be detrimental to the work ethic of the locals, a perspective shared by Bendixson and crucially, Sutch. "The only secret is why there has not been an attack. Even then, people think I am paying the communists off." To answer the soldiers' inquisitive look, he said, "I have been seen to give Raza money sometimes. The natives gossip. Some of the Brits probably think it's true." He finished his drink. "Let's stop this pretence about the National Amy coming here."

"Tony, that is true," said Bendixson.

"Fine. But everyone knows—well, apart from the army until now—the army is here because Shi Baru has joined the communists and is going to lead an attack."

"Tony, we don't know for certain." It was Bendixson.

"It's my workers and my people. I would rather be prepared." He addressed Oldham directly, "Your guys going to protect my plantation?"

"Of course." Oldham was buoyed up though that was what his platoon had been doing since arriving in Shala.

"But I still don't want them trampling over my land and damaging my trees."

"My problem is that I don't have enough men. This is really a company task."

"I'll speak to John Sutch about getting more men. So that means there's no chance of your guys helping out collecting rubber when they're off-duty." A grin.

Oldham laughed. "No chance."

"You better stop them going to the bars."

Knight knew it was in jest but thought a serious point should be made. "I don't think we should do that. If the CTs see a change, then it's likely they'll change their plan."

"That suits me if there is no attack."

"They'll just wait. I would have thought it's in your interest to bring this to a head now and not in the future when it will be the National Army."

Hockin thought for a moment and then said, "Good point."

"Does anyone have a photograph of Shi Baru?" asked Oldham. Hockin offered a group photograph taken when Chila Baru had visited him. "Can we get copies made in the station?" Bendixson agreed. "Sergeant Knight, can you deal with it." A nod from Knight.

"Shouldn't I get the DO back in?"

"No. I'll speak to him," said Hockin.

"Just a moment," said Jerome. "Why a photograph?"

"So my soldiers know what he looks like."

"He's not done anything wrong."

"Let's hope we get him before he does," Oldham replied.

"Get him!"

Knight tried to appease him. "Eddie, it was you who first mentioned him to me."

"What are you going to do when you *get* him? Murder him!"

Oldham, now angered, responded to Jerome, "We don't murder anyone. That's left to little thugs like Baru."

"He's an educated human being!"

"So was the bastard who shot a planter's wife last month. *In the back*!" Oldham stared hard at Jerome, then relaxed slightly. "Look, if he's innocent, then we will have done him a favour. The son of Chila Baru is a natural target. You know him so you can help us."

Jerome stood rooted in the same spot, his eyes staring ahead, thinking over the officer's request. He shook his head. "What's the point! He has been tried, judged and condemned. Sorry, but I still have some integrity left." Oldham's eyes blazed about to square up to Jerome but Knight's shake of his head was a call for restraint, with which he complied and turned his back on Jerome, purporting to speak to Bendixson.

"Goodnight, Tony, Terence." Jerome left.

Jerome paused for a moment outside Bendixson's home. The night was cool but invigorating and it tasted better than what he had left. His mind was puzzled, possibly fuddled, not so much by what Oldham intended if he had understood correctly but by Knight's acceptance. He found it difficult to believe that Knight could willingly help capture a man who was guilty only of disappearing. This was in sharp contrast to his words in the convent. No doubt pious humbug! Or was he guilty of the same, remembering his own reaction when Baru had left suddenly. Maybe if he was still working for Hockin, he would still be there, not walking back to his home, the bar, with anger and bitterness infecting him.

Only a few locals and four soldiers were in *The Golden Eagle*. The music was too loud and the girls were sitting desultory at their usual table in the corner to the right, furthest from the door; obviously, their advances had been rejected or not enough beer had been drunk. Unusually, he did not speak to the mama-san sat in her usual place at the far end of the bar with the stairs up to the rooms behind her. She seemed concerned. He was struck again by how young the soldiers looked. He went upstairs and turned left, his room being the second on the right. On opening the door, his left hand curled around to the light switch. "Don't switch the lights on, Mr Jerome." The voice was English, coming from, he thought, the shadows to the left of the windows that were flung open to their fullest extent. "Come in. Close the door. Go to the window and close them." Jerome knew it would be prudent to comply. He closed the window but remained facing out towards the dimly lit lane.

"Shi Baru, isn't it?" Though frightened, his voice sounded calm. There was a rustling noise and then the light was switched on. Jerome turned slowly, his eyes on the same level as Baru's whose body and face appeared to be thinner than before. Jerome's eyes dropped to the black pistol in Baru's right hand and he thought it was the same type that Phil Knight carried. The Englishman's face was now pale and anxious, his body stiff.

"Don't worry. I'm not going to shoot you." His voice was not threatening. Shi Baru explained, "One because I want to talk to you and two, it would be silly because there are English soldiers downstairs." Jerome felt his body relaxing at the Oxbridge-accented words. He could not imagine Knight giving *silly* as a reason for not shooting him. "Sit down." He indicated the chair at the small table to the right of the window. Jerome pulled the chair out, turned it so his back would be to the wall and sat down. There was a large, brown envelope on the table beside the chair. He lay his right arm from the elbow down flat on the envelope and stuffed his left hand into his trouser pocket. Baru sat on the bed, which ran along the opposite wall from the door to a wash basin. The furniture was completed by a single wardrobe along the wall to the right of the door. Baru laid the Browning on the bed. "British service weapon. They are not all that easy to come by, unlike American revolvers. But I prefer it. One may call it poetic justice to kill the British with their own weapon."

"I would call it tragic irony." It was a reflective response, which surprised and calmed him.

Baru smiled. "As long as they are dead." Just braggadocio by Baru who probably had not or could not shoot anyone, though Jerome would not test this hypothesis.

"You have changed, Shi. There was never hatred in your eyes before."

"I have never seen my country in the same way as in the past few weeks." He paused, his head quivering like a nervous tic. "People think I have been with the communists as they call them. I haven't. I have been travelling the country…incognito. Of course, I used my father's name sometimes to gain entry to certain places. I saw my people—the way they were patronised by the British, the cruelty of your army. The newspapers and radio proclaim the patience and disciplined restraint of the British Army." Now he was sneering. "No! I did not see patience and disciplined restraint, only callous disregard for human life…because we are just little wogs, too numerous so another death doesn't matter." He paused, head quivering again, looking at the window trance-like and ignoring Jerome who did not consider even fleetingly an attempt to overpower Baru. His mind was back in the room. "Take out the photographs. In the envelope." Jerome picked up the envelope and took out four half-plate prints. He held up the first one that showed a man on his knees, face blood-splattered and a British soldier standing over him with the butt of his rifle raised over the man's head. "He is just a suspect. He was released later but still has the scars—the indelible scars of the British Army, which has stained the pages of history." Jerome thought it was a phrase memorised from a propaganda inventory. Jerome did not respond but he felt anger not only at the soldier but also at Baru. He was British and he felt a defensive emotion when his country was attacked. He flipped to the next photograph. Baru described the scene. "A fourteen-year-old Chinese boy lying dead, shot by a British bullet. Note the lack of compassion on the soldier's face. *Only callousness!*" Jerome grimaced. The soldier was young like the ones downstairs in the bar. He saw a grim, blank face that never expressed what the soldier was thinking. He moved quickly onto the next photograph, taken from behind a soldier, his raised rifle aiming at a girl who appeared to be running away. He estimated the girl was about twenty yards from the soldier. There were other civilians in the photograph, most of whom seemed to be looking towards the girl's left. "Another innocent wog! This time a girl who was too frightened to stop when called upon. So the brave British soldier did his duty and shot her dead." Jerome closed his eyes and put the photograph back on the table. But Baru had not finished. "Look at the last one. Or are you too ashamed to see another example of your brave soldiers. Look at the last photograph!" He commanded. A British officer and two soldiers standing over six bodies. Baru's voice became harsher, losing some of its Oxbridge timbre, "Six people this time, a family wiped out by these disciplined soldiers: an old man, the parents, two boys of seventeen and sixteen and finally a girl of eight. It was a well-disciplined act of butchery except the family hadn't been completely wiped out. The eldest girl is studying in England thanks to the benevolent British Empire."

Jerome controlled himself. What Baru had described could all be true but his commentary was so pat, rehearsed, the inventory of propaganda. "Are you quite finished with this tirade?" He had forgotten that the other man was armed.

Baru stood up. "No, I'm not. When the last British soldier and their last imperialist master leave my country, either walking or in a box, then I will be finished." Something in Jerome's brain told him that Baru's declaration was from a picture or a speech. He looked at the floor, shaking his head.

"You're wrong, Shi. More killing isn't going to help your country. What has happened to you?"

Baru's arms stretched out in front of him. "You ask what has happened to me." He shook his head, an incredulous smile on his face. "You ask me that after seeing those photographs." Jerome clasped his right hand around his forehead trying to find the right words in reply. "Is your conscience bothering you?"

Jerome sprung up, facing Baru. "No, it's not. I know I have always treated people like human beings, no matter their colour. What is bothering me? I'll tell you. That a man the last time I met had been young, idealistic, tolerant, concerned about his country and people...nationalistic without being dogmatic, has now turned into a cold, callous individual who seems willing to plunge his country into more bloodshed." He paused, his face within inches of Baru's sullen eyes. "I thought you were the bright hope for your country...the Jack Kennedy and all that. You're too educated to let a few atrocities, which have always been committed by soldiers, British or not, to blur your vision. No, Shi. Something has happened to you or someone has influenced you. I can tell by your eyes. It was all so well-rehearsed." He stepped back from Baru and sat down again. He threw up his right hand in a dismissive gesture. "Forget the guns and the bombs. Return to Shala and help your people get ready for independence." Baru lowered his head, his fervour dampened briefly. He knew and had met well-meaning Englishmen who did have genuine feelings for their 'adopted' country. "I ask you, no beg you, for the sake of your country not to get involved in violence. Think what it will do to your mother and sister if you end up in conflict with your father." Baru's eyes darted up towards Jerome but the latter continued, "Once, not long after you had gone up to Oxford, your family came to tea at Tony Hockin's. Your mother was so proud of you. She was grateful to Allah that her husband and son wanted to help the people, like those in the poor village that she came from. Your sister marvelled because a poor, coloured boy could be accepted by the British. I have no time for the empire but I am still English with a pride in some of her achievements. Not a blind patriotism, my country right or wrong. You know the quote. Think about it."

Baru shook his head, smiled and in a calm and controlled tone said, "I came to ask you to help your 'adopted' country. Now I realise that you are worse than Hockin who at least is honest. He just wants to make money from us. You seek a status. To be seated on a plinth of moral authority. Of course, you will criticise the British but," wagging his right index finger at Jerome, "you want to be looked up to, not on the same level as the poor, coloured natives." Now Jerome was shaking his head in a mixture of sorrow and anger. "You mention my mother and sister, and their pride at me going to Oxford. That's exactly what you don't understand. You send people to England to be educated, thinking they will return as an English gentleman imbued with British values of tolerance and fairness. We do." He paused. "But when we ask for what the English value above all else—their freedom…" Another pause. "We become ungrateful wretches. Never could trust the wogs. Look at Nehru and Jinnah. Both educated in England." He sat on the bed. "Eddie, you would think that the English with their great seats of learning and their many learned intellectuals would understand. If you reveal something, put temptation in their way. It's Adam and Eve, the apple, the seed of your Christianity. You must have read Milton?"

Jerome nodded. *"Paradise Lost."*

"Remember?" This was the authentic Shi Baru. "You can't say the *apple* is on an English tree. You showed us the apple. Why should it be denied to us? We are told of our liberal, efficient, colonial administrators. Sutch!" He wagged his right index finger, not at Jerome but at an imaginary audience in the wall. "Why does he and others tolerate a corrupt, rotten police force? They have no interest in change. They would rather we remain in our subservient position. They want to maintain the fabric of colonialism with their jobs, pensions and privileged lives. What else have the English brought us!" He looked down, inwardly structuring the response. "Your medicine and religion. Your propaganda is so skilful that people believe they are benefits. No! Both are alien to our culture and traditions. I think your great Kipling put it in simpler terms: *Wot do they understand.* Even he, the great narrator of Empire, saw its folly eventually." Jerome did not think they were correct readings but understood his point.

"Independence *is* coming."

"Not on our terms. I want for my people democracy, real democracy, good jobs and national pride. It's only because the Labour Government wants to cut military spending and abandon here and everywhere east of Suez that independence is coming. Independence is in name only because we will still be a colony." He picked up the Browning and pointed it at Jerome. "Put the photographs back in the envelope."

"Can I have them?"

"Why?"

"I might be able to get an enquiry going—"

Baru was abrupt. "Don't meddle! Go back to England. Go back to your silly ideas of Western democracy and justice." Jerome put the photographs in the envelope, passed it to Baru who picked up a canvas bag from the bed and put the envelope together with the weapon in the bag. "I'm sure you are sensible enough not to leave this room or call anyone for the next ten minutes." The two men stared at each other and then Baru was gone. Jerome buried his face in his hands and then laid them flat on the table. There was the sound of a motorcycle from the lane. He realised that his shirt was soaked in sweat from fear and the exertion of keeping calm.

Chapter 13

One of the HQ clerks had informed him that his two visitors would be about thirty minutes late. GBH was amused by how most Branch officers were enthralled by 'special forces'.

The two Special Branch officers were meeting 513 Troop: the number was the height of Panti Ridge. The Troop had flown in from Singapore the previous day and were now isolated in an old loggers' camp ten miles north of the capital. GBH had decided it was best not to accompany them and waited in his loaned office in army headquarters in the capital. Prior to the designation of the unit, the soldiers had suggested names: the Panti Panthers, a reference to the amount of time spent going up and down Panti Ridge during their training; the No I Johore Assault Group, a nod to their home base, and GAG, Grievous Assault Group though the author feigned ignorance and then surprise at the term. He had indeed been the author of the letter to the CFELF the previous year in which he had proposed, due to the unavailability of the SAS, the creation of a dedicated assault unit that could act on sensitive intelligence. He was not of the view that soldiers of an infantry battalion could not execute the actual mission but was alert to the sensibilities of the Branch and other intelligence agencies in protecting their sources. If a regular platoon was deployed and as was often the case, the target did not appear, the soldiers would bemoan another waste of time and useless intelligence—he had until he had met Branch officers in Malaya, especially one Jimmy Doherty. If the operation went ahead next time, it would likely be a different platoon and this increased the threat to security. There was no doubt the CTs would have an intelligence network. Soldiers were prone to talk and consequently, he had reasoned to the CFELF that a dedicated assault unit was essential. He had proposed an organisation of 24 junior ranks commanded by an experienced captain and sergeant. There would be the requirement for a Royal Signals detachment to ensure good communications for the patrols operating deep in the jungle as well as Iban Trackers. Volunteers could come from battalions in Singapore and those in transit. GBH would be responsible for training the unit with support from staff at JWS. With experienced soldiers, a three-month training period would be sufficient, mainly to ensure that fitness levels were at the required standard and for the individuals to train together. He had not been trying to reinvent the wheel as far as basic infantry tactics were concerned and that was why he had proposed the volunteers receive the normal pay rates. The volunteer soldiers needed to be fit and resourceful, self-reliant but specifically able to endure tough, degrading conditions though he tried to avoid putting his men through these unnecessarily, believing some officers seemed to take pleasure in boasting of the conditions their soldiers endured. Nevertheless, soldiers needed to be challenged, which would result in a sense of achievement in overcoming the challenge.

The CFELF agreed to the proposal as well confirming that he had received confirmation from the SAS that they could not cope with an additional task but would be willing to provide an officer to command the unit. The commander's response had included a rebuke for going outwith the chain of command but accepted that on exceedingly rare occasions, it might be the proper approach. He had concluded by including copies of directives to relevant formation and unit commanders to cooperate with the plan and not erect barriers. GBH's superiors had not been impressed by his action but had known it would be unwise to cross the Commander Far East Land Forces.

GBH did not have a high regard for the officers of the Special Air Service Regiment considering them public school boy adventurers who had read too much John Buchan and Rider H. Haggard; notwithstanding that he had encountered excellent troopers and non-commissioned officers from the SAS. Thankfully, GBH was able to inveigle the Royal Marine Commando in Singapore to allow a captain coming to the end of his tour as an instructor in JWS to become the unit commander as well as managing to scoop up a sergeant from the Royal Hampshire Regiment returning from Borneo who also had served with the SAS. The new Troop commander was reasonable and temperate and had been able to encourage six JNCOs and marines to volunteer whilst the other volunteers had come from the resident battalions in Hong Kong and Singapore.

GBH had returned from Palestine with a bitter taste and contempt for the Jewish terrorists groups—the Irgun and the Stern Gang. He knew of one infantry major who had had a good war and a promising army career ahead being so disgusted by the Jewish terrorists that he had left to return to Glasgow to teach. GBH's brother, David—now up at Oxford—was more sympathetic to the creation of the Jewish state stemming from his involvement in the liberation of concentration camps. He urged his brother to consider the emotional impact of the Holocaust on the worldwide Jewish community. GBH thought even if it was right for the Jewish people to be given a 'homeland', it should not be at the cost of forcibly evicting Palestinians whose families had lived there, some for over a thousand years. If the Jews could reclaim their ancestral lands, then the same argument should apply to the Red Indians in America, though he did not expect the moneymen of New York to be eager to support their 'return'. He had heard from another officer of the massacre in the village of Deir Yassin by the Irgun and the Stern Gang. If he had been there and had managed to capture any of the terrorists, he would have had them summarily executed. His antipathy to the Zionists was reinforced by the support they received from left-wing Labour MPs whose first loyalty was to Stalin in Moscow.

He spent time as an instructor at the regimental depot, making a few visits to his grandmum in Dundee and the Mackenzies, still working for the estate's new

American owners but never visiting Fi's grave. He did not require a physical memorial. In November 1950, the UN forces were forced to retreat south from the Yalu River on the North Korean border with the People's Republic of China, following an attack by vast Chinese forces. When his battalion was deployed to Korea, GBH returned as a company second-in-command. He was to travel out with another battalion officer who was spending the last few nights with his fiancé in Glasgow before embarking on the troopship. Reluctantly, he agreed to meet Robbie Finlayson and his fiancé in the Central Hotel's *Malmaison* restaurant. It was a mistake because after introductions with GBH being described by Robbie as the best officer in the regiment, a glass of wine was poured for him and the couple ignored him. He intended to finish his drink and leave but recognised the man deep in conversation with an attractive, young lady in a corner beside the windows. He confirmed with Robbie that it was Alastair McFadzean and the fiancé said it was his daughter. "Excuse me." He stood up and went over to the corner table. "Excuse me, sir. Sorry to bother you." McFadzean looked up; his daughter's head was bowed. "I think you knew my father, David Buchanan-Henderson."

He stood up and grasped GBH's hand firmly. "Indeed I did."

GBH looked down at Una. "I think you went to school with my sister Fi, Fiona."

She looked up, her eyes roaming over him. "You must be wee Gordon. Yes, I did but that was a long time ago…a lifetime ago." She dropped her head. GBH felt hurt by her reaction and decided to leave but her father almost man-handled him into a chair.

"Sit. Have a drink." He poured some champagne into an unused third glass. "Your father was a good man. The most honourable man I have ever met. He sold the estate. Where is he?"

"In France, sir, running a wine business with an old friend…who is French."

"Was that to get away from our socialist government? Not real socialists, Clem and Bevin made sure of that. Mind you, there are lots of Reds in France, crawling with them."

"So I understand from my father."

"So you are still in the army unless…you going to a fancy dress party." He laughed, GBH smiled and Una ignored them. "So what are you doing in Glasgow?"

"Catching a troopship out to Hong Kong tomorrow."

"Korea?" GBH knew that he was not meant to say but it was common knowledge or would be soon. He nodded. "Well, you need a drink or two. Stupid getting involved. Mind you, good for my profits." He looked towards Finlayson. "Is that young Robbie Finlayson?"

"Yes sir."

"Do some business with his dad. The girl?"

"His fiancé."

He turned to Una. "You should marry a soldier, not that lawyer."

She replied angrily, "He is an advocate!"

107

"Much older than Una. Supposed to be here tonight but couldn't make it. He spends most nights in Edinburgh."

"Father, that is where he works."

"Sure! I know all about these Edinburgh lawyers and their activities. Why is he marrying now? It's a cover for him so that he can become a judge. Don't think he's getting any of my money." GBH felt embarrassed and an intruder.

"Father, that's enough. This is not the time or place." GBH stood up and put on his tam o'shanter.

"I need to go. Thanks for the drink, sir." McFadzean stood up and shook his hand warmly.

"Good luck and you take care, son." It was said with genuine feeling.

"Goodbye, Miss McFadzean."

"Bye." Without looking up. He saluted, turned, said goodbye to Robbie and his fiancé and at the door caught a glimpse of the McFadzeans obviously arguing.

Shortly after arriving in Korea, he was informed that his grandpapa had died. When his CO, his company commander in Shala, told him that arrangements could be made for him to return to Britain via Hong Kong to attend the general's funeral, GBH felt insulted and replied, "My duty is here with my soldiers." His tone on the cusp of insolence blended with derision for the crass proposal. A drumhead service was held to honour and commemorate GBH's grandpapa. In his eulogy, the CO spoke of General David Buchanan-Henderson's gallant and honourable service to the Regiment and their country. His grandson was perplexed and torn because he could not imagine his old grandpapa as a commander leading soldiers into battle. Certainly, he had been a general: he had seen him resplendent in his general's ceremonial uniform but... He could not erase the image of the amiable, old man sitting at dinner sending him into spasms of laughter. A smile erased the sombreness on his face. This was observed by others: some thought it was inappropriate on such a solemn occasion; others that it was typical of his enigmatic character.

His company was deployed on the battalion's left flank above the Imjin River bordering the right flank of a company from another Scottish battalion. One of his duties was to liaise with that company to coordinate patrols and ensure there were no incidents of friendly fire. The neighbouring company commander was impressed by GBH's calmness and tactical acumen. When he was injured in a collapse of his dug-out requiring to be removed to the rear for medical treatment, he proposed that GBH was the right man to replace him because he knew both companies' positions, his own second-in-command was too inexperienced and could not get a replacement company commander in time because the attack was imminent. After quick discussions on the brigade radio net, it was agreed. Fortunately, or luckily, GBH had 24 hours before the attack. He had no qualms on taking over a 'foreign' company, never having subscribed to the uniqueness of battalions stemming from their recruiting area. In past wars, soldiers had not always served with their home regiment. The concept of loyalty in an infantry battalion was a facade. An infantry soldier was an infantry soldier. During the terror of war, individuals needed each other, relied on each other for support, creating a unique bond but still motivated by selfishness, the instinct to survive. He had recognised that the paradox of soldiering was its Janus nature, bringing out the best and worst in man. Despite the high ideals of the military code—comradeship, honour and duty—the savage must be beneath the surface. In fighting the Japanese, he had come to learn both from his own experience and from some of his superiors that leadership included knowing when to resurrect and re-inter the savage.

Most of his new command knew him by sight and most had been impressed by his calmness and natural authority when he had toured the company position providing direction and encouragement. Attached to the company was a Royal Artillery captain, the forward observation officer known as the FOO to provide fire support and as an observer a tall, burley American army captain, Louis L Williford from Richmond, Virginia, who had not taken the opportunity to return to his own unit.

The Chinese attack was as anticipated, waves of soldiers with the noise from the screams, bugles and whistles deafening. The defenders were robust and determined but GBH was aware that ammunition was low with little chance of resupply. He had determined that he would lead the rear or depth platoon in a counter-attack in an effort to clear the Chinese from one of his forward platoon's position to establish a base to support the other forward platoon. In his dug-out, while briefing the others, the FOO suggested that he could call down fire on the position. To the others, a moment's hesitation but in fact a moment's battle appreciation by GBH, who then said resolutely, "Do it!" He ordered, by means of field telephone and shouting, the company to get to the bottom of their trenches. His company sergeant-major ran out of the dug-out screaming at the soldiers to burrow deep into their trenches and was shot dead whilst doing so. The FOO had relayed the fire mission whilst GBH was informing the CO and his own battalion's CO of his action. 'Shot over.' He screamed for everyone to get down before the FOO could acknowledge. GBH had never been so terrified as the shells exploded on the position for what seemed an eternity. The night had been bitterly cold but now he, like the others, was drenched in sweat and caked in mud and dirt from the collapsing dug-out. They were being hurled around the dug-out by the blast waves. Shocked and dazed, it took them a little time to realise the shelling had stopped. They had to clear debris from the entrance to get out onto the position. The Chinese were retreating now, well away from the position despite the efforts of their officers to make them turn and continue the attack. There were pieces of Chinese bodies everywhere and many were on top of the sergeant-major's body, thereby preserving it as a recognisable corpse. Slowly and gingerly, heads emerged from the trenches. The smell of the dead blended with the cordite created a nauseating stench, which the bitterly cold air could not disperse. The appearance of the soldiers reminded him of miners caked in black, some vomiting, faces dazed and strained, some covering their mouths with their sweat rag or other material to keep the stench out. They had been miners digging frenetically and in terror to make their trenches deeper. He ordered his still dazed second-in-command to get the platoon sergeants to do a head count and ammunition check. He knew it was important, essential to keep the men active. The FOO was leaning against the parapet of the trench in front of the company HQ dug-out, appalled by observing for the first time the consequences of his work. "Thanks, Nigel." The FOO gave a puzzled grimace. "It's not Nigel? Doesn't matter."

The FOO, his head over the sandbags topping the parapet, was retching, shaking, spluttering, "Sorry, sorry."

"Easy. Easy." He resisted the urge to comfort him by tapping him on the shoulder. They were now joined by the American.

"You two are crazy bastards," the American shouted. "Let me know where you are going next so I can go in the opposite direction."

He was replaced as the company commander by a major returning to his own battalion and left with the heartfelt gratitude of their CO to be greeted with a reprimand by his CO. "Your action was reckless."

"With respect, colonel, I disagree."

"You endangered the lives of your soldiers."

"I thought the thousands of Chinese attacking my position were doing that. I took a calculated risk. It's called battle appreciation."

The CO's eyes flared with anger and sneered, "This regiment does not belong to the Buchanan-Hendersons."

GBH, riled by this malicious comment, inclined forward aggressively, alarming the CO. He was certain that the CO had been waiting to express his malevolence towards his family for many years. "I think that comment is unworthy of you." But he would not be reckless. "Remember, colonel, that you are only a lease-holder of this battalion."

"I have had enough of your insubordination. It's time you learned of the real army." GBH realised that his CO did not have the wit to understand the absurdness of this comment the day after a battle.

He found himself inexplicably on the staff of Field Marshall Montgomery at Supreme Headquarters Allied Powers Europe known as SHAPE near Versailles. He never really understood Montgomery's or even his role. Time was spent drafting plans to repel a Soviet attack in Europe. He was bored by Montgomery with his interminable briefings and reports. The colonel, who was the chief exercise planner, impressed him as an exceedingly competent, professional soldier and a decent individual. The colonel was not impressed by GBH telling him that his staff work was slapdash and verged on the negligent. He reminded him that Fourteen Army under Slim would not have defeated the Japanese if it did not have an efficient resupply system to ensure that the fighting units had what they needed. GBH did not forget this advice.

The only advantage to the posting was being able to see his parents on a regular basis. Their wine exporting business with Charles Planet was successful and growing though he sensed his father was not happy. His father found the French lazy and was always complaining of their lot as well as most of them being communists whereas his mother seemed to have been liberated. She was comfortable with the language, able to shop, order in restaurants and hold simple conversations, making her popular with the villagers. She had learned to drive and owned a small sports car in which she hurled around the roads and narrow country lanes. Her son was absolutely terrified on the both occasions she drove him. In response to his mother's probing, he confirmed he had begun a relationship with the sister of a contemporary of his brother's at Oxford.

"They're good boys, Grievous. Wouldn't want to fucking tangle with them." Doherty looked at Godden for confirmation.

"Very impressive." Doherty shook his head at Godden's less than enthusiastic support and exchanged glances with Grievous.

"When are you going to use them? They can't sit up there indefinitely. Has there been any movement?"

This time the glances were between the policemen. "No. They're still on the border. They seem to be waiting for something to happen or new instructions. We think there might be some conflict between the political boys and the armed wing."

"But we can't be sure. Who the fuck knows what's going on." Doherty was not prepared to reveal his intelligence even to a man he respected. Grievous thought, *I would hope you know what's happening, otherwise what are we doing here?* From his experience particularly with Doherty, he felt certain that the Branch had control over some elements of the enemy and was able to manipulate them into acting. He would dangle an enticement.

"I have managed to wangle Royal Navy helicopters to support any operation. Though only available for another seven to ten days at most because their carrier will be leaving soon."

"How did you swing that?" Doherty asked.

"I have friends too, Jimmy." He smiled. His only friend from school, Jonathan Ballingall, who had become a naval pilot and was now a rear admiral in Singapore, had said he would do what he could to get him helicopters. It was not a commitment but he did not have to tell the Branch officers as they did not share all of their information. "The problem is if we can't get the helicopters, then my boys would need to tab into position. That could take some time. Could set up a base closer to the target area?"

"Could be compromised," said Doherty.

"What about the RAF helicopters here?" asked Godden.

"Never can depend on them. They never put you where you want to go. We had a problem with them during our final exercise on Panti Ridge. Better to fly Navy." He could see that he had unsettled them and decided to let them stew a little longer by changing the subject. "How is the situation in Shala?"

"Fine. Apart from the army getting their knickers in a twist over not knowing about young Baru." Doherty knew he had made a mistake.

"What do you mean?"

"The army wasn't told about Shi Baru's possible involvement. Their captain, Oldham, made a bit of a fuss to Sutch and Bendixson."

"Why? Whose decision was that?"

"It was decided after consultation with the commissioner, the DO and HE."

GBH despaired of 'consultation', the new way by which decisions emerged. Why didn't someone just accept responsibility? "I think that was wrong. Soldiers don't like being misled. It's likely we will need them for support, QRF, cut-offs, cordons. A stupid decision." He paused. Doherty, discomfited, avoided Grievous' eyes. Godden was unmoved. "Another factor. If this drags on, then it's likely the present platoon will be replaced. New platoon will need to get to know the ground. Not helpful." There would be no need to replace the platoon if the police requested they remain for operational reasons. But GBH knew their CO from the Malaya Emergency and when his battalion had come to the Jungle Warfare School for their training and test exercise before deployment. He was confident that after an explanation, the CO would support him. This was the first time in his many years of dealing with them that he had ever felt the Branch were dancing to his tune, though Godden's apparent indifference was a concern.

Chapter 14

Later that day, Knight was at Hockin's for dinner or what was called supper. He felt uneasy at Hockin's insistence that he could come to the plantation anytime he wished. It was an open invitation. He was in a quandary in that Hockin represented what he disapproved of most—privilege and the sense of entitlement—but he found Hockin to be reasonable and not arrogant like many of the expats. Ho's approval of him was influential. Knight had told Oldham several times that he should be spending more time with Hockin and the other civilians, which was met usually with a snort. Oldham considered them products of a minor public school, describing them as lower middle class, shopkeepers, *petite bourgeoisie* with small-minded attitudes. The female camp-followers were competing to be the dowdiest in the colony. Except Miss Kanna. He socialised with Sutch and Bendixson only because the CO had told him it was essential. Oldham was ill at ease with this new requirement of public relations though he understood that it was probably the future, being unlikely that Britain would ever fight a sustained, conventional war again unless in Europe and even then it would be over in a few days once it went nuclear. He operated on a three-day cycle of two nights commanding one of the standing patrols and the third night in the ops room, stagging on as it was called.

Knight adhered to his policy of staying away from his former platoon as much as possible though on occasions, some of the corporals and lance-corporals would come to his office after a patrol to inform him of some important piece of information. Occasionally, there would be implied criticism of their platoon sergeant usually with the opening of 'things not the same' but Knight would cut them short. To stop the complaints, he instituted the practice that they would be debriefed by Eileen Kanna who knew how to handle them and now there were almost no requests to give Sgt Knight 'a vital piece of information'. The only NCO who came on a regular basis was Horrocks and it was mostly just for a chat. Knight sensed that Horrocks found his fellow NCOs, including Sgts Nash and Williams, boring and limited. Corporal Jubb was rated by Horrocks but unfortunately, the former spent all of his time in the police OP. In one conversation, Knight asked him of his reputation for the ladies, especially the rumours about the wives of senior NCOs. "Fucking hell, sarge! Have you seen them?" He pushed his hat to the back of his head, eyes wide, mouth partially open in mock shock.

Knight laughed. "Some respect. You're talking about the wives of my fellow mess members."

"Bet you wouldn't." He laughed. "Anyway, I'm a good Catholic boy. But the rumours are good for my reputation." He paused then said, "Anyway sarge, I don't see you spending much time with your fellow mess members."

"Probably for the same reason as you…and we will leave it at that." He liked Johnnie Horrocks and surmised he would be a good guy to have around if things got a bit hairy.

Knight arrived with Eileen Kanna, whose response to Hockin's surprise at her attendance was that it would give them, the other guests, something to talk about. A mischievous female. The buffet curry dinner was excellent. Hockin had dispensed with his house servants and was an attentive host. Knight was surprised to see the Robertsons there, knowing their low standing with the other expats but Hockin was inclusive by nature and he liked George Robertson who had taught him scuba diving up at Jacques Bay. Jerome was not present. After dinner, Knight and Eileen stood in a corner. The others were seated on sofas and chairs with Hockin reclining in an armchair. They were reminiscing about their school days, dances, masters, debates and sports. He caught a glimpse of Julie observing him as did Eileen. "Looking for an opportunity to speak to Julie, Phil?" He smiled. "Impress her more with your views on how we are not fit to run an empire unlike the French… Remind me…Algeria and Indochina are still French." He laughed. "You're right, I'm not just a pretty face."

"Did you learn that from Martin at your bridge party?!"

"Is that your best response?"

"Yes. I thought it was good."

"I need another glass of that dreadful wine."

"I'm going to get some hot water. I'll get your wine on the way back." As he reached the door of the kitchen, a scream came from the sitting room. "What the hell!" His hand went to the holster as he spun back into the sitting room. Hockin was holding Julie Ryan. The others were on their feet looking towards the windows, which overlooked the river.

"What's up?" Brusquely.

"She saw a face looking in." Hockin was agitated.

Knight rushed over to the window, dropping to his right knee and cocking his weapon. "Turn the lights off and get down!" Holding the Browning in both hands, he moved the weapon slowly from the left, searching the tree line that was about twenty metres beyond the veranda, not spotting any movement. "What was he like? Chinese?"

"Phil, she's upset."

He ignored Hockin. "Julie! What did he look like? His clothes?"

She shook her head, trying to regain her composure. "He was smiling and…"

"Go on." Knight's voice was softer.

"Something shining…a knife…large one."

"Good girl." He scanned the tree-line again, still nothing. "I'm going out." He was angry with himself for not having his Armalite. He noticed Robertson was beside him holding what he thought was a 38 revolver.

"I'll come with you."

He nodded. "But keep a few feet behind me and don't move until I tell you." He ordered Alston who seemed calm, "Lock all the doors, barricade them, shutter the windows! Tony, you've some weapons?" Hockin nodded. "Get them!"

A calm Eileen Kanna said, "I'll phone the ops room."

"Do that."

"Where's the vehicle?" Referring to their Land Rover and crew.

"Further away tonight." He told Hockin to lock the door behind them and then to Robertson, "Let's go!" Knight was first out the opposite side from the river, vaulting the veranda and crouching beneath it, scanning the ground. He turned to his left, indicated Robertson to follow him and, still keeping low, ran to the corner of the house. Again, he indicated Robertson to follow him to the corner where by hand gestures, he told the teacher to stay there whilst Knight made his way along the side of the building to the corner facing the river. Once there, he poked his weapon around the corner followed by his head. His night vision was fully focussed now. There was no one beneath the veranda and he could not see any movement in the trees to his right. He gestured back to Robertson to join him. He thought, *He might be a bore but at least he has spunk and he is probably touching forty.* He surmised that if it was CTs, then they were likely to have opened fire by now. It would be foolish to go into the trees, and he also knew it was rather foolish to leave the house but felt he had to react even if it was only as reassurance to the civilians.

The lights of the Land Rover flared on with full power with the beam forming a right angle to them about fifty metres away. Almost instantaneously, there were three metallic pops. Knight knew it was an SMG. This was followed by the crackle of the radio. He heard 'contact' and 'wait out'. "Let's go!" They were about thirty metres from the vehicle. He threw himself flat on the ground and indicated Robertson to do the same. "Don't want to get shot by my own men...Collins!"

"Sarge!"

"Coming in from the direction of the house...and turn those bloody lights off!"

They got to the Land Rover as Collins was sending another message. "Hello zero, this is three three echo, one enemy wounded, no casualties." Collins was standing at the driver's side, door open, headset on, handset in his left hand, his SMG in the other hand still pointing forward towards the ground. Knight could hear low moaning and saw the body on the ground about five metres from the Land Rover. At the passenger side, Lance-corporal Mullan had his weapon still in the aim but to the left.

"Who fired?"

"The Welsh git with his pop gun. Want me to—"

"Just shut up!" Knight was aware of Robertson still there, looking towards the casualty. He spoke to Martin who had come from the back of the vehicle, "Go with Mr Robertson back to the house and get Doctor Alston up here. No one else! And let them know you are outside; don't just barge in!"

115

"Understood," said Robertson. There were two more pops. "Jesus Christ!" There was the sound of a motorcycle moving at speed.

"That's low velocity. Well to the south of the house," declared the lance-corporal.

"Get going!" To Robertson and Martin. He indicated to Mullan to follow him the short distance to the casualty. He was Chinese, barely conscious, wounds to the top of his right shoulder and left side of his chest. A knife, not a machete but more a large kitchen knife, was lying to his right and above his head. He returned to Collins. "What happened?"

"Heard a noise like someone stumbling through the trees. Told Trev to switch on the lights. Guy was running towards me. Waving his knife. Shouted a warning."

"Sign language," interjected the lance-corporal sarcastically.

Knight asked, "Any first field dressings in the wagon?" Then to the lance-corporal, "What are you doing here?"

"Black cat," replied the lance-corporal.

"What?"

"Tea."

"I know but…" He could hear people approaching, then saw them—Alston, Robertson and Hockin as well as his driver Martin. "Fucksake." Faintly. He showed Alston the casualty.

Hockin looked at him. "I know him. I'm sure he's the guy I sacked the other day for stealing." Knight gave Alston, who was kneeling down by the casualty, the first aid pack from his vehicle.

Knight told Hockin, "Tony, I think you and George should go back to the house. Police will no doubt take a statement from you."

"You're right." There was more radio traffic.

"Sarge. A policeman has been shot at the entrance to the plantation." That explained the low velocity rounds. "They want Dr Alston down there ASAP. There's an ambulance on its way."

"This guy needs to go to hospital." Alston called after Hockin who was walking away, "Tony, can I use one of your vehicles to at least get him down to the gate."

"What! For him? What about Phil's vehicle?"

"Mine's short-based. Not get him in."

"I'll drive it," said Robertson.

"OK. I'll go back and look after the girls."

Collins resisted the urge to say, 'That's all you're fucking good for. White prat.'

"Tell Eileen we'll pick her up on the way out."

"Will do."

"Sunray for you." Collins handed him the headset and handset. The policeman had been wounded. There would be a police patrol with him soon and he should return once he had briefed them. Oldham had decided he would remain in the ops room in case there were further incidents. He would speak to Knight on his return. The returning silence was submerged by the sirens of police Land Rovers blended with the bell-like sound of an ambulance.

Oldham's elation at his platoon's first contact was spiked by a number of facts: the enemy was a sacked worker with a kitchen knife and not a terrorist armed with an AK47, shot by a Welsh member of the battalion's signals platoon and it had happened by mishap. He was in his office with Knight and Nash doing a debrief whilst Eileen Kanna was taking statements from Collins and Martin in her office at the opposite end of the corridor. She would then type up a report incorporating the short-hand notes she had made of Hockin's and Robertson's accounts once they had returned to the house. The police did not take statements saying it could be left to the next day once the situation had settled down. Nash's reminder of his first briefing that they were all C Platoon was met with Oldham's normal sign of irritation, the imperceptible half-shake of his head, lips curled in tightly, looking straight ahead. "What's this *black cat*?"

"Sir, my understanding is that it's a company thing. Hot tea if possible is taken out to the boys during the night when they are deployed." Oldham knew about it, having been introduced by the company sergeant major who believed the best morale booster for the British soldier was a cup of tea. During operations, if possible without compromising the operation, tea was taken out to the soldiers deployed. The CSM reminded people, especially new officers, that it could be cold during the night in the ulu, the jungle. The code word *Black Cat* was used to let people know tea was on the way. The CO was aware of the practice. Knight was not aware that there was an urn of tea in the back of his vehicle, which the patrol commander had asked Collins to bring out. Knight had told Martin not to park just at Hockin's house but to put it under cover in the trees. Oldham had moved one of the standing patrols closer to the house and consequently, the patrol commander that night—learning Knight was going to the house—had arranged Black Cat with Collins. Initiative! Knight knew it was often by such mishaps that the army experienced success or failure.

Oldham narrated the shooting of the policeman at the entrance to the plantation. As had been agreed, a police Land Rover was positioned each night at the entrance to the plantation. A motorcycle had come at speed down the road from the west and when a policeman had tried to stop it, he had been shot by the motorcyclist. When Oldham asked him for an assessment of the night's two incidents, Knight said possibly the incidents were connected but without further information simply did not know but thought it was likely the motorcyclist ended up in Kampong Tengu, area Z.

These incidents led to an increased police presence in Shala and around the plantation. Oldham had spoken to the CO who told him they were fairly minor incidents and not to overreact. The other companies were dealing with more serious incidents. If the police asked him to undertake operations for which he, Oldham, felt he did not have the necessary men and resources, he was not to agree to anything until he had cleared it with the battalion operations officer.

Chapter 15

Godden arrived in Shala.

After a brief meeting with Bendixson, he spent almost an hour with SSgt Ho behind closed doors. A joint conference was arranged by Bendixson in his office with Godden, Inspector Khan and him for the police and Oldham, Nash and Knight representing the army. The two casualties shared the same ward with one being protected and the other guarded. Police constable Abdul had sustained bullet wounds to his left arm and his right thigh from a low velocity weapon, possibly a British Browning, which would be confirmed once the recovered empty cases had been examined. The arm wound was not serious but the other injury could lead to the loss of his leg. He was described as an excellent officer with two commendations for bravery and had been due for promotion. Married, with his wife expecting their first child. Alston had recommended Abdul being transferred to the hospital in the capital, which had better facilities. A helicopter was on its way. The other less seriously wounded man, now a detainee, was Tan Tse Chin who had been dismissed over two weeks ago for stealing. Although it was his foreman Mehad who had been responsible for the dismissal, Hockin thought it was his responsibility to confirm it and inform the man in person. The alleged stealing had not been reported to the police, which was met with raised eyebrows by Godden.

"One of my men has been shot, almost killed. Something must be done!" Knight was amused by the way commanders, army officers included, became protective and almost familial towards the casualty whom they probably did not know or not very well. It was like having to put down the family Labrador. Godden was asked for an assessment.

"We are investigating. We cannot be certain the two incidents are linked. Tan might have been after revenge. A sense of grievance at an unfair sacking, possibly. Of course, his sense of grievance might have been stoked and used by the communists. Could have been a recce but we simply don't know. We are making enquiries. Only one definite I would say is the motorcycle and shooter probably ended up in area Z." Oldham gave Knight a nod as if to say, your assessment wasn't far wrong.

"Thank you, Arthur." He placed both hands flat on the desk, looking around and striking an authoritative pose. "A cordon and search of area Z? William?"

"I don't have the men to provide a cordon. It would take days for a proper search of that area. It would mean taking my soldiers out of the OP and stopping the patrols."

"Sir, I don't see what it would achieve." It was Inspector Khan.

"What do you mean?"

"Even if we found the motorcycle and the gun, which would be unlikely because of its size, they could move it around even as we search. Very unlikely we could link it to the gunman. And we would need to reduce our patrols."

"That's not helpful, inspector. Somebody has attempted to murder one of my officers. We *need* to do something." Khan obviously was not a *favourite Labrador*. An interruption, his telephone. "Yes. I said not to be disturbed… Yes… Put him through." He put the receiver against his chest. "Doctor Alston." Informing the room. "Yes, Doctor Alston." He listened, the others straining unsuccessfully to hear Alston. Bendixson's face red with anger, shaking his head, then he erupted, "No! No! No! Transfer him by road! I will not allow it…" Though the others could not hear his words, they deduced Alston's tone was calm and reasonable. Bendixson's face went even redder and the volume increased. "That man is a criminal, a thief, a terrorist! He is not going on the same helicopter as my brave officer!" A pause for Alston to reply. "I don't care. It's not to happen! That's my decision! Goodbye!" He threw the receiver on the desk, shook his head, leaned back in his chair and looked around. "Well, you all know what that's about. Alston wants to transfer Tan in the same helicopter as…eh…Abdul. I won't allow it."

"Terence," Godden spoke quietly, "strictly speaking, you can prevent him from leaving the hospital but not from going on the helicopter. That's a decision for the Royal Air Force. Is that not the case, William?" Bendixson replaced the receiver surreptitiously in the cradle whilst Godden was speaking.

"Yes. And the RAF can be very difficult, even irrational. They decide who goes in their choppers."

"It could have serious consequences if you prevent Tan from being removed. The medical staff would be unhappy. Alston, that paragon, would no doubt raise it with the DO and possibly HE. Likely to get into the newspapers and the communist leaning ones would have a field day. Even could affect our intelligence gathering." Godden looked at Oldham. "He was shot by the army. We have already detected some disquiet amongst the plantation workers. It might look bad if he is refused essential medical treatment." Oldham was going to speak up in defence of his men but realised the Branch officer's comments were not intended to criticise the army but to change Bendixson's mind.

"He's a thief…in collusion with the communists."

"Alleged thief, and we don't know if there was any collusion." Even though Bendixson was senior in rank, Godden treated him like a spoilt child. "Also, we might get more out of him if he's away from here."

"All right." He pressed a button on the intercom. "Telephone Doctor Alston and tell him I consent. He will know what I am talking about." An attempt to regain authority as the noise of the helicopter could be heard on its way to the landing site near the hospital. He paused until the sound faded a little. "No search then." Answered by confirmatory head shakes from Godden and Oldham. "Don't think we need you anymore, Khan."

"Sir." He stood up, replaced his hat, saluted and left.

Bendixson waited for a moment then said, "Some of the girls are becoming concerned." He meant his wife and Mrs Alston. "I think we need to increase security in London Crescent." He looked at Oldham for support then. "Oh. I forgot that journalist is arriving tomorrow. Tony's friend. An international journalist. Don't want anything to happen to her."

"Is she not staying with Tony?"

"No, Arthur." A disapproving frown. "She is staying as before in the Crescent with that nurse."

"I could patrol it but on a random basis," said Oldham.

"I was thinking of something more permanent. Closing each entrance. Initially with vehicles, army at top and police at bottom until we get barbed-wire barriers."

"Think that might be possible."

"The last bungalow, a three-bedroomed one, is empty and…" He hesitated. "I thought you could put some of your men in there permanently." Even Godden was taken aback. Knight thought, *You scheming, devious sod. That's why you got rid of Khan.* "Of course, we would need to get authorisation from the DO. A 24-hour guard would reassure the ladies."

"I need to look at my numbers. Some of my guys are not fit for duty at present." He looked at Nash.

"Five at present, sir."

"And I assume," he said to Godden, "the standing patrols need to continue." A nod from Godden.

"Terence, why don't you get the DO's consent and we can consider it later?"

"Fine. Good."

"One other matter." Knight had asked him to raise it. "There are no objections to Sergeant Knight continuing his strolls around town? We don't want to show that we have been intimidated. Maintain our regular routine."

Godden shook his head. "I don't like it. Make sure there's a police patrol nearby."

"Sir," said Knight, knowing that he always did.

"Still with Miss Kanna?" asked Bendixson.

"She's a great asset," replied Knight. Godden's response was a wry smile.

"William, think you should stop your boys going to the bars."

"Terence, if we have increased commitments, then none will be free to go to bars. But I will stop it for the next few days at least."

"Good. Can we have another meeting later, this evening possibly? I'm keen to get the security arrangements in place for the Crescent." Godden, Oldham and Knight had the same thought, *To avoid grief from Mrs Bendixson.*

As they were leaving, Oldham told his two sergeants that they would go to his office to consider options but were interrupted by Godden who asked if he could have a chat with Oldham, to which he agreed. "My office?" Godden nodded in agreement. "OK, gentlemen." To the sergeants. To Godden, "Twenty minutes?" Godden nodded. "Right, twenty minutes in my office and bring Williams."

Once seated in Oldham's office in the police ops room, Godden said, "You probably think what I told you at our last meeting is a crock of—"

"Or their jungle navigation is as poor as ours?" A blank face.

Puzzlement on Godden's face then a slight smile seeped through. "Touché." A pause. "But the intelligence remains extant. I do acknowledge that you should have been told about young Baru." Godden was not stupid or obstinate that he would ignore an experienced soldier when he said the decision was wrong but not an apology. Apologies were for occasions such as forgetting a wife's birthday or an MP caught in a sex scandal, not for public servants implementing government policy. One adjusted the approach, not indulged the vanity of a putative aggrieved. "We had hoped to bring him back into the fold so there would have been no need to advise you of his possible involvement with the CTs." Oldham thought it a feeble justification but had no grounds to challenge it. "Now we need to address the present situation." Oldham thought Godden spoke from a memorised written brief. "What I am going to say is for you only and I ask that you do not discuss it with anyone, *even* the DO." Oldham nodded. "There is conflict between the political faction, the commissars and the armed wing. You might be surprised that it is the political boys who are pushing for an attack. The militants use Shala and the surrounding area as a sort of R and R area, also for dumping weapons and stores as well as recruits in transit from their training camps north of the border to other areas. We could waste time and resources mounting search operations but unlikely to find much, if anything. Inspector Khan was right about searching for the motorcycle and weapon. Besides, the weapons and stores are not important because they can always be replaced."

"I understand." The soldier was hooked.

"We have been able to monitor some of the fighters in and out of Shala, which has resulted in some success in other areas without disabusing the military leaders of their belief that here is a safe haven, a base for them. The military don't want that to change. They know an armed attack, especially on the plantation and possibly resulting in the death of some whites, would lead to a major security crackdown."

"Whites including women have been murdered in other areas—"

"I know but you need to understand that Hockin is highly thought of in the capital…not because he's a nice guy." A sardonic smile. "He is a nice guy…but his plantation is considered the best run in the country with the best conditions for the workers, an example to other plantation owners. An enlightened, colonial tuan." An ironic smile led Oldham to suspect that Godden did not approve of or did not like Hockin. He surmised school jealousy.

"Though, according to Sergeant Knight, he is not the largest employer and the logging and textile industries are more important to the local economy."

"That's right but he is a visible symbol of British imperialism, not the hidden imperialism of capitalism. He does have some admirers…supporters amongst the locals because of some act of altruism a couple of years ago. That old fool Raza—you know about him?"

"I know of him but have never met him."

"He tells all who will listen that Hockin is a good man. Not really helpful to Hockin because it makes the commissars more determined to kill him."

"Kill him?"

"Well, destroy the plantation…but I think they would like to kill him…well, some would." Godden realised he had misspoken but hoped Oldham would not realise the import and immediately changed the subject. "But Baru is the real target…not to kill him…but as I told you before, if Baru can't protect his own town and people, then they might turn to the communists."

"Why not the other fellow? Jafar?"

"Onn bin Jafar. He is seen as being for the bumiputras and a bit too keen on Islamic law being applied. The Chinese and Indians will not support him."

"I understand. So what's the state of play at the moment?"

"The armed band is possibly on our side of the border waiting for a decision. We could try to locate them and mount an attack including airstrikes but it suits us to have Shala violence-free like a no man's land."

Oldham wondered who the 'us' were but asked, "What's your assessment of the outcome? Who will win?"

"The commissars. Like ours, they hold the purse strings. Their backers, not just the Chinese and Russians but some business people in the country, will deal only with them. If the military faction don't play ball, they can cut off supplies and money. Could leave them starving in their jungle bases."

"So there will be an attack?" A plan was originating in his mind.

"We think so, and we should be able to give you warning once they are on the move."

"How much?"

"Could be just a few hours, maybe less. That's why we want you to be close to the plantation." This caused Oldham to think his plan was viable. "Another reason is if we hit them away from the plantation, they will claim that wasn't their target and we would be back to square one. But this time, we might not have knowledge of the attack. We need to hit them close to Hockin's place to demonstrate that we can protect it and hopefully it will stiffen support for Baru."

"What happens if they attack somewhere else?"

"Chance we need to take. If they attack and destroy a logging camp, well, so what! There are plenty of trees in this country. As I said, Hockin is a symbol both of the Brits and also Baru. They got on well though I think the relationship has cooled."

"Knight and I are both concerned about the convent, especially because of its proximity to the plantation and area Z. It's not just the nuns, there are a couple of English females working there."

"Do you think they would attack there?"

"Why not, especially if they are frustrated in an attack on the plantation. It's an easy target and certainly would cause widespread fear and panic."

"Have you been up there?"

"No, but Knight has. They are not too well disposed towards us."

"No. They are in a difficult position in trying to provide services to area Z, which is where the CTs get most of their support. I understand my predecessor used to spend time up there. He is Irish and now my boss. I proposed cutting off their government funding to bring them to heel but the DO wouldn't agree." Oldham thought it could not possibly be within the remit of a Special Branch officer to make such a proposal until he remembered his CO's warning that Godden had the ear of senior officials both here and in London. "Think he was convinced by Tom Alston. He's a quiet but determined man as you saw today...probably the only principled man in Shala." He paused. "And as you know, principles, moral qualms, are impediments in our business." Oldham did not share that view. He was an officer and a gentleman who, though it might be considered old-fashioned, adhered to the ideas of honour and duty, suspending his warming to Godden

"Maybe you should go up and see if the shooting had had any impact on the holy sisters?"

"Probably better if Knight goes."

"If you think so."

"Can we just clarify matters so there are no misunderstandings?"

"Go ahead."

"You want me to continue standing patrols, ambushes around the plantation?"

"Yes." Oldham was writing down Godden's instructions.

"The only problem is Hockin is resistant to soldiers on the plantation. It's not a problem during daylight hours but need to be closer to the house at night."

"I will speak to him. You need to cover the river."

"Doing that. An obvious approach."

"Good. I would like you if possible to give some protection to the convent."

One moment he wants to cut their funding, now he wants to protect them. "The OP overlooks it but will look at putting a standing patrol near it." His plan could incorporate some protection for the convent. "I am running out of men so Bendixson's proposal for the quarters." He did not tell him that on arrival, he and his sergeants had considered ways of forming another infantry section.

"Ah! I would like to see that happen. I know the station overlooks it but I would like to see soldiers there on a permanent basis. It's an obvious target...and I would like, William, if your guys could be responsible for the protection of Miss Croxham, the journalist. She's high-profile not just because of her job but her family."

"Never heard of her before."

"Don't feel too bad. I hadn't until I came out here but she is well respected in Southeast Asia. I wouldn't want anything to happen to her. She could be helpful. Can't leave her safety to Hockin. And if he objects, I'll go to HE." They agreed that once Oldham had discussed matters with his sergeants, who were waiting outside his door in the police ops room, they would reconvene with

Bendixson. "However, if you think you don't have the manpower, I would appreciate if you speak to me first."

Oldham said, "I will need to clear this with my CO."

"Of course, but if you need more men, I'll see what I can do. I'm not leaving until tomorrow. I'm having supper with the DO and Bendixson tonight. Are you coming along?"

"No. Not invited."

This was the first time that Oldham had ever had such a detailed briefing from a Branch officer, or any intelligence official. Usually, the tasking Branch officer would give details of location, timings, numbers and weapons though never once had the target turned up. Godden had painted a picture akin to the army's measuring of distances: the rear—the planning of the terrorists with the machinations of the different factions, the middle—the armed gang waiting on the border and in the near ground—an ambush of the terrorists near Hockin's home. He felt though there had been lectures on it, he now understood the interaction between politicians, police and army in this type of conflict. The buoyed up and enlightened officer beckoned his sergeants in. What Godden had left out was that Oldham might not even make it onto the canvas and if he did, it would be as a small figure in the bottom left-hand corner.

Knight had briefed Sergeant Williams on the meeting with the police. Oldham told the three sergeants that the platoon would assume responsibility for protecting London Crescent and Miss Croxham's safety, with Cpl Horrocks being responsible for the latter. Williams made a reference to the corporal's reputation, which Knight stated firmly was just malicious rumours with which Oldham agreed, then said, "Mind you, if it were true, I would love to see the looks on Sutch's and Bendixson's faces knowing…" He did not finish the inference but it was received with laughter even from Nash. They were interrupted by a call from Bendixson informing Oldham that his CO was on the secure telephone. He told the sergeants they would resume their discussion later and went to the chief inspector's office.

Bendixson handed him the telephone receiver and said he would leave him, closing the door to give Oldham privacy. "Yes, Colonel."

"I understand you have just had a meeting with the police on future ops."

"Colonel. Also had an interesting chat with Mr Godden."

"Well, what happened and have you come up with a plan?"

He informed him of Godden's update on the threat, the tasks the police have requested and his proposed plan. He expressed reservations about protecting London Crescent and the journalist. He could hear the CO jotting down notes. "Give me a moment while I have a quick word with the ops officer." There was an interval of nearly three minutes, which Oldham used to begin drafting his orders. "William, when do you propose to deploy?" He told him the next night if he could do a proper recce. Another intermission. "Sounds a good and workable plan. Go ahead." The CO anticipated his next question. "Think you need to protect our civvy friends and this journalist. Do you have sufficient men?" Oldham explained how he intended to form a section commanded by

Horrocks, those on light duties and from the detachments. "That should work. Horrocks should be able to handle that. A bit bolshie but a good man. I know you would probably prefer not to, but. There's always a *but* in these situations. If the bandits kill a couple of white women, especially this journalist, you know who will be blamed." He was surprised by the colonel using the term 'bandits' because the soldiers had been told to call them 'communist terrorists'. "Be in no doubt that our friends, both the civil servants and the police, would blame us. *The army refused to protect our pretty white girls!*" Oldham did not think he had ever heard the CO using such a caustic tone.

"Yes, Colonel."

"A few more points." It was not feasible because of the numbers and the ground to protect the convent though the CO said personally he would prefer to protect them than the pretty white girls but that was only because he was a Catholic but added quickly that he was joking. A company of the National Army was being deployed the next day to an unused camp about ten miles south of Shala. The Royal Engineers would provide a couple of sections to help make the camp habitable. It would be a few days before the company would be operational and initially would patrol up to but not in Shala. "The police have not been informed yet but likely the DO will receive the signal tonight or tomorrow." Oldham smiled, thinking that first time he had known something before the police. The CO informed him that the company commanders of the replacement battalion were arriving for a recce but he would do his best to keep them away from him. If need be, Knight could brief them.

Oldham realised that it was only four weeks to the end of the battalion's tour. There was also going to be a visit by a colonel, a staff officer at Jungle Warfare School. Oldham groaned inwardly. "He gave us a couple of lectures at JWS." Oldham remembered the tall, red-haired officer from a Scottish regiment who had been surprisingly knowledgeable and interesting though had seemed rather austere with an Oxbridge accent. Oldham knew from his time at Sandhurst that most officers of Scottish battalions came from anglicised families and even those who didn't, spoke in a refined accent and were called 'posh jocks'.

"When is he coming up?"

"Not finalised. But William, no matter where you are, you must meet with him."

"Yes, Colonel." Another inward groan.

"Colonel Buchanan-Henderson is not a kinglehead. None of your sardonic remarks." The CO knew that he indulged Oldham but he considered him his best officer. He had not engaged in the silly antics of subalterns, and indeed he tended to avoid them. Oldham had a tough inner core that he felt most modern officers lacked. "Might go over the heads of most officers but not Buchanan-Henderson. He is liable to rip your tongue out." He had succeeded GBH as commander of a Federation company in Malaya.

"Yessir." Not the usual 'Colonel', Oldham almost coming to attention.

"Anything specific that would assist you?"

"Like some helicopter support."

"See what I can do. In the meantime, anything else, sort it out with the ops officer. Also send me a copy of your platoon orders."

"Yes, Colonel."

"Good luck."

"Thank you, Colonel."

He returned to finish briefing the sergeants on his plan. Nash stated there were five men on light duties but that would not prevent them doing static duties in London Crescent. Further, the platoon sergeant said that they did not have enough individual ration packs for a ten-day deployment and could have centralised cooking, which his platoon commander did not want because it caused too much noise and disruption. He told Nash the type of ammunition he wanted. He would hold an orders group the next day with the time to be confirmed and asked his sergeants to anticipate any problems as well as providing the solutions.

At the reconvened meeting with the police, only Bendixson and Godden being present, he outlined his proposed plan and confirmed that he would share with the police the protection of London Crescent as well as assuming responsibility for the safety of Miss Croxham. The police understood that protection could not be given to the convent but Oldham said he would ensure that the OP keep a watch on it and be ready to deploy if there was an attack. The police accepted that there would be no movement except by military vehicles on what they called the border road after 1700 hours. The police would deploy two Land Rovers and a total of eight police officers at the entrance to the plantation from the same time. The local populace would be informed that due to the recent incidents, the border road was out of bounds after 1700 to 0700 hours and anyone who needed to travel on it during the hours of darkness would be required to contact the police station for permission. In reply to Oldham's question, Bendixson stated that the locals did not tend to go into the forest on the other side of the border road; in fact, they were reluctant to go into the forest anywhere at any time. If they did, they would not stray far from roads or logging tracks. Bendixson agreed to remove his officers from the OP for the foreseeable future.

Oldham's final request was for a boat, the police having three small motorboats, to take him and his section commanders up the Kanu early the next morning to reconnoitre an ambush position and he would prefer no police officers on the boat. Bendixson suggested that it might be better if he arranged for Hockin to take him in his boat. The police tended not to go up the Kanu but Hockin did. Godden said that he had been fishing with him. Anyway, the police officers thought it would be best to brief Hockin on the plan, which was against the army officer's instinct and professionalism, though he agreed. Oldham was again surprised, more astounded, at the deference that the two of them showed to Hockin who did not own a huge plantation—though he was now aware of its political significance—and who did not seem to have any influence from what he saw or could gather in the capital. Bendixson said that he would arrange it and confirm either before he went to the DO's for dinner or would telephone from there. Oldham said that he did not have a prior social engagement and would wait in his office for the phone call. The caustic comment seemed to go over Bendixson's head but not Godden's who produced a neutral smile from his smile hangar. Oldham said that he wanted to leave before first light.

Chapter 16

Oldham was buoyant and confident on his return from the recce. He had found an ideal ambush position on the west bank about 120 metres from the bridge on the border road. It was just before the river curved to the right, the northeast, where an arrowhead-shaped feature jutted out, which was a perfect place for the cut-off/early warning group. The enemy boat would need to slow down to take the bend and then they would be in the killing area with his soldiers behind the raised bank. Hockin stopped the boat before the cut-off position and secured it to a tree, covering it with branches and foliage. Hockin had been concerned at cramming five soldiers into his boat and had been insistent that they sit where placed, especially going north as they cleared the bridge. They walked back to the selected ambush position, which on the ground was even better because there was a trench-like dip running from the spur for about thirty metres towards the bridge that would provide cover and protection to the ambush section, though heavy rain could cause flooding but that could be resolved by a drainage system. Corporal Hammond's section would initially mount the river ambush, instructing him to select firing positions that he would confirm once he had selected the positions for the other sections.

He left Hockin with Hammond and the others and walked around thirty metres in a straight line west from the river, hoping he was parallel to the border road. Oldham halted at two slight rises separated by another trench-like feature about thirty metres behind the ambush position where he could site his platoon HQ as well as a cooking and rest area. He left Corporal Price and his signaller at this spot for the latter to establish communications with the police station and the OP whilst the former—whose section would be responsible for the rear protection—identified firing and basha areas.

The officer with Corporal Lewis made a ninety-degree turn to their left walking forwards, thereby forming an L between the river and road, which was around 100 metres away. Oldham did not wish to break the tree-line and end up visible on the road. He was silently counting his steps; each soldier should know how many paces he takes over a hundred metres but the number changed depending on the nature and incline of the terrain though it was not an exact methodology. Oldham estimated that he was about around twenty metres from the road. Now, the two men were flat on the ground, crawling forwards, having to gently push away twigs and other foliage. He could see the grass verge lining the road. He took two twigs and leaned them in an inverted V against the tree to his right, then, having adopted a low half-crouch, began moving to their left.

After about ten metres, Oldham halted, glanced around and saw the tell-tale signs of a standing-patrol including the wrapper for hard-tack biscuits, which angered him. His soldiers had been told and trained to pick up everything, including cigarette ends, and carry it back to camp. Knight had been the instigator of this action. The captain and corporal had a short discussion selecting routes across the road to the plantation. Oldham picked up the wrapper, placed it in a pocket, made their way back to the tree marked with the inverted V and back to the selected platoon HQ position.

Meanwhile, Hockin sat with his back to a tree watching Hammond moving from left to right along the high bank, pausing every few steps to look over the bank or through gaps and sometimes aiming his weapon out towards the river. He thought he should have brought one of his revolvers, though he did not like carrying a weapon unlike Robertson, the school teacher, who seemed to revel in carrying guns and talking about them. The others returned and Oldham spent further time with Hammond and the other two section commanders, discussing the ambush position, selecting firing positions and also for the claymore mines. He began telling Hockin of his plan but the civilian was disinterested and seemed distracted. He asked him if there was anywhere they could ford the river so that they could get up to the OP. In response to Hockin, no, he had not seen the trees painted with large crosses, one on each bank just above the bridge. People could wade across the river there and boats had to stay exactly in the middle and that was why Hockin had been insistent on them remaining still on the route in. He would point them out to the officer on the way back.

Knight left for the convent after Oldham returned from his recce. The platoon commander was brimming with confidence and ideas. He confirmed he had found an ideal spot and that Knight did not need to attend his orders later in the day; nevertheless, they would have a chat before the platoon deployed. Eileen Kanna was adamant that she was not going to the convent, which suited Oldham because she could type up his platoon orders. He explained that the CO wanted a copy. It was unusual for a CO to want a copy of a platoon commander's orders but it was Shala. Soldiers tended to have an explanation for most things normally because of an individual, delay, loss of equipment or weather. Oldham and Knight had both reached the same conclusion: Shala.

Collins and Martin as usual accompanied Knight with a new member of the team, one of the privates on light duties. They had returned to carrying their personal weapons though Knight retained his sidearm. Sister Mary Spinola greeted him warmly. He was escorted into the same room, sat in the same chair and was grateful for a cup of tea without milk.

"No doubt you have heard of the recent shootings?"

"Yes."

"We are still concerned about your safety."

"Just mine?"

"Everybody's."

"It has upset the children. Of course, there are rumours."

"About what?"

"Their parents talk. Well, it has been said that the soldiers killed others and buried their bodies in the forest."

"What about the policeman who was shot!"

The nun sighed and said, "The reality is that there is not much sympathy for the police…especially down in Tengu. They can treat the people quite roughly." Ho's image came into his mind. "Of course, I'm sure many of them behave properly."

"At least, both the wounded men are receiving the same treatment." His tone was terse.

"I'm sorry." There was a short interval of silence.

"It will be different soon when they get independence and we'll be gone."

"Do you think so?" He shook his head and the nun smiled. "You are right. Independence will not change anything…just different, corrupt men abusing their power." She changed the subject. "What are you going to do after here?"

"After Shala? Another posting."

"And after the army?"

"I don't know. What about you?"

"After the army?" They laughed.

"After independence?"

She became serious. "I hope to go on teaching and helping as much as I can."

"What about home? Scotland?"

"Yes. But when I put on these garments, my home becomes where I am. Shala is my home." Her eyes told a different story. "I miss Scotland and my family. I haven't seen my family in seven years. Mother-General has promised me a holiday in Scotland when I leave here. God willing, if I am spared, I will see my family again." She looked towards the window. The soldier sensed in her a tinge of sadness, even regret. Turning back to Knight, she smiled and said, "You and I are the same in some ways. We both wear uniforms, do the bidding of others and are far from home." Knight admired her stoicism. "But yes. I hope to see Loch Lomond again. Have you ever been there?"

"No, Sister. I have never been to Scotland… Though I had a friend who told me the Highlands are God's own country. Someday I hope to go." A twinge of guilt. The Scots had never been one of his favourite races, always moaning and somebody else, usually the English, were to blame for their woes, though he did like McGraw from the platoon and he had met on training courses some Glaswegians who had all shared a biting, irrelevant sense of humour that he had enjoyed. He knew it was time to go. He advised her that the border road was out of bounds during the hours of darkness and required police permission to travel on it at night, though as expected, she said that they did not use it. He reminded her if the nuns had any concerns about their safety, they should contact the police; he knew they would not. He pondered whether his visit had been necessary but the short time there had been calming, a retreat from Shala for a brief time.

After his brief discussion with Knight, Oldham had written his platoon orders and given them to Eileen Kanna to type. Afterwards, he went to find his platoon sergeant. Oldham's manner was brisk, confirming ammunition and rations, and telling Nash to get onto the CSM for more individual ration packs; notwithstanding he did not consider the lack of individual 24-hour ration packs a major problem. The soldiers took the minimum from the packs, such as hard tack biscuits, tea, coffee sachets, chocolate bars, curry powder, tins of sardines, water and usually noodles, which the soldiers preferred because the packets were lighter. Weight was always a consideration for the soldiers because as well as rations, they had to carry their weapon that for most was the SLR with four full magazines together with extra ammunition for the machine guns, claymore mines, trip flares, radio batteries, hexamine blocks for cooking, a change of clothing including extra socks. Thankfully, they had been issued with Australian lightweight groundsheets, which could be used for their bashas. Many of the soldiers had bought American or Australian boots, webbing and packs, in particular the American A frame pack, in Singapore. Wearing non-standard uniform was acceptable when deployed. However, Oldham did not consider weight would be a problem because resupply would be possible using the OP. He returned to make some changes to his orders only to be told by Eileen that she had trouble reading his writing, which was almost as bad as Knight's. She suggested that it would be quicker if he dictated his orders while she typed. It was.

On completion, he went to the OP to issue orders to Corporal Jubb and re-familiarise himself with what the OP could see and note the dead ground. With Jubb, he sited the claymore mines, when to use the searchlight and cut a hole in the perimeter fence at the back so that he could come to the OP from the ambush site without using the gate that faced the convent. After that, he gave Horrocks his orders for London Crescent and that he was to personally escort Miss Croxham throughout her visit. He would have one of the chefs in the house to cook for his section. One of the two Land Rovers was to be a permanent block at the north end of the Crescent whilst the other was to be used for transporting the journalist. Oldham agreed that Horrocks should drive that Land Rover so the lady was not stuck in the back. His final comment to the corporal was that he was not to have any parties. Horrocks was unsure whether he was serious.

Knight's vehicle returned to the station and as arranged, collected Eileen Kanna to make the short trip into the square, parking the vehicle close to Raza. Eileen greeted him and introduced Knight who said that they must have a chat sometime.

"But always with a beer." Raza grinned.

"Always," Knight retorted, knowing it was an odd reply. Knight and Eileen, accompanied by the new addition to their team, walked to and entered the *Golden Eagle* whilst Collins and Martin remained at the vehicle on alert, though there were two police Land Rovers at opposite ends of the square, their occupants lolling around outside the vehicles. In the bar, they exchanged greetings only with the mama-san whilst Eileen had a coke. Jerome was not in so Eileen left the money for her coke and they left, walking back towards the vehicle.

As they approached the vehicle, they heard the mama-san calling, "Miss, miss, you forgot your change." She pushed a dollar note into Eileen's right hand who had the composure to thank her, then stuffed the note into her bag without looking at it. Knight was astonished at her coolness in assessing the situation immediately. They returned to the police station without discussing what had happened. The others were told to go for lunch and the remaining two walked slowly up the stairs into their office.

Knight sat at his desk with Eileen on the seat opposite. She removed the dollar note folded in four, unfolded it and disgorged a smaller piece of cream-coloured paper. She read it then passed it to Knight to read. He looked up at Eileen and then down for a second read. The writing was in English and mostly in capital letters by an apparently unsteady hand probably caused by nervousness, possibly fear: *BARU in SPOKE TO JER THINK. Day HO in WITh NIGHT THINk.* He passed it back to Eileen and asked her to read it.

"Baru in spoke to jer think. Day Ho in with night think." She laid the piece of paper flat on the desk. "I don't think there is any doubt. Baru was in the bar and spoke to Jerome…well, at least she thinks he spoke to him. And the day you were in there with Ho. When was that?"

"Should be in the log." She went to her desk, unlocked her bottom right-hand drawer, removed a file and flicked through it. "Here it is." She returned to the chair at Knight's desk, placed the open file in front of him and sat down.

"The day of Bendixson's cocktail party. When we found out about Baru. Think in my report, I said about Jerome leaving in a sulk."

"Will I get the report?"

"No need." He looked at the note again. "By the way, why did you not mention young Baru to me?"

She was now behind her own desk about to type up and log the report. She looked over the typewriter at him, smiling. "I told you that Sutch told me not to disclose anything." He nodded his head in understanding. "Anyway, I thought a sharp guy like you would find out, especially as the expats can't keep their mouths shut."

"I did, twice, but failed to recognise what I was being told. I got my Barus mixed up. Not so sharp." He laughed. "Old mama-san is taking a risk. I assumed she was likely to be passing stuff to the other side."

"More likely she is but maybe insurance. Can never be certain in these situations. Possible she doesn't like Baru."

"How do you know that?"

"My aunt told me never to be surprised. You are not very good at this intelligence business." She teased him.

"Your aunt?"

"I told you." He shook his head. "Oh. She was a spy. In the SOE…you know about them?"

"Yes."

"And in Malaya during the Emergency."

"You said about not liking Baru. Young Baru not being popular was mentioned at the party. Think it's in my report."

"You might be good at this intelligence business!" She was mocking him.

"I'm a simple, infantry soldier."

"Thought that was the essential requirement for an infantry soldier."

He shook his head in mock disgust, then asked, "How come you could be so calm and collected when mama-san gave you the note?"

"Aunt again. Told me not to show surprise at the unexpected or something like that."

"Seems quite a woman."

"She is. She's married to a vicar. You would get on with her. Neither of you are impressed by someone's status."

"What do you think we should do with this?"

"I suspect you have decided."

"Yes. Need to speak to Captain Oldham first. Then our man." He picked up mama-san's note. "You better log and secure this."

"Right. Then I'll do the report." Knight picked up the telephone receiver.

The platoon—apart from those allocated to London Crescent, Knight's team and Horrocks who was manning the ops room—was in their accommodation waiting for orders. Oldham decided to give orders to the platoon rather than just the section commanders. He was intercepted by Bendixson outside the accommodation block. As he began to speak, he was drowned out by the sound of helicopters that was growing louder. They moved to the side of the police station to have a better view. There were four helicopters, a Belvedere and three Wessex, which were just south of the town, now curving to the east, and one of the Wessex broke formation losing height and seemingly going to land on the eastern side of Shala. "Think they were dropping supplies. There is a National Army company being sent to Numa. It's…" He realised there was no need to shout as the sound faded. "They are putting a company in an old camp about ten miles south of here. There are some Royal Engineers coming with them to get the camp up and running. Using the helicopters to bring in the material will speed it up." Oldham thought it was Royal Navy marking on two of the Wessex but did not mention it to the policeman. "Don't worry, they will not be coming into Shala for the present. Just patrolling up to the outskirts. There is going to be a coordinating meeting with them when they are ready to start patrolling, which I think will not be for another few days."

Oldham did not disclose that he knew of the deployment but not of the helicopter support though he recalled the CO's reply to his request for air-support. Bendixson continued, "I have just come to tell you that the lady journalist will not be arriving tonight so your men can stand down."

Oldham thought for a moment, then said, "I would prefer they still move in tonight so that they can set up and iron out any potential problems."

"Right. I'll tell Ho it's going ahead as planned. He will sign over the keys and check the inventory. It should be the accommodation walla from the DO's but the less people who know of it, the better."

Oldham refrained from pointing out that people would know once they saw the two army Land Rovers blocking one end of the Crescent and armed soldiers patrolling. He was eager to get on with his orders group and didn't bother to ask why Miss Croxham was not arriving that night but did ask, "Are you coming in to hear my orders?"

"No, no. Sorry. Off up to tell Tony Hockin that she won't be arriving tonight. She's having dinner with HE. The helicopter was picking up the DO and his wife who're attending. High-powered dinner with the commissioner and the army commander."

Oldham was thinking, *As if I am really interested*, but asked, "Could you not just phone?"

"No, no. Better in person. Probably need to pacify him." Oldham shrugged and walked away.

Chapter 17

"Orders."

He held the long wooden pointer in his left hand, which Nash had obtained, standing over the model on the floor. "Ground!" He explained the ground, pointing to the model and indicating the relevant features including the river, the bridge, the border road, the plantation. "Situation! Enemy forces. A group of armed communist terrorists, CTs, estimated at about ten to twelve, moving from the border to launch an attack on the plantation. Here." Using the pointer to indicate the movement from the border to the plantation. "We have no information on their weapons but probably the usual mix of AKs and other Eastern European weapons." He paused, allowing the section commanders to finish their notes. "Friendly forces. It's only us." He departed from his written orders. "A section under Corporal Horrocks, callsign 33 Golf, will be guarding the married quarters in London Crescent." Murmurs of 'lucky bastards'. "Our friends, the police, will be patrolling in the area during daylight hours. And will respond after contact to carry out their investigations." Another pause.

"Mission! To kill or capture the communist terrorists!" He looked slowly from left to right and then repeated, "To kill or capture the communist terrorists!"

He looked at his notes. "Execution. General outline. We will move from here by vehicle along the border road to a holding area in the jungle around here." He was indicating the route as he spoke. "Before last light, we will move off on foot just inside the tree-line. I will lead followed by one and two sections, platoon HQ and three section. One section will stop around here but will confirm on ground to set up an ambush and during hours of darkness, the ambush will be sited within the plantation near the big house. Remainder of platoon will move here, platoon HQ as well as a rest area. Two section will be responsible for the security of this area as well as supporting one section. Three section will mount an ambush along the west bank. Here. It's a perfect ambush position!" His enthusiasm was greeted with the same expressionless faces though there were a couple of smiles. "Four section in the OP will continue with its normal tasks but in addition can cover the road with machine gun fire and illumination. It will be used as a base for resupply if required. It will react to any attack on the convent. Here, just below the ambush site, the river can be forded. My intention, if necessary, is to use the OP for rest. I want minimum noise and movement. No cooking after last light. If the ambush is not sprung within the ten days and depending on the intelligence, we could extend our time in position. For withdrawal, I will give orders in situ."

He paused, observing his men, recognising the signs of disgruntlement.

His mentor at Sandhurst had told him the relationship between the commander and the commanded eventually broke down with the worn cliché applying—familiarity breeds contempt. Some relationships broke down at an early stage, some later. He understood that most of them had been with him for over two years and had been on this operational tour for almost a year. C Platoon had carried out more patrols and ambushes than any other platoon. Despite the insistence from Special Branch and army intelligence guys that the intelligence was good, they had never had a contact except for the shooting a few days ago, which had been a cock-up. He understood his men's attitude of 'heard it all before'. He felt the enthusiasm and confidence he had after his meeting with Godden ebbing away; nevertheless, as a good officer, he would crack on.

"Detailed tasks." He gave more specific instructions to each section and that the platoon's light mortar group of two men would be deployed to the OP so it could provide illumination being replaced by two of Jubb's section. Oldham continued giving details for timings, dress, medical, ammunition, feeding, laying communication cables, nicknames and code words. He emphasised that if the code word 'Ulster Fry' came over the radio, he must be told immediately even if he was sleeping.

He concluded, "Any questions?" Unusually, there were none.

"You needed to see me?"

Knight stood up. "Yessir."

Oldham said, "I need to speak to you." He sounded deflated. "Eileen, if you could excuse us?"

She stood up, picked up her bag, walked to the door, turned and said, "I'll go and wash my hair. " She ruffled her hair." For the big welcome drinks party."

Oldham, now seated in Eileen's chair, guffawed. "Wouldn't bother. She's not coming to Shala tonight. Dinner with HE. Don't think Hockin's too happy."

"Do you want me still to go?" Eileen asked.

Knight nodded. "Just in case he turns up. The team will be on stand-by. Just give me a call. I'll be here." He saw Oldham's puzzled expression. "That's what I want to talk to you about." He turned back to Eileen. "Have fun."

She clicked her tongue, smiling. "Always do. Leave you boys to compare the firepower of your personal weapons." She was gone, the door closing behind her.

Oldham, another puzzled look on his face, asked, "Was she being crude? Not very lady-like." Knight didn't respond. "She's a bit different from the others."

"Certainly is. But she's good."

"At…"

"Her job."

"You do like her. I know you… Anyway, what do you want to see me about?"

Knight leaned across his desk. "You better have a look at that." He passed to him mama-san's note, now in a plastic cover. He read it, glanced at Knight and read it again. "Jerome?" Knight narrated the circumstances of mama-san giving Eileen the note, including Eileen's composure and their assessment that it was the night of Bendixson's cocktail party "Hell. If this is true, he has committed an offence?" An agreeing nod from Knight. "You have not told the police? Your scouser mate?" An agreeing double shake of the head. "Why?"

"Want to be certain it's true before telling the police."

"How are you going to do that?"

"Confront him. We think he'll turn up at Hockin's place tonight and—"

Oldham interrupted, "Thought they don't get on. Remember their disagreement over Baru. And didn't Hockin sack him?"

"Still haven't been able to find out what really happened. But he turns up, especially if there is booze and food on offer. Got the Belhaven connection. You know the way it is with public school boys."

"I wouldn't call Belhaven a public school, more a public secondary modern. Anyway, why do you think he would confess to you?"

"I think he will want to tell me. People don't like to keep secrets."

"Why has he not told anyone?"

"Maybe he has or he's waiting for the right moment or right person."

"Why you?"

"When I first met him up in the convent, he told me without prompting about the Belhaven connection. I think he's a bit of a gossip. And I think he likes me. Well, that I'm OK."

"Right." Oldham leaned towards the other man. "Remind me. Is this not the guy who refuses certain free benefits?" He arched his eyebrows, angling his head to the left. "You better have Collins in with you. Have they made it legal yet?"

"I didn't go to public school." A smiling retort from Knight. "I'm banking on him not knowing that he has committed an offence. So may I proceed?"

"Of course. But if it's true, you'll need to tell Bendixson."

"Yessir." He took the note back from Oldham. "How are things? All set?"

Oldham, having been pumped up, the air of confidence was going out again. "I think I have lost the platoon." Knight sensed it was not appropriate for a quip such as 'your navigational skills were always crap'. Oldham wanted to tell someone his concerns about the platoon, which he did, telling Knight of the platoon's collective sullen attitude and in particular no questions at the end of orders, which was unusual for C Platoon.

He had come back from the recce full of energy and belief that the platoon was going to achieve its first kill, in most part because of Godden's briefing on which he admonished Knight that it was just between them. He couldn't tell the platoon of Godden's information and even if he had, he suspected the reaction would have been the same. "I know the men are tired because it has been a long and arduous tour. I know they have no faith in any intelligence." He paused with his look of irritation, looking down and tapping a few keys on the typewriter in front of him. "The sergeant major was probably right that I should have moved on." He saw Knight's surprise. "Nash told me."

Knight thought that was wrong of Nash to betray his CSM's confidence. Knight did not repeat what anyone told him in confidence about others unless it would have an effect operationally, concerned the mistreatment of soldiers or was dishonest. People did bitch about their subordinates or their superiors but Knight thought it was wrong to repeat it. The CSM on occasions expressed criticism of officers and also SNCOs in other companies, which Knight never repeated. It was also helpful in learning of the antics and behaviour of others, which influenced Knight in his dealings with them. Some he knew to be wary of and not to depend on.

Oldham was irate. "But did he tell anyone. No! The sergeant's mess is good at saying 'I told you so'. No fucking moral fibre!"

Knight was not prepared to let that pass, no matter how pissed off Oldham was. "Don't think the sergeants' mess has a monopoly in lack of moral fibre."

Oldham's eyes flashed in anger, then a nod of his head. "You're right. I'm sorry."

"When do you go?"

He looked at his watch. "About forty-five minutes."

"Lot of noise making weapons ready."

"Thought of that." He grinned. "Doing final inspection in the accommodation, straight onto the wagons and we'll make ready at the drop-off point with the noise of the four tonners covering it." Knight nodded. "I know everyone will know most of the soldiers have gone. No doubt the terrs will have people out looking for us. Hoping the helicopters continue, So we can dig some pits. I've told Williams and Groves to make sure there is plenty of vehicle movement even along the border road. Can you make sure they do?"

"Will do, sir."

"No doubt you and Miss Kanna will be taking a few spins. Never know what might happen." His infectious grin was restored fully.

"With Collins and Martin there." There was a brief period of silence.

"The police will use the code word 'Ulster Fry' when—if—they know the enemy are on the move towards us. I have told the guys that I must be told immediately. Also told Williams to let you know but I suggest you listen out for it. Think it's in tribute to Godden's boss and predecessor here."

"Ho seems to have a high opinion of him."

"You know, Bendixson thinks he's an alcoholic…suppose I would be if I had to work with him." Knight grinned. "Another thing. I wish you were coming. Our first… It seems unfair. I thought about asking the CO."

"Sensible not to."

"I'm leaving first with the section commanders and the guides. Will you come down and say a few *bon mots* to the boys as they get on the trucks?"

"You know I don't speak French."

Oldham stood up. "Forgot. U r from up north. Even English is difficult for you. Jist want me fags and me stout." A mock northern accent.

"French!"

Oldham smiled. "Time to put on my warrior face."

Knight was also standing and had put on his floppy hat. "The boys won't let you down." He held out his hand. "Good luck, sir."

They shook hands. "Thanks." Knight saluted Oldham who was half-turned towards the door and who returned it with a slight wave of his right hand.

Chapter 18

Thirty-five minutes after leaving the police station to pick him up, Jerome was sitting across from Knight who had instructed Collins to play it low-key, not insisting but asking Jerome to come to the station because Sergeant Knight would like a chat. When asked what the chat was about, the Welshman shrugged saying he wasn't important enough to be told.

"How are things at Tony's?"

"He's not happy. Expected to see you there."

"I knew the guest of honour was not going to be there."

"Think he's rather taken with this young lady. He was going to bed when I left. No doubt the others will stay on to eat his food and drink his booze." He paused and changed the subject. "I hear you were up at the convent today."

"Yes. We're concerned about their security."

"Think the good sisters are safe. They have nothing to fear."

"You can guarantee their safety," Knight said in a jestful way.

"No, I meant—"

Knight interrupted, "I've been going through some reports, mainly about Baru, Shi Baru. The shooting of the policeman, the guy with the knife at the plantation…well, Baru seems to have been involved, possibly behind them. Of course, I can't tell you our information or the sources but …well, Eddie, I'm asking you to take my word. I'm not asking you to betray him but help us build up a picture of his character." Jerome was struck by the sincerity in the other man's voice. When the soldiers had arrived at the plantation, he was convinced that they knew about his meeting with Baru. From the plantation to the station, despite the soldiers' relaxed attitude, there had been a gnawing pain inside, fear. Now, he relaxed. "We know it's sometime since you've have seen him." An opportunity to come clean. "But try to remember. Please." Knight was looking at the wall to his left and not at Jerome.

Jerome shook his head, adhering to his position. "It's so long ago."

Knight, still looking to his left, said, "You're lying." Turned to stare hard at Jerome who was visibly jolted. "We know that you saw him the night of Bendixson's cocktail party." Though he could not be certain it was that night. "When you left, you were angry." His tone was still curt. Jerome was panicking whilst speculating that they had followed him. "Did you go see him?"

"No, no."

"Met him in the *Golden Eagle*." It was not a question.

Jerome felt tricked as if it was a scene from a film. Was it really him there! His heartbeat increased and he tried to create some coherent thoughts. "Do you still deny meeting him? Possibly you are helping him!"

Jerome sprung up, his fists clenched by his sides. "No. But I would not sink as low as to help anyone or do anything that might cause bloodshed."

"No?" Knight arched his eyebrows.

"Don't be so bloody smug!" Jerome did not recognise this Knight.

"Sit down!" Knight was looking up at Jerome whose mouth was twitching. "Sit down." Slow and deliberate.

He sat down. "You asked me to believe your word. Now I'm asking you to believe me that I offered him no support."

"Was he armed?" Jerome nodded. "What type of weapon?"

"Does it matter? I—"

"Yes, it does!"

Jerome sighed. "It was the same type used by the British Army, 9 millimetre or something."

"You know, you could be charged for this." Jerome closed his eyes, wondering what the soldier wanted. "What did you discuss?"

"No. I've still got my integrity. He came to see me. We argued but I'm not going to betray someone's confidence."

Knight sprung up. "You what! It wasn't the confessional. Constable Abdul was shot with a nine mil." It had not been confirmed officially. His arms folded, legs apart, he looked down at Jerome.

"I'm sorry." He closed his eyes. "I'll tell...what I can remember." Knight sat down and picked up a pen. He did not interrupt Jerome as he related the details of meeting Baru, instead concentrated on making accurate notes. When the civilian was finished, the soldier asked a few questions to clarify some points. He reminded him that photographs could be doctored and that they might not have even been taken in the colony. He concluded the interview by saying, "Thanks. If you remember anything else, get back to me."

"I'm sorry. I'm prepared to take the consequences."

"That's a decision for the police."

"Can I ask you? Who told you? Was it Ho? He's always in there talking to mama-san."

Knight shook his head. "Can't tell you." He thought surely Jerome would know if Ho had been informed; he would then have been interviewed by the police. "Can I go now?"

"Yes. But I don't think you should go back to the *Golden Eagle*. It will get out that you have been here. They may think you have reported your meeting. I think you should stay somewhere else. I can organise something for you in London Crescent. Sure the Robertsons would give you a bed."

"No thanks. I have to take that chance. I don't want to risk anymore lives because of me." Knight was not referring to other people's lives.

"I can get you dropped off."

"No. It's OK. I prefer to walk." He stood up, went to the door and opened it.

"Keep in contact." Jerome nodded and left.

Knight reflected on the meeting. If Ho had been told, why had he not acted on it? Speculating on some possibilities including whether he could trust him, though he had always been positive about Jimmy Doherty. He had served in the British Army and there was no way in which he would work for the communists, though he recalled Eileen relaying her aunt's words of never being surprised. He decided as agreed that he would tell Ho first about Jerome. Knight realised that he did not have any sympathy for Jerome. It was fine having liberal thoughts on the evils of colonialism even though he tended to share them, having seen the disparities of wealth in Hong Kong and other places but he had a job to do. Liberal thoughts were fine in London but not in places where people used guns, especially against his soldiers. He picked up his pen to finish his report. He wished Eileen was there so she could type it up. No. He just wished that Eileen was there.

When told about Jerome, the soldier was unable to discern anything in Ho's speech or facial expression that indicated he knew already. Ho was impassive. The policeman made some notes and asked some questions, which made Knight think this was new information to him. "How did you find out?"

"Rather not say but it was given to Miss Kanna."

He smiled. "I will need to tell Bendixson and of course, Godden. We'll need to speak to Mister Jerome…and of course, the mama-san. She could be facing charges."

"Is that wise?"

"Maybe not. I'll speak to her and give her a friendly warning." Knight thought it was likely to be a rather harsh warning.

"Do you think he'll be charged?"

"Don't know. He could be useful. Bendixson would be against it. The DO could be the problem. He believes in everyone being equal before the law." He snorted. "Think it will depend on Godden's attitude. Some tea?"

"Yes. Thanks." Ho produced the tea from a large flask that sat on a small table beside the window. Each took a couple of sips of the tea.

"Didn't get much out of Tan Tse Chin," said Ho. "The man shot at the plantation."

"Right."

"Still a bit out of it because of the drugs. He didn't know the guy who had dropped him off at the bridge. Didn't think he was local and it was not Baru." Ho explained that the man on the motorcycle had suggested that Tan go back to the estate and ask for his job back. It was the end of the working day and Tan had walked from the bridge. He said that he spoke to a few workers but does not know where he got the knife. He went to the house, saw people there, panicked and ran away. He became disorientated. When the Land Rover lights were switched on, he raised his arm to cover his eyes, not to attack anyone, and he did not see the soldiers. The unknown man had told him that he would pick him up at the main entrance to the plantation.

"Would your guys not have stopped Tan on the way out?"

"No reason to. He was a worker finished for the day. They wouldn't have known he had been sacked a few days before…and being picked up by someone is not unusual. The motorcyclist, when he heard the shooting, probably thought best to get away. When our officer tried to stop him…well, if he had been found with a gun on him then he would have been for the drop."

Knight shook his head, his elbows on Ho's desk, his clasped hands forming an inverted V. "Odd. A guy you don't know advises you to go and ask for your job back. 'No problem. I'll drop you off and pick you up at the other end.'"

"I'm never surprised by what goes on here. We will be speaking to him again."

"Unless…" Knight unclenched his hands, with his right cupping his chin. "Let's accept it's true. He goes to see Hockin who does or doesn't give him his job back. More likely he would say need to discuss it with his foreman."

"Mehad. Someone I need to have a chat with. What about the knife? Go to ask for your job back carrying a large knife?"

"Yes." Knight pondered this factor. "Forget the knife for a moment. Say he asks for his job, no, decides not to for whatever reason and simply walks down to be picked up. What would the man on the motorbike do?"

"Ask him questions about what happened."

"And if he is a CT?"

"Ask him if he saw any security forces in the plantation." Ho looked at Knight. "Which he didn't have to because Tan was shot by the army, which confirmed soldiers on the plantation guarding Hockin."

"Even though it was just my team waiting to take me back." The police, apart from Godden and Bendixson, did not know about the standing patrol close to the plantation house. He was not about to tell Ho. Notwithstanding that Knight had sent Lance-corporal Mullen away and he had not been interviewed by the police, the enemy knew there were soldiers on the plantation. Even if a story could be spread that it was a pick-up party, it would not be believed and even if it was, it would be unthinkable that following the shooting of an armed man, there would be no soldiers on the plantation.

Undoubtedly, the communists would know from sources in the police—the officer in the room possibly—that it was only army in the OP, the border road was out of bounds during the hours of darkness except to the army who were now guarding London Crescent, and most of the soldiers had left the police station. It would not require much brainpower, and Shi Baru had an abundance, to come to the conclusion that it was most likely that the soldiers were in the forest between the border road and the border. The logical conclusion to Knight was that C Platoon were wasting their time but, and here was the catch 22, if they withdrew then Hockin was not being protected, though having refused an army escort, he would be an easy target driving around; a man on a motorcycle could take him out. He would have to inform Oldham of his assessment. He thought it rather surreal, a Mad Hatter's tea-party.

Ho was now standing. "I better go and tell Bendixson about Jerome as well as the probability that the bandits know that soldiers are guarding the plantation.

No doubt he'll pass it to Godden." He placed his hat on his head, taking time to ensure it was on correctly. He turned back to Knight and said, "I'll make sure he knows the information comes from you." A mischievous grin. "Don't want him to think that I am being malicious. He knows I have my doubts about Mr Jerome." He was halfway out the door. "Especially when it comes to girls."

Chapter 19

The journalist had accompanied the DO and his wife on their return to Shala in a Royal Navy helicopter. The helicopters were continuing to deliver material to the camp south of Shala, which was being refurbished for the National Army. Knight and others were surprised that the helicopters continued to Shala before turning east. It seemed a waste of time and fuel. It had been made clear to her by the Governor at his dinner that she must have a military escort at all times; otherwise, her press credentials would be revoked and she would be required to return to Hong Kong. She was told her father had thought it a sensible precaution. Croxham bridled at this attempt to restrict her movements and the use of her father, the diplomatic network. Men had been trying to put chains on her since school.

She had graduated from St Andrews with a second in English. She had abandoned her post-graduate course after three months and found employment with a woman's magazine in London, travelling around England interviewing various personalities in the fashion world whom she found dreary and boring like her life. Replying to an advert by a magazine for a features writer willing to travel, the magazine's editor was amazed when this young English girl with all the mannerisms of her class had appeared in his office in Rue des Dames in Batignolles, a communist leaning working-class area, which was a far cry from her upbringing in Kensington. The *L'Eitre* was a left leaning paper. The editor had refused initially to discuss the position with her but after heartfelt pleadings—without any tears—he had agreed to take her on probation for three months. She was given a feature to do on the aftermath of Algeria's War of Independence, particularly the effect on individuals.

She had travelled to Algeria speaking to individuals including politicians, former terrorists or freedom fighters, teachers and shopkeepers among others. On her return to France, she had sought out *pieds-noirs* and former French soldiers in bars and restaurants in Paris, Nice, around Rues Smollet and Beaumont and in Marseille's dangerous old town around Place de Lorette, Rues Saint-Antoine, du Panier and de Muettes. The former soldiers had displayed casual acceptance of the use of torture and willingness to commit atrocities, attitudes shared with their Algerian enemy. She had found an absolute hatred of Charles de Gaulle among many of the former soldiers and *pieds-noirs*. In a single sentence in her article, she had thought that there could be attacks on De Gaulle. Her editor had been stunned but delighted to find a female who could write a story about people without being schmaltzy. There had followed a few more stories but Jennie had finally gained acceptance and recognition following a feature on the death of President John F. Kennedy. Travelling mostly at her own expense, she went to Berlin, Addis Ababa, Nairobi and New Delhi to find out how ordinary people reacted to his death. She obtained a reputation for honesty and bluntness interwoven with understanding. Her father had expressed disquiet at her working for a left-wing, French magazine, though she had decided it was time to move on.

She had turned down offers from the *Economist* and *Time* as well as one from an elegant Englishman who had given her tea in the Raphael Hotel on Rue Kleber. He had been vague about the job on offer with her interest only being maintained because she had thought it was the actor Alec Guinness at the neighbouring table. Eventually, she had accepted a position with the *Far Eastern Economic Review* in Hong Kong. After six months, she had decided that she was not the right fit for the *Review* and went independent, though staying in Hong Kong, which she loved. She continued to provide features to Marcel, her former editor, on the embryonic home-grown fashion industry, though Hong Kong's reputation still was for cheap clothes and other goods. In addition, she provided articles on the attitudes in Hong Kong to the Vietnam War. She was aware that Marcel had connections with the Vietnamese community in Paris and she was trying to obtain the necessary accreditation to visit Vietnam. Shortly before leaving for Shala, she had received a telegram from Marcel informing her that it was likely she would be granted permission to enter Hanoi and she had to be ready to go on short notice.

Unlike other colleagues and contemporaries, she maintained a frugal lifestyle, renting initially a studio flat in To Kwa Wan near Kai Tak Airport and as her income rose, a still small two-bedroom flat off Hollywood Road, full of antiques shops, on Hong Kong Island. She avoided the hard-drinking culture associated with the expat journalists in Hong Kong but made sure that she attended as many receptions and functions hosted by the colonial and other governments as well as those by the business community. A respected journalist one evening in the Foreign Correspondents Club had steered her in the direction of Shala and the possible rift between the expected first leader on independence and his Oxford-educated son. His paper was not going to touch it at present because he sensed such a story might upset HMG and due to other circumstances, they could not offend HMG at present. Jennie thought that she might be getting sent on a wild goose chase but she felt that he, unlike most of the others would not shaft her, though there was always the possibility that there was no substance to the story and his information was wrong. She would take the chance. It certainly was not Algiers.

She had been annoyed—no, angered—by the polite insistence that instead of going to Shala, she would have dinner with HE, which would be attended by the police commissioner, the army commander, the Shala DO and their wives. Her escort was a Grenadier Captain who was HE's ADC. She found the food ghastly, the white wine warm and the conversation ludicrous. It could have been in Tunbridge Wells in that the natives, the ruled, were absent from the conversation:

146

the Governor rambled on about rearing pigs in Dorset; the commissioner, a very tall man from Galloway in the Scottish Borders, talked incessantly about his children who were at university and that his son had secured a job with a financial institution in Zurich; the rotund army commander spluttered, none of which Jennie understood; Sutch, who had impressed her on her first visit, said little of note and the ADC's sole role was to chortle like one of the Governor's pigs at attempts at humour by the Governor and the army commander.

The Governor's wife, whom Jennie had observed drinking a fair amount before and during the meal, asked to be excused before the pudding. There was sympathy from the men who rose as she withdrew whilst the other wives exchanged knowing glances. Jennie felt some sympathy for her in that alcohol seemed a sensible solution in order to endure her life. The journalist thought they were second—no, third-raters—sent to a colonial backwater and had fared badly against some of the officials she had met in Hong Kong, like Cowper who was dynamic and decisive. The two army officers like the ones she had encountered in Hong Kong were mostly polite and charming but did not impress as warriors compared to the tough, former French soldiers. She was glad to withdraw with the other ladies whilst the men had their brandy and cigars, or whatever they did in their closed world. During coffee, Mrs Police and Mrs Army complained about their allowances though it would be worse once they were back in England because of the socialist government, which caused both to speculate that they might have to find some suitable employment. Sutch's wife said almost nothing and Jennie had heard her say only yes, no, please, thank you, during the whole evening.

The journalist was thankful when she finally got to her room in the governor's guests' bungalow where the Sutches were spending the night. She fell asleep quickly but woke after a short time, feeling upset. She wondered what she was doing there and began to cry, which she had not done for a long time except sometimes when moved by a movie or a particularly fine piece of literature, but tonight it was because she was feeling sorry for herself. There was no story here and would catch the next flight back to Hong Kong, though she realised that she had not returned for the story. On her first visit, she had been surprised to find that she had liked Tony Hockin who did not fit her image of a colonial plantation owner. She found no evidence of a split between Chila Baru and his son with Tony saying that as far as he knew, the son was still in Oxford finishing his degree. The District Officer Sutch admitted that he had heard of it but was not aware of any evidence to substantiate it. All the Europeans dismissed the idea of conflict with the only one ambivalent being the Special Branch officer, Godden, who hinted at ongoing enquiries but in the context of the overall political situation. He reminded her of the elegant Englishman in the Raphael Hotel in Paris. On her final night of her first visit, Hockin had turned up at the government quarter where she was staying, telling her the story of an old woman. He had let slip that British soldiers were being deployed to Shala. She would keep to her plans and return to Shala but for personal reasons.

They were escorted by police vehicles to London Crescent where she was again sharing with Susan Cahill, the government nurse, whom she had found cold and hostile on her previous visit. She had noticed the soldiers and two army vehicles at the far end of the street. Susan Cahill confirmed that the army was guarding the quarters. The knock came as she had placed her case on the bed, and hearing her name being mentioned, she returned to the living room.

"Miss Croxham?"

"Yes."

"I'm Corporal John Horrocks." He had a grin on his face. She had been irritated by having to accept an escort, and her irritation was exacerbated by this confident, fair-haired soldier. "Your hair's rather long for the army? A hippie!" She felt foolish as soon as she said it and was about to apologise.

He pushed his hat to the back of his head. "I am. My bosses don't like me but they reckon I am good with this." He jerked his head towards the sub machine gun slung over his shoulder. He had refused the offer of an Armalite, preferring the Sterling SMG.

"Are you?"

"I hope I don't have to prove it…nor do you." He regretted saying it. "I'm in charge of your escort while you're here." Susan Cahill behind Jennie smiled. "I understand you are going up to Mr Hockin's place this evening. What time do you wish to leave, ma'am?" She was irritated at being called 'ma'am'.

"I would prefer you do not call me ma'am."

"Yes, miss." Exasperation but decided not to respond. "In forty minutes."

"Right. There's no need to rush back tonight. Seeing we are neighbours." She glanced at Susan who was nodding. "We're in number 9 where the wagons are." She nodded, turned to go back to her room as the corporal spoke to the other woman. "Susan, do you want a lift?" Her reply was that she was not going. Jennie sensed the soldier's attitude pleased Susan.

Knight, despite his reluctance, attended the delayed drinks party to welcome Jennie Croxham because it would seem unusual if he was not there and it was to enable Knight's report and assessment to be passed to Oldham, using the 'black cat' procedure that had been arranged using coded radio messages. He avoided the journalist, spoke briefly to Alston and his wife, then left. The evening for the journalist had been pleasant but she had not been able to speak to Hockin on his own and she felt she was being scrutinised.

The following day, she had visited the government clinic speaking to Dr Alston but made a point of speaking to the locally employed members of staff. She visited the convent, surprised that Sister Spinola knew of her work. During their discussions, the nun was frank, critical of the police and in particular their harsh treatment of those who lived in area Z as well as accusing them of being corrupt by taking bribes from the larger businesses but extorting from the hawkers and small traders. Bendixson was a pleasant man but Spinola doubted whether he knew or cared about the conduct of his officers. She praised Sutch and Hockin but they did not understand the community. They lived in a bubble. Alston was a good and decent man whom she admired but he, like most of the other whites, wanted to return home as soon as they could after or even before independence.

Spinola had had no dealings with the army except two visits by a sergeant who was the community liaison officer or something like that. She was aware that the army had concerns for their safety but she did not. The army was not that visible around Shala and most people presumed they were in the forests and protecting Hockin's plantation but the people remained frightened of the soldiers. The locals or certainly those in Kampong Tengu did not believe that the man shot had been armed and he had been removed to hospital in the capital so his family could not see him. The nun knew that it was Alston's decision to transfer him to the capital but the people believed what they wanted. Facts were not always relevant and could not compete with prejudices and perceptions. The journalist speculated whether the nun also was living in a bubble because most likely, her interactions were with the people in the shacks.

On the way back, they stopped in the square. She meandered around the square, aware of Horrocks a few paces behind her with another soldier further away to her left and slightly ahead of her. The Land Rover remained stationary outside the *Golden Eagle* bar. Horrocks had not made any more irritating comments, still calling her 'miss', which she could live with. She did admit to herself that he was professional and friendly towards the other soldiers, though there was no doubt who was in charge. She turned towards Horrocks as they were walking to the Land Rover. "Is that old Raza?" Her head indicated the old man to her left sitting at the edge of the square surrounded by children.

"It could be. I have heard of him but don't know him." He did not tell her that for most of his time, he had been in the police station manning a radio and it was only now as her escort commander that he was getting to see Shala.

"Shall we go over and talk to him?"

"I think it's best you speak to Sergeant Knight first."

"He's the liaison officer or something. That's probably sensible."

Jennie had refused his invitation to dinner because she had needed to write up on her visit so far and she had thought it impolite to ask if any of the other expats would be there. His home seemed to act as the British Club in Shala. She was not surprised when he turned up at her accommodation. Susan Cahill was at a bridge party at someone's house. She had not eaten yet. He would take her for dinner. She refused, saying she had a corporal who was required to escort her everywhere.

"Bet you have broken rules before! I'll take you around this beautiful country, introduce you to Raza." He regretted mentioning him because her mind would now be back on work. "After seeing Raza, you can forget your work and I will take you to Jacques Bay where you can watch the most beautiful, spectacular sunset in the world and..." He smiled and held up his right hand, index finger extended. "It will only take me a few hours to drive you east to watch an equally spectacular, phenomenal sunrise." Her wistful expression encouraged him.

"And drink gin in the well-practised manner of the British Raj!"

His frown turned quickly into a smile. "You are mocking me. So what! What is wrong with being a colonial? I'm willing to carry the white man's burden…and most of my burdens are white men…and women."

She turned serious. "Is that not the most dangerous part of the colony." An assertion, not a question.

His usual jest punched out. "You'll be safe. Everyone knows I pay the communists protection money." He nodded his head, becoming sombre. "Yes, it would be stupid." The grin returned. "Always preferred the sunset…more romantic. But that's for tomorrow. First, dinner in the market, then tomorrow Raza and onto Jacques Bay." He looked at her. "The market is not the most salubrious dining room."

"I'll go and change. I won't be long."

"Take as long as you want. I'll still wait." She had closed the door to the bedroom.

The soldiers in London Crescent had given each other knowing looks when the couple came out. Hockin remarked sheepishly that they couldn't be more wrong. They turned left on London Crescent towards the road leading to the market with the powerful arc-lights shining out from the police station to their right. As they approached the market, Jennie took Hockin's hand, needing the confidence and security on seeing the people.

The market contained stalls, some covered and lit up by one or two bulbs that had been connected from the surrounding buildings with the connecting wires running overhead, creating a maze. Each stall had cookers mostly fuelled by gas cylinders, though a few had electric stoves not good for cooking but to heat tea and water. Again, each stall had its own dining area consisting of different sizes of metal and wooden tables, chairs and benches. It was not too busy and some stalls were more popular than others due to the quality of the food or the price. The locals sat at the tables of their chosen stalls, eating noodles and rice sometimes with meat and seafood and vegetable dishes and bottles of beer and soft drinks were spread liberally around as well as the ever-present tea or hot water.

"Tony. Are you sure?"

He gripped her hand tighter. "Don't worry." They were aware of the eyes on them and the hum of conversation lowered. He was known to most people but his regular eating there was in the past. Hockin guided her to a long table with benches. They sat at one end facing each other with two young men at the other end. The stallholder, the cook, an older Chinese man, came to them. "Good evening, tuan. What would you like?"

"Jennie?"

"I don't know. Is there a menu?"

"Will I just order?" He didn't wait for a reply. "We'll have a plate of fried prawns, some vegetables and two bowls of rice. And a large bottle of cold beer. Two glasses." He turned back to Jennie. "You don't mind the beer?" She shook her head in agreement. The cook thanked them and went to prepare the food. They sat in silence, observing their fellow diners whilst a young boy brought the beer, glasses, cutlery and napkins, actually toilet paper. There were a number of policemen patrolling the market in pairs and other obvious off-duty police officers, some with wives or girlfriends. The normality of the scene made Hockin consider the recent meeting in Bendixson's house about Shi Baru surreal.

"I'd not seen much evidence of the army today." She was prying. "Think they are hiding in the jungle."

"Thought you would be pleased about that. Are you not anti-army?"

"Why do you think that?"

"Somebody. Think our Scottish teacher said it. Probably read your stuff."

"But you haven't." She laughed. "Tony, I'm not against soldiers. They are like dentists, unpleasant necessities."

"Good description of Captain Oldham." She did not respond to a typical Hockin quip because of the two men sitting at a couple of tables behind Hockin whom she was sure were talking about them, which might be natural but she was alarmed by the coldness, even basic evil in their faces. She wished her moustachioed escort was there. A few minutes later, the food was placed in front of them, freshly cooked and hot. Jennie was surprised by the size and quality of the prawns.

"Good?"

"Excellent. I was just thinking that the food is almost as good as the Poor Man's Night club in Hong Kong." In response to Hockin's puzzled expression, she added, "It's— Have you never been to Hong Kong?"

"Been to Singapore a couple of times and KL. But here has everything I need. Want to go to the beach then Jacques Bay is not far away."

"Think you would like Hong Kong."

"Isn't there some trouble there? Rioting?"

"Not serious. They don't bother the gweilos. That's us. White ghosts."

"Have heard it used here sometimes by the Chinese. So you think Hong Kong is worth a visit?"

"Honkers—we call it that sometimes."

"I have heard that too."

"It's good and different from Singapore."

"When do you go back?"

"Not confirmed but probably a few days."

"I'll get the same flight." She shook her head but laughed at his impetuosity. "No. You're right. A couple of days later so you can write your story and cancel your appointments. That's settled." He ordered another beer to celebrate.

"Who do you usually come here with? One or all of those pretty girls?"

His smile faded. "No. Eddie and I used to come here after we had been on the sauce. In fact, this is the first time I have been here since Eddie left me." She noted mentally 'leaving him', not the plantation or quitting. She surmised that they had had a close relationship and must have cut a quite a dash, Hockin with his boyish grin and the more good-looking Jerome. "The girls never really wanted to mix with the locals." He was thoughtful for a moment. "Anyway, you didn't tell me how dinner went?"

151

"I thought I was in Tunbridge Wells. In fact, I wish I had been in Tunbridge Wells. The governor…HE…a small town bank manager who wants to breed pigs. Mrs HE, an alcoholic."

"She makes no effort to conceal it." Hockin knew of the lady's reputation.

"Sutch was quiet. I had been impressed with him the last time. The commissioner is a complete and utter bore. They are all second-rate. I'd rather not talk about them."

They finished eating, not speaking, and after Hockin paid the bill, they left, walking hand-in-hand back towards the police station. Jennie saw the two evil-faced men still in their seats but she did not spot Horrocks and another soldier sitting to the men's left but in another stall's area.

Horrocks had been alerted by the soldiers in London Crescent. Horrocks and the other soldier were now in civilian clothes, their shirts outside their trousers to conceal the Browning 9mm pistol each carried. They had alerted the patrolling police to their purpose, though at first, the police officers had not thought that with his long hair and drooping moustache, Horrocks was a soldier. He had made his companion wear a bandana to hide his short hair, more like hippies who had forgotten to get off at Goa. The corporal sensed a possible threat from the evil-faced men because of their sustained interest in Hockin and Jennie, and they also looked out of place because of their clothes and the pallor of their skin compared to the locals. Horrocks knew he could be wrong and that's why he did not ask the police to check their identity nor did he want to spoil Jennie's evening. They positioned themselves so that they could observe the front of the two men in order to be certain they were taking out money from a wallet or bag to pay the bill and not weapons. If they were armed, Horrocks was confident they could take them down with little risk to any bystanders. They shadowed Jennie back to her accommodation in London Crescent though Horrocks regretted not getting the police to check the identity of the two men. He would speak to her but not report her for breaking the rules; it was his stock-in-trade.

Chapter 20

Knight was later than normal. On his return from Hockin's, he had shared a couple of beers with the chef sergeant who was cooking now for a small number. He stopped at the ops room to check whether there were any messages from the platoon or battalion. Oldham had sent a coded message confirming he was going to remain in position for another few days at least. Knight thought that Oldham was probably happier out in the ulu even if it was possibly pointless. He was surprised to find Eileen Kanna at her desk poring over papers, making notes, her typewriter on the floor. She normally sauntered in about an hour after him, which did not bother Knight because she was flexible in her working hours, depending on what was required. Without looking up, she said, "I'll be with you in a moment." He realised that she was reading his report of the interview with Jerome. He sat down, placed his Armalite on a small table to his right, took off his belt, wrapped it around the holster and placed it on his desk to his right, then unclipping the stud fastener, he eased the weapon out slightly. He folded his arms flat on his desk waiting.

"I couldn't sleep last night. Your report on the position likely being compromised made sense but...some of the points from your debrief or interrogation of Jerome kept coming into my mind." She smiled. "So I got up early and came here expecting to see you."

"A couple of beers—"

"How was the party for the esteemed Miss Croxham? Never mind, I don't care." She picked up the report on Jerome. "Assuming that most of this is accurate. Of course, he could have forgotten something or deliberately concealed something. It's the question that I have been asking myself since working here... And I think you have been asking the same question?"

"Go on."

"Why would anyone want to kill Tony Hockin?" Knight's arms were now in the inverted V position, leaning forwards, listening. "I know that it's claimed that he is the wicked face of colonialism, British imperialism." She scoffed. "He's a pretty inconsequential figure. If they had wanted him dead, he's an easy target driving around on his own. His plantation is not very big compared to others in the colony. He does not employ many people here compared to logging and textiles."

"Which I have heard him acknowledging."

"What difference would it make if they killed him? A few upset people here and back home but someone would take over. Impact on HMG? None."

"In fact, he owns very little of the plantation. His uncles are the main owners." A quizzical look from Eileen. "Jerome told me. The first day I met him. He's a bit of a gossip."

"They could destroy, burn the plantation, but it would take time and effort. And of course, the security forces would just stand by and let them." She did derision perfectly. "They could destroy a lot more logging trucks in a single night, which would cause significantly more economic damage." Shaking her head, she leaned back in her chair. "He's just not important enough and would have little to no effect on HE or HMG."

"They all seemed to show great deference to him…even Sutch."

"Maybe they think he is important. That he is an obvious target though I think they just like his food and booze. He is a fun type—not my type—full of energy, though not so much now. But…" She picked up the report, turning to the numbered paragraphs already tabbed. "Baru was critical of the British Army with their disregard for human life because the locals are wogs."

"We are always targets but there has been a growing reluctance to take us on."

"He brought the photographs. I know they might not be genuine."

"You're not suggesting we have been lured into a position to be attacked. They would need a lot of men. And Oldham will have made sure the position is secure. They would be stupid and reckless. They are not the Vietcong."

"I agree. I want you to consider this though there are caveats. It's not verbatim, possibly not exactly in the order Baru said. We are relying on Jerome's memory."

When she was finished, he said. "So Sutch, Alston, even the good Sisters are the likely targets?" She nodded. "I'm really not any good at this business. I would be better off in the ulu with the platoon."

"So what next?"

"I think we need to speak to Jerome again. Can you draft an assessment?"

"Your name on it?"

"Of course!" Shared laughter.

Doctor Alston had finished his round of the wards. He had noticed the expressionless faces of his patients, their eyes showing a detachment, even coldness to him. Despite his efforts, he felt some resentment towards them, asking himself why they could not just be grateful for his efficient and effective care. He knew that he saw life mostly in black and white with some traces of grey but had never been able to understand the social and psychological nature of the Asian. He had worked hard and gained additional government funding for the clinic as well as for the services provided by the Holy Rosary Convent. His wife had never settled and kept begging him to return home to their families and friends. Being a government doctor in a colony was not as rewarding financially as some thought or claimed. He was aware that some of his contemporaries were earning much more money back in England. The Belhaven connection was a cul-de-sac. The nurse recently appointed as his secretary-cum-receptionist told him that Mr Jerome was waiting to see him.

Alston shook the other man's hand, taking in the unhealthy appearance of a friend once known for his zest and devotion to the good life. The Hockin-Jerome axis of *bonhomie*. Alston pondered briefly over the fact that a man could be so changed notwithstanding that it had nothing to do with him. He motioned for Jerome to take a scat and waited for him to sit before moving around his desk to sit down.

"How are you?"

"I don't know, Tom." He sounded weary. "I just seem to feel faint and sick these days. Maybe…it's nothing." He shrugged, followed by a nervous laugh. "Maybe I should see a quack."

Alston arched his eyebrows, resisting the temptation to tell Jerome what he really needed. "You don't look well. Are you still living in the *Golden Eagle*?" Though he knew he spent most of his time in the convent.

"Oh, sometimes but I'm mostly up at the convent."

"How is Sister Spinola? Not been up for a while." He did not want to discuss what the expats called 'the situation'. "I think what you need is an involvement with a job or a girl."

"Gawd, Tom, not—"

"Look!" He stood up, deciding to be frank. "There's nothing wrong with you except feeling sorry for yourself. No one is happy about the situation at the moment. We all wish we could go back to the old days." He walked around to the other side of the desk. "Eddie, why don't you go home?"

Jerome stood up, facing Alston. "I don't need a lecture. I came to see you as a doctor."

"No, you bloody well didn't. You're looking for sympathy, understanding. You think it's you against the world. We can't change anything here."

"Oh Christ!" He flopped back into his chair. "I'm sorry, Tom. I just don't know what to do. Can I tell you something in confidence?"

"Always is."

"It's not medical." Alston nodded. "You'll probably find out. No secrets here." He recounted his meeting with Baru and the resulting meeting with Knight.

"Have the police spoken to you?"

"Yes. That Staff Ho. He frightens me. Told me if I was approached by Baru or anyone who seemed connected to the terrorists to tell him immediately. Whether there would be any charges would likely be decided by the commissioner." He shook his head. "Bendixson didn't have the bottle to tell me."

Alston did not say anything, pondering how Jerome could be so foolish and irresponsible in not reporting the encounter and the seriousness of the offence that he did not think Jerome had fully grasped. He was astounded by Jerome's next suggestion.

"You know. I think if Baru, Sutch and Tony just sat down together then they could resolve things."

Alston laughed. "Maybe you could arrange a secret meeting."

Jerome said, "That's a good idea." Seemingly oblivious to the intended humour. "I think I might be able to make that work." He stood up, a return of enthusiasm. "Thanks."

"Eddie, I was joking." Jerome was gone. The receptionist noticed the difference in Jerome's demeanour. Was Alston really such a good doctor?

The 'good' doctor knew Jerome sometimes could be silly and impulsive but this had potentially grave consequences. He might not face any charges because Baru had come to him but the authorities could not ignore Jerome contacting terrorists, which could lead to a capital charge. He had to tell someone in order to protect Jerome from himself. Bendixson was not an option in that Jerome was likely to ignore him. Hockin, despite their history, would most likely help but at the present seemed totally besotted with the journalist. Knight? That was a possibility. He had been impressed by him on the few occasions they had met and Jerome thought that Knight had been sympathetic to him.

Knight agreed to see Alston immediately. He was concerned by the doctor's grave tone on the telephone. The doctor would come to the station but asked if Knight could meet him outside. Knight took him to a room in the empty soldiers' accommodation and listened. He agreed with Alston that the consequences for Jerome could be severe. He suggested going to his office so Alston could have some tea or coffee—he didn't say brew—while Knight gave it some thought. Knight knew that he, the army, had the power to detain Jerome for a period without charge, then release or hand him over to the police who would want to know why he had been detained. The Governor had the power to deport any civilian expat from the colony for security reasons without revealing the reasons to the individual. "Give me a moment." He knew what he intended to do was a risk. If he passed it up to Battalion, the CO would tell him to pass it to the police.

There was the usual "Enter!" when he knocked on Ho's door. He knew it could be a mistake, an error of judgment but he thought that by telling Ho first about the *Golden Eagle* incident, he might have banked some credit with the policeman. He told Ho about Jerome's proposed action but said it might just be talk, though Alston would not have come to him if the doctor had thought it was bravado. He told Ho that he planned to detain Jerome immediately and requested that the police not stop him. There was silence for a short time whilst Ho considered the matter. He opened his left leg desk cupboard and took out a phone, which he placed on his desk on his right side. Knight did not realise that Ho had a secure telephone in his office. "Don't tell the chief inspector!" He grinned. "He does know but it's not on his inventory. Refused to sign for it."

There seemed a long wait for it to be answered. "Thought for a moment no one was working." Pause. "Is Mr Godden there?" Pause. "Yes. I'll speak to him." He put his hand over the mouthpiece and said to Knight, "It's the boss, Jimmy Doherty." Removed his hand. "Sir." Knight thought it was swearing coming from the other end. "Jimmy. You know that report that came from our friends about that individual?" Pause. "Yes, him." Ho was laughing. "Comes from the same source who is with me now." Pause. Knight stood up to leave but Ho signalled him to sit down. "Well, it seems he wants another meeting with the same individual... He thinks he can resolve things if they all sit down. They are reasonable men." Alston or Knight had not mentioned 'reasonable men'. Ho covered the mouthpiece again. "Jimmy asks if he thinks he's in *Julius Caesar*. The play by Shakespeare?" Knight nodded. "He's thinking about it." Knight thought it was slightly odd that even on a secure telephone, they were talking in a sort of code. He wondered if Special Branch officers were trained not to use simple English.

In Special Branch HQ, Jimmy Doherty sat down, wondering how to play this. He did not mention it to the other officers in the room knowing sadly that he could not trust some of them. He thought, *Julius Caesar. Wasn't even funny*, then another thought, *You're a fucking idiot*. He picked up the handset. "Is our friend still there?" Pause. "How did he get it?" Pause. "He's OK. Right, this is how this is to be played. And get...what's his name?" Pause. "Who the fuck cares what his rank is. His first name?" Pause. "Right, tell Phil. And he's to handle this himself. Not some fucking public schoolboy officer. Tell him I'll clear it with his CO. Think he is the only fucking sensible army officer in this place. In fact, put Phil on." Pause.

"Phil. Jimmy Doherty here." He shook his head. "You don't have to fucking sir me. Probably heard of me?" Pause. "Probably all bad and true." Pause. "Excellent. Should be able to keep the doctor out of it. He'll also think he's not facing any charges. Now listen. Don't write anything down. This is what you are to do." Doherty gave his instructions in a slow, clear manner without swearing. "Repeat them back to me so I know you got them. I know most of you cabbages are thick. Especially the fucking infantry! Also so Ho knows what is going on." Pause. "Good. Keep Ho in the picture. My instructions will come via him, though I might speak to you direct." Pause. "Tell the good doctor that it's being dealt with and he should not tell anyone else. If our friend raises it with him again, then he should report back to you. OK." Pause. "Good man. Better speak to that fucking slope again." Pause. "I'll ensure Godden knows and you're not going over his head."

Returning to his office, Knight escorted Alston outside where he told him that the police would deal with it and not to worry. He should not tell anyone else because if it came out, the police would have to act so this was to protect Jerome, and not to discuss it with Jerome. "I won't." But if Jerome did tell him something, Knight would be grateful if he told only him. Alston appeared satisfied when he left. After Alston left, he told Eileen that it was better that she did not know for now what was going on and went to the ops room for them to track down Jerome. He was in the Holy Rosary Convent. Yes, he would be happy for Knight to come up to have a quick chat. Eileen told him that she would like to send the assessment report away as soon as possible and the DO's senior secretary was working late so Eileen could use their secure machine to send the report but only after Knight had spoken to Jerome in case there was a need for changes. They dropped Eileen off at the GAB on the way to the convent.

Jerome was in a jovial mood. The nuns and other staff were all busy so Jerome was in the parlour by himself. He was going to a dinner for Jennie Croxham. Hockin was sending one of his drivers to pick him up and might even spend the night. Knight was once more confused by their relationship. No, Knight was not going because he had work to do. Whilst the platoon was deployed, he did not think it right to socialise; anyway, Williams and he shared the watch-keeping duties during the silent hours. He slept on the camp bed in Oldham's office, telling the reliable signallers to wake him in the event of an incident. Knight suggested they go outside in case someone came in. Jerome understood. In response to a question on any expat being mentioned by name, Baru had, as far as he could recall, mentioned Hockin once and it had been fairly favourable. Sutch was mentioned representing the colonial administrators but was sure not Bendixson, but Baru's ire was directed at the police as well as the colonial government. Baru was very critical of the police. He added as was Sister Spinola whom Knight remembered had criticised the police in his presence. There had not been another approach by Baru. Tentatively, Knight suggested if there was another approach either directly or indirectly, then he could listen to what was said—if Baru was being reasonable and not indulging in a tirade against the British. But he must not offer any help or make any suggestions, which was necessary for his protection. Further, he should not initiate any contact. Jerome should report any approach of whatever kind only to Knight. He agreed without seeking reasons or asking any questions. Knight, unsure why, asked if Baru had said anything specifically about him, Jerome. He nodded and said, "He told me to go back home to England."

Knight thought it was sensible advice that Jerome should heed.

His visit to the OP refreshed and enthused Knight, thinking to himself that this is what he should be doing instead of playing silly games with…no…for Special Branch. He had been disconcerted on leaving the convent on the short drive up to the OP. He knew Corporal Jubb had a good reputation before joining the platoon, and after each visit, Oldham came backing raving about him. Jubb had established a good routine with lists detailing who was on stag either observing or security, resting, fatigues or cooking. It was too easy, when a section was on its own, to fall into a slapdash routine with meals taken when convenient or weapons not being maintained. It was not Jubb's way. They were outside on the flat roof. Jubb showed him the arcs for the two machine guns, where they had cut back some of the shrub to the north to give a better field of fire, the locations of the claymore mines but only out to the north and the gap in the fence for Oldham and others to enter without coming to the front.

Jubb was sceptical about the terrorists coming down the river to attack the plantation. Even with the ambushes, they could slip across the border road or come around through the jungle to the east of the OP without being spotted. A whole company of CTs could be hidden in the shanties beyond the convent. No wonder the DO had moved out of his house because there, he would have been a soft target. The task of keeping an eye, even reacting to an attack on the convent, was a tick in the box. If there was an attack, they would be gone before the army could react and most probably would have another group to fire on the soldiers as they deployed. In Sarawak, while they had manned the hilltop observation posts, the SAS and others would patrol right up to the border even across it to identify likely crossing points to hit the Indonesians there. The guys in his section were not complaining because they were better off in the OP with hot food, rest and being dry except manning the GPMGs when it rained, unlike the others sitting in the ulu. He was not complaining but it seemed all unreal. Knight spent time observing the surrounding area through binoculars and Jubb helped him locate the camp to the south being refurbished.

"Doesn't seem to be any choppers around today," said Knight.

"No, but if you come around here, sarge…" He guided Knight around the parapet until they were facing east. "See that ridge line to the east running north to south."

"The first one? Not too high?" He took the binoculars from his eyes and faced Jubb. "So?"

"Well, there are usually four choppers, three Wessex and a Belvedere. Some of the choppers are navy. A couple of times, two of the Wessex would drop down below the ridge line out of sight. The other two would remain above." A facial question from Knight. "I thought they might be landing. I thought it was strange so later when I heard the noise, I came up and the same thing happened. I told the boys to keep a look out for it. Only one reported it happening. They did it again yesterday but no choppers today so far."

Knight himself had thought it a rather odd return route and asked, "You think they were landing troops."

Jubb nodded. "According to my map, there is nothing there."

"How far is that rise?"

"About fifteen clicks."

Knight had initially resisted using 'click' for one kilometre but it was now common military jargon. "We can't be sure how many clicks beyond the high ground they landed if they did." He considered the possibility further. "How high or steep is it on the other side? My map is in the wagon."

"According to the map, a gentle climb but you can never be sure with these maps."

Knight grinned. "Don't I know that from experience." Jubb gave an empathic nod. "Even if it is another unit, might not be coming this way. There have been actual incidents to the east. Why didn't they land on this side of the ridge… Don't answer that. So they couldn't be seen except they didn't know about Jubb." Another grin. "So if at least six choppers landed, how many men?"

"Depends on how much they were carrying and for how long. If really loaded, about thirty."

Knight nodded in agreement. "Keep it to yourself for the moment. I'll make a few discreet enquiries." He thanked Jubb; he was seldom excessive in giving praise but did so when deserved. Oldham had said Jubb should be a sergeant though Knight considered that he had officer potential.

On the way to the GAB to meet Eileen Kanna, Knight felt flustered by two factors: the Branch's attitude towards Jerome and possibly another unit of soldiers coming into their area without their knowledge. His discussion with Eileen Kanna was brief in that his conversation with Jerome apparently confirmed her assessment. The assessment ended with:

It is assessed that Mr Tony Hockin or his plantation is not the likely target for the armed group of CTs sourced to be moving into our operational area.

Knight signed it. It would be with the battalion before the end of the day, passed up to the brigade who would decide whether it was passed to the police. Just before midnight, the ops room informed Knight that the CO would speak to him on the secure line at 0900 hours the next morning. He assumed that the CO had read the report. The CO also had a meeting with GBH.

Chapter 21

In his office, Doherty had opened a bottle of whiskey for his late-night meeting with Godden and GBH, with the former declining a drink. The latter usually took one small dram to appease the Head of Special Branch and as Doherty was pouring the drink passed a brown envelope to him. "Have you seen this?" Doherty put down the bottle and extracted the report, scanning it quickly, then shaking his head. "Thought not. Bob Marchant gave it to me at supper." Doherty read the report quickly and passed it to Godden.

"If we are lucky, we'll get our fucking copy tomorrow. I have been insistent that all reports, no matter the source, come to us immediately. HE is too friendly with the brigadier and my dickhead boss won't fight for it." GBH caught the disapproval on Godden's face at the remark about the police commissioner even while he was reading Knight's report. When finished, he passed it back to Doherty who pushed it back to GBH, who shook his head. "Keep it."

"Well, he is right," Godden said.

"You can tell it's not written by a professional intelligence guy." GBH looked at the two Branch officers with a slight smile. "It has a firm conclusion, no caveats, not like the drivel that comes from army intelligence, even some of the stuff from this office with your *maybe, possibly, on the other hand.*"

Doherty laughed. "Grievous, you're some man." Godden's laugh was more restrained.

"Did you get anything out of the man shot on Hockin's estate?"

"Yes, we did," replied Doherty. The sacked worker had been going to ask Hockin for his job back. The idea had been put in his head by a guy called Peng or Ping. He did not know him well and had only recently started to live in the shanties. "But Grievous, you could be living in the shanties for years and still never meet or know everyone. It's like fucking sardines." Doherty continued, stating that Peng or whatever his name had told him to keep an eye out for soldiers and he would pick him up at the main entrance. He would be on a motorbike. It had been his own decision to take a knife in case he met Mehad whom he hated and insisted that he had been sacked unfairly. He said that Mehad was extorting money from some of the workers, especially those living in the shanties, and was cheating Mr Hockin. "We're going to have words with Mehad after this. Think he's been playing for both sides." Doherty was inclined to believe the wounded man and wanted him relocated. He could be useful. It was another battle with the uniforms who wanted him charged so it would be a matter for the commissioner.

"What's happening at your end, Grievous?"

"First thing. I told Bob Marchant today. I know what we had agreed but with this report, I think circumstances have changed."

"Fair enough," Doherty said.

"And it's not gone to brigade yet. I managed to persuade him to sit on it for twenty-four hours. That's why I had to tell him about the op."

"Fair enough."

"They are his soldiers up there."

"You're right." Godden did not make any comments.

"Anyway, the boys are in a patrol base. They are just inside Bob's area so another reason to tell Bob Marchant. But they will need at least a full day to get to the ambush positions. That's only about eight hours of daylight so it would be better if two days. We need to get the trackers up close. And that's without anything unexpected happening. I'm ready to go up to Shala at any time."

"First class. Are you set to go, Arthur?"

"Yes. Bendixson is going to put me up. He can give you a room."

"No. I'll basha down in the station. They will have a bunk for me?"

"We'll make sure," Doherty said. He drank his whiskey and poured himself some more. "They haven't moved yet but I'm confident if all goes well... What?" The other two were smiling. "Fucksake!" He smiled. "I know. Professional. Anyway, I think there will be movement within the next couple of days."

"I hope so. The navy helicopters will be gone in a few days and I wanted to fly up. In fact, I will fly tomorrow afternoon so I had better arrange a briefing with Marchant." He paused and then said quietly, "It's been twenty-two or -three years since I was last there."

The two police officers looked at each other before Doherty said, "You never told me."

"Did I not? Must have slipped my mind. I'm just an old staff officer visiting old battlefields for my memoirs. If Mountbatten can do it so can I, though he will be staying with the general in Singapore." He turned to Godden and asked, "Do you want to come up with me? You'll need to be at HQ's LZ for 1400."

"Thanks. I will be."

"If the time slips, I'll let you know. I'll be taking my Royal Signals rear link detachment and their kit on the chopper so there will be limited space. What about you, Jimmy?"

"No. I have a man to see. Depending on what happens, I might need your boys again but it will be easier." There was silence for a couple of minutes with GBH and Godden making notes whilst Doherty staring ahead, seemingly lost in thought.

"You know, I think we missed a fucking trick with Baru. I think we should have encouraged that dickhead Jerome to keep in contact with Baru. And if he wasn't prepared to play ball, then we could have applied some pressure."

GBH sensed Godden's disapproval and asked, "Is he being charged?"

"Not yet. Probably not ever... The old boys' network will look after him! Won't they, Arthur!?" Godden knew it was pointless to respond. Doherty leaned forwards over his desk towards GBH. "The general-secretary or his assistant is likely to be close by to exploit politically their successful attack. He's probably sitting in the shanties at this moment with Baru, waiting like us. If I had been on the ball, we might have been able to lure them. Fuck...too late."

"What was your intention?" GBH asked.

"To deal with them. Remove them." The soldier had been aware of Godden's less than enthusiastic expression, obvious disapproval. "Arthur here was fucking queasy about it." Godden did not respond. "I would have used any opportunity to take these fuckers out!" GBH was also uneasy. He had assumed that because Doherty's information was so good, it had to come from someone near the top, a party official such as a general-secretary. He had even speculated that Baru was his source. Doherty laughed. "But I'll be gone soon."

"Have you decided where?"

"No. Possibly Hong Kong. Even private security work. It pays good."

"What about home?" Godden asked.

"No. I would..." He shook his head. "I would hunt down the fucking priest who killed my brother." He responded to the surprised inquisitiveness from the other two. "He didn't actually kill him but drove him to..." His eyes were welling up. "Wee Sean killed himself because he couldn't take anymore abuse...and he couldn't tell his ma and da because they wouldn't have believed a priest would do that." His accent was becoming broader. "But we all knew what the fucking priests were doing. But we kept silent." He took a drink of whiskey, not looking at the other two but at the memory. "We kept silent. The English and the fucking Prots were our enemies, not our own priests. Bastards!" He drank more whiskey. "That's why I became a peeler." He saw the surprise on both faces. "What! Think it was out of loyalty to Lizzie?" A snort. "I wanted to get justice for wee Sean...but the RUC weren't interested. The church helped keep the people in check, keep them down... And the fucking Prot ministers were doing the same to their kids...the scout leaders and them who ran the Life Boys. They were abusing them!" He poured more whiskey into his glass. "Arthur, you know that priest at the convent?"

Godden nodded. "McElroy?"

"He was his fucking brother. He denied it. Think he was messing about with the kids there but that old bitch covered for him. It wasn't until the Scotch nun came... She managed to get him removed..." He laughed but still tears. "Just as well because I was going to get him done by the terrs. I fucking was!" GBH was impassive but again, Godden showed disapproval. "That's your problem, Arthur. You're a good peeler but sometimes..." Another slurp of whiskey, his head shaking. "Sometimes...it's the only way to get justice." He was quiet, wiping his nose and eyes. "I'm sorry, Grievous. I'm a fucking wreck. Too long doing this... It corrupts you inside." He stuffed his handkerchief back into his right trouser pocket with no one speaking for a few minutes. "Anyway, Grievous. What about you? How long do you have left?"

163

"Like you, Jimmy, this is my last op. I really shouldn't be here but the brigadier agreed."

"That's so you take the blame if anything goes wrong."

"You could be right, Jimmy." He smiled. "I have decided to leave the army when I am finished in JWS. About six months."

"You're the best soldier I have ever met."

"Now out of date. No need for jungle fighters anymore. They want people who can command armoured brigades and divisions. I know nothing about that. Anyway, time for a change."

"What will you do? Where will you go?" Godden asked.

"To Glasgow first—"

Doherty laughed. "Glasgow! Went there a couple of times. It's wild. Are you not a laird from the Highlands with a big estate?"

"Sorry to disappoint you. Not anymore. My brother is in London and I have no more ties with home."

"So what will you do?" Godden again.

"Travel. There are places I want to go to." The image of Fi and him sprawling over maps and books in the library reeled through his mind.

"Fucking hell, Grievous. Have you not been to enough places?"

"This time I will not be looking for ambush positions and patrol bases. Nor looking at people and wondering if I will have to kill them, or them me." A gentle laugh. He stood up. "And I will prepare for my new life as a traveller by visiting the sites of Shala." He turned to Godden. "See you at the helipad." Then to Doherty. "Will I see you before I go?"

"Probably but just in case." They shook hands. "Good luck."

"Thanks. I am sure we will have one more drink together. Goodnight."

"I better go as well. Things to sort out."

"Okay, Arthur. I wish you could have seen him in Malaya. Unlike some of the others, he never said this is too difficult. He was always positive. Mind you, that didn't mean he wouldn't tell you if he thought something was crap but he always came up with solutions. He was the first officer I knew who took the time and trouble to understand what Branch was trying to do. First class!"

Godden had been queasy about the proposal to lure Baru into a trap using Eddie Jerome who was delicate and combustible. Had Doherty not read Knight's report that Baru had told him to go back home? Baru was not stupid and if Jerome had been sent back to Baru, it's likely he would have been murdered. Doherty backed off when Godden opposed it even though his superior knew the opportunity had already been lost.

Since arriving in the colony, Godden had been dismayed by the conduct of both the government and the expats. The colonial government made decisions without any real consultation with the locals over their future. To Godden, the expats were crass and dim, exploiting their status that most would not have obtained at home. They employed servants, though most did not even try to interact with them or any of the locals in order to understand their different cultural and social mores. He was guilty too but his was going to be a short stay in Southeast Asia. It would be for most of the expats once the Labour Government's plan was implemented; what some called scuttling but he thought was sensible, reflecting Britain's real standing and power in the world. He recalled an American friend, a diplomat in London, telling him that his boss in the State Department had opined that an insurgency was a political struggle with military elements, or words to that effect.

Godden considered that Shi Baru could be an effective ruler despite his anti-Britishness, which was likely to be softened by the realities of power. His Mr Ormsby had told him that it was unwise to view individuals as permanent enemies or friends. There was always the requirement to take a long-term view that Special Branch was supposed to do but Doherty had considered killing Baru. It was foolish but also potentially dangerous to the future stability of the colony and the new country. He thought Doherty was becoming paranoid. He spoke always in extremes: there was a bad Catholic priest so they were all bad. He was quarrelsome and Godden thought he could well be having a nervous breakdown, which would not be surprising considering the work. He did not understand the close relationship between his boss and the poised and restrained army officer. Again, Ormsby had told him never to be surprised by seemingly mismatched relationships. Godden pondered how GBH could remain so calm and in control if even half the stories he had heard about him were true.

Godden was from a working-class background and only his grandparents' savings had enabled him to attend Belhaven as well as a bursary from the school when his talents were recognised. He had attended the LSE, not exactly a breeding ground for colonial police officers. Just before he had graduated, he had been invited to have lunch with an old school friend in St Ermin's Hotel in Victoria. He was surprised because they had lost touch when the friend had gone up to Cambridge to read law. The friend gave some story about bumping into another mutual friend who had passed on his number. Godden had thought it was contrived but was interested and it would be a free meal.

They had sat not in the restaurant but in the cocktail bar in the lobby, served by a small, slim Italian waiter. Godden had, on his friend's recommendation, a club sandwich, which was very good and filling accompanied by a small beer. The conversation was obligatory about mutual school friends and life at their respective universities. Another man had appeared—almost middle aged, well-dressed in a pinstripe business suit like his school friend—and suddenly Godden had felt out of place in his cheap—but not to him—John Collier's jacket. It was a 'hello, good to see you' encounter, which again Godden thought manufactured. There were the introductions and the new man would have a drink but just a tea, Darjeeling. He asked in an effete voice the school friend about his parents and how Cambridge was, though it was lesser than Oxford, a smug smile to Godden. The school friend realised that he had to meet his mother and left abruptly with apologies. Godden thought that the friend, thinking they shared the same homosexual tendencies, was trying to organise an assignation with one of his older male friends. Godden, even though homosexuality was illegal, had thought it was amusing and decided to remain. They both watched as the friend walked down the steps from the entrance into the hotel's open courtyard, striding—no ambling, no poncing—towards Caxton Street. Another slim waiter, this time Irish, in the same attire of white, short jacket and black trousers as his colleague removed the plates and asked if they required anything else.

"A couple of whiskies." He looked to Godden for consent who nodded, though he did not really like whiskey.

"Particular brand, sir, Glenmorangie? Laphroig?" The waiter's voice was subservient.

"Your cheapest." A voice of authority unlike the earlier one. "Expenses aren't what they were." The waiter scuttled away, a small or no tip to come. "A poofter like the Italian one and your friend." He saw the curious look on Godden's face. "Our job to know these things. Can be useful. Apart from the obvious pressure point, for people who live in the shadows, they tend to be great gossips. The Windsors could not function without them." He said nothing further until after the waiter had brought the drinks and returned, now in a sullen mood, to behind the small rounded bar. "Arthur. May I call you that?" A nod from Godden. "I'm not going to play obtuse games as expected by my office. I am an officer in the Secret Intelligence Service. Ignorant people call us MI6."

"British?"

The man laughed. "Very good. My name is Simon Ormsby. My real name. Someone suggested that you might be a suitable candidate."

"Can I ask who?"

"Should be 'may' and 'whom'." Godden felt deflated as when his English teacher had corrected him on his poor grammar. "In our work, exactitude is essential." He smiled. "LSE and your left-wing tendencies may be considered obstacles."

Godden was hurt. "I consider myself—"

He held up his hand. "I have no doubt you are a loyal Englishman. Your father and your grandfather served in the army…with great distinction. The problem is that some in my office think that unless you went to Oxbridge…" He smiled again. "And we know how well we were served by some of those." A hard and cynical tone. "Would you be interested?"

"Yes…well, I'm—"

"Good. We don't need exactitude this time. I am always dubious of anyone who accepts without thought." He observed the confused young man for a moment. "I need to run this past my masters. I will contact you soon if that is acceptable to you?"

"Yes. Of course."

"We'll have another chat but probably not here." He signalled for the bill, paid it and said, "This is not Richard Hannay or James Bond stuff." Godden nodded but was still a little dazed, confused. "By the way, it was your physics master." Godden thought of his old, crusty physics master who had always insisted on exact experiments and calculations. "No need to mention this to him or anyone. I'll be in touch."

166

Godden sat for a time thinking about what had happened, even ordering another cheap whiskey to the Irish waiter's annoyance.

His next meeting with Ormsby was about a month later in a staged, unexpected encounter in Gower Street. The older man had suggested they take a walk and had ended up in a pub in Caledonia Road, which was frequented by prostitutes and hardened Irish and Scottish labourers. They had sat outside and Godden was glad that the older man had not been in his pinstripe suit, and in fact seemed to merge in well, unlike him who was an obvious student. It was not unexpected and in some ways a relief when he was told that he was not considered a suitable candidate at this stage; nevertheless, sometimes they used what Ormsby termed as unofficials. He thought a stint in a colonial police force might be helpful.

The SIS officer, despite his masters' disapproval, believed in cross-fertilisation in that experience in a colonial police force could be advantageous and could lead to employment by the Security Service. He had to explain to Godden the functions of the Security Service. He opposed the thinking that a member of the security service was not suited to his Service in that experience in catching spies was useful to people like him who recruited spies. There was a colony in Southeast Asia that was about to become independent but there was an insurgency that had to be defeated or at least contained before independence. Godden was surprised and elated that Ormsby did not know he had old school friends in the colony.

The next meeting had been in a pub near Waterloo Station. Godden had applied for and been accepted as a colonial police inspector though he was certain that Ormsby had ensured his acceptance. Ormsby was enthusiastic. He had no doubt that Godden would move up the chain of command quickly. Colonial police officers were not often very bright.

Although he would be a police officer observing the chain of command, he would report as required to the SIS station in Hong Kong. He was to be wary of the Special Branch because sometimes their officers could go rogue. The Governor, a limited man, would be told to take heed of Godden though he was never to have a one-on-one with HE. His advice to HE would come via HK. If all went well, he would join the Service. Godden was confused but found Ormsby's web exhilarating and his career had proceeded as Ormsby had predicted or arranged.

Chapter 22

The CO's telephone call to Knight had been delayed by two hours. Bendixson was reluctant to leave Knight in his office on his own. It was different when it was Captain Oldham but he was persuaded by Colonel Marchant saying he had to discuss personal matters with the sergeant. "Good morning, sir."

"Good morning, Sergeant Knight. Two good reports from you, especially the second one. Caused a bit of a stir with our friends."

"Thanks, sir, but it was actually Miss Kanna who wrote the threat one."

"Thought so. You're bright," he laughed, "but not that bright. Pass on my thanks to Miss Kanna."

"Will do, sir." Knight liked his CO's frankness.

"How are things going? Anything else to report?"

"Sir, I was up with Corporal Jubb at the OP." He told him of Jubb's sight of the helicopters apparently landing to the East of their operational area.

"Right. There's activity to your east. There is a colonel flying up this afternoon. Should be leaving here at 1400. Told Oldham about him but didn't know when then. Did he mention him?"

"No, sir."

"He's from Ulu Tiram. Ostensibly, he's coming up to update himself and to visit Shala because he was there during the war. Now listen, Knight. He's landing at the government helipad and being picked up by the police. He will have a copy of my orders for Oldham. There is an operation being mounted north of Oldham's position. Orders are going out by radio to Oldham as I speak. Got that?"

"Yessir." Knight was almost certain he knew this colonel.

"In addition, his sigs det need an FFR three quarter ton for the duration of his visit. You better have your mt guy there to sign it over." The CO also told him that he was to escort the visitor and other admin requirements.

"Yessir."

"As I told young Oldham, this guy is not a kinglehead. He's tough. He will be in overall command. Do what he tells you. No need to refer anything back to me. And don't you and Oldham think that the rest of us are doing nothing. Things are bubbling away here." Knight smiled. "I know you two think your platoon is the only one doing any operations."

"Sir."

"Any questions?"

"No, sir."

"Good. Now we are going to be leaving this place soon. What am I going to do with you? You could go to the depot but I think you rather not go. Am I right?"

"Yessir."

"Have a think about it. I should tell you but you probably know that some of the officers don't rate you. One or two of them could be the next COs."

"Sir."

"A wife on the horizon?"

"No, sir." Knight knew what he was referring to; in the army, especially in an infantry battalion, it was preferred that senior NCOs were married, which denoted stability and expunged doubts about sexual preferences. The same applied to officers who should be married before becoming a company commander as a major. Knight thought it was twaddle having known a few married officers and senior NCOs whom he suspected of being homosexual.

"What about Miss Kanna?"

"I wouldn't have thought I'm her type."

"Too posh for you! That's one of your problems. You need to ditch your outdated mores. Class doesn't matter so much these days. We even have a Labour Government."

"Yessir."

"We'll have a chat soon. One other thing, just keep an eye on young Oldham. He might get a bit pissed off with what's happening."

"Sir."

"Good luck." The CO ended the conversation.

Chapter 23

GBH was told that the helicopter would be about forty-five minutes late. He decided to remain in his bunk and told the brigade watch-keeper to inform him when the helicopter was inbound. He sat on his bed perusing his notebook but it was all in his head. One could over-think an operation, a plan, so he put his notebook away and reflected on his career.

After NATO, he was back with his Battalion as a company commander in Malaya. He had had the time to train and mould his company without interference: the CO was content to leave such matters to his company commanders. During the tour, there was only one battalion-size operation with the majority being at company or platoon level. His company had spent most of its time on ambushes or cordon-and-searches with limited success, killing two terrorists and capturing five. Another company had more success while the other two companies had less with one company not firing any rounds in anger. This was the first time he had experienced the police Special Branch having the lead in intelligence. He enjoyed working with the Special Branch, though he realised quickly that it was not the British officers but the local sergeants who had the best sources. The security forces also depended on the information from turned and surrendered terrorists.

The opportunity arose to remain in Malaya as a company commander with the Federation Regiment. In a letter, the Regimental Secretary had cautioned against remaining in Malaya if he wanted to follow his father and grandfather in commanding the 'family' Regiment's First Battalion, the highest accolade as well as the last time a regimental officer would serve with his parent regiment. His prospects were slim already because he had not attended Staff College but his record and family name might overcome this obstacle. They could have a chat when GBH was home on leave. It would be rude not to attend a 'chat' with the Regimental Secretary.

The death of his mother in a car accident in France had pre-empted this 'chat'.

Initially, GBH had assumed that it might have been some fault on his mother's part because he had experienced and been terrified by her driving through the narrow roads and lanes of rural France, but the fault had been on the other driver's part though it was not a great comfort. His devastated father had insisted that his wife be buried in France because she had settled down there and had been popular with all. Charles Planet was able to arrange with the local priest for Elizabeth Buchanan-Henderson to be buried in a secluded corner spot in the graveyard of the local church with a short service conducted by an army chaplain from NATO. It was agreed that his father would go to live with David in London, selling his share of the business to Planet for a nominal amount. The selling of the family estate had provided a sizable fund that they had not needed to dip into because the income from the business was sufficient with them not having a lavish lifestyle. The two brothers feared for their father in that he seemed disinterested in anything. David had encouraged his father to attend lectures and military functions but he had attended only three or four.

GBH had been appalled by the pusillanimity of the Government over the Suez Canal with the army being stopped a few days after the operation had started. The accepted wisdom amongst many of the officers was a stab in the back by our so-called allies, the Americans. GBH did glean the truth behind Suez from his brother, including the collusion with Israel that had shocked and appalled the soldier. The Americans had not stabbed Britain in the back. President Eisenhower had made it clear that he would not sanction military action though Harold MacMillan seemed to have convinced his cabinet colleagues otherwise. Many of the senior Foreign Office officials were against the operation but resignations were few, justifying their stance by saying their role was to implement and not make policy. GBH was contemptuous, suggesting that the real reason was to protect their pensions and future knighthoods. One of the damaging consequences of the Suez fiasco was that it was difficult to condemn the Soviet invasion of Hungary whilst two European powers were attacking a small, defenceless Arab country. David did not hold any illusions about Nasser, considering him to be a nasty and dangerous dictator, but David's principal conclusion was that it demonstrated the economic, military and political weakness of Britain.

David told his brother in the strictest confidence that he had written a memorandum for his minister advising that Britain should consider reducing their military commitment East of Suez as well as try to reach a deal with Communist China on the return of Hong Kong. He had not gained overt support from colleagues and it had impeded his career progression. GBH had protested that it would be a failure of duty to run away from their obligations. It would be like the King's abdication. Dave had replied in his detached Foreign Office style that what was a real abdication of duty was to pretend to your friends and allies that you could meet these obligations.

GBH decided he would return to Malaya and this time he would be accompanied by his wife. They were quartered in Terendak near Malacca on the west coast of Malaya. He commanded a company of the Federation Regiment, being surprised by the quality of most of his soldiers, especially the senior NCOs and in particular the Liverpool-born Sergeant Tony Ho. He encountered an Irish Special Branch officer Jimmy Doherty and they established a good working relationship. Doherty was bright and enthusiastic about his work though he did seem to drink to excess. Doherty often wanted GBH's company for particular operations and GBH was drawn towards, but only on the cusp of the secret world of informers, surrendered terrorists and the importance of the village or Kampong headman. On occasions, GBH and Tony Ho would accompany Doherty and an SB sergeant, usually Chinese but sometimes Malay, to rendezvous and meetings with agents, or so he presumed. The soldiers were there to provide security, though on some occasions Ho's language talents were used. GBH found commanding a Federation Regiment company challenging but satisfying.

At a cocktail party in Kuala Lumpur to which he had been invited because of his family name, he had bumped into Louis L. Williford whom he had last seen scarpering down a hill in Korea. "I remember you. Korea, right?" A mordant smile from GBH. "You're that crazy guy!" They shook hands. "I tell guys about you. What about the arty guy?"

"Never met since."

Williford was out of uniform but still employed by the Pentagon, working out of the US Consulate in Hong Kong but spending time in Singapore and Malaya to learn from the British on how to fight communist guerrillas. GBH thought he was deceitful though his wife found the American charming and full of witty and interesting tales. GBH had hoped his wife with their new son would become accustomed to the military life though after a short while, he feared his wife was not happy, making frequent trips to Singapore, often leaving their son with the amah.

His helicopter was inbound. He put on his belt, picked up his backpack and left for what would be his final operation.

Chapter 24

At the helipad in Shala, after a brief introduction to Hockin who was saying goodbye to Jennie Croxham who was returning to Hong Kong via the capital, GBH was driven in a police vehicle to the police station. There was the usual formal welcome by Bendixson outside the station, the front not the rear. He would not need a briefing and because of the delay, he would not be able to make a quick tour of the town. Reluctantly, he had accepted an invitation to dinner with the DO, with Godden and Bendixson also attending. He had uniform only and he was sure that he preferred to bunk down in the station in case there was any activity, though he knew that was unlikely. If the chief inspector didn't mind, he would have a wander around the station and hopefully a chat with Staff Ho as well as ensuring his signals detachment had all they needed. It was only right that he speak to the soldiers still in the station. Godden and Bendixson had some police matters to attend to including ensuring that boats were available for the follow-up but would RV at 6 pm to go to the DO's. GBH had relayed via Godden that an early supper would be more convenient because he had some work to do and needed to rise early to go the OP to meet Oldham at just after first light.

Once he had dumped his kit in his bunk on the third floor, he made his way to the ops room. He found the noise from the police radios incessant and loud. This would not do for his ops room and he would need to find an alternative. His Royal Signals sergeant was in discussion with Sergeant Williams so he told them they would need to find an alternative and the sigs det had to be ready to leave at first light for the OP to set up.

He was directed to Staff Sergeant Ho's office at the other end of the corridor. He gave the two police officers a wave as he passed the chief inspector's office. Knight and Kanna heard the two men greeting each other. "Namaste." Eileen said that it was not Malay only to be informed by Knight that it was Gurkhali. After a few minutes, Ho brought the Colonel into Knight's office to introduce him. Knight had been right that the visitor was Colonel Buchanan-Henderson, wondering why the CO had not told him but it was irrelevant. The Colonel's dress was unchanged, faded OG shirt and trousers almost grey and his boots not the issued British jungle ones but the same leather high boots made especially for him somewhere around Arab Street in Singapore. The two lanyards around his neck—one to the left attached to the 38 Webley's butt, facing outwards because he favoured the cross-draw. The second lanyard attached to a compass on his right side. Holster and compass pouch were made of leather, again crafted for him.

Knight stood up, put on his headdress and saluted. "Hello, sir." A handshake.

Eileen, now standing, said, "Good afternoon, sir. Eileen Kanna." Another handshake. Ho said he would see him later and left them.

"I have heard of you, Miss Kanna." Though he was looking at Knight. "I know you, sergeant."

"Yessir. I was—"

"You commanded the enemy on my test exercise."

"Yessir."

"Sit down."

"Can I get you a drink, sir. Tea, coffee?"

"No thanks, Miss Kanna. I'm not a great one for brews." Knight recalled that the one complaint about Grevious was the almost lack of brew and smoke breaks. "You were with the Gurkha section when it was chased by an elephant."

"Yes sir."

"Has he told you about it?" To Eileen, who shook her head. "Tell you his war stories?"

"No sir. He seems to live an unexciting life."

"Wasted a complete afternoon looking for the bren and the SLR thrown away. Wasn't yours?"

"No sir." He didn't tell him that he had lost his machete and after finding the weapons, he had told the Royal Marine officer that he was willing to pay for it so that they could continue the exercise.

"You were a bit of a jungle bunny. A few times you led my guys a merry dance up Panti. You miss it?" Knight thought of the steep feature with a flat top LZ and a sheer drop on one side. On a number of occasions, soldiers had to be casevac'd from the top. He recalled one particular time when one of GBH's unit had sustained a broken leg and it was almost dark. An RAF helicopter had approached then turned back because it was too dangerous in the fading light but thankfully, a Royal Naval helicopter had turned up and taken the casualty off. He reflected that it was such incidents that coloured a soldier's mind against another regiment, corps or service, and he remained a little biased towards Naval flyers.

"Not really, sir."

"It's a mystical place!" Another smile though Knight could not be certain that he did not believe it. "Anyway, you know what my group was trained for?"

"Yes sir."

"I should have recognised the name when I read your Int reports…though don't usually associate intelligence with infantry sergeants." GBH smiled.

"Actually, sir, Miss Kanna is mainly responsible for the reports."

"I know that." Another smile. His tone became authoritative. "I understand you are going to be my escort. I am having dinner tonight with the senior civvy fellows. Be ready to leave just before first light. We are going up to the OP where my sigs det will operate from. Problem is I need an ops room here and the police one won't do. Too much noise. I need a secure direct line to the OP."

"It does get quieter during silent hours, sir."

"Maybe so but any contact or incident might not be during silent hours!"

Knight felt it was a rebuke. "Chief Inspector Bendixson has a secure line to the OP in his office." He did not want to mention Ho's secure telephone before asking him and it might not be to the OP.

"Rather not take over his office but might have to. Godden, a Branch officer, is going to be with me. Do you know him?"

"Know of him, sir."

"Told my sigs sergeant and your sigs man to come up with a solution. If you have any ideas, let them know. I will brief you tomorrow with Captain Oldham. He's coming into the OP. Anything else?"

"Breakfast at 0400?"

"That's fine. My basha is upstairs. Think it's the platoon sergeant's one."

"I'm next door."

"Where will you be if I need you later?"

"Ops room, sir."

"Good." He turned to Eileen. "You understand, miss, none of this goes out of this room."

"Yes, Colonel." Knight pondered whether she had called him 'colonel' deliberately because Knight as an SNCO would only call him 'sir'.

"Good." He stood up, followed by the others. "Never had a lady on my team." He chuckled. Eileen felt annoyed by the admonishment but pleased to be considered part of his team. He was gone in a swift, elegant movement before Knight could complete his salute.

Eileen said, "I like him. A real man. Have I found what I have been looking for!" Knight gave her a behave look. She laughed. "Jungle bunny! Chased by elephants! Might have to consider you if the Colonel Gordon Buchanan-Henderson is not free."

He shook his head at her irrepressible style. "I'm going to speak to Ho."

The whine of the two Land Rovers had disturbed the early morning not being possible to mask the sound but people were used to the sound on an almost 24-hour basis. And in keeping with Oldham's orders, vehicles had been along the border road and to the OP at different times of the day. Martin, Knight's usual driver, was on light duties being replaced by Private Paton a small, bespectacled soldier from Mansfield and an additional escort, McGraw, equally small, tough soldier from the Raploch in Stirling. There was a brief introduction to Jubb whom GBH's sigs det commander knew from Sarawak and told the Colonel that the corporal was a good, reliable man.

GBH spoke to the soldiers in an easy manner asking them how they enjoyed life in the OP but most agreed that they had had enough of here and wanted to return home as soon as possible. One soldier told GBH that he did not understand what they were doing here looking after white prats. As politely as he could, Jubb explained to GBH that it was the name C Platoon had given to the expats. Oldham and Knight had both found it amusing but the Platoon had been told never to use it in front of civilians or the police. As far as Knight was aware, there had been no infringements.

GBH gave Oldham time to have a brew and sandwich that the cook had prepared. The Captain and his four men were cold and wet. GBH, Oldham and Knight were in the observation post with the soldiers on stag outside observing. GBH gave Oldham the written orders from the latter's CO, giving him a brief time to read them but pointing out that the salient point was that he, GBH, was in operational command. GBH explained the mission of 513 Troop and that Knight had been on their final test exercise. Oldham understood now why Knight could not tell him what he had been doing in Malaysia. There was a group of about ten CTs about to or had crossed the border to mount an attack in Shala.

Originally, Hockin and his plantation had been the target but thanks to an assessment by Knight…well, Eileen Kanna, the fear was the target might be the government buildings, even the DO himself and possibly senior policemen. C Platoon's ambush remained the primary part of the operation. Oldham concealed his scepticism. Nevertheless, there was the possibility that the enemy might go around the OP into the shanties below the convent where there was a communist network. It was thought unlikely they would go west because they would need to go through more jungle and once out of it, would be likely to be spotted by the loggers. Branch would soon find out because they had sources.

The Royal Signals det would be in the OP to ensure communications with 513 as well as monitor Oldham's net. GBH would be in the police station with Godden. Oldham must not patrol north or west of his position unless ordered by GBH. The ludicrous *Ulster Fry* remained the code word for enemy on the move. In event of a contact further upstream from his position, police boats would be sent up to recover bodies or prisoners. He could not be certain how long they would need to remain in position but he would expect if no activity after two or three days, Branch would know what was happening. A derisory look from Oldham to Knight. The only question the young officer had was if he was not to move north, did this mean 513 Troop would not move south? Unlikely they would but if the situation developed, GBH's unit knew exactly Oldham's position and would come onto his net in clear. He gave him the relevant callsigns. GBH ended with a few encouraging words and Knight could see in Oldham the enthusiasm and warrior face returning.

The visitor did not want to go to the convent, instead drove around the town including the border road and areas X and Z but not going into the plantation. "The white prats." He chuckled saying, "I like that. Never heard it before. So obvious. Not very polite though. Wish I had thought of it. Who came up with that?" He turned towards Knight in the rear who nodded towards Collins.

"Private Collins, sir."

"Good man. But I hope you just as good with the radios." GBH's signals sergeant had tuned in one of the sets to 513 Troop's frequency though they would send in clear only in the event of a contact because the rest of the time they used Morse.

The Land Rover on GBH's instructions had parked on the square just outside the post office. The Colonel stood in front of the Land Rover observing the scene whilst McGraw was at the rear of the vehicle and Knight to the Colonel's left but

176

slightly forward holding his Armalite at the ready position with a contact being the last thing he wanted. Knight could see Raza across the square surrounded by children taking a not unexpected interest in GBH who, his hands clasped behind his back, took a few paces to his right then came back to stand close to Knight. Raza's interest was not because it was a stranger but he thought he had seen the tall officer before. GBH spoke quietly, "It seems the same but there were not so many buildings beyond the square and not as high."

"Sir, have you been here before?"

"Yes. At the end of the war. Didn't I ask you about Shala in JWS?"

"Yessir but I hadn't been up here at that time."

"No. Of course." He looked around trying to replay the first time in his head. "My company was the first to get here. Some Americans had been here before us. God knows what they were doing here. Think they had been parachuted into the wrong LZ." A titter. "Always many mistakes made in war. The people were almost emaciated. They had suffered terribly at the hands of the Japs. We learned of one officer who…if I had got ahold of him, I would have killed him with my bare hands…" Knight had heard soldiers, especially after terrorist incidents threatening what they would do if they got their hands on the bastards, but he knew most of it was hot air. This time was different; he had never seen such a chilling, determined look on any soldier's face. He took off his hat and wiped his forehead with his sweat rag. "I'm sorry." Knowing it was the same *ang mo lang*, Raza stood up and walked towards the two soldiers who spotted him.

Knight answered before GBH asked, "Old Raza. Shala's wise man. A Merlin type figure." Recalling Jerome's description.

"Excuse me, sir." He was speaking to GBH.

"Yes."

"Were you in Shala in 1945?" Knight was surprised by his English. When he had been speaking to Eileen, it had been a combination of English, Hokkien and Malay.

"Yes."

"You have not changed much, sir."

Knight was curt. "What do you want?" Raza ignored Knight.

"I think you are the officer who helped the old woman."

"Go on," said GBH.

"She had suffered. The Japanese had killed all her family. She gave you a paper with a message written by a British officer."

GBH nodded. "Major Fleming, Donald Fleming. Yes." He paused then looked down at Raza. "Were you here?"

"Yes, sir. I was standing beside Fong Siu Wai when—"

"That was her name. I had forgotten." A pause for reflection and recollection. Raza continued to speak, recounting how GBH had built a home for the old lady on the plantation and how Tuan Hockin had allowed her to stay. "Sorry. What did you say about Hockin?" Raza told GBH how Hockin had allowed the old lady to stay in her home while others in the plantation had wanted to remove her. "I see. I assume that she…Fong…"

"Fong Siu Wai."

"Right. Fong Siu Wai is dead?"

"No, sir. She is in the hospital…being cared for by Doctor Alston…a good doctor and a good man. But I think she is close to the end."

"Sergeant, we passed the hospital." GBH, pointing to his right, said, "Is it not over that way."

"Yessir."

"Right. Let's go."

"Mount up!" ordered Knight.

GBH held out his hand, which Raza took. "Thank you, Mr Raza. I hope we meet again before the end of my visit."

"Thank you, sir."

Nurse Tan was startled that a British Army officer was asking to see Fong Siu Wai who was an old woman close to death and could not possibly be a terrorist or bandit, whatever the British called them. She stuttered that she would need to speak to Doctor Alston and was told to get him immediately. "My sergeant and I will wait here."

McGraw was standing at the back of the vehicle, Paton outside at his door, both scanning the grounds of the government building and the area beyond the fence, whilst Collins remained in the back monitoring two nets.

"Why's the colonel bothered about some fuckin' old chog woman!"

Collins with his best scowling look replied, "Didn't you listen to the colonel?" GBH had told them an abridged version on the short drive to the government clinic. "She saved the life of a British officer. She helped us during the war."

"So fuckin what!"

"Can't see any of the white prats saving us." McGraw snorted. "Jock, don't think you should say anything about her in front of the colonel." Another snort. "He seems a mean bastard to me."

"Whit—" Collins silenced him by holding up his left hand, beginning to write on his signals pad.

"Jock, I think that's good advice," said Paton.

The nurse returned with Susan Cahill. Both soldiers stood up. "I'm Sister Cahill. Nurse Tan tells me you want to speak to Mrs Fong. Why?"

GBH held out his hand and said, "Good morning, Sister, I am Colonel Gordon Buchanan-Henderson." Despite an initial reluctance, she granted him a brief, loose handshake. "And this is Sergeant Knight."

"Oh, I'm sorry, I didn't realise it was you." Knight held up his left hand to indicate it was not a problem.

"Sister, with respect, I think it would be better if I spoke to Doctor Alston. Is he available?" She smouldered a little at this rejection but his air of authority persuaded her to comply and she muttered about going to find him. The two nurses walked off, with GBH saying, "We will not go anywhere." They resumed their seats. Memories of GBH's gentle but biting humour in Malaysia caused Knight to smile.

After a few minutes, Doctor Alston, flanked by Sister Cahill and Nurse Tan to his right and left respectively, appeared. The two soldiers stood up, both thinking the positions of the nurses reflected their status.

"Phil."

"Doctor Alston. This is Colonel Gordon Buchanan-Henderson." The doctor and soldier shook hands.

"I understand you wish to see the old Chinese lady. Can you tell me why?"

"I would prefer to speak in private." In Alston's office without the nurses present, GBH gave an abridged version of meeting Fong Siu Wai in 1945 and preferred that the story remain private. When he mentioned speaking to Raza, Alston laughed.

"It will be all over Shala by now." He was thoughtful for a moment. "You know, Colonel, in the early days, we used to go to speak to Raza. Thought he was harmless...not so sure now. Anyway, I vaguely remember him telling us the story of the young British officer. So that was you." GBH nodded. "That was wonderful what you did for her..."

"Not as much as she did for Major Fleming."

"Yes, indeed. She showed me the piece of paper. She keeps it in a plastic folder."

"Is she conscious? How is she?"

"Officially, I can tell you nothing because you are not a relative but..." He picked up a file and flicked through it. "She is not doing so well. She slips in and out of consciousness. Sometimes she is lucid, other times...well, she doesn't know where she is. She is close to the end. I am surprised, no, astounded at how long she has lived."

GBH had learned of her life story in the few days he had been in Shala, both from Fong Siu Wai and others. "She probably has had more resilience and courage than all of the soldiers today in Shala." He reflected that the British had failed to do more for her. Fleming's operational report had been mislaid. She should have received a decoration. Chin Peng did though he went on to lead the CTs during the Malaya Emergency and probably had had some influence in this colony. Alston would allow GBH a few minutes with her but not Knight unless he got rid of his weapon but he could look in through the window from the corridor. Alston was glad that he had put her in a private room.

Alston spoke gently to Fong Siu Wai telling her that she had a visitor, a British officer she had met in 1945. There was no response. GBH felt awkward. Then slowly her eyes flickered open. Alston took the plastic insert from the drawer in the small bedside cabinet and gave it to her, saying that she had shown it to this officer in 1945. She indicated she wanted water and Alston poured some from the plastic jug into a plastic beaker, then raised her head tenderly to allow her to sip it, then gently eased her head back onto the pillow.

She looked at GBH and said in a low but clear voice, "Sir...thank you... Have forgotten English... Please?" Her right hand holding the plastic cover moved towards him. GBH looked at a puzzled Alston.

179

"Does she want me to keep it? Read it?" He took it from her hand and unhurriedly read aloud, "'I, Major Donald Angus Fleming, declare that Fong Siu Wai has been my brave and loyal comrade. She nursed me back to life when I was ill. She has provided valuable assistance to the British Army. Her two sons fought the Japs. They, their wives and children were brutally killed by the Nips. She now wants to end her life in this small piece of God's earth. I ask, no, beg that she be allowed to do so. I would hope that we or the civilian authorities could build a more permanent home for her. I will provide more details in my op report.'"

"Yes." A weak smile but her voice was clear. He gave her back the paper, which she took then released from her hands to let it fall onto the bedcover, moving her hands back towards him. He cupped both her hands as delicately as he could as if he was holding the finest bone-china cup. She tried to say something but slipped back into unconsciousness.

"I have never seen her look so serene," said Alston. "Time to go."

Knight, ill-at-ease holding the Armalite, muzzle pointing down, in his right hand with the arm extended fully down, looked at the two nurses to his right both impassive and he realised that apart from a hello, he had never spoken to Susan Cahill. Alston came out of the room and closed the door behind him, saying that the colonel wanted a moment alone. They watched as GBH laid his right hand on the top of her head for a moment. He put on his floppy hat, came to attention and saluted Fong Siu Wai. When he came out of the room, he thanked Doctor Alston and saluted the two nurses before turning and walking away, followed by Knight.

Chapter 25

GBH asked if he could commandeer Knight's desk so that he could write up his notes. Once seated, he took out his notebook, opened it, lay it flat on the desk and said, "I would be grateful, Sergeant Knight, if you did not include our hospital visit in your log or report."

"I had not intended to because it was not part of our operation here."

"Thank you."

"Sir, remember what Raza said about Hockin helping that old woman."

"Yes. Why?"

"Just wondered whether that might have influenced the CTs."

"Tender terrorists." A cynical grin.

"Just a thought, sir." The two men sat in silence, writing up their respective reports.

"Do you think he's paying them?"

"Sir?"

"Hockin. Could he be paying them off? Protection money?"

Knight shook his head. "Don't think so."

"Why not? I know it happened in Malaya."

"Well, sir. He's not the sole owner of the plantation. Uncles back in England own most of it—"

"How do you know that?" Interrogatory!

"Jerome told me." He expanded to avoid another stab. "He worked for him as his manger. It's all in my first report."

"Not read that one." Another jab. "Could Jerome be lying?"

"Don't think so, sir."

"Why?"

"He seems honest and open…especially his reaction about Shi Baru. I just think…well, that he's a bit idealistic."

"Is he homosexual? Jimmy Doherty seems to think so. Do you know Doherty?"

"Only of him, sir. Staff Ho thinks highly of him. They worked together—"

"I know. In Malaya. Ho was one of my sergeants. First met Doherty there." A sardonic smile infiltrated his impassive face. "Irish and Chinese. Both would sell their mothers!" Knight was unsure whether he meant the races or just those two individuals. "Jerome. Homosexual?"

"I don't think he's the type." He stopped from mentioning public school, anticipating that GBH had gone to a public school.

"The type? And what is the type?"

"He seems to like females. Think he has a girl at home in England. It's my impression, sir. I suspect it would have been mentioned by one of the expats if he was. I quite like him."

"But if you thought he was a homosexual, you would avoid him. You think it's right that they are not allowed in the army?"

Knight looked down, feeling uncomfortable at GBH's unexpected question. "I just don't think it would be good for morale and good discipline, especially in an infantry platoon. It could…"

GBH wanted to tell the sergeant that his view was because he had not fought in a war, which was not his fault, but instead said, "Yes. You are probably right." GBH had learned in the ferocious fighting against the Japanese that a soldier's colour, religion or sexual inclination was irrelevant because what mattered was the ability to endure, then endure some more, be willing to shoot and throw grenades to kill. He knew it was not a popular view and he had shared it only with one other person, his only school friend who had understood.

"So you think Jerome is fine. Not helping the communists intentionally or otherwise?"

"Yessir. Probably a bit foolish and too idealistic to be in a colony."

"You seem to be quite good at this job. I noted the doctor called you by your first name. Other people have also said good things about your work here."

"I have been lucky with having Miss Kanna but to be honest, sir, I would rather be out in the ulu with the platoon."

"So would I but we need to use people's talents in the most effective way. We sometimes don't realise what we can achieve. It was a surprise to many, myself included, that I made the grade as an infantry officer." He noted Knight's surprise. "It's true. But back to you. Any half-decent corporal will make a reasonable fist of being a platoon sergeant and company sergeant-major. Your CO sees you as an observer, a chronicler of people and events. His words, not mine." Knight did not respond but did not agree. "And also bloody left-wing!" He smiled. "Don't worry. Had one in my family." He changed the subject. "It should be a major in command here and a captain or at least a lieutenant doing your job. I know it's a criticism of your CO but he won't mind. We have known each other a long time. Also, I know the battalion has other tasks. So it's a compliment to Oldham and you that you have been left to your own devices. The CO has not been up?"

"No, sir."

"How do you feel about that?"

"I'm fine with it. I know there are problems in other areas, but I think the boys would have appreciated a visit. They say they are not bothered but most of them like to see their OC or CO."

"A chronicler! And criticising your CO."

"You asked me a question, sir."

"But if the op goes well, could be a downside for Oldham and you, probably more you."

182

"Sir?"

"There will be resentment and jealousy because of your ranks. Also, you and young Oldham are clever. The army doesn't really like clever people. Might be easier for Oldham because he will spend most of his time away from the battalion and should pick up good reports. But you will depend on the patronage of company commanders who are probably captains at present." Knight was certain GBH had discussed this with the CO. "You want to think of your options away from the battalion."

"Thank you, sir."

"I better get on."

"What time do you want to leave, sir?" GBH was going up to the plantation to brief Hockin on the possible threat against him. Godden would be present, was already there having lunch with Hockin.

He looked at his watch. "1400."

"Yessir."

"I'll see you down at the wagon."

"Sir."

"And, Sergeant Knight, our conversation comes under the same rules as our hospital visit."

"Yessir." Knight saluted and left.

The three men were in Hockin's study. GBH accepted a tea whilst the other two had wine. "Tony," Godden said, "as you know, there is a threat against you."

Hockin grinned. "You know I think it's nonsense."

"Colonel Buchanan-Henderson is here to answer any questions on the military side." Godden explained that they expected a group of ten to twelve terrorists to cross the border very soon, if they had not already done so.

"This was the same story you gave me...what, four weeks ago."

"Tony, there was a delay because of internal divisions but they are on the move and—"

"How do you know, Arthur?"

"You know I can't go into that." The soldier thought it was akin to a family squabble.

"Does it come from one of Doherty's drinking sessions with one of his local mates?"

GBH intervened. "Mr Hockin, I have worked with Jimmy Doherty in Malaya during the Emergency. He is an excellent Branch officer. My men would not be here if I did not believe his intelligence."

"Sorry." He looked at GBH. "Colonel?"

"Yes."

"What are you doing here?" His tone was curt. "I was told a colonel was visiting just to update himself or something. Now you say your men?"

White prat flashed through his mind. "Captain Oldham has most of his platoon in an ambush position close to here. I think you are aware of that." Hockin nodded. "There is the possibility that the terrorists might go into

Kampong Tengu first and their route is likely to be around the police OP. Oldham's CO could not provide any more men so my unit was deployed north of Oldham's to cover the route around the police OP." His tone was measured and controlled.

Hockin sighed. "This is so inconvenient. I'm supposed to be flying to Hong Kong tomorrow."

"Well, go. No need for you to be here."

"No, Arthur. I'm not going to be like my grandfather. I need to telephone Hong Kong. Probably better to send a telegram." Hockin was speaking to himself. "Well, Arthur, you might as well stay for supper. Colonel?"

"No, thank you. I need to get back to the station." He sensed Hockin was pleased at his refusal.

"We'll get Tom…and Eddie if we can track him down." He looked at his watch. "Still time to send a telegram."

"Might not be wise, Tony. Using the post office."

"Gawdsake. I'll just say I'm detained by business."

"Prefer not. Just to be on the safe side."

"You and your security! Are there communists everywhere!" Godden did not respond and thought Hockin might change his mind when Mehad, his foreman, was arrested after the operation.

The telephone jangled on the desk. "Tony Hockin here. Who?… What?… Sure?… When is she coming back?… OK. Thanks. Bye." He held the receiver in his hand, smiled and placed it back in the cradle, then explained, "That was an Aussie journalist from a Hong Kong newspaper. He has just arrived. He had bumped into Jennie in Hong Kong Airport and she asked him to phone me. He said that she had tried to phone but couldn't get through. She had just got permission and was on her way to Hanoi. Didn't know when she would be back." There was disappointment in his eyes.

"I better go, Mr Hockin."

"Right. I'll see you out." He turned to Godden. "Get cracking on those phone calls. Also try and round up a few of the girls. That Eileen Kanna. Like her."

Godden shook his head, grinning. "You want to send a telegram to a female telling her you can't make it. Hanoi's a better proposition than you. Now you are telling me to round up the girls." Hockin shrugged his shoulders in 'you know me' look.

Outside on the veranda, GBH mentioned that Fong Siu Wai was in hospital. "Who?"

"I understand you allowed her to live on the plantation."

"Is that her name? Might have been told once but have forgotten. I heard she was in hospital. Not so good."

"No. But what you did was a generous act."

"Oh, you know, need to do the decent thing sometimes."

"I might not see you again so I will say goodbye."

"Right." They shook hands. Hockin watched the soldier walk down the steps, get into the Land Rover and drive off. Hockin waved but there was no returned acknowledgment. GBH was being told that there was a message for him to contact the OP. Hockin wondered why the colonel had mentioned the old woman and felt foolish for not asking him. Tom Alston would know.

Knight and the others were not to stand down yet until GBH knew what the message was from the OP. He went up to the ops room. Paton and McGraw got out of the vehicle to stretch their legs and for the Scot to have a cigarette.

"Sarge, didn't want to say in front of the others but there was a Morse message as well. I know a bit of Morse." Knight was surprised. "Think the message was something about having fixed their position."

"OK. Just keep me informed if any more." Again Knight speculated why Oldham had opposed his promotion; being Welsh was not a credible reason.

On his return, GBH informed them that he was going to be in Oldham's office probably for the rest of the op. There was a camp bed there already. They would have to use the police ops room because Ho's secure phone was only to Branch HQ; he was not going to set up in Bendixson's office because the chief inspector had normal police business to deal with. He would prefer if all his team could basha down in the main building. Knight said that he would arrange it but anyhow, he and Collins were sharing the night stag with Sgt Williams and the other signallers. GBH was satisfied and returned to move his kit into his new basha. Collins was surprised by the news that he was now stagging on in the ops room and was told he should not have revealed his Morse code skills.

GBH told Sgt Williams to waken him if there were any messages. He sat at the desk and took out from his American A-frame rucksack a bundle of letters and set them on the desk. They had been addressed to him in Jungle Warfare School.

Chapter 26

Command of his Regiment's Territorial Army Battalion had followed his time in Malaya, though his wife had elected to remain in London, which was not in keeping with the expected role of the CO's lady, and its secretary had expressed the collective Regimental displeasure. GBH, aware of the Regimental conventions, knew that he should have insisted on his wife's presence but he lacked the inclination and resolve to insist. Some individuals from the wider Regimental family professing knowledge of his family background had claimed that GBH was intimidated by females. One result of being separated was that rather than using the allocated marriage quarter, he had found a cottage between Perth and Dundee. He seldom used his staff car and driver, driving himself to Battalion HQ.

He had not found the TA challenging and it seemed to be no more than a social club. His efforts to improve their military skills and introduce more demanding exercises had led to his brigadier's assertion that he was probably expecting too much of the part-time soldiers. The brigadier's advice had been that he should enjoy himself by going to the many social functions including shooting parties and balls. He had ignored the advice.

On several occasions, he had returned to London on leave but had felt that he was only interrupting his wife's social life. When he had proposed that she should move up to Scotland, his wife had declared that she could not possibly take her son up to the wild, desolate highlands of Scotland. Malaya had been bad enough. In the second year of his tour, Willard had been posted to the American Embassy in Grosvenor Square, which GBH's wife claimed had enlivened her social life.

He became aware of soldiers being paid but not turning up for duty or leaving after the first parade. He had felt the paymaster had been complicit in the fraud. One retired TA CO had told him not to worry and that it was a way for the soldiers to earn some more money and anyway, it was not his money. GBH had been appalled but had never been able to prove anything; however, he had felt that he had stopped it to a certain extent in that he would turn up unannounced at different locations when a drill night was scheduled. His company commanders learned quickly when he turned up two nights in succession in the same location; on the second night, most of the soldiers had left. Notwithstanding his abhorrence of this practice of soldiers being paid but not working, GBH felt guilty because he realised he was not fully committed. His moral stance was hypocritical because he had cheated the army when a staff officer in NATO, being paid though he had done little and was now ambling through the tour as CO of a TA Battalion.

It had been the most unsatisfying and dispiriting time in his army career though morale had been raised learning his next posting would be to Singapore as a staff officer responsible for training in Land Forces Headquarters. Just before the end of this tour, his grandmother had died.

The entrance hymn *Faith of our Fathers* had been sung with tribalistic gusto:

Faith of our fathers, living still
In spite of dungeon, fire and sword;
Faith of our fathers! Holy Faith!
We will be true to thee till death,
We will be true to thee till death.

David Buchanan-Henderson sat with his wife and two sons in the right front pew facing the altar whilst across the aisle, GBH sat, without his family, with the Mackenzies. The church had been almost full though GBH had not recognised anyone, probably some friends of Deoiridh though Mrs Mackenzie had told him that people attended out of interest and for the purvey. The two veiled women dressed in black seated in the back pew on David's side had seemed familiar.

The Irish priest of the Passionists Order welcomed everyone. "Thankfully, today we do not face the threat of dungeon, fire and sword. In Scotland more so than any other country in Europe, even including Ireland, we Catholics are fortunate, blessed, to have our own education system."

The first limited murmurs of disapproval.

The priest said he intended to leave the eulogy or oration to the end of Mass, unusual in a Catholic Requiem Mass. The Buchanan-Hendersons sat or stood throughout the service though David did kneel when required. The thought flickered in GBH's mind that his brother might be considering becoming a Catholic because he attended the high church services of the Church of England.

At the end of Mass, the priest gave his eulogy, beginning with a brief history of her life. He had not known Deoiridh well. She had spent her final two years in a nursing home. Both brothers had presumed the other was paying the costs: they did not discuss finances. GBH felt guilty because he had visited her twice in the two years and their conversations had been stilted and brief. The priest continued that on his visits, her mind had been sharp and clear. "I understand that she had strong opinions and could be an obstinate woman. No doubt if I had met her earlier, we would have argued." He had heard that some of the congregation had been thankful that she had returned to Holy Mother Church. "Oh yes, I know what goes on. The most important skill for a parish priest after knowing Latin was to have a network of spies."

There were more murmurings and heads shaking in disapproval.

"People said that she had strayed." A pause as his eyes scanned the congregation. "The Holy Catholic Church is not a home for stray cats and dogs!" A wry smile on David's face: the priest had forgotten the *Parable of the Prodigal*

Son. The priest's voice rose, not in anger but declaratory. "The church is for human beings with emotions, needs and weaknesses who have free will. People come to me to ask that I speak to Jimmy or Jeannie who is not going to mass…even worse, they are going out with a non-Catholic, a Protestant!" Another pause. "Remember the first question of the catechism. Who made you?" Another sweep of the congregation. "I can see many of you mumbling 'God made me.' So…if anyone is to blame for individuals straying…it's *Him*." His right index finger pointed upwards.

More murmurs, even gasps of disapproval and shaking of heads.

"I'm not here to judge our sister." Waving his right hand in cutting movements. "Neither is anyone else here. Only…" Once more an upwards right finger.

"What I can say about Deoiridh is that she was a pilgrim, her name told us that. She did not pass on the other side. She opposed what she saw as injustice, inequality and did what she could to eradicate, or least mitigate, their effects." Another pause, now a stern look at his audience. "We have a new young American president, a Catholic. And if I may take a little pride." A twinkle in his eyes. "Also Irish."

Some laughter and self-satisfaction amongst his listeners.

"I'm sure many listened to his inaugural address. He said, 'Ask not what your country could do for you but what you could do for your country.' Well, our sister Deoridh did not need to be asked that question: she had been answering it for a long time." A pause. "As did her daughter's family, the Buchanan-Hendersons. Yes, much is expected of those to whom much is given. They have given much more than what was expected. They, also like the Good Samaritan, did not pass on the other side."

Confusion and some anger in the congregation at this praise.

"It was suggested to me by a young friend of Deoridh's that I should read from the book, *Sunset Song*—one of Deoridh's favourites—the minister's eulogy." He looked down at his notes. "It *was* powerful and emotional, but…she was not of the old Scots folks. She never clung to the past but wanted to change society, seeking a better life for everyone. She suffered the most grievous rejection there is…from her parents. But!" A slow, sweep of the congregation, his eyes challenging them. "She still said, 'Here I am, Lord.' She did tend the poor and lame. She was true to her faith until death."

More censorious gestures and murmurs.

"So I will go down now to bless our sister on her onward journey." He moved down and blessed the coffin with holy water. The two brothers exchanged glances before leaving their seats to follow the coffin out. It had been announced that the service at the graveyard was private though all were welcome to the hotel for the purvey. On the way out of the church, GBH recognised the two veiled ladies, Una McFadzean and Catriona Mitchell. He stopped, shook hands and insisted on their attendance at the graveyard.

The purvey was well-attended whilst David spoke to people, thanking them for coming, GBH sat in a corner restraining himself from challenging those so-called Christians who disapproved of his family like those at the time of Fi's death. He considered that most Catholics and Protestants shared two traits, their hypocrisy and lack of Christian compassion. He found Fi's friends, Una and Catriona, seated in the public bar. Catriona had to leave but Una asked him to join her for a quiet drink to which he agreed, but he had to speak to his brother first. When he returned, the bar as well as the hotel was almost empty, the free food and drink finished.

She apologised for her brusque treatment of him in the *Malmasion* so many years ago. "I treated you badly. You must have thought I had forgotten Fi...but I hadn't. I wanted to forget that time in my life." Her marriage to Roderick Farquarson had been a failure. Her father had been right in that he was more interested in the other sex. He was now a high court judge, a senator in the Court of Sessions, an esteemed figure in the Scottish Judiciary. She had inherited her father's wealth and continued to live in Glasgow but had not remarried. Not long before her father died, Catriona had contacted her to tell her that Deoiridh was sick. Her family had seemingly forgotten her.

The memories had come flooding back of this wonderful, energetic woman who had taught them so much of Scottish history and caring for others, and made them sing. She had gone with Catriona to visit Deoiridh in her Dundee home but they had realised that she was unable to look after herself. Her grandsons were far away. She had told her ailing father—the American wife long gone—who had remembered the vibrant woman. He had been insistent that he would pay for her care. He had loved her despite their age differences, though she had never known. She was a real woman, not like the flossies he had spent his life with, not including Una's mother.

"So your father paid for the nursing home? I thought it was my brother."

"When he passed away, I continued the payments. My father left everything to me and told me that I could spend it anyway I wanted. I am now a very rich lady." She looked at her cup of tea. "My father was not a nice man. Some people thought he was evil." She looked at him. "He thought your father was the most honourable, decent man he had ever met. He knew that he had given up his career for..."

"Fi?"

"Yes. My father had stuck his wounded and damaged brother in a home. He hadn't cared for him physically or emotionally." She sipped her tea. "But...I still loved him. He refused any awards after the war. It was said that they were not offered because of his dalliances with women...not fit to mix in proper society...he was a Glasgow gangster...which he was." She paused, looking down at the cup then at him and smiled. "He knew what he was. An immoral, amoral, decadent and vile person who had made money out of war. That his efforts, his weapons had killed hundreds...no...hundreds of thousands of people, not just German soldiers but innocent men, women and children. He didn't regret it. There was no road to Damascus. He didn't find Christ." She looked at him in a sanguine way. "You are a soldier. You believe in duty and honour." He nodded. "My father hated that...hated all those who glorified in it. He refused an honour.

Yes." This was news to GBH. "He was offered a peerage." She smirked. "He turned down the offer and had contempt for those generals who took them. They had killed thousands of people but they were acting honourably. Some even now have shows on television telling us how they won battles. It was a parlour game!"

GBH was not aghast by this criticism that chimed a little with his views. "His work did save the lives of many including my own soldiers."

"Thank you. Another decent Buchanan-Henderson." He did not add that he too felt no remorse for the enemy he had killed, particularly the Japanese. Some now spoke with admiration for the tenacity, the fighting spirit of the Japanese. He found them cruel and evil who inflicted suffering and death not only on their prisoners of war but also on their own wounded. They did not prevent their own mothers and wives killing themselves and their own children.

He was surprised that with her wealth, she continued to live in Glasgow. She had travelled but Glasgow was home, a real, vibrant, amoral city like her father whom she had not deserted, though had come close several times. She said, "Glasgow is not a city of sights but of words." Visit her and she would show him Glasgow, a city with a life alien to the rest of Scotland with its mountains, glens and lochs. He said he would try. There was an awkward silence; though he wanted to, he did not know how to continue the conversation, then he spluttered out that she was a very fine woman. More silence, then she said, "Should we get a room?"

"Not this time."

She put her right hand over his right hand. "May I write to you?"

Chapter 27

Ulster Fry came later than normal. Nearer to noon.

GBH was calm when Sergeant Williams told him that the code word had come from callsign one, which was the Royal Marine commander of 513 Troop. This was the joint net with C Platoon with 1, 2, and 3 allocated to the Troop and 5 to Oldham, 7 to GBH and 8 to the relay station in the OP. These callsigns had been decided to keep the net simple. After an update from the OP on the secure telephone in Bendixson's office, he called Knight and Williams into Oldham's requisitioned office to give them more but limited details. Having expected the source for the code word to be the Branch, Knight surmised that this indicated that 513 Troop had eyes on the terrorist group and if so, why had they not engaged, though he did not ask. GBH had not disclosed the details of 513's deployment. A four-man patrol commanded by the troop sergeant with two Iban Trackers had located the armed group's position just across the border. This was the information relayed by Morse that Collins had partially decoded. *Ulster Fry* meant the CTs were now moving towards Shala.

Sgt Williams offered the opinion that considering how close the border was, the enemy were likely to be close to Shala by that night or the next morning, only to be told by GBH—annoyed by SNCOS who speculated—that he expected any contact to be not tomorrow but the following day, though he could be wrong. The sergeants did not know that the terrorists were moving on the west bank of the Kanu whilst 513 were on the east bank though the salient factor was that the terrorists were carrying two long-tailed type boats because the river was not wide or deep enough at the border. The first possible insertion point for the boats was around two kilometres from the border with the first and best debarkation point on the east bank around four kilometres further where 513's main ambush was set with a cut-off group further downstream. The enemy would be at their most vulnerable when leaving their boats and the aim was to kill or capture all of the enemy. Engaging the enemy from the opposite bank, apart from the size of the patrol, was that some might escape.

Almost immediately, a telephone call requested GBH to return to Bendixson's office and he asked the two sergeants to wait. On his return ten minutes later, he told them that he was going to the DO's house for a conference. The police seemed to be in a bit of a panic caused by new information, which he did not disclose. He would take his Land Rover team but did not require Knight whom he asked to look at manning; in particular, raising a reaction section though still guarding the government married quarters. It would only be for 48 hours so might be able to take a few from that task. He did not know how long the conference would last. Opening the door of Oldham's office to leave, he paused in thought, closed the door and asked, "Have you anything that might suggest that there are already CTs in Shala? Don't mean party officials or low-level hacks, eyes and ears stuff but hardcore fighters." Knight mentioned one report from Corporal Horrocks who was responsible for the safety of a visiting journalist, the word contorting GBH's face as if he had taken the vilest tasting medicine. Miss Kanna was summoned to bring and leave the report. GBH read the brief report.

"Horrocks accepts he should have gotten the police to check the two men but his priority was to protect Miss Croxham. Think it came down from the Governor, sir."

"Your loyalty to your corporal is laudable. No need. I understand. May I take this?"

"Yessir." A refusal was not an option.

The meeting in the DO's dining room with Sutch and GBH on one side of the long table facing the two police officers was opened by Sutch saying it was at the request of the police and invited Godden to speak first. The Branch officer told the others that he had received, about an hour ago, a telephone call from Chief Inspector Doherty who told him that there was reliable intelligence that three to five armed terrorists were already in Shala, probably in area Z. Doherty would not disclose the source even over the secure line, which Godden defended by stating that there were concerns over its security and even HE did not use it for sensitive discussions. GBH was surprised that Godden professed this knowledge.

"I understand, Colonel Buchanan-Henderson, that your men are reporting only six CTs moving from the border?"

"Well, sir." He used the salutation though he considered that in protocol, he outranked the civilian DO. "That is the estimation but you must appreciate that it is from a distance through foliage. It is possible there may be more coming up behind them but...I think because of certain activity, that is probably unlikely." The DO's pursed lips expressed annoyance at the failure to give more details but did not press the soldier. "Further, I have a report here that does not confirm but might support the Branch's intelligence." He passed the Horrocks report to the DO who read it quickly then passed it to Godden who after reading it said that he had not seen it before.

"I would be surprised if Sergeant Knight had not sent it up."

"I don't doubt that. It's only a few days old and possibly not come down from brigade intelligence yet...though sometimes they don't send us everything if they think it's not important." He shook his head in frustration. "They still haven't grasped that Branch has to see everything." Sutch ignored this and turned to Bendixson who was quite agitated. His officers over the last few days had been reporting disquiet and unrest in the town. There was nothing concrete but when two of his normally level-headed and unexcitable officers, Inspector Khan and Staff Ho, were also raising their concerns, and especially with Arthur's information and the fact that six armed terrorists were on their way, he felt it would be irresponsible not to bring it to the DO's attention. GBH was again surprised that Ho did not go to Doherty. He did not know Khan.

"I am concerned about the safety of our people. I know the army is at the Crescent." He shook his head vigorously. "But I fear that is not enough. People, yourself included, DO, and others like Doctor Alston are having to travel to their offices. I think we need more soldiers on the streets." Bendixson was not an unexcitable officer; his tone conveyed a hint of panic.

"So we seem to be missing some CTs who could be in Shala or close by." He raised his right hand to prevent Godden interrupting him. "I know that sometimes figures are not always accurate. A gang of five when they appear are only three." This was inconvenient and potentially dangerous because Sutch knew the date for independence had been brought forward and was now only three months away. A successful attack in Shala could undermine Baru. "Gentlemen, what is important is the need to deal with this immediate terrorist threat and prevent a successful attack."

"I knew I was right that we should have cordoned and searched area Z after my officer was stabbed!"

"We don't have the men," Godden, not concealing his exasperation, responded to Bendixson.

"Possibly we can have a fresh opinion." Sutch turned to GBH, asking, "Do you know area Z, Colonel?"

"Yes. Kampong Tengu." Sutch and Bendixson, but not Godden, were surprised that he knew the Malay name.

"Terence thinks we should cordon and search it. I am aware that you probably have not had a chance to have a look at it but could you estimate the number of troops it might take to mount such an operation?"

"Well, it is larger and denser than on the map. But I would say it is at least a battalion-size operation. Possibly could do it with three good and fresh companies. It could not be done thoroughly in one day. Of course, there would need to be police support."

"Thank you."

"There are two other factors to be considered. One. Where do the troops come from? I understand all the battalions are overstretched. It's unlikely Land Forces could provide any units." He paused. "Two. What would happen if there are armed terrorists there? Would they fight?" He looked at the Special Branch officer.

"I think so," responded Godden.

"Surely, they could not beat the army!" It was not a question from the uniformed police officer.

"Yes, we would prevail but there could be civilian casualties not necessarily caused by us though we would be foolish to discount a nervous, frightened soldier overreacting." The others nodded in unison being aware of a few previous incidents.

"Any civilian casualty would hand the communists a propaganda coup and make no mistake, they would exploit it to their advantage. British soldiers murder innocent women and children."

"Mr Godden is right."

"That did cross my mind," said the DO who clasped his hands together on the table and leaned back in his chair. "That would be completely unacceptable. It would be a political nightmare." He could visualise the headlines in some newspapers, 'British Army takes their revenge before running!'

"Sir, I say we still need more soldiers on the streets and protecting our people."

The DO asked, "Terence, where do we get them from?"

A light seemed to come on in Bendixson's brain indicated by a large grin. "What about the National Army soldiers? There are some just south of us." He looked at GBH.

"I am not part of the chain of command. It would require a request from the police or…I am not sure of the Governor's exact powers here but he usually can deploy troops in an emergency by an order in council."

"I'm sure, DO, that you could arrange that." Bendixson was upbeat now.

"I do not think it would be helpful to my operation if troops began flooding Shala." GBH knew he was being a bit dramatic but it was for effect.

"I agree," said Godden. "The group in the jungle might abort their attack."

"How will they find out? Jungle drums!" Bendixson chortled.

"Yes!" GBH said with disdain. "In the form of American radios that they have been buying in Singapore or getting from North Vietnam."

"That's true." Once more, Godden supported GBH. "We don't know if they have any radio communications."

"But it is a possibility."

"How come they can get this stuff?" asked the DO.

GBH provided the explanation. "Unlike us, the Americans are awash with equipment. The Chinese and Indians in Malaysia, Singapore and here are past masters in trading. Some American soldiers, especially in the Q side, are always willing to make a few dollars. So the equipment is stolen, bought or captured."

"How enterprising," said the DO, which surprised GBH, believing that the DO should be aware of the nature of the people he was administering. A flash of *white prats* in his mind made him smile. He liked the expression and regretted still that he was not its author. He refrained from telling the DO that he and most of the infantry soldiers used American clothing and kits, which they had bought.

Godden hoped to soothe Bendixson's agitation. "This is Friday. Why don't we advise, tell all government staff to take the whole weekend off?" Saturday until noon was normally a working day for government staff with some of the expats working the full day. "Is there a feast day around now? Saint George's, Patrick's?" Shakes of the head. "Royal birthdays?" Negative response.

"It's a possibility. I could say I have to work from home, which I sometimes do, and my assistants know I have a report to complete for HE. Apart from the duty assistant, I can give them the option to work from home, which I have done

194

before. Terence, you tell them discreetly…no. Instruct them! And they are not to discuss it with anyone. I want them all secure inside the Crescent. They can party. No." His elbows on the table, his arms formed an inverted V with his palms flat and swaying lightly back and forth to his closed lips. "The Robertsons are due to go soon?"

"Think still about two months before they hand over, sir," Bendixson said.

"Yes, but I am a busy man and with the approach of independence likely to be spending more time holding HE's hand." A gentle smile. "It's probably the only date when I can give them farewell drinks…and they deserve my thanks for all their contribution to the education of their charges." He looked at the others. GBH remembered he had had teachers called Robertsons. Surely not the same ones. They would be about ninety years old. He refrained from asking.

"I think that's an excellent idea, sir."

"I am delighted you think so, Terence, because you have to organise it. I will get my secretary, the formidable Miss Garland," For some reason, a smile towards GBH. "to do the invitations and have them dispatched. My wife will organise the food and drinks. I am positive the other girls will come onboard." GBH thought the DO showed more commitment to a cocktail party than the terrorist threat. "Terence, tell everyone it is a three-line whip and I will not brook any rebellions."

"Sir. But I am worried about Tom Alston. He practically lives in the clinic." Godden thought he would do the same with a wife like Alston's.

"Do not fret. I will handle Tom…anyway, I think he gets on with Robertson." *Sotto voce.* "He's the only one."

"Now, now, Arthur." Acknowledged with a manufactured apologetic expression. "I will ensure Tony attends."

"Jerome?" Bendixson asked.

"Track him down. If required, get some of your police officers to pick him up. Where is he?"

"Probably the convent."

"Sir, we need to discuss the convent," Godden said.

"Oh yes. The two girls up there. I'll get them picked up."

"No, Terence." Irritation in Godden's voice. "I mean their security."

"The good sisters have made it clear that they don't want protection from Her Majesty's forces." Dismissive, from Bendixson.

"That's not their decision!"

"Stop!" the DO ordered. A brief interlude to allow the policemen to calm down. "Arthur, I thought the official threat assessment concluded there was no threat to the convent."

"Sir, a low risk. However, a recent report, an assessment following a review of Jerome's meeting with Shi Baru, by Sergeant Knight—"

"Actually, by Miss Eileen Kanna. I think she used to work for you."

"She still does." A tad abrasive from the DO.

"Well, sir, following this review, they concluded the convent was a potential target as well as government facilities and individuals. You will recall I briefed you personally."

"But you did not mention the convent." A reprimand for Godden.

"No sir. We were still assessing it and doing our own investigation. Speaking to sources. It will be included in the next risk assessment."

"That is indeed helpful." A sliver of sarcasm. "Why? I have seen reports suggesting the nuns have aided the communists. Terence thinks they would give medical help to the CTs. Don't you?"

"Yessir." His voice betrayed his nervousness. "To be fair, sir, Captain Oldham from the beginning considered there was a threat to the convent. Rogue elements. Think he said something about hard nuts not from the area killing…though he used another term… In fact, it was Sergeant Knight who said that. His language can be a bit blunt. He upset some of the girls when he gave a talk on personal security."

"Mm, yes, my wife said something about that. I thought the communists are discipline and controlled?"

"Normally, they are. But sometimes one or two of our people have acted outside the law."

"That's putting it mildly."

"And we tend to offer excuses and protect them. They do the same, especially if any act turns out to be beneficial to them. It might have the effect of intimidating people."

"Colonel?"

"I agree. If their intended target is unavailable or they suffer losses, they might lash out at a soft and unprotected target. The convent would come into that category. Also, these people fight according to their rules, not ours. I would not be surprised by anything they do. They are not tender terrorists."

"Alliteration. Ever the English gentleman."

"I am neither a gentleman nor English."

The DO was flummoxed by the content and directness of the reply. "Oh, excuse me, Colonel." GBH nodded. "After my faux pas, what are we to do?" The newspaper headline he was now seeing read, 'Defenceless nuns slaughtered while the British held a cocktail party!'

"I thought we had no more available men," said Bendixson, his agitation crawling back.

"We are looking at that at the moment. I think we might be able to put together a section taking some from the OP. But I can't be certain until I get back."

"I understand, Colonel. I do not think we need to detain you any further."

"Thank you." He asked the two policemen, "Will you be back in the station? We might need to finalise a number of matters." Both confirmed they would be returning to the station and another meeting was fixed for 1600 hours. GBH stood up, replaced his headdress, walked to the door, turned and saluted—not the DO specifically but towards the three of them.

"Colonel, you are more than welcome tonight."

"No, thank you."

"A wise decision. The Robertsons are quite boring."

"That's rather mild for you, Arthur. They are the most boring people in the colony." A sniggering Bendixson. They were gently scolded by Sutch. GBH resisted saying they had competition.

"You have a party to go to, tonight," GBH told Miss Kanna, "and it's a scale A parade at the DO's home." They were in Knight's office.

"Are you going, Colonel?"

"I am not. I have another party to attend." A youthful twinkle.

"Short notice," commented Eileen.

GBH explained it was to say goodbye to the Robertsons though it was a bit early but the DO could not be certain of being available on any other date; he did not disclose the actual reason. He mentioned the common attitude towards the Robertsons.

She launched into a defence of the Robertsons. "They are OK. He does go on but they are so enthusiastic. I have helped out at sports days and galas. The children love them. They keep challenging and stimulating the kids but always with encouragement to achieve more. They are very popular with the parents. I would say, apart from Doctor Alston, they have done more for the locals than anybody else. I know they…well, he in particular, is a figure of fun amongst the expats with his thirst to learn about everything. Anyway, I think apart from the DO, those two are better educated and more knowledgeable than any of the others."

"You can defend me at my court martial," declared a smiling GBH.

"I am sorry. Some of the—"

GBH interrupted her, "No need. I understand." He told her that she could leave now to get ready and if she was needed, they would come for her.

After she was gone, he briefed Knight on the outcome of the meeting that the civilians were going to be confined to their quarters for the next 48 hours, and the need to protect the convent. Knight was surprised when GBH made critical remarks of the other three, in particular Bendixson, but the sergeant concentrated on how another section could be formed and suggested he could command it, though GBH did not agree. After his arranged meeting with the police, GBH would send a coded message to Oldham to tell him what was happening, and then he would go up to the OP to issue orders to Corporal Jubb. "I intend to remain at the OP to control the operation." A faint smile.

He explained his thinking to Knight. There were now, including London Crescent, six different deployments, almost a hundred men so almost a company. If there was an attack, he could direct and control the response, being the only one with not only the knowledge of the overall deployment but with the authority to act. The Brigadier and Colonel Marchant had relinquished to him command of 513 Troop and C Platoon respectively. It was his duty. Another smile, boyish. "I was excellent as a platoon and company commander." He had decided not to tell the nuns that there would be soldiers near the convent. Knight would drop him off at the OP and could hear the orders to Jubb so that he knew the full picture. He needed Knight to remain at the station to liaise with the police and he would tell the police that Knight would be acting with his authority. He had considered taking Collins as his signaller but would leave him with Knight. In fact, Knight's team would be the last reserve and needed to be ready to deploy to any of the locations. The platoon ops room would now be a listening station. GBH said that he felt both a little excited and nervous. That disclosure came with the same caveat as applied to the hospital visit.

The posting to Singapore had been delayed for a year to accommodate the incumbent's next posting and GBH had found himself a temporary lecturer at Sandhurst with the officer cadets enjoying his lectures on being a platoon commander in the jungle, usually unlike Europe on one's own with the accompanying responsibility. When time had come for the Singapore posting, the allocated married quarter had not been available initially and his wife was not prepared to move into a major's quarter even on a temporary basis so it was decided she would come to Singapore when the quarter was available. Willard had offered to facilitate a visit to South Vietnam to which Far Eastern Land Forces had consented immediately because the Americans had shown a reluctance to agree to visits by British officers, and further, the defence attachés were constrained by petty bureaucracy. The rationale for the visit had been the possible deployment of British troops, although his brother David had informed him that it was highly unlikely that British troops would be sent to Vietnam for both political and military reasons. GBH had accepted the invitation out of interest and military lessons, even negative ones, could always be learned.

In Saigon, he had been given a positive briefing by a major of the Military Advisory and Assistance Group Vietnam always called MAAG, before being delivered into the hands of a Special Forces colonel. At all times, he had been escorted by volunteer officers and sometimes CIA personnel as they toured by road, boat, helicopter and even light aircraft around various areas with names he found difficult to pronounce or remember, far removed from the Malay language. The officers had been enthusiastic and confident though disparaging of most of the South Vietnamese units and their officers, insisting that with American combat troops, the enemy could be defeated quickly. These earnest officers believed that they could achieve anything. He heard the young Americans officers scoffing at the French experience: they were French and useless militarily. The Americans ignored or had forgotten their difficult experiences in Korea. However, caution was expressed by one American colonel, and then a journalist who, one evening after a few drinks and with no one else present, had told GBH that the military were full of piss and vinegar.

On his last day, he had had lunch in the Continental Hotel beside the Opera House with a diplomat from the British Embassy who knew his brother. GBH had wanted to sit outside on the street but the diplomat had insisted on being inside, which was more discreet and safer though the soldier had not told him he was carrying a side-arm. One of the Embassy's conditions for the visit being he was not to carry a weapon. The diplomat enthused that this was the hotel in which Graham Greene had written *The Quiet American* and a visit to the room could be arranged. GBH thought it was absurd that one would want to visit a room where someone had written a book.

Whilst the diplomat had droned on about supporting the Americans and defeating the Vietcong, which would defend Malaysia and other British interests in the region albeit without British military support, GBH had pondered his attitude to the Arts. He had been to the ballet and opera on a few occasions, always finding them tedious. Shakespeare had left him indifferent. Deaths were not dramatic tragedies that left people poorer emotionally. Simply Lear and Hamlet had made poor decisions. Cordelia should have appeased her old and ailing father. He would never have treated his grandfather or father in that way.

Succumbing to pressure from both Una and David, he tried to read two of Graham Greene's novels but had been put off by the emphasis on Catholic guilt, which he did not share, and he was not torn or haunted by decisions in his life. He realised that he was a philistine and probably amoral. Was this what had attracted Una to him, a surrogate for her father? His father would have been appalled and disappointed by the thought of his son being like MacFadzean. A laconic smile, not noticed by the droning diplomat. The diplomat and soldier parted, the former thinking he had influenced the other, the latter not taking in the other's message and not interested in it.

On his return to Singapore, he wrote his report.

He was scornful of the British military and civilians who urged the Americans to learn from the British success in Malaya. Yes, the Brits had won in Malaya but Vietnam was different. The Americans were aliens, ignorant of the culture and language with only a few making any attempt to understand or learn. The Americans retreated to their insular compounds following their day working with their Vietnamese allies. The British, no matter the reasons, had had a footprint in Malaya with British norms having been imposed on society. There were British teachers, doctors and other professionals in the country, not just the military and other security agencies. Further, the military situation was very different with the Vietcong having the support of a country, North Vietnam. The Vietcong were experienced, skilful and ruthless. He concluded that British military involvement could be costly in both lives and costs unless it was a token presence for political reasons.

His wife had decided not to follow him to Singapore because it would disrupt her son's education. Again, he had accepted it without question, and again there was talk of him being cuckolded by another wife. He had spent his time visiting units throughout the command and writing training exercises that had been eagerly grasped by unit commanders, saving them time and thought. It was unclear the location of his next posting until a training position was manufactured for him at Jungle Warfare School with the rank of acting colonel. He considered it a sop, because he would not command again, and in recognition of his distinguished career. He had to return to London for six months between

199

postings to deal with personal matters. He had lost two wives, one to a Swiss banker and the other to Willard, with each wife and son relocating to Paris and Washington DC, respectively. He was glad that neither child had been a daughter. He had never loved his wives: it had been just sex. There had been two meetings with Una before his final weekend, which they had spent in the Rathbone Hotel just off Charlotte Street in London.

The final detail in the operation was to obtain Hockin's consent for the police to use his boat in conjunction with the two police boats to move police and soldiers up the Kanu River in the event of a follow-up after the ambush had been sprung. The company of the National Army, south of Shala, was put on stand-by to begin patrolling in Shala from the Monday, which had always been the plan. The expats remained within the confines of London Crescent except for Bendixson who was required to carry on with his normal duties and Hockin who insisted it was right that he return to the plantation, taking Jerome with him and both giving a commitment to the DO that they would remain in the house until Monday morning or until they received further instructions. The DO remained at home.

Chapter 28

Twin explosions, almost simultaneous!

The initiation of the ambush followed by the thundering rattle and clatter of small arms fire.

"Jesus Christ!" shouted Sgt Williams in the ops room with the newly arrived Knight standing between Williams and the signaller. The firing stopped after about thirty seconds.

"Contact, wait out!" Over the shared net.

"Not Oldham. 513. Explosions probably the claymores initiating the ambush," Knight stated.

"That sounds as if it's just outside. Did you know that was going to happen?" His question had been prompted by Knight entering the ops room as the contact happened but the response was a shake of the head. Bendixson dashed into the police ops room, a muddle of panic and fear imprinted on his face; a quick knock on the army ops room door as he entered the already crowded small room.

Small arms fire again. The normal procedure in an ambush of sweeping the killing area with more fire.

"Where's the shooting?"

"513 Troop." Knight hoped he was right.

"Oh, thank God. Seemed so close I thought it might have been the Crescent or the GAB."

"Contact at eleven forty-six hundred hours." The Royal Marine Captain's voice was calm and deliberate. A BBC announcer reading the shipping forecast, not someone just involved in a brutal and deadly act of violence.

There were six enemy dead, a number of weapons and ammunition captured, two walkie-talkie type sets as well as two small long-tail type boats. No friendly casualties. The area was secure. GBH acknowledged and waited for the other stations to acknowledge the contact report. After each callsign had responded, GBH said, "Will return to you after speaking to our friends, wait out."

The secure phone from the OP rang in the police ops room. Godden was now in the ops room. After a brief discussion, Bendixson deployed the police follow-up party by boat of which GBH informed all callsigns and that they were to remain in their present positions. Bendixson and Godden retreated into the former's office to report to their superiors whilst Knight returned to his to begin drafting his report. He agreed in response to her telephone request for Eileen to come into the office. He briefed her on the events whilst she told him that Dr

Alston had gone to the clinic in response to concerns about an elderly patient with both sharing the same unspoken thought on the identity of the patient.

A tap on the door with a simultaneous opening brought Bendixson in. It was just under four hours since the contact. "Just to let you know, Sergeant, that the follow-up search has been completed and the police party are on their way back."

"Thank you, sir. I'll come along."

The tapping of the typewriter alerted Bendixson to Eileen Kanna's presence. "What are you doing here, Miss Kanna?"

A slight, right twist of her head towards the police officer. "Working." A dismissive tone, the equivalent of a smirk.

"Do you have the DO's permission?" A shake of the head but not accompanied with a turn of the head. Knight knew her abrasiveness was not helpful and it infuriated Bendixson who turned to the soldier saying, "Sergeant, this is not acceptable. I don't have time now. But you have not heard the end of this." Knight was glad that Bendixson could not see her slender smile of contempt.

A conference by secure telephone was held with GBH in Bendixson's office with Knight present at GBH's request. It was agreed that the army would be at the landing jetty to demonstrate the joint nature of the operation and to provide additional security. There was also agreement that they would need to proceed on the assumption that there were CTs in or around Shala, probably waiting for the weapons so GBH would leave C Platoon in their positions whilst 513 Troop would redeploy to two already recced positions—one covering the river and the other near the OP to support, if necessary, the convent protection group. Godden reported there was no further intelligence from Doherty. The police would block the border road in the morning to allow the recovery of the ambush troops. National Army troops should still deploy into Shala the next morning as planned. Godden left to brief the DO and Bendixson handed the receiver to Knight. GBH told Knight that he wanted him to go to the jetty just to confirm numbers of captured items, and agreed to Knight's proposal to take Horrocks in case any were the market tourists. Bendixson was bemused but did not ask. Finally, GBH asked if he could be picked up from the OP at 0800 hours if all went to plan.

The jetty was a few metres north of London Crescent before the Kanu disappeared underground before re-emerging, curving to the west south of the square. It had been decided in around 1930 or 31, for some forgotten reason, to divert the river underground away from the square before reappearing on its way to Jacques Bay. The necessary work had been planned and supervised by a French engineer.

The six dead terrorists, each covered with a poncho up to their neck leaving their heads exposed, were laid out in a single straight line. It had been decided by the DO that a colleague of Alston's would confirm death. Behind them was laid out the captured equipment, including the two boats with both having been struck by rounds. The captured weapons consisted of four AK47s, three Chinese-type SKS, two Armalite M16s and one Belgian FN as well as two Browning automatics and a Webley 38. There were 15 magazines of rounds of varying types as well as bandoliers, together totalling just under 1,000 rounds. The two walkie-talkie type radios were homemade and not functioning, and some maps and written documents in a plastic folder that would require further examination.

After the doctor had completed the formalities, Inspector Khan and Staff Ho walked down the line pausing at each body, followed by a police officer photographing each body with the poncho on and off. Khan and Ho told Knight and Horrocks the dead CTs were not known to either of them and did not think they were local. Knight sought Khan's consent to Horrocks looking at the bodies, which he granted after Ho had told him of the events at the market.

The corporal, accompanied by Knight, walked slowly down the line of bodies looking at each one, pausing longer at the one second from the right. Knight realised that this was the first time he had seen the enemy up close. He had been involved in the arrest of suspects but he had never seen hardened terrorists; he did not consider the knife man at Hockin's a terrorist. There was now a small group of spectators looking down at the scene, which the police did not discourage because it sent out the message that this is the consequence of taking on the security forces. Horrocks told the police officers and Knight that he could not be certain but thought the second one from the right was one of the men he had observed in the market place. Whilst the three others were making entries in their notebooks, Horrocks scanned the small crowd gathered near the police and army vehicles. He turned back towards the other three and said quietly that he thought the second one from the market-place was standing to the left of the bonnet of Knight's Land Rover.

Ho took charge, telling the other three to go examine the captured weapons, then he shouted in Malay to a constable who went to his Land Rover behind the army vehicle and brought out a large plastic bag. Ho shouted again, indicating that the constable had not gotten the right bag, shook his head and bounded up to the Land Rover to rectify the matter. He rummaged around in the back of the Land Rover before moving to the side and shouted—not in his scouse accent— to Pte McGraw standing at the rear of Knight's Land Rover, asking whether he had any evidence bags.

"Whit? Dinnae know whit yer sayin'." In response, Ho shook his head in frustration, indicating to the constable to follow him and muttering loudly, "Gweilos!"

He stopped at the rear of the army Land Rover, looking into the back but at the same time indicating the suspect whilst briefing the constable to go to the left and McGraw to follow him to the right. Ho pinioned the suspect's arms shouting in Mandarin to stand still and not resist while McGraw levelled his weapon at the suspect's head. On instructions, the constable handcuffed the suspect. Ho beckoned another police Land Rover to come forward.

Khan and the two soldiers ran up the slight incline to join Ho. The inspector directed other police officers supported by Knight, Horrocks and McGraw to push the small crowd away but not in an aggressive manner. The suspect was bundled into a police Land Rover and taken to the station. Khan turned his attention to organising the bodies to be taken to the mortuary and the captured equipment to the police station. Ho explained to Knight that he would have preferred to have followed the suspect but probably would have lost him in the shanties as well as adding that Knight could be present for the interrogation.

Chapter 29

On his return, GBH went straight to Knight's office. The sergeant confirmed that GBH knew of the death of Fong Siu Wai though neither spoke further of it. He read the first draft of Knight's report, announced he was going to sleep for a few hours, Miss Kanna should be present for 1300 to type up the completed report followed by a final debrief with the police and Oldham, and that helicopters would be picking up the Troop and he at 1500 hours from the border road below the OP. When, on leaving the office, Bendixson informed him that HE was making an important statement on the radio at 1000 hours, he shrugged.

The important statement was that the date of independence had been brought forward by three months with the first of December, Independence Day, or Hari Merdeka. Chila Baru followed the Governor, announcing it had been agreed that he would lead the new government with Jafar as his deputy, which would be provisional, and that elections would take place after independence and not before as planned. Knight decided to see for himself the local reaction to this news.

The single Land Rover had taken a short tour of Shala observing the National Army troops guarding the GAB and London Crescent having replaced Horrocks and his section but life seemed like any other morning. Knight stood beside the Land Rover, now stationary in the square near the post office. He exchanged glances with Raza as usual surrounded by children. He considered but decided against going over to express his condolences on Fong's death. With the platoon departing in three days, it was unlikely he would speak to Raza directly and he would not have the opportunity to decide for himself whether the old man was a sage or a charlatan.

Knight pondered on whether the people going about their lives were talking about the killings by the army, the earlier date for independence or neither. The words of T. S. Eliot's *Little Gidding* resonated in his mind. He had written of knowing a place only after exploration. For Knight, *And know the place for the first time* would not apply to Shala. This was the reality in that even after dramatic and shocking events, these stoic people just carried on with their lives: its mundanity suppressed such events. He would be leaving Shala as he had arrived, ignorant and a stranger.

GBH thanked C Platoon for their part in a successful operation and wished them well in the future. The once wet and tired soldiers, now fed and relaxed, had shorn their grumpiness and were pleased by his appreciation. There was a final meeting of the two army officers with Bendixson and Godden, with the former conveying to them the DO's congratulations. Godden reported that Doherty's intelligence on armed terrorists in Shala was not accurate—the result of an error in translation. According to Bendixson, the arrested individual, thanks to Ho's skilful and forceful interrogation, was providing usable intelligence. A wry smile was on GBH's face. Knight had told him how the prisoner had cracked within minutes. He had been at the end of his tether. His spirit had been broken by long periods in the jungle, contradictory orders from bickering superiors and seeing his friend from childhood, also his sister's husband, dead. GBH said that once he had debriefed 513 Troop, he would pass on any information that might be helpful to the police for further operations and the Troop would be remaining in the colony as brigade troops for tasking. Oldham remained silent. There were polite handshakes as GBH left. He went out of the front entrance of the station and spotted his crew, Collins, Paton and McGraw, lined up at attention beside the Land Rover.

"Colonel." He had sensed during the platoon debrief and the meeting with the police that Oldham was unhappy, deflated.

He stopped and turned. "Yes, Captain Oldham."

"May I be frank?" A nod from his superior. "Well, Colonel, I feel that my men have not been treated fairly." There was no reaction. "We sat in the jungle getting cold and wet for nothing. There was never going to be an attack on Hockin."

A few months earlier, he would have ripped into the young officer for the remark but he had some sympathy for him. "It was your Sergeant Knight...and Miss Kanna who were responsible...well, for confirming it. But you should know, from experience, that intelligence is not always accurate. We could not discount Hockin as a target." He paused. "Yes. You were a decoy. Part of the deception plan; them knowing you were there caused them to take a different route." Not the whole truth.

Oldham remained despondent.

GBH stepped out of character. "I think you are a good officer. Your CO, Bob Marchant, thinks highly of you. You have the ability to be CO of your battalion. But!" He grabbed the captain's eyes. "An officer, especially a CO, has to make decisions, often difficult, sometimes ruthless. And at times, his officers and men cannot know the reasons...often best not to. The mission must come first."

"Colonel?"

He stepped back into character. "Rank, mess nights, regimental balls, drill, parades, sport, battalion rugby, regimental silver, regimental history are mere trappings, fripperies to our sole aim."

"Sir?"

"To defeat the Queen's enemies!"